# ROSE
# HILL

# ROSE HILL

## Pamela Grandstaff

Books by Pamela Grandstaff:

Rose Hill Mystery Series:

Rose Hill

Morning Glory Circle

Iris Avenue

Peony Street

Daisy Lane

Lilac Avenue

Hollyhock Ridge

Sunflower Street

Viola Avenue

Pumpkin Ridge

As always, for my mom, Betsy

# Chapter One – Saturday

Theo Eldridge fortified himself with half a bottle of good Kentucky bourbon and several lines of coke before he got behind the wheel of his bright yellow Hummer. As he wound down the two-lane mountain road toward the town of Rose Hill, he reviewed his list of grievances. He was irritated by several things but was mad as hell about being stood up for dinner, and was determined to take it out on somebody.

When he got to town, he drove slowly past the veterinary clinic. He considered setting it on fire but decided it might be more fun to trash the place instead. It was conveniently located right across the street from the newspaper office, which was also on his list. His third target lay several miles outside of town. With three places to hit and one night in which to do it, he needed an accomplice.

He found the ferrety-looking handyman Willy Neff trying to argue his way into the Rose and Thorn, where the little man was banned for life. Theo parked the Hummer by the curb a few doors down, clamped his cigar between his back teeth, and eagerly entered the fray.

"He's with me," Theo told bartender Patrick Fitzpatrick, who not only refused to let him bring Willy in, but also refused to sell him a bottle of whiskey he could take with him. Theo communicated his indignation at this affront by threatening to remove one part of the bartender's body with the intention of inserting it in another.

"You could try it," Patrick said, "but you wouldn't survive it."

Theo cursed the bartender but walked away with little Willy in tow. They drove out to Hollyhock Ridge to make mischief at the home of somebody else Theo hated

1

but found the inhabitants awake and armed. After a shot was fired over their heads, Theo decided it might be wiser to focus their efforts on less occupied premises.

When they returned to Rose Hill, Willy dropped Theo off at the Rose and Thorn, where Patrick again refused to sell him any whiskey, telling him, "You've had enough to drink."

Theo turned to the row of amused locals seated at the bar and demanded, "What are you looking at?"

When they refused to be provoked, he made a crude pass at Mandy, the young waitress.

"Not in a million years," Mandy told him. "Not if you was the last man on earth and I was so horny my pants caught fire."

"Leave her alone, Theo," Patrick said.

Theo turned and glared. The mirror on the wall behind the rows of liquor bottles reflected a brutish looking man, well over six feet tall, with a thick neck, a meaty red nose, bloodshot pale blue eyes, and a joker smile punctuated by a rancid-smelling cigar. Theo leaned over the bar and put his face very close to Patrick's, but the bartender did not flinch.

"You'll never have her," Theo said, in his gravelly growl. "I'll make sure of it."

"That's enough," Patrick said.

He picked up a wooden bat that was kept behind the bar and pointed it at Theo's head.

"You can walk out of here or get carried out. It's up to you."

Theo sneered at Patrick but left the bar, sweeping a table full of glassware onto the floor as he went. As he departed, he could hear the locals snickering behind his back. He consoled himself by imagining violent acts of retribution for which he was sure to be credited but never arrested. The most difficult part of taking revenge on the people who crossed him was not bragging about it afterward, especially when he'd had a few too many drinks.

Having reached the next low point in what had so far been a real pisser of a day, Theo decided he needed someone to cheer him up. He turned the corner and lurched down Peony Street toward the mobile home park. As soon as he left the curb to cross the street, however, he stepped into a deep pothole full of icy water camouflaged by slush. Within seconds the frigid water had filled his boots and soaked through his socks. To make matters worse, the shock of the cold water unhinged his jaw's vise-like grip; his cigar fell out of his mouth and landed with a plop in the icy water. Theo cursed the pothole, cursed the weather, cursed the town, and cursed everyone who had conspired to thwart and frustrate him all day.

A few minutes later, standing outside a shabby trailer where he had expected to find a warm, willing body, some booze, and an alibi for what he planned to do later, he instead found himself in the middle of another heated altercation.

"It'll be a cold day in hell before you or that little snot-head get a penny of my money!" he yelled as he left the mobile home park.

The neighbors were used to these little dramas, and only a few curtains twitched in the nearby trailers.

With sopping, frozen feet, Theo squished his way down the icy, brick-paved alley behind the businesses on Rose Hill Avenue toward the spot where he'd told Willy to wait. The little man's rickety truck was parked in front of the antique store, but Willy was passed out across the front seats with both doors locked. Theo pounded on the windows and the hood of the old truck, but Willy didn't stir.

"This is what I get for leaving that good-for-nothing idiot alone with a twelve-pack of beer," Theo grumbled, and then thoroughly cursed the unconscious man.

Determined to punish Willy for being such a worthless piece of excrement, Theo looked for something with which to break the windshield. He found an aluminum baseball bat in the bed of the truck and was just about to swing it down on the glass when he heard a trashcan fall over in the alley behind him. He turned, almost throwing himself off balance, but couldn't see or hear anything in the darkness of the passageway.

"This whole damn town is covered with cats," he muttered.

As he reached into his coat pocket for his phone, he realized he'd left it in the Hummer, along with his keys. Swearing over his bad luck, he leaned back against Willy's truck and considered his options. It was 1:45 a.m., Willy was useless, and even if he could somehow get his SUV unlocked, he was in no shape to drive back up the mountain. Looking down the street, he could see the fog creeping steadily uphill toward him.

Music and raised voices from a party in a nearby apartment building drew his attention. He considered crashing it, if only to use the phone, but couldn't think of anyone to call. There was no one left in this town he hadn't pissed off or ripped off, and certainly, no one who would be willing to come out in the cold and drive him home, let alone give him a place to sleep. He briefly considered rousing his previous night's playmate, the one who'd stood him up for a repeat performance earlier in the evening, but discarded that idea as way too risky.

A dog barking in the distance reminded him of what he intended to do when he told Willy to park where he did. He gripped the bat tightly in his hand as he crossed the deserted street and stumbled up the steps to the back door of the veterinary clinic. He took a swing at the motion detection light above the door and was rewarded by the gratifying thwack of impact and shattering glass. With a swarm of bitter resentments, festering grudges, and petty irritations buzzing around inside his head, Theo attacked the back door.

Once inside, he was disappointed to find only empty cages illuminated by a nightlight. He paused to catch his

4

breath while deciding what to destroy next, and heard the crunch of someone stepping on the broken glass and splintered wood on the floor behind him. He started to turn but was struck on the back of the head with such force that he was already unconscious before he landed face down on the cold tile floor, where he would bleed to death within fifteen minutes.

After his assailant fled, the party music thumped and wailed for another half hour, and a few dogs in town barked back and forth to each other. Meanwhile, the fog from the Little Bear River continued to creep uphill until it had engulfed the entire town of Rose Hill.

ROSE HILL by Pamela Grandstaff

# Chapter Two – Sunday

M aggie Fitzpatrick was sitting across the table from police chief Scott Gordon in the break room of the Rose Hill police station at just after 4:00 in the morning. Scott had hauled in one of her bookstore employees for public drunkenness at around 3:00 a.m., and she was waiting for the young man to sober up enough so she could take him back to his dorm.

The crime committed by twenty-year-old Mitchell Webb, the college student currently snoring loudly on the couch in Scott's office, consisted of standing outside the apartment building where his ex-girlfriend Yvonne lived, singing "Let's Stay Together" in an effort to win her back. This idea had taken several shots of tequila to seem promising.

Mitchell, with his dreadlocks and multiple piercings, had frightened some of the older residents of the neighborhood, and a concerned citizen had telephoned Scott. The chief of police was a little more sympathetic to Mitchell and felt more as if he was rescuing the young man from further embarrassment than apprehending a dangerous criminal.

Scott called Maggie partly because he didn't want to get Mitchell in trouble with his parents or the college administration, but mostly so he could get Maggie out of bed and into the station. She had refused to have dinner with him (yet again) only hours previously.

Scott was much like Mitchell in his romantic devotion, if not his methods.

At his call, Maggie threw on a coat over her flannel pajamas, stuffed her feet into snow boots, and now sat across from him, red curls tangled about her head, mercilessly beating him at Gin Rummy.

They were listening to the radio as they played cards, and Scott was making Maggie laugh by singing along (in a flawless falsetto) with Al Green as he performed "Let's Stay Together."

"I can't believe you requested that song," she said.

"You should be impressed," Scott said. "I have connections. I know people. I can make things happen."

"They probably don't get many requests this late at night."

"This is a classic," Scott said. "I'm surprised Mitchell has such good taste in music."

"He loves all that old stuff," Maggie said. "He says he has an old soul."

"I have an old soul," Scott said. "There is more depth to me than you can even imagine."

"I'm not interested," Maggie said, "and quit letting me see your cards."

When Ed Harrison rushed into the station, Scott thought at first he must be drunk, but his eyes were wide open, and his face was pale. When Scott grabbed his arm to keep him upright, he could feel it trembling.

"A dead body," Ed said, "at the vet's."

Maggie dropped her cards. From the rambling, partially coherent explanation that followed, Scott determined Ed had found someone dead behind the veterinary clinic, across the street from the office of the Rose Hill Sentinel newspaper, which Ed owned.

"Oh no, not Drew," Maggie said.

Drew Rosen was the new veterinarian they were all still getting to know.

Ed shook his head, saying, "I don't know. It's dark. The back door's gone. The dog's gone."

Maggie's face paled as she looked back and forth between Ed and Scott.

Scott called Frank, his full-time deputy, and asked him to meet them at the veterinary clinic.

"Are you well enough to come back with me?" he asked Ed and got a nod in return.

Ed's color was a little better, but Scott felt some prescient nausea at what he was going to find behind the clinic, based on Ed's demeanor. Ed was the most no-nonsense, level-headed person Scott knew. If he was this upset, it must be bad.

Scott asked Maggie, who was trying to stay quietly out of the way yet still hear everything, if she would remain in the station to keep an eye on Mitchell. She reluctantly agreed.

Rose Hill Avenue was lit by streetlights that seemed to float in the thick mist. Scott could hear the sound of ice melting and dripping from every roof, which was not a good thing to hear in January. A freak thaw like the one they were experiencing could loosen an entire roof-full of snow and ice, sending it sliding onto the sidewalks below, or right on top of someone's head. If the temperature stayed warm there would be flash floods and empty ski resorts; if it plunged back below freezing everything would be covered with a thick layer of ice.

As the patrol car drew up in front of the newspaper office, Ed said, "Tommy's not here."

Twelve-year-old Tommy Wilson was Rose Hill's only paper carrier, but he wasn't waiting outside the newspaper office, as he usually would be at this hour. Tommy delivered the daily paper, published in the nearby town of Pendleton, and delivered Rose Hill's weekly Sentinel on Sundays.

"He probably overslept," Scott said. "We'll check on him."

Scott made a three-point turn in the alley between Ed's newspaper office and the newly renovated antique store and parked in front of the veterinarian clinic across the street. Ed sat frozen in the passenger seat, staring ahead, his jaw clenched.

"Where's the body, Ed?" Scott asked him.

Ed moved stiffly, as though he were sleep-walking. He looked over toward the newspaper office, then turned and pointed toward the driveway that led to the back of the clinic, where there were two additional parking spaces and a dumpster. He got out of the cruiser and led Scott around to the back of the building, but slowly, as if his limbs didn't want to carry him back to the scene.

The motion-sensitive light was missing above the back entrance, and the beam from Scott's flashlight reflected off broken glass sparkling against the melting snow on the concrete porch and stairs. What was left of the back door dangled from hinges still attached to the battered doorframe. Scott's boots crunched the broken glass as he climbed up three steps to the entrance and looked inside. There was a nightlight on inside the room, which was lined with three levels of kennel cages along each wall. On the tiled floor, Scott could see a man lying face down in a dark puddle.

Scott directed the beam of light up over the body from the feet to the back of the man's head. He could see the skull was caved in near the crown, and the hair on the scalp was sticking up around the indentation in clotted, bloody clumps. The coppery, sour smell of blood was rank and overwhelming. Scott stepped quickly to the edge of the small cement stoop and vomited in the snow.

When he turned back around, Ed said, "I puked too."

Scott pulled the neck of his parka and sweatshirt up over his mouth and nose so he almost couldn't smell anything. His eyes watered and his stomach rolled, but he forced himself to look at the scene until he gained control of himself. From his first look around everything seemed tidy in the kennel room. Except for the violence done to the light, the door, and the man, the back room appeared untouched. What seemed likely to Scott to be the murder weapon, a metal baseball bat, was lying on the floor next to the body.

There were also bloody paw prints on the tile floor, and from the size of them, Scott thought they probably belonged to Duke, the veterinary clinic cat. He entered the backroom, carefully picking his way through the glass and splintered wood. He stepped over the body and crouched down next to it, bracing his back against one of the kennel cages.

The man was lying on top of his left arm, with the right arm outstretched from his body toward the nearby kennels. Scott reached out and felt the underside of the exposed wrist. There was no pulse. Blood covered the part of the face that was visible so Scott couldn't tell who the man was, but from the size of him, Scott could tell it wasn't the vet. This man had a very large frame, with short hair, and Dr. Andrew Rosen was thin and lanky, with longish brown hair and sideburns.

Scott stepped back over the body and went out the way he came in, just as Frank's SUV pulled into the driveway behind the clinic. With dismay, Scott realized he had not asked his deputy to park on the street, and now his slushy tire tracks had corrupted any evidence beneath them. He thought ruefully that he and Ed had already ruined any footprint evidence left by the murderer in the driveway and on the steps and porch.

Scott turned to look at his friend Ed, whose eyes were shut tight, gloved hands clinging to one of the iron poles holding up the porch roof.

"You touch anything in there?" he asked.

Ed shook his head 'no,' but did not open his eyes.

"It's not Drew," Scott told him.

"That's good," Ed said, but still did not open his eyes.

Frank walked up, looked past Scott into the room, and said, "Holy shit!"

Scott told the younger man to put Ed in his SUV, park on the street, and wait for him there.

The paper delivery truck pulled up in front of the newspaper office with a loud huff and squeal of air brakes and then idled at the curb while the driver unloaded bundles of papers onto a bench in front of the press office.

"I need to deliver the papers," Ed said, finally opening his eyes.

"Just wait with Frank until I get us some help," Scott said. "If Tommy shows up, Frank will give me a shout."

To Frank, he said, "Call Skip and tell him to go get the vet and bring him down here. He'll know if anything was taken. And tell him to park on the street."

Scott used his phone to call the county sheriff's dispatcher. A movement caught his eye as he punched in the numbers for the county desk, and he turned quickly, but it was only Duke, the clinic's huge tabby tomcat. Scott shooed him away from the back door and wondered how he was going to keep him out of the crime scene. Duke quickly returned and twined around Scott's legs, purring loudly. They were old friends.

Scott Gordon had only recently been promoted to chief of police and had no illusions about his abilities as a police officer. He considered himself more of a watchdog than a detective, and he was by no means a skilled crime scene investigator. Since he had established the victim was, in fact, dead, and it was obviously not from natural causes, he didn't want to contaminate the scene any more than he already had for those who knew what they were doing. The county sheriff's office had the resources and the expertise Rose Hill's small station lacked, and when there was a serious crime in Rose Hill, the county stepped in. Scott told the officer on duty at the county dispatch desk what he had, and the officer forwarded his call to Sarah.

Sarah Albright was the lead homicide investigator for the county sheriff's department. She had trained at Quantico and worked several years on a violent crimes unit in DC before moving back to the area. Overqualified for her current position and a woman, she could have had a miserable time of it save the county sheriff was an intelligent woman herself and was confident and secure enough to skillfully manage team members with more specialized expertise than she possessed.

By the time Sarah arrived at the crime scene, it was 5:30 a.m. and Scott's part-time deputy Skip had secured the area with yellow tape.

"What the hell, Gordon?" she said. "When I saw your number I thought maybe I was finally getting that booty call I've been dreaming about."

Scott gave her what facts he had. He had the vet in the patrol car (with the cat Duke, who wasn't happy about being stuffed into a pet crate), and the man who found the body, Ed Harrison, in Frank's SUV.

"You probably ruined any evidence there is," she said, "but we'll see what we can do."

Sarah was a petite woman with a shiny cap of dark hair and sharp, dark brown eyes. She, Scott, and a deputy with a camera donned surgical gloves and paper booties and then entered the veterinary office from the front. Scott followed Sarah in at her invitation and only came forward as she directed him. It was a courtesy he was allowed in at all, and if not for his curiosity and a sense of obligation to the town, he would have preferred to wait outside in the fresh air.

The veterinary clinic was a small cottage conversion with a cinder block addition built on the back. The waiting room and reception area looked clean and tidy, and the examining room and bathroom seemed to be in good order. Sarah pushed open the door that led to the addition, which housed the surgery, office, and kennel room. Sarah flipped the light switch using the end of her pen. Scott took a deep breath before he followed her in and steeled himself for the smell.

"There's hardly room to turn around in here," Sarah said.

The deputy began taking pictures of everything in the room, careful not to step in the puddle of blood. Scott studied the dead man's bloody profile, now bathed in bright fluorescent light, as Sarah surveyed the scene and spoke into a hand-held digital recorder.

Scott estimated the victim was around six feet tall and weighed over 200 pounds. The hair on his head not gummy with blood was salt-and-pepper gray, with a longish brush cut, as if it were overdue for a trim. He was wearing khaki pants, dark brown leather boots, and an expensive looking dark brown leather coat; a far cry from the durable, insulated canvas coats most of the local men wore, or the puffy nylon ski parkas the college students and tourists wore.

Scott got a whiff of the blood smell and turned his head, hoping Sarah wouldn't notice.

"What's wrong, Gordon?" Sarah said with a smirk.

A seemingly idle thought drifted into Scott's head just then, and he stopped to allow it to the forefront. Scott looked at the dead man and mentally applied the features of the person who had come to mind.

"Sarah," he said.

Sarah clicked off her recorder and fixed him with a dark hawkeye.

"I know who this is," he said.

Back at the Rose Hill police station, while her assistant supervised the removal of the body from the veterinary office via county morgue van, Sarah led Scott and Ed into the break room.

"Sit down," Scott urged Ed, fearing the man might fall down if he didn't sit.

"I need to deliver the papers," Ed protested, and Scott gently took the keys from his hand.

"We'll take care of it, Ed."

Scott stepped outside and instructed Skip not to enter the newspaper office, but to take the bundled papers and make sure every house and business in town got one. With just over a hundred homes within the city limits, it wasn't that daunting of a task. Scott also asked him to check on the boy who was supposed to deliver them.

This assignment made, Scott poured Ed some coffee, and attempted to stay calm and conversational with the man, who displayed every sign of still being in shock. Ed held the coffee cup in both hands and stared at it as if dazed. Sarah informed him she was going to tape their conversation and Ed nodded.

Scott experienced a moment of thinking more like Ed's friend than a police officer and opened his mouth to suggest Ed might ask for a lawyer to be present, but Sarah began, and he let the moment pass, feeling guilty as he did so. She pressed the record button and described who was present and what they were doing. Sarah indicated Scott should begin the questioning.

"Start at the beginning," Scott said. "Tell me everything you did today, I mean yesterday."

Ed took a deep breath and blinked several times as if he were just waking up. He took a moment to concentrate before he spoke.

"I had to approve the final proofs of the paper for the printer, so I worked on those for most of the morning. I called in some corrections and approved the updated pages online. I checked out the new antique store, to see how the renovations were progressing. I wanted to interview the owners, but they weren't around. Hannah stopped by to place an ad for a new stray she had taken to the vet's. I went over to take a picture of it. Then I went to the diner for lunch. Theo was there. We got into an argument."

"What about?"

"Theo asked about my dog Goudy, and I told him he died last fall. I made the mistake of telling him about the stray Hannah had picked up, saying if no one answered the

ROSE HILL by Pamela Grandstaff

ad for it I was going to adopt him. Theo said he'd lost a dog a few months ago, asked me what it looked like, so I told him it was a black lab. He said, 'That's my dog.' "

"Theo has a dog breeding business," Scott told Sarah, who rebuked him with a sharp look.

"It's no secret how Theo treats his dogs," Ed told Sarah. "He keeps them kenneled all the time, and they barely get fed or let out to run. I couldn't stand the thought of him getting another one. I told him it wasn't a purebred; it was just an old stray."

"What was Theo's response?" Scott asked.

"He said he would see about that."

"And then?"

"Well, I guess you could say we had words."

"Did the fight get physical?"

"No."

"Did Theo threaten you?"

"He said he'd like to tear my head off just to spit down my throat. I guess you could call that a threat."

"Did you say anything that might have been interpreted as a threat?"

Ed looked at Scott with a perplexed expression.

"Well, I might have. When Theo said I'd get that dog over his dead body, I said that was perfectly fine with me."

"And then what happened?"

"Pauline told us both to get out. Theo was still yelling at Pauline when I left."

"What did you do next?"

"I drove out to the lake and put a line in the water. I wasn't dressed warmly enough, so I left as soon as the sun went down, about 5:00. I got back to town around 5:30. I did some laundry, ate some dinner, watched the news, spent a couple hours in the Thorn, and then went back home to bed."

"Who was at the Thorn?"

"The usual bunch; Patrick was bartending, Mandy was waitressing, and Ian was entertaining tourists. I talked to a few people, watched part of a basketball game, and had a couple beers."

"Was Theo at the Thorn?"

"Not while I was there."

"Did you go anywhere else?"

"Not until 4:00 this morning, when I went to work."

"So the diner was the last place you saw Theo."

"Why are you so interested in Theo?" Ed asked, and looked at Scott in bewilderment. "You think Theo killed that guy?"

"What time were you at the bar?"

"From eight 'til ten," Ed said.

"Was there anybody with you afterward?"

"No," Ed said, and the realization that he was being questioned as a suspect seemed finally to dawn on him. His face lost what color it had regained. He looked at Scott, and then at Sarah.

"I didn't kill that guy, I found that guy."

Sarah said, "The victim didn't commit suicide by whacking himself on top of the head, Mr. Harrison. This is a homicide investigation, and we have to question everyone this way."

Ed looked back at Scott, crossed his arms over his chest, and sat back in his chair, defenses now firmly in place. Scott took a deep breath and tried to do a credible job of interrogating his best friend.

"Anybody call you while you were home?"

"Drew called me right before I went to the Thorn," Ed said. "He had neutered the stray in the afternoon and wanted to let me know the dog was waking up from the anesthetic. He said I could come get him in the morning."

"And after that?"

"Nobody."

"Why did you go to the vet's office so early this morning?"

"To look in the back window, to see if the dog was okay."

17

"And then?"

"I saw the door bashed in and the body on the floor, so I came and got you. The dog's gone."

His voice quavered slightly.

"We'll find the dog," Scott told him.

Ed just shook his head and seemed to struggle not to give in to his emotions. He turned to Sarah.

"Just because I had a noisy disagreement with the town bully yesterday and then found a dead guy this morning doesn't mean I'm a murderous psychopath."

"Do you own a baseball bat?" she asked him.

"I have some sports equipment at my house, and there are probably some bats. I play softball in the summer."

"Ed and I play on a league team," Scott told Sarah, and started to say something else when Sarah interrupted, loudly, saying, "Did you kill him, Ed?"

"Who?" Ed responded.

"Theo," Sarah said to Ed. "Did you kill Theo?"

All the blood seemed to drain out of Ed's face, his eyes rolled back in their sockets, and he fell sideways to the floor.

"Jesus," Sarah said. "Are all the men in this town so sensitive?"


Scott insisted Ed be taken to the twenty-four-hour medical clinic out by the highway, even though Ed said he was fine. Holding an icepack to the goose egg raising up on the side of his head just above his eye, Ed allowed Frank to lead him to the squad car.

"He could sue you," Sarah said, as she watched the squad car pull away.

"He won't," Scott said.

"What are you so pissed about?" Sarah said.

Scott clenched his jaw and said nothing.

"Do you think he's telling the truth?" she asked.

"I've known Ed my whole life," Scott said. "There's not a straighter arrow in this town."

"Except you, of course," she said.

"No," Scott stated, "including me."

"I thought you were the oldest living Boy Scout in America," Sarah said. "I thought you were your mama's little altar boy."

"What's your plan now?" Scott asked.

"Let's get the other one done," she said, "and go from there."

Veterinarian Andrew Rosen seemed keyed up and jumpy as he recounted his Saturday. Scott knew the man was in his early thirties, had purchased the practice from the previous owner's widow the summer before, and had moved to Rose Hill from Philadelphia, where he had worked in an emergency veterinary clinic. Animal control officer Hannah Campbell knew him the best of anyone, and she'd told him Drew was a 'crunchy granola Peace Corps' type with a friendly, laid-back personality. She got on well with him, which had not been the case with the former vet.

During Drew's recitation of the events of his day, Scott did not interrupt him until he mentioned Theo stopped in his office.

"What did he want?"

"He heard I had a stray black lab and thought it might be one of his."

"How did he seem?"

"Same as always," Drew shrugged, "rude, impatient, insulting."

"Theo's a client?" Sarah asked.

"He has a dog breeding business, and pays me a certain amount per month to provide medical treatment."

"Does he take good care of his dogs?"

"I haven't seen any evidence of abuse," he said.

"Ever heard about any abuse?"

"I think Hannah may have heard complaints about him. She keeps an eye on all the animals in these parts. She'd deal with it if there were."

"Any chance the lab you neutered could have been one of Theo's?"

"This lab has a huge white star on his chest."

"Meaning?"

"The standards for purebred labs allow for a small white spot on the chest, even though it's not desirable, but this guy has a huge splotch. A breeder wouldn't want to replicate that."

"Was he satisfied the dog was not his?"

"No. He demanded to see the dog and got pretty loud. I had other patients waiting so just to get rid of him I told him the dog wasn't on the premises. He argued with me for a few minutes, then left."

"Did you feel threatened at all? Physically, I mean."

"I have a second-degree black belt in Taekwondo, so I feel confident in most situations. If you stand up to bullies like Theo, they usually back down."

"Did he threaten you?"

"He said he ought to beat the hell out of me. I told him I didn't think violence solved anything between civilized people, but I was certainly willing to defend myself, so he cursed me and left."

"Has there ever been any physical contact between the two of you?"

"No, none."

Scott watched him closely but couldn't tell if he was lying.

"Anything else unusual happen during the day?"

"I don't take appointments after noon on Saturdays, so my receptionist went home. I neutered the stray, cleaned up, did some paperwork, and got caught up on e-mails."

"You did the surgery without any assistance?"

"Hannah was there. She assists me with surgeries, and in return, I vet all her strays. She left about 2:00."

"Ed said you called him."

"When the dog started coming out of the anesthetic. I knew Ed wanted to adopt him and was concerned about him."

"What time was it?"

"Between 7:30 and 8:00. I left the office shortly after, and took the dog home with me."

"Why didn't you leave the dog in the kennel?"

"There were no other boarders, so it meant I could keep an eye on him at home and not have to come back into the office on Sunday, today."

"Did you tell Ed you were taking the dog home?"

"I don't think so. I think I decided to do it after I called him."

"Did anybody else come to the surgery while you were there last night?"

"No, nobody."

"Anybody see you leave?"

"I can't remember seeing anyone. Someone in the apartments over the insurance office was having a loud party, and I could hear their music as I left."

"And you went straight home."

"The dog was still pretty groggy."

"And you stayed home all evening."

"After I left the office I was home until your deputy came by."

"Any reason you can think of why someone would want to break into your surgery?"

"Some of the animal tranquilizers are popular with addicts."

"You reported nothing was taken, though."

"Skip let me see inside the drugs cabinet, and everything was the way I left it."

"When was the last time you inventoried the cabinet?"

"Yesterday afternoon, actually, while I was killing time waiting for the dog to wake up."

"Any previous break-ins?"

"Not while I've been there."

"Anyone besides Theo giving you any trouble lately?"

Scott noticed some color rise into Drew's cheeks, just subtly. He felt Sarah stir beside him and knew she noticed too.

"No," he said. "Other than Theo being so thoroughly unpleasant, everyone else has been very kind."

"Ever had a malpractice lawsuit filed against you?"

"No," Drew said, "and I hope I never will."

Whatever uncomfortable feelings the subject of threats had brought up were subdued, and Drew was as cooperative and calm as it was possible to be with a dead body in his clinic.

"When Skip took you in to review the contents of the drug safe, you saw the body. Did you recognize the man?"

"No," said Drew. "I did not recognize him."


"What do you think?" Sarah asked Scott after Drew wrote and signed his statement, and one of her deputies escorted him back to his home.

"If everyone who ever had a fight with Theo Eldridge is a suspect, we may as well start at one end of town and interview everyone," Scott replied.

"Keep an eye on the vet. I think he's hiding something. JT will ask for the clothes he wore yesterday, and snoop as much as he'll let us without a search warrant. If we find anything, we'll hold him. Meanwhile, you can do a thorough background check on him."

Scott nodded and forced himself not to react, although he bristled inside at being assigned a task more suited to one of his deputies.

"Okay, Scott," Sarah said. "I'm going to go, but my team will nose around asking your fine citizens where they were on the night of, etcetera. When Mr. Harrison gets back, we'll look over his office and house and ask him for his clothes. I'll leave it to you to get a written statement and send it to me."

"If there's anything more I can do I'll be glad to," Scott said, and forced a smile he hoped seemed cooperative.

"Be careful writing blank checks like that," Sarah said with a smirk, eyeing him up and down. "Right now I could use a back rub and breakfast in bed."

"Regarding the case," Scott said, and then pretended to check the message light on the station phone system to put the front desk between them. "I meant can we be of any help to you professionally?"

"You really are no good at flirting," Sarah said. "Why can't you just relax and enjoy it instead of taking everything so seriously?"

"I just think it's a bad idea," Scott said. "I'd prefer we keep our working relationship on a professional level."

"Suit yourself," Sarah said. "But I'll keep the offer on the table. On the floor, in a bed, up against the wall, wherever. Who knows, someday you might decide to take me up on it. Until then I'll just have to assume you'll make it well worth the wait."

"It's not going to happen, Sarah," Scott said. "I don't know what else I can say to convince you."

"We'll see," she said. "When you get tired of waiting for your chubby gal pal to get off the fence, you give me a call. Meanwhile, would you mind taking a couple of my people out to Theo's house to have a look around?"

"No problem," said Scott. "I'll see if I can't find Willy Neff while I'm up there, and ask him a few questions as well."

"Who's Willy Neff?"

"He lives in the garage apartment out at Theo's, and takes care of the dogs," Scott replied. "He served some time for receiving child porn through the mail a few years ago. He's had some public drunkenness issues, but we keep a close eye on him."

"Sounds charming," Sarah said.

As soon as the door shut behind Sarah, Scott said, "All right, Maggie, you can come out now."

Maggie came out of his office and made a pretense of yawning and stretching as if she had just woken up.

"Did you get all that?" he asked her.

"I don't know what you're talking about," Maggie said, unaware that red grill marks from the heating vent between Scott's office and the break room were clearly visible on her pale, freckled cheek.

"How's our friend Mitchell?" he asked.

"Sleeping like a big drunk baby. Who do you think killed Theo?"

"I don't know," Scott said, rubbing his face. "We're just getting started."

"I can't think of anyone who won't be glad he's gone," Maggie said.

"That narrows it down."

"I might have done it," Maggie said. "I had as much reason to hate him as anybody."

"Lucky for you the chief of police is your alibi," Scott said.

"If I were going to start a vicious killing spree," Maggie said, looking over his shoulder at the county car parked out front. "I can tell you who I'd start with."

"I'm not interested in Sarah," Scott said. "You know that."

"It's the principle of the thing. If you were hitting on her, it would be sexual harassment. She shouldn't be allowed to get away with it just because she's a woman."

"I appreciate your concern," Scott said.

"I don't really care," Maggie said. "It's none of my business."

"You say that," Scott said, "but you don't mean it."

Maggie glared at Scott, but he just smiled.

"We need to get started on this right away," Maggie said. "Someone must have followed Theo to the vet's office or lured him there. I'll ask around and see what I can find out."

"You need to stay out of it. I'm the chief now, and you're going to have to let me do my job. If the killer's still in town, you might make yourself a target by being too nosy."

"I'm not stupid, you know. I'll be careful. Besides, people won't tell you the things they'll tell me," Maggie said. "Hannah will know everything there is to know by noon, anyway."

"I guess there's no point in trying to stop you."

"Not really," Maggie said.

She buttoned her coat over her flannel pajamas and left the station.

ROSE HILL by Pamela Grandstaff

# Chapter Three - Still Sunday

Scott was looking forward to seeing the lodge again, even though it was in tragic circumstances for the owner. He drove his own vehicle, leading the way for the two sheriff's deputies, who had a signed search warrant.

The house was perched on one of the ridge tops of Pine Mountain, at the end of a long, curving driveway. It faced southeast, overlooking Gerrymaine Valley, a high alpine valley encircled by mountains on protected state forest land. When the humidity was low, and the sky was clear, you could see all the way to Bear Lake, which shone like glass, reflecting the lush green of spring and summer, the burnished gold, and red of fall, or the stark grey and white of winter. This part of the Allegheny Mountains still displayed a largely unspoiled natural beauty, mostly due to the laws that protected it from people like Theo.

Sarah's team members used the dead man's house key to enter the house, and pointedly did not ask Scott to join them, so he went in the opposite direction, up the drive toward the kennel. Willy's old truck was not parked anywhere Scott could see, but the county animal control truck was parked between the garage and barn.

Hannah Campbell was supervising Theo's dogs as they ran and played in the deep snow of a fenced meadow. Scott hailed her, and she walked up to the fence to meet him.

"What are you doing out here?" Scott asked.

"Hello to you, too, Chief Gordon," Hannah said, as she held up a net bag of tennis balls. "What does it look like I'm doing?"

"I can see that, but why?"

When she handed Scott a ball, he threw it down to the end of the meadow. Baying and barking, a multicolored pack of retrievers sped off to find it, kicking up snow as they went.

"Well, Theo can't very well do it himself, now, can he? Being dead and all."

Hannah hitched herself up and over the fence.

'She couldn't weigh 100 pounds,' he thought, as he helped her down the other side.

No one could call Hannah pretty, with her prominent nose, closely spaced hazel eyes and thin lips. She did nothing to try to enhance what she had with makeup or hairstyle, preferring to slick her mousy brown hair back into a stubby ponytail anchored down by a baseball cap and to leave her plain face clean.

"Why are you doing it, though?" Scott asked. "Isn't this Willy's job?"

"Drew called me this morning and asked me to check on the dogs," she said. "He said Theo was dead and Willy wasn't answering his phone."

Scott followed Hannah into the barn, where she picked up a pressure sprayer attached to a long hose and turned on the water spigot. Hannah sprayed the concrete floor, so the muck in each kennel rolled into a grate-covered drain.

"How did Drew say Theo died?" Scott asked.

"Said he didn't know the details and I shouldn't tell anybody."

Scott took the hose from Hannah when she handed it to him and washed out the kennels on the other side as she disinfected the clean side. The mess was stinky, but it seemed a wholesome kind of smell compared to the foul stench at the murder scene. Hannah sprayed the disinfectant from a gallon jug connected to a sprayer and hose. It smelled like pine and reminded Scott of scout camp outhouses.

"And your good friend Maggie didn't call you early this morning?" Scott asked.

"No comment."

"And you haven't been on the phone all morning gathering information from various sources?"

"I'd like to call my attorney before I answer any more questions."

"All right," Scott said. "Off the record, just tell me the local consensus."

"Well, by the state of him last night I'd say he either drank himself to death or drove into a tree."

Scott turned, dowsing Hannah's feet.

"You saw Theo last night? When?"

Hannah turned off the spigot, took the nozzle from Scott, and coiled the hose back up.

"Around midnight. He and Willy Neff came out to the farm in Willy's truck. When we got outside, Theo was yelling about the black lab I found out at the state park a few days ago. He said it belonged to him and he wanted it."

Hannah began disinfecting the kennels Scott had washed out, and Scott sat down on the stairs to the hayloft.

"Was he driving?"

"Willy was driving, and he was none too sober himself."

"Tell me everything that happened, from the beginning."

Hannah turned off the valve, set down the disinfectant sprayer and canister, and then hopped up to sit on top of several forty-pound bags of dog food stacked on a pallet. Ignoring Scott's disapproving look, she took out a pack of cigarettes and a lighter and lit up. The doors and windows were open, so a cold, stiff breeze blew the smoke out of the barn as quickly as she could exhale it. She was far enough away from Scott so that he wasn't bothered by it, but he hated seeing her do it.

Hannah picked a piece of tobacco off her tongue and flicked it away.

"The dogs woke me up when they heard Willy's truck come over the ridge. It was after midnight, maybe 12:30. I don't remember but Sam might; he was still up working. I got up and threw on some duds, thinking there must be some kind of emergency. When we got outside, Theo was yelling he had come for his dog. Sam took a shotgun out with him and that, combined with our dogs barking at him, convinced Theo to get back in the truck."

"He was drunk?"

"Mean and crazy drunk; you know how he gets. Said I'd kidnapped his dog and Drew was going to castrate it, and we were all in cahoots to steal this prize black lab, worth thousands of dollars."

"Thousands? Could that be true?"

"Oh, yeah. I heard a guy bought a German shorthaired pointer from Theo for four thousand and the dog turned out to be gun shy."

"Expensive house pet," Scott said, thinking fast and furiously, trying to work out a timeline. "So how long was he at your place?"

"I'm not exactly sure. It seemed like a long time but was probably only ten or fifteen minutes. I told him the dog was not in my kennel, that Drew had him at the clinic. He called me a liar and a few other things. My darling husband took exception to that and fired a warning shot over the truck, so they left. Willy could probably tell you if he wasn't too drunk to remember. He's not home, though. I checked."

Scott wondered again what Willy Neff's part in all this had been, and where he had gone.

"If Willy's passed out in his truck somewhere it may be hours before he comes home," Scott said.

"He could also be dead in a ditch, and who would care?" Hannah said. "Nobody, that's who."

"And when did Drew call you about Theo's dogs?"

"About ten. I was in my truck, headed to the store."

"Which means the scanner grannies heard every word."

Hannah nodded, saying, "Yep."

"Any idea where Theo was headed when he left your place?"

"No, but I wouldn't be surprised if he went to Drew's house."

"He knew where Drew lives?"

"He should have; he was the landlord."

Scott reflected that Drew hadn't mentioned that fact.

"Are you going to tell me what happened?" Hannah asked. "You might as well, you know. The scanner grannies will tell me anyway."

The scanner grannies were a group of senior citizens in town who kept their hearing aids glued to their older model police scanner radios. Using anything other than a landline in Rose Hill was akin to using a party line in the old days, as these now illegal type scanners could pick up many mobile phone and cordless phone calls as well as firefighter and police radio communications.

"Somebody whacked him over the head in the back room of the vet clinic," Scott said.

"He must have gone there looking for the dog," she said. "Who do you think killed him?"

"I don't know," Scott said. "He had plenty of enemies."

Hannah slid off the pallet of dog food, put her cigarette out in a puddle of water on the cement floor, and threw it in the trash bin.

"No one in Rose Hill will care who did it. Everyone will just be glad he's gone," she said. "That doesn't make your job any easier."

"The sheriff's department has the case, and I'm just helping out as they let me."

"Ohhhh, so you spent the morning with the defective detective?"

"Officially, Hannah, only officially."

"That woman is hornier than that whole pack of dogs," Hannah said. "She'll be humping your leg by nightfall."

"That's not gonna happen," Scott said. "I've established strong professional boundaries."

"You better watch out," Hannah said. "She's got a pointy head and a sharp tongue, and you are on her to-do list. I was conferring with my investigative partner on this very subject just this morning."

"You and Maggie need to stay out of this one. I mean it."

"I can't help it if people tell me things," Hannah said. "I'm just a very good listener."

"This is serious," he said. "I don't want you two involved. It could be dangerous."

"Yeah, yeah, yeah," Hannah said. "I get it."

"I may need to talk to you again, and I've no doubt someone from the sheriff's office will be around to talk to you and Sam," Scott said, preparing to leave.

Hannah clicked her heels together and saluted.

"I will make sure all my papers are in order, sir."

"You might as well have your gun permits handy. They will probably want to see them."

"Yes, sir. Anything else, sir?"

"At ease soldier. Have you told me everything?"

Hannah followed him out of the barn, shrugging in response to his question.

"I'm working on a comic book name for Sarah," Hannah said. "I'll let you know what I come up with."

The dogs were now lounging around the meadow, panting, and some were rolling on their backs in the snow. When Scott helped Hannah climb up and over the fence the dogs boosted themselves up from the ground and swarmed around her. Hannah took turns patting and rubbing them as they jostled each other for a position near her.

"How do the dogs seem to you?" Scott asked.

"Frisky and frustrated, just like your pint-sized policewoman," Hannah said. "They need to run nonstop for a week just to get their ya-yas out. I'll keep an eye on them."

Scott admired the shiny coats and lean muscles of the different breeds represented in the pack. There weren't any black labs, but there were two chocolate and two yellow.

"Do you think that stray was his?" he asked.

Hannah herded the dogs toward the barn entrance, and some of them veered off, not wanting to go back inside. She produced a bag of treats from her coat pocket to lure them back.

"If Theo had a black lab there's no paperwork for him," she said. "I checked that first thing when I got here. Everyone else is accounted for, and their tags match the records in the office. You want to hear something weird, though?"

"Always," Scott said.

"They're all males."

"So? Aren't they supposed to be?"

"It's a funny way to run a breeding business is all," Hannah said. "Usually a breeder keeps some females and raises litters to sell or replenish stock."

Scott didn't know the first thing about the dog breeding business, so he just shrugged.

"Just thought I'd mention it," Hannah said.

Scott leaned over the fence so he could still see her as she walked backward into the barn, enticing the dogs back in their kennels with the treats.

"So why would he claim the dog was his if it wasn't?" Scott asked.

"Sheer cussed meanness," she called out as she backed out of sight.

Scott went around to the side of the old stable, now a garage, where a flight of steps led up to Willy's apartment. He knocked and called out, but no one answered. He tried the door and found it was unlocked.

As he entered the apartment, the stench hit him first. His eyes watered and he was immediately made nauseous by it. He propped open the door and went back outside to gulp a few deep breaths of clean air. A quick inspection revealed an apartment filled with garbage and filth, but no Willy Neff.

Willy skulked around town, a target of abuse and derision, and Scott could hardly stand to be in his presence for more than a few seconds. Willy avoided him for the most part, which was understandable, and when he did talk to Scott, it was in a whining, pitiful tone that irritated the hell out of him.

He wondered what would happen to Willy now with his protector and benefactor dead. As small and physically weak as Willy was, and as much as he depended upon Theo for his home and any money he could earn, Scott couldn't imagine him killing the much bigger man. He may have seen who did do it, however, and was hiding.

Scott went back to the lodge house, but stayed outside, out of the way. He wanted to sit down somewhere quiet with a pen and paper and try to figure out the timeline and to make a list of people to question.

He had been awake now for almost twenty-four hours and was feeling a little bleary-eyed. The sun was burning off the fog, and he could see a portion of the silvery surface of Bear Lake down in the valley. Scott sat down in one of the rockers on the porch and closed his eyes for just a second, enjoying the warmth of the sunshine on his face.

One of the deputies cleared his throat and woke Scott up. He looked amused as Scott apologized.

"I want you to verify the list of what we're taking," the deputy said.

Together they went through the items the deputies had gathered in several cardboard file boxes. They had a large stack of Theo's paper files, his day planner, and the hard drive from his PC. Among the personal belongings were a zip-lock plastic bag half-full of pot, several prescription bottles of pills, a few vials of white powder, and an old-looking gold coin.

After one of the deputies gave him the house key and left, Scott called Sarah from inside the house on Theo's landline. He told her Willy was missing and about Drew calling Hannah to tell her Theo was dead. Sarah thanked him and abruptly ended the call, leaving Scott feeling dismissed and left out. This was the county's case now, but it was his town, and he wanted to do something.

Scott admired the interior of the house. The spacious entryway was paved in flagstone, and separated two large rooms on either side, framed by tall, timbered archways. This central corridor was open to the exposed timber framed ceiling, peaking about 40 feet above the ground floor, and ended in a broad, carved oak stairway that led to the rooms on the second floor.

Just to the side of the central stairway was a narrow hallway back to the kitchen, and Scott went back there to look around. The kitchen had been updated with newer commercial grade appliances since his last visit, as a teenager. The large, heavy wooden work island in the center was the same as he remembered, scarred by many knives and heavy ceramic bowls. Scott could remember seeing an entire roasted pig being cut up on this work surface by several staff members during a summer barbecue. Theo had chased girls with the pig's tail all afternoon.

The kitchen was centered between a dining room on one side and a study on the other. Scott walked through the spacious wood-paneled dining room and noted that although the table was set for two, only one of the place settings had been used. He went through to the spacious front sitting room that featured a high ceiling, a polished wood floor, ornately patterned rugs, heavy dark furniture in the mission style, and a large fieldstone fireplace.

He then crossed through the entryway to the library, which had the air of a room rarely used. Scott studied a collection of silver-framed family photos displayed on a polished grand piano. He remembered Theo's father as a larger than life, red-faced man with an upper-class British accent, a potbelly, purple, bulbous nose, and a bad temper. He was pictured here holding a large shotgun broken down over the crook of his arm, kneeling next to the carcass of an elk with an impressive display of antlers. Scott wondered if it was the same elk head as the one prominently displayed over the fireplace in the sitting room.

Theo's photograph, snapped at his college graduation, proved he had inherited the majority of the paternal DNA. Theo had attended a succession of boarding schools but came back to Pine Mountain Lodge every summer with his British accent refreshed and new methods of torture devised for anyone weaker than himself.

Twenty years ago Theo had broken Scott's nose for trying to interfere with him torturing Sean Fitzpatrick, one of Maggie's brothers. It had required several lodge staff members to pull Maggie's brother Patrick off Theo afterward. Those old animosities never dissipated over the years, but just simmered beneath the surface.

Theo's mother, a fragile blonde with a gracious, poised demeanor, looked young and delicate in her black and white bridal photo. She had been a lovely, kind woman who seemed overwhelmed by her domineering husband and belligerent eldest son.

There was a photo of Theo's sister Gwyneth as a teenager, her long blonde hair haloed in sunlight, seated in an Adirondack chair on the dock down by the lake, reading a book. Like Theo, she was a boarding school student, and affected the same pretentious accent and snobbish disdain for "the locals." From what Scott remembered, Gwyneth spent her summers sighing dramatically, perceiving slights, complaining about being too hot or too cold, and looking down her nose at everyone.

It was through younger siblings Brad and Caroline that Scott and his friends were invited to Pine Mountain Lodge. Brad was a good-natured, good-looking kid who was popular and athletic. He and his sister Caroline, several years younger than Theo and Gwyneth, had been allowed to stay in Rose Hill to attend school.

There was a photo here of Brad as a teenager, embracing his mother with one arm as they stood on the front porch of the lodge. He had sun-streaked blonde hair and bright blue eyes, looked mischievous and good-humored. While he faced the camera, his mother was looking up at him in delighted adoration. He was fifteen the summer he drowned.

Caroline was the youngest, a sweet, outgoing girl who loved horses, so it was no surprise to see her portrayed in full riding gear seated in an English saddle on the back of a glistening Tennessee Walker. She, like Brad, had many friends, and there was always a pack of kids running about the place all summer. After Brad died, Caroline was sent away to boarding school as well, and there were no more fun summers at the lodge.

Scott left the library and entered the billiard room. He lifted a tablecloth draped over a small-scale model set up on the pool table. It was a development model for a large tract of land, with subdivisions of homes, condos, hotels, and a golf course around a lake. Scott shook his head at the absurd logo for "Eldridge Point." It was a very muscular looking eagle in flight with a comically fierce look on its face, its talons gripping a bouquet made up of a golf club, a fishing pole, an oar, and a ski pole. Scott covered it back up with the tablecloth and entered the study.

Although he could tell the sheriff's deputies had thoroughly searched the premises, Scott looked through the desk in the study anyway but didn't find anything interesting. He felt underneath all the drawers and the desktop, but nothing was taped under there. He looked behind all the books on the bookshelves, pressed on the wood molding around them, and looked behind the pictures on the wall. Maybe he'd watched too many crime shows, he thought to himself, but if ever there was someone likely to be hiding something it was Theo Eldridge.

The study closet was full of boxes, and Scott pulled them all out and went through them. They were full of clothing and other promotional merchandise with the ridiculous Eldridge Point logo on them. Before he put them back in the closet, he checked the walls of the closet in case there were any dummy panels with a hiding space behind them, but they were solid cedar. The floor was made of thick pine planks, and the ceiling looked to be made of the same cedar as the walls. Scott put all the boxes back in the closet and shut the door.

Scott found the housekeeper's name and number by the phone in the lodge kitchen; Gail Godwin was a woman he knew from town. He wondered if she would know who it was Theo expected for dinner, and why this person didn't show up. He called her house and left a message, telling her not to bother coming to Theo's until he notified her, and to drop off her keys at the police station. Being a church-going woman, he assumed she probably already knew more than he did, or would immediately dial one of her friends to get the details.

Scott was a church-going person himself, and although he saw many of his fellow congregants perform selfless good deeds, he also broke up their domestic disputes, heard their bitter complaints about the neighbors they were supposed to love, and bore their constant criticism.

Scott stretched the yellow crime scene tape back across the front door after he locked up. With only one full time and one part-time deputy, he didn't have enough staff members to leave someone on guard here.

Hannah's truck was gone, and the dog kennel was quiet. The day was getting on, and he could feel a headache developing from lack of sleep and food. He shook out the last migraine pill from a small bottle he kept in the center console of his SUV and took it, hoping he caught it in time. He didn't need a setback right now.

Back in town, he checked in at the station, where Frank told him the physician at the emergency care clinic had examined and released Ed. Frank said he brought him back to the station to write his official statement, and then took him home. Skip also said a lot of people were just happening to drop by the station to ask questions about the yellow tape around the vet's office.

Scott left Frank in charge and drove up the hill to his house on Sunflower Street. Sitting at his kitchen table, he wrote out his notes before he gave in to exhaustion and went to bed. As he fell asleep, he happened to think of Tommy, the newspaper delivery boy, and got back up to call Skip.

"He was waiting outside the newspaper office," Skip said. "Said he'd overslept and seemed really sorry about it. We sat on the tailgate of my truck and rolled papers, and then I drove, and he threw. He didn't say more than ten words to me, but the kid has a great arm."

Scott thanked him and hung up. Relieved to know the boy was safe, Scott let himself sink into the sweet oblivion of sleep.

As Maggie left the church, flanked by her mother Bonnie and Aunt Alice, she saw Hannah's animal control truck parked a little way down the block. As they approached, Hannah waved out the window and then leaned over to open the passenger side door for Maggie.

Watching her mother and Hannah's mother in the side mirror as they pulled away from the curb, Maggie said, "I'll get an earful about this later."

"I don't let my mother bother me anymore," Hannah said. "Why worry about pleasing the unpleasable?"

"My mother just assumes if you and I are together we must be doing something wrong."

"That's because we so often are," said Hannah.

She drove Maggie home so she could change, and then drove them both out to Hannah and Sam's farm.

Maggie and Hannah were first cousins whose fathers were brothers, and they, along with their cousin Claire, had been friends all their lives. They were "as tight as ticks" or "as thick as thieves," according to their mothers, and had an unbreakable bond of loyalty and love between them that, so far, no man or woman had been able to sever.

Even when they weren't speaking over some disagreement, Hannah could always call up Maggie and say, "I know we aren't talking right now, but did you know the English professor with the bad comb-over has run off with the bursar's wife?"

"I guess you heard all the gossip at church," Hannah said. "Who do all the good Christian people think killed him?"

"Someone he screwed over," Maggie said. "Someone he lied to or cheated."

"That includes most of the county, doesn't it?"

"Pretty much. Why do you think he was at the vet's?"

"To get that stray. Unless there's something more going on we don't know about."

"We need to talk to Drew."

"I was thinking of having him over for dinner this week. Want to come, too?"

"Yes," Maggie said. "I'm dying to know why the guy really moved here."

"Good. We can grill him for dinner."


Hannah and Sam Campbell owned a couple hundred acres outside of town, accessed by a long, curvy dirt road which branched off of Hollyhock Ridge. Their farm sat in a small valley surrounded by mountain ridges, with a pond and a large meadow. They had converted the barn into a kennel to house the strays Hannah brought home on her job, and although it wasn't nearly as fancy as Theo's was, it was clean, warm, and dry—conditions her canine inmates rarely experienced in their often short, painful lives.

As they crested the last hill of the long driveway, all the kenneled dogs started barking, yelping, and howling, and the two house dogs, Jax, a Husky mix, and Wally, a Border Collie, came running to meet them.

"If Sam wasn't awake before he will be now," Hannah said.

Sam was a network security consultant who worked from an office in their home. Years ago, while escorting a convoy outside Kuwait during the Gulf War, his unit was attacked. Because of the injuries he received, both legs had to be amputated just below his knees. After an extended recovery period, Sam married Hannah, and they renovated the farm to accommodate Sam's wheelchair, adding wide doorways and a series of wooden ramps and walkways to the various outbuildings.

A quick check inside proved her husband was working, so Hannah and Maggie took some beer and chips and retired to the "parlor," their word for the tiny, messy office in the barn. It consisted of two old horsehair-filled armchairs, a battered desk and chair, a filing cabinet, and an electric milk house heater. Hannah turned up the heater, and they slumped back in their chairs to smoke and gossip. Hannah never smoked in front of Sam, who hated it with a passion, and although Maggie had given up nagging her about it, she still refused to breathe it second hand.

Hannah found an empty soda can to use as an ashtray and lit up. Squinting to keep from getting smoke in her eyes, she cranked open the window more so the draft would suck the smoke out, and then waved her hands to try to clear the air.

"You ought to put Scott out of his misery," she said as she sat back down.

"Not gonna happen," Maggie responded. "He's too nice."

"A man is like a kit. You have to put him together to suit you. Look at Sam. I made him what he is today."

"A technology genius slash virtual recluse?"

Hannah flicked ash in Maggie's direction, and Maggie had to jump up to avoid the glowing embers that came with it.

"No, smart ass, he's a well-behaved husband. We get along great."

Maggie thought but didn't say Hannah's description of her husband was true when Sam was feeling well. When Sam was feeling down he could be very difficult to live with, but Hannah pretended it rarely happened, and when it did, it didn't count.

"I would only disappoint Scott," Maggie said. "He has this ideal image of me in his head that I can never live up to. He doesn't think I'm being myself when I'm always being myself, just not the person he wants me to be. He drives me crazy, saying, 'don't say that,' 'don't think that,' and 'you don't mean that' until I can hardly stand to be around him."

"You can tell yourself that, but you can't fool me. You turn bright red every time he shows up."

Maggie thought of Scott. He had hazel eyes with long, dark, curled up lashes, a crooked nose, and a beautiful smile. His chestnut hairline might be receding, but he was a powerfully built, good-looking man with a great ass, and even the smell of the laundry soap he used on his clothes could make her weak at the knees.

"I am attracted to him, and I'm fond of him too. He's a good man," she admitted. "But he makes me crazy, and we would fight all the time. And that mother..."

"She hates any woman who might steal her little precious," Hannah said and lit another cigarette off the one she'd just finished.

"She's vicious," Maggie said. "Except it's all so passive-aggressive, and you know how that kind of hatefulness always goes over a man's head."

"Why is that?" Hannah demanded. "It's like only we can see the barbed wire wrapped around the seemingly innocent comment."

"If I married Scott she would constantly interfere and try to tell me what to do. I don't think I could bear it, and eventually, it would split us up."

"Sharon found out the hard way," Hannah said, and Maggie nodded.

Scott met his ex-wife Sharon at a community college, where he was studying criminal justice, and she was taking paralegal courses. A petite blonde with big, innocent-looking blue eyes, she had a mind like a steel trap, which she took care to keep hidden behind a studied naiveté and a breathless little girl voice. She set her sights on Scott and applied herself to win over his mother as if it were an Olympic event. His mother Marcia enjoyed being flattered and catered to until her guard lowered. Before she realized what was happening, Sharon had snagged her son, married him, and installed him in a house of her own, right under Marcia's nose. Not, however, out of her reach.

Marcia and Sharon had Scott stretched tight between them for a while, as Sharon desperately tried to get pregnant and Marcia became ill with a succession of nonspecific complaints involving fainting spells and continual weeping, which required her son's constant attention. After a humiliating round of doctor appointments confirmed Scott was unlikely to father children, Sharon assessed her quality of life married to him and his mother and decided to cut her losses to pursue bigger game in the city.

"Sharon had the right idea," Maggie said. "Abandon ship."

"Not me, baby," Hannah said. "I made Sam's mom walk the plank."

Maggie smiled, thinking about the fight Hannah and her mother-in-law had at the reception after her and Sam's wedding when Hannah told Mama Campbell she needed to pull the self-pity bug out of her ass and accept the fact her son could have a good life married to Hannah and living in a wheelchair.

"You have to admit Mama Campbell's hostility wasn't veiled with anything," Maggie said, "and her aggression was anything but passive."

"That's true."

Maggie picked at the horsehair sticking out of a hole in the upholstery and pictured herself walking down the church aisle toward Scott. Each time she did so, his mother barred the way.

"I just don't see it happening," Maggie said.

"Is it also maybe because you think Gabe might come back?" Hannah asked.

Just then, both women heard the unmistakable sound of Sam's wheelchair rolling down the wood plank boardwalk toward the barn, and Hannah hurriedly hid all signs of tobacco usage.

"Hey," he called out, as he got closer. "You two juvenile delinquents aren't smoking in my barn, are you?"

Hannah cranked open the window as far as it would go so she and Maggie could stick their heads out.

"Your barn? I think you mean my barn," Hannah said. "We're having a prayer meeting in here. It's the Lord's Day, you know."

He grinned at them as he stopped his chair just beneath the window.

"So I guess you're using my good microbrew for communion," he said.

"That's right, mister, and your organic-shmanic blue corn chips for wafers."

"Blasphemer," he accused.

"Godless heathen," Hannah replied.

"Come fix my lunch, woman," he said, but the tender look he gave Hannah warmed Maggie's heart. The man was drop-dead gorgeous, a certified brainiac, and his mother lived over a thousand miles away. She could see how Hannah could forgive a few episodes of depression.

'When he was good, he was very, very good,' she thought to herself, neglecting to finish the rhyme.

Maggie and Hannah got Sam caught up on the gossip as they tag-team cooked a big breakfast for their lunch while he set the table. Just as they put the food on the table, they heard a vehicle coming over the ridge, and the house dogs took off barking.

Hannah looked out the window and reported, "It's Patrick, and he's got Ed with him."

"I better get some more plates," Sam said. "Get a bottle of whiskey out of the cupboard, will ya, Maggie?"

When the men arrived Patrick stuck his tongue out at his sister Maggie by way of greeting, but Ed looked pale and wouldn't meet their eyes. Everything felt odd and uncomfortable, so Maggie and Hannah decided to have lunch in town, leaving the men to eat the feast they had prepared.

"He looked awful," Maggie said to Hannah as they got in the animal control truck. "Did you see the huge knot on his head?"

"Better leave them to eat, drink, and compare conspiracy theories," Hannah said, as they bumped up the rutted drive.

"We have to help Scott figure out who did it," Maggie said. "We can't let Sarah beat him to it."

"I bet the scanner grannies are peeing their pants over this," Hannah said. "They've all had time to compare notes and eat lunch by now. I think it's time to check in with a few of my regulars and see what's what."

She got out her phone and pulled over as soon as she had service.

Hannah was a virtual repository of Rose Hill gossip due to her frequent visits to the homes of these shut-ins, often arriving with a kitten or puppy they could hold and cuddle while Hannah made sure their prescriptions were filled and they had enough heat, food, and toilet paper. There were three different church committees in town whose members also performed these charitable visits, but Hannah free-lanced without regard to denomination. She was more popular because she shared her cigarettes and could be counted on for the occasional bottle of beer.

When Hannah got off the phone, she gave her report.

"Gladys Davis lives closest to the clinic, but Marlene Thompson says the students who live over Delvecchio's Insurance Agency were having a wild party last night and Gladys couldn't sleep, so she turned off her hearing aids. She didn't hear anything after that."

"That's helpful."

"Alva Johnston says she heard the Jamaican man you have working in your bookstore got arrested last night, so she thinks he might have killed Theo over a drug deal gone bad."

Maggie's face flushed.

"First of all, Mitchell was born and raised in Charlottesville, Virginia, and his dreadlocks represent a hairstyle, not a drug habit. Secondly, he was not arrested;

46

he was picked up and held overnight for being drunk and disorderly. He is not a drug dealer. He is a sweet, gentle young man, a political science major, and my second best barista."

"So you say," Hannah teased her.

"You tell those old busybodies if they persist in slandering my innocent employee, his father, who is a prosecuting attorney, will haul their hip replacements into court."

"Yeah, yeah, yeah," Hannah said. "Someone else said they saw you out on the street in your pajamas early this morning. Care to explain that?"

"You know where I went, to the station to baby-sit Mitchell."

"Uh huh. Looks mighty suspicious to me. Maybe you were bailing out your Jamaican drug-dealing lover. Admit it! He was having an affair with Theo, who you killed in a jealous rage!"

"Who said they saw me?"

"Nobody. I was just messing with ya."

"You stink."

"I smell better than your Jamaican drug dealer's dead lover does about now."


The two women settled on Dairy Chef for lunch and had the place pretty much to themselves. They sat in their usual booth, as far away from the front counter as it was possible to get, near the restrooms.

"I guess Sarah's taking over the case," Hannah said, around her first mouthful of fries.

Maggie did a great, although unwitting imitation of her mother's pursed-lipped look of disapproval.

"She can have him," she said, but her tone lacked conviction.

It seemed to Maggie that county sheriff's investigator Sarah Albright had everything she lacked.

47

Maggie was a tall, curvy woman with blue eyes, pale, freckled skin, and bright red curly hair. She never felt like anything about her appearance was under control. Her shirt was always coming untucked, her pants always felt too tight across her hips yet too loose at the waist, and a wild curl was always escaping from her hairdo. On top of that, she was cursed by a rash-like blush which blossomed across her chest and face whenever she felt the slightest emotion.

Sarah, on the other hand, was tiny and perfectly proportioned. Her clothes were always a coordinated, fashionable ensemble; her shiny, precision-cut hair and flawlessly applied makeup were both flattering and stylish. She was well-educated and confident and had a natural authority which people seemed to respect.

Sarah was courteous to her, but Maggie knew she was secretly wondering what Scott found so attractive. Maggie didn't know, either, but she resented the mental comparison she imagined Sarah made between them, in which the younger, slimmer woman easily won. When Sarah was around Maggie felt like a giant red and white Macy's Day parade balloon.

"You should have heard her coming on to him," Maggie said. "She's shameless."

"You better not let him simmer too long," Hannah said. "He might just boil over for someone else."

Hannah tucked into her lunch with gusto while Maggie brooded some more.

"We need a comic book name for her," Hannah said. "What should it be?"

"You're better at that than me. You pick."

"Tiny Crimefighter?" suggested Hannah.

"Better yet," Maggie countered. "Tiny Trollop."

"Tiny Trollop, the crime-fighting kitten," Hannah said. "She's the tiny paw of the law."

Maggie took a bite of her now cold hamburger and made a face. Hannah had already finished her hamburger and a large order of fries and was keeping an eye on what remained of Maggie's lunch.

"What do you think can be wrong with her?" Maggie asked. "She seems so perfect."

With this admission, Maggie lost her appetite and put her sandwich down on the tray.

"Well," Hannah replied thoughtfully, as she picked up the discarded sandwich and added a thick layer of mustard and ketchup to it, "maybe she has really bad breath, like a coffee-drinking skunk with post nasal drip."

"That's what I like to hear," Maggie said. "Go on."

"And unfortunately I fear there's a bit of a chronic farting problem," Hannah said.

"Poor thing," Maggie said. "I hate that for her."

"It's very sad," Hannah said. "These aren't lady-like tooters we're talking about. These are noxious methane gases that melt polyester and set cotton on fire. So dangerous is her flatulence that she is forced to wear asbestos panties."

"Thanks," Maggie said. "I feel much better."

"That's what friends are for," Hannah said. "Are you going to finish those fries?"


Scott was deeply asleep when his mother called to see why he had not come to dinner. He hurriedly showered, dressed, and ran over there, where she was pouting at the front door.

"It won't be any good now it's cold," she said. "You could have at least called."

Scott kissed her temple and apologized, then went to the kitchen, where a perfectly prepared meal was waiting, and it was still hot. She refused to eat, saying she wasn't hungry. She cleaned the spotless kitchen instead, sighing heavily, while he ate.

His mother abhorred gossip so he couldn't ask her if she'd heard anything about Theo. He asked about his sister, got a blow-by-blow account of her latest phone call, and dutifully admired the newest pictures of his niece and nephew.

"They've invited me to come for two weeks next month so I can be there when the twins are confirmed," she said.

This led her to lament his missing Mass that morning.

"I was investigating Theo Eldridge's murder," he said.

"I don't appreciate your tone, young man. You could still have let me know you were going to miss church and be late for dinner."

"I'm sorry, Mom," he said, as all his resistance drained out of him. "I got busy and didn't think."

"Didn't think about me, you mean," she said. "I'm just your mother, I know. I don't rate up there with murderers and people from the county sheriff's office. I didn't know where you were or what had happened to you. You could have been lying dead by the side of the road, for all I knew."

She dissolved into tears, and he got up and hugged her, even as she pretended to turn away. It felt stuffy in the house, and Scott had an urge to open a window and let some air into the room. His mother had a horror of drafts, however, and he knew from experience that all the windows were painted shut.


When Scott left his mother's house, awake again from several cups of coffee, he drove out the narrow dirt road known as Possum Holler to Drew Rosen's house. As he pulled up, he could see Drew was attempting to shovel his walkway with a flimsy plastic shovel. Scott pulled a heavy steel shovel out of the back of his SUV and assisted, making better headway using the proper tool. After they had the path cleared, Drew thanked him, but he was obviously not glad to see him. Scott returned the shovel to his vehicle and faced the man.

"You want to do this outside or inside?"

Drew invited him in.

The old house was shabby and drafty, and Scott felt sorry for anyone who had to live like this. The recuperating black lab was stretched out on a broken down couch on top of a puffy sleeping bag, and merely acknowledged their presence with a wan lift of the head and listless thump of the tail before going back to sleep. A fire blazed in the large gas box stove, but the warmth only radiated out a few feet before a perpetual icy draft dissipated it.

Scott pulled a chair out from a wobbly kitchen table, on top of which sat a big wooden bowl with an oversized tabby cat in it. Duke opened one golden eye to consider Scott before yawning, stretching, and repositioning himself for a better look. Scott accepted Drew's offer of tea and reached over to rub the top of the big cat's head.

"I wouldn't do that if I were you," Drew said, watching with some concern.

"Duke and I are good buddies," Scott said. "He sometimes accompanies me on my rounds at night."

He scratched Duke's head, and the big cat erupted into a deep, rumbling purr, his eyes squeezed closed in pleasure.

Drew gave Scott a dubious look, but Scott nodded.

"He does. And sometimes he comes home with me and sleeps in my kitchen."

"I'm sorry if he's making a nuisance of himself," Drew said. "I advise my clients to keep their cats indoors, but if I try to keep him inside, he attacks me."

"He's good company," Scott said. "I don't mind at all."

"When I bought the practice, the vet's widow told me Duke was the clinic's blood donor cat. The first time I tried to draw blood from him, he got more out of me."

"Owen loved cats, but his wife hates them," Scott said. "That was probably the excuse he gave her for keeping the cat around. No wonder he doesn't like you."

There was a short, reasonably comfortable silence, and then Scott reminded Drew why he came.

"You need to tell me more about the altercation you had with Theo," Scott said. "You didn't mention he was your landlord. You also claimed you didn't recognize his body, but you called Hannah this morning and told her he was dead. When you lie to me and leave stuff out, my imagination fills in all sorts of horrible reasons why."

Drew stiffened, and at first, Scott thought he was going to deny it, but then he sighed heavily.

"Okay," he said. "You were probably going to find out anyway."

Scott sat back and sipped his tea while the vet talked.

"Before I took over the practice, I looked at the books, so I knew a large part of the revenue came from the retainer for Theo's breeding business. He paid Owen a set amount per month for vetting all the dogs, plus bonuses for each litter. I recently discovered, however, that there were no litters, except on paper."

"What do you mean?"

"Theo had a kennel full of male dogs he would stud out for a fee, but Owen's files contain documentation, including AKC registrations, DNA results, and vet records, for females Theo didn't have and litters that were never born."

"I don't understand," Scott said. "How can it benefit him to have fake dog papers but not dogs?"

"Let me explain," Drew said. "Theo probably figured stud fees were easy money. He takes a horny male dog to a bitch in heat and nature takes its course 99.9% of the time. Whether or not a litter results, Theo gets paid something. If there's a litter, he gets paid more, or gets his choice of pups, depending upon the deal."

"How much did Theo make on each try?"

"Anywhere from a couple hundred to a couple thousand is my guess. Breeders are willing to pay more for champion bloodlines, and to prove lineage he needed AKC registration papers, DNA results, and vet records. He probably started out with some purebreds, but those dogs are expensive. Also, breeding dogs is a risky business. Bitches and pups can die during whelping, there's no guarantee any of the pups will be show quality or good breeding stock, and it's a lot of hard work. Plus, the more dogs he had, the more clients he could service."

"So he supplemented his authentic dogs with dogs who looked like purebreds but weren't?" Scott asked. "How could he claim they were pedigreed without DNA proof?"

"He could provide DNA from purebreds he did have when he registered them," Drew said. "Once he had established the legitimate sire and dam at the AKC, he had only to provide DNA evidence from their real offspring when submitting the DNA of subsequent imposter dogs. It's a mail-order test. Unless someone suspected something and did subsequent testing, he'd get by with it."

"So he could claim this stray black lab was one of the pedigreed offspring?"

"Once he dyed the white star on his chest, it would have been almost impossible to tell by looking that he wasn't pedigreed. Theo could have used the AKC registration from one of his fake litters and DNA from his actual purebreds. He may also have procured bad breeding stock from legitimate breeders."

"What do you mean by bad breeding stock?"

"Due to the limited availability of new breeding stock, dogs will sometimes have medical problems due to line breeding, which means a breeding couple has at least one ancestor in common. When this happens, some offspring may display genetic mutations, like odd color coats, physical defects, or behavioral problems, which keep them out of competition. If the breeders don't put them down as pups, they have them neutered so undesirable traits won't be passed on."

"Put them down for the wrong color coat? That's pretty cruel."

"It's called culling," Drew said. "Raising and showing dogs is expensive. You're making an investment you hope will pay off in titles, stud fees, and puppy sales. Why would you waste money on stock that will never earn its keep? Breeding champion bloodline dogs is not a business for the faint-hearted."

"I had no idea," Scott said.

"Most of the breeders I know personally are in it because they love the dogs," Drew said. "They make sure healthy, non-standard pups are spayed or neutered so as not to be bred further, and then they keep them as pets or find homes for them. In this way, they keep their reputations and the integrity of their businesses intact. But you can see how indiscriminate breeders might create a surplus of non-revenue-producing dogs, and how they might be tempted to sell them to Theo. They'd have the champion DNA he needed to submit for the non-purebreds."

"Why didn't the people he sold his services to figure out his scam when they got funny colored pups and gun-shy bird dogs?"

"My guess is he stayed clear of professionals and preyed on backyard breeders, who are often amateurs inexperienced enough to be fooled. If someone complained, Theo could provide paperwork to back up the sire, and suggest it was the dam at fault. If that client escalated their complaint to the AKC, Theo's dog would have its DNA retested, and if it did not match the registration, he would not only lose his AKC registration but be fined and banned for life."

"So with Owen gone, Theo needed a new vet to sign off on the paperwork."

"He may have had paperwork stockpiled with Owen's signature, or he may have been forging Owen's name since he died. Either way, using a dead vet's name was bound to catch up with him, especially if he sold his services anywhere locally. People do call and check out these dogs. They're spending a lot of money, and if they want to know about temperament and health, the vet can give them that information.

"The reason he came to my office yesterday, besides looking for the black lab, was because someone he sold stud services to was accusing him of substituting a non-pedigreed dog, and had taken his complaint to the AKC. The AKC was demanding a DNA retest performed by a vet, and he wanted me to provide it. Once I did that, he knew he could coerce me into being his new co-conspirator."

"And you told him no," Scott said.

"Not only did I tell him 'no,' but I also threatened to go to the police–you," Drew said.

"I assume he wasn't pleased with your answer," Scott said, imagining Theo blowing a gasket.

"Well, first he fired me as his vet," Drew said. "Then he said I ought to sleep with one eye open because I was living in a fire trap. And he would know, being the slumlord."

"Did you know the house next door to this one burned down after the owner refused to sell it to Theo?" Scott asked him. "No one believed it was an accident."

"I knew it burned down but not how," Drew said. "Wasn't that Maggie's house?"

Scott nodded, tipped his chair back, and ran his hands through his hair, putting these new puzzle pieces in place. Drew rose and lit the fire underneath the kettle to make more tea.

"So why didn't you tell us all this in the station?" Scott asked him.

"Because I hadn't come to you to report Theo's breeding scam. I was just bluffing when I told him I would. Not reporting a crime is a crime as well, right?"

Scott thought this over and decided not to respond.

"Why did you say you didn't recognize the deceased?"

"Because I didn't," Drew said. "I heard who it was over the radio in the squad car when your deputy drove me home."

Scott mentally cursed whoever it was who gave out the information over the airwaves while they had a suspect in the car. The kettle began to whistle and Drew offered Scott more tea, but he declined. Drew sat back down at the table with his own mug refilled.

Duke flicked his tail over the edge of the large bowl, turned over on his back, and then curled around in the opposite direction. Drew reached out to rub the big cat's head as Scott had done but drew it back when Duke made a low, ominous sound in his throat.

"So Theo had this fight with you, fired you, and then waited until early this morning to come to the clinic to do what?" Scott said. "Wreck the place? Burn it down?"

"Hannah said he was out to her place looking for the dog. I think he came to the clinic to steal the dog before I could neuter him. Other than the white star on his chest, the dog meets all the breed standards. He could steal the dog, dye the star black, give him new papers, get the DNA docs however it was he always did, and claim it was his purebred black lab. Wrecking or burning down the clinic afterward was probably also his plan, just to get back at me."

"But you would have known the dog was the same one, wouldn't you? You would have figured it was Theo who'd done it and could have pressed charges."

"Maybe," Drew said. "If he just stole the dog and didn't destroy the clinic I probably wouldn't have minded very much. It would be an awful lot of trouble to go to for a stray that would have food, water, and shelter at Theo's."

"You have a very elastic moral fiber," Scott said.

"I've treated so many victims of animal abuse," Drew said. "I may not have approved of his breeding practices, but compared to the lives most dogs lead, Theo's dogs have it made."

"Will you be able to make it without Theo's monthly fees?" Scott asked him as he stood to leave.

"We'll see," Drew said. "I may have to move into the office."

"It would be a distinct improvement over this," Scott said, not bothering to hide his look of pity.

"There's not a lot to choose from in this town that isn't student housing, and my late night partying days are way behind me."

Scott agreed, but made no suggestions, even though he knew of a couple available places. It wasn't that there weren't any, it's just that arrangements were usually made among Rose Hill families, and rarely accommodated outsiders.

Scott said goodbye, got in his SUV and then turned around in what used to be Maggie's driveway next door. The man who plowed the narrow gravel road still plowed that driveway as well, even though there was no house. It was now just a handy place to turn around, an empty lot covered in snow.

Scott was dead tired, but he wanted to see Maggie. When he got to the bookstore, he found her helping a student find textbooks using the young woman's class schedule. As soon as she had the stack of heavy books piled on the counter, she turned the customer over to a clerk and led Scott back to her office.

"I thought classes had already started," Scott said.

"They have," Maggie replied. "She's a late registration transfer."

"Has it been a good semester so far?"

She shrugged, and Scott thought she wouldn't admit it if it had been. When it came to business, Maggie took after her mother, a savvy businessperson descended from a long line of tight-lipped, frugal Scottish tradespeople.

He followed Maggie into her office and closed the door behind them. She sat at her desk and, after removing a stack of books lodged on the seat, Scott sat on the chair next to it. The monitor and keyboard took up half her workspace, and a pile of trade magazines and publisher's catalogs covered the other half. There was an inbox filled to the brim with what looked like packing slips and invoices, and the glass of the window into the bookstore was covered in yellow sticky notes vying for her attention.

"You look busy," he said.

"I am," she said. "In between everything else I'm expected to do, I still have a business to run."

"Would you rather I didn't take up your time talking about the case?"

"Of course not," she said and gave him her full attention.

"Well, first of all, I need to ask whether you saw anything unusual last night when you walked down to the station."

"I've been thinking about that. I did notice Theo's Hummer parked in front of the Thorn, but it often is, so I didn't think it was unusual. The fog was so thick I could barely see across the street. Evidently, there was a big party in Mitchell's ex-girlfriend's building, which may be why no one heard Theo breaking into the vet's office."

"What are the scanner grannies saying?"

Maggie told him what Hannah found out about Gladys Davis turning off her hearing aids because of the party noise. He made a note of it. She also told him the vicious gossip going around about Mitchell, and he shook his head.

"Tell him to let me know if anyone gives him any crap. I won't tolerate it."

Scott got her caught up on all he had done since he saw her last, and although he stayed on the subject, internally, he was swooning from her proximity. He couldn't quit looking at her mouth, no matter how often he reminded himself to maintain eye contact.

'I have got to get hold of myself,' he thought. 'I'm acting like a love-starved teenager.'

"So who killed him?" Maggie asked when he was finished talking.

"Too early to tell," Scott replied, noting the oversized blue oxford shirt she was wearing was gapping in the front just below her bust, giving him a peek at the pale pink lace bra she was wearing underneath.

"It will be harder to find someone who didn't want him dead," she said.

"Including you?" Scott asked her teasingly, admiring the rosy color in her cheeks and the freckles sprinkled over her nose.

"He burned my house down because I wouldn't sell it to him," she said. "He as much as bragged about it afterward in the Thorn."

"There was no proof, though," Scott said, noticing a long red curl escaping from Maggie's ponytail, and resisting the urge to wrap it around his finger. "The fire chief said it was the wiring."

"There was something fishy about that," Maggie said. "You know as well as I do there was nothing wrong with the wiring. I had all of it brought up to code after I bought the place."

"Chief Estep was an honest man," Scott said, conscious of the smell of her hair and skin now he was close enough to discern them. Her perfume was delicate and floral. "I find it hard to believe he could be bribed. He hated Theo with a passion."

"Too bad he's dead," Maggie said. "Or you'd have another good suspect."

"Mmm," Scott said, wondering what color panties Maggie was wearing, and imagining something lacy to match her bra.

"What's wrong with you?' Maggie asked him, in an irritated tone. "Are you drunk or something?"

"I think I might be," Scott said, with a grin.

"Then go home and sleep it off," she told him crossly, and reluctantly he did as she suggested.

# Chapter Four – Monday

When Scott checked in at the station at eight a.m., he had a message from Sarah, sounding irritated he wasn't in yet. She wanted him to pick up Theo's mail from the post office and arrange for it to be held. She also mentioned she would be in Rose Hill later and wanted to go over some to-do lists with him.

Scott sighed. It was bad enough he couldn't be in charge of investigating a murder on his own patch, but he hated having Sarah boss him around as well. He wanted to check on Ed, follow up on the whereabouts of Willy, and talk to everyone who might have seen or spoken to Theo on his last day alive, but instead, he dutifully headed toward the post office.

Scott walked down Rose Hill Avenue to the small post office, which was across the street from Maggie's bookstore. When he entered, he could see postmaster Margie Estep was attempting to help Mamie Rodefeffer–a cranky, wealthy senior citizen–buy some stamps. He almost backed out again, but Mamie turned and regarded him through thick lenses.

"Ah, good, the police," she said and waved her cane in Margie's direction. "You can arrest this woman for highway robbery."

Margie said, "The price of stamps went up, Mamie. I can't help it."

Scott went around the dividing wall and pretended to look at notices posted on the bulletin board opposite the post office boxes, while he listened to Margie and the wealthiest woman in town bicker over less than two dollars' worth of stamps.

"And I know you've been taking my *National Geographic* magazines," Mamie accused Margie as she left.

Scott smiled in sympathy at Margie, whose small round face was bright pink with irritation. Margie Estep was a short, pudgy woman in her late forties, with a graying brown Dutch-boy haircut and a plain face made all the more unbecoming by dated-looking large-framed glasses. Her wool cardigan was sprinkled heavily with dandruff, and her round-collared blouse was buttoned up to the very top. She had never married, nor dated anyone as far as Scott knew, and lived with her invalid mother, Enid. Her father Eric was the fire chief for many years before he died in tragic circumstances.

When Scott asked for Theo's mail, she pumped him for information, but he told her he couldn't discuss the case. He was not about to supply grain to the head grinder at the rumor mill. He was sure she was harmless, but he didn't underestimate the town's ability to jump to conclusions ahead of the facts. He hoped Mitchell wouldn't encounter any unpleasantness due to the latest vicious gossip, but he half expected it.


Scott took Theo's mail back to the station break room. He put on some latex gloves and went through the stack of envelopes.

There were three insufficient funds warnings from a bank in Pittsburgh. There was a statement from the same bank, which showed Theo had been fined for each instance of insufficient funds, even though the bank had covered the checks.

He had very little in his savings account, had virtually emptied out his retirement account, and had three credit cards maxed out at high balances. His trust fund still had an impressive balance, but the only income he seemed to receive was the quarterly payouts from its dividends and the occasional check from a dog breeder.

It was easy to see that Theo was cash poor and in financial distress.

There was a letter from a fracking company, saying they were waiting for him to provide proof that the land for which he was offering the mineral rights was legally his to sell. There was also a letter from a logging company asking him to call them about their proposal.

Scott knew the Eldridge land was part of the family trust so Theo would not be able to legally accommodate either.

There was a letter from the AKC informing him that, pending the outcome of their investigation into his breeding practices, and due to multiple complaints filed against him, his AKC affiliation was suspended until such time as their investigation of his records could be completed, an inspection of his facility could be performed, and the results from the DNA retesting of his dogs by a licensed veterinarian were received.

There went his other form of income.

There was a letter from an attorney representing an investor in the Eldridge Point development, demanding that an updated financial report and project status report be provided, or the investment principal refunded. It included a threat of litigation if he did not comply.

There were a few utility bills and some larger envelopes, among them a thick envelope sent from a law firm in Pittsburgh. It contained a sales contract for the vacant Rodefeffer Glassworks property, and Scott could not believe how much Theo was getting for it.

Realtor Trick Rodefeffer, the grandson of the man who sold the property to Theo, was not listed on the contract or on any of the attached documents as the seller's or buyer's representative, although Scott had heard he was handling the sale. Had Theo cut Trick out of the deal? Scott had seen Trick taking the prospective buyer, a young man reportedly made insanely rich from the sale of a dotcom start-up, around town on Friday, and this was postmarked Monday. Theo would have had to request the contract early on Friday, and then have it completed and put in the mail on the same day to make the Monday delivery.

Did Theo have the kind of clout with his attorneys where he could demand same day service? Would Trick's cut be big enough to supply him with a motive for killing Theo if he were cheated out of it? Trick might not even know about it yet. Or would he? Did someone in the lawyer's office tip him off? Knowing Theo, he might have told Trick he was doing it just to piss him off. Scott added those questions to his list and set aside the documents.

Among the manila envelopes, there was one with Theo's name and address computer-printed on a white label with no return address, postmarked Saturday. When he sliced the end of the envelope open, a card and a photo fell out. He picked up the card first. There was a painting of a vase of white lilies on the front with the words, "He is just away..." printed in a calligraphy font, and "But will live on in our hearts through our memories," printed on the inside in the same font. Under the pre-printed message inside the card was another large white label like the one on the front of the envelope. This computer-printed label read, "You will pay for what you did."

Scott felt his stomach roll as if he'd driven over a bump in the road too fast.

He picked up the photo and felt the rollercoaster sensation begin again. It was a faded color photo of three adolescent boys posing on the end of a dock with Bear Lake behind them, holding up fishing poles with a small fish hooked to the end of each line. They were puffing out their chests and grinning, sunburned and dirty in cut off shorts and grimy, unlaced tennis shoes, looking like they were having the time of their lives. Scott knew they were because he was one of the boys in the photo. The other two boys were Brad Eldridge and Sean Fitzpatrick.

Ed Harrison was the photographer. He took the picture with the camera he got for his sixteenth birthday. The date printed on the photo confirmed Ed and Scott were sixteen and the Sean and Brad were fifteen when it was taken. It was just two days before Brad drowned, not twenty feet from where they were standing.

Scott shook his head, trying to make sense of it. He never thought about it if he could help it, and certainly never reminisced over photos taken back then. Seeing himself and his friends so young and happy brought it all back.

That particular summer was a difficult one for everyone in the photo. Scott and Ed had been dumped by their best pals, Patrick and Sam, right after school let out, because the older two, now seventeen, were much more interested in drinking, parking, and necking with their girlfriends. Neither Scott nor Ed had a girlfriend who was willing to do any of that, nor a car in which to do it. For teenagers, a one year age difference can seem like a decade. Scott and Ed were still very much boys that summer, while Patrick and Sam were anxious to prove they were men.

Brad's older brother Theo, home for the summer and eager to remind his younger brother who was in charge, bullied Brad constantly and viciously. Their mother and sisters were away, visiting relatives in the UK, so there was no one to intercede on Brad's behalf. Their father considered physical violence a normal part of family relations. To him, it was just part of the toughening up process that turned sensitive boys into men who could easily kill any living thing and were willing to use any underhanded means necessary to gain more money and power.

The day the picture was taken, the boys spent the morning fishing in Bear Lake, drinking icy sodas from a battered metal cooler, munching on sandwiches and corn chips provided by the Eldridge family's cook. They had three weeks until Scott and Ed began wrestling practice, and Brad tried out for junior varsity football. Sean ran track, so he didn't have anything to do until the next spring.

To them it was just another long, sunny day in the middle of summer, most of which had been spent riding bikes, swimming and fishing in the lake, or playing pick-up baseball games in a dirt lot down by the river until it got too dark to see. Two days after the picture was taken, on the morning of July 4th, a group of girls paddling canoes across the lake found Brad's lifeless body floating face down among the cattails beyond the boathouse.

Because the lodge was outside the city limits, the investigation into Brad's death was performed by the county sheriff's office. Brad's friends were all questioned. Scott and Ed had spent the morning with some other boys, setting off fireworks down by the river, until the fire chief came and ran them off. They spent the rest of the day swimming in the city pool, eating popsicles they got for free from Hannah, who was working at the concession stand. Sean said he was with his brother Brian, helping out at their uncle's service station all day.

Brad's father may have wanted to quickly put the loss behind him, or just didn't want any scandal attached to the Eldridge name, but for whatever reason, he applied considerable pressure on the county to wrap up their investigation by the day of the funeral. He only waited for his wife and daughters to return home to have the service, and then sent them all away immediately after. Brad's father may have grieved terribly, but if he did so, it was done in private.

The official determination was death by accidental drowning. Brad was known to swim across the lake and back on occasion, and it was decided he probably experienced a cramp and drowned. Everyone knew Theo like to grab kids and hold them under the water until panic set in, only then letting them up, gasping and crying, so he could laugh at them and repeat the performance. Most of the kids who had experienced this torture thought that was probably what happened, that Brad's death was a horrible accident. Brad's closest friends thought it might not have been an accident at all.

Scott wanted to take the photo and letter to show Ed, but under the circumstances, with his good friend a suspect in Theo's murder, he knew he shouldn't. He considered showing it to Maggie instead. Sean was her brother; maybe she would know something that would help.

He heard Sarah enter the station and ask Frank where he was. On impulse, Scott put the card and photo into the copier and had just enough time to produce a photocopy of each, slip them under the machine, and return the evidence to the table before she walked into the break room.

Sarah looked professional and attractive in a blazer, turtleneck, form-fitting pants and high-heeled boots. She looked Scott up and down and shook her head. He had on jeans, work boots, and a sweatshirt.

"I've heard of casual Friday," she said. "But isn't today Monday?"

Scott was embarrassed but did not defend himself. This was supposed to be a day off for him, and he had slept very little since Theo's murder.

Sarah set her briefcase on the table and opened it.

"What do you have for me?'

Scott showed Sarah the mail he had opened.

"Looks like he was in some financial trouble," Sarah said, "and these are some seriously disgruntled people we can interview. Good work."

She put everything in a folder and put it in her briefcase.

He showed her the card and photo and explained whom everyone pictured was and what had happened. He expected her to be impressed, ask pertinent questions, and take some notes.

"It's probably just a prank," she said instead. "Some people have a sick sense of humor."

"But it's postmarked Saturday," Scott insisted. "Before he was murdered."

"We'll look into it," Sarah said, tossing it into her briefcase. "Anything else?"

He showed her the sales contract for the glass factory, explained who Trick was, and suggested he might be upset to know he was being cheated out of his percentage of the deal.

"Anything else?" was all she said.

He told her there was still no sign of Willy Neff or his truck and handed her a copy of the man's mug shot, which he had dug out of the files.

"Willy has no family," he told her. "As far as I know Theo was his only friend if you could even call it that. Theo employed him and bullied him is more the truth."

Scott felt like he was back working as a lowly deputy, presenting his findings to the chief for inspection and approval. Everything he'd carefully put in plastic bags, Sarah carelessly tossed into her briefcase.

He waited to see if she was going to be equally generous with what she knew. He couldn't demand she share anything with him and he didn't know exactly what his position was in this conversation. Was he a peer, or a peon?

Sarah removed a report from a file folder and went over the highlights of what was found at Theo's.

"Tig is still exploring the hard drive of Theo's PC," she said as if Scott knew who Tig was, "and J.T. is still going through his paper files."

Scott nodded. He did know who J.T. was. He was one of the deputies who followed him out to Theo's; the one who woke Scott up on Theo's porch after they searched the dead man's home. Scott really hoped J.T. hadn't told Sarah about that.

"He was being sued by quite a few people," she said. "Investors in a luxury housing development he was supposedly building, a fracking company he accepted money from for mineral rights he couldn't legally sell, and a timbering company for breach of contract."

"I saw drugs," Scott said.

"Lots of prescription narcotics," she recited, going down the list, "all from a Dr. Machalvie. Practices here in town, I suppose?"

Scott nodded yes.

"He had a prescription for the marijuana, and there was a small amount of cocaine, but it looks like personal use rather than distribution; and this, between the nightstand and his bed."

She showed him photos of both sides of the gold coin, enlarged to show detail. It had Greek lettering on it, a profile of a man's face on one side, and a seated figure on the other side, holding out a winged creature. Sarah instructed him to take the photos around and see if anyone recognized the coin. She said she was going to see Dr. Machalvie, and she'd like to meet Scott afterward for lunch to touch base. Scott agreed to meet her at the diner.

Clearly, he had his marching orders, but he chose to do something else instead. As soon as Sarah left, Scott took the photocopy of the threat card and photo out from under the copier and put it in a clean folder. He then went through the old files until he found the case folder for Brad's death. Because the county had taken over the case, the file was not very full, but there were some handwritten notes and newspaper clippings.

An hour later, he had finished studying the documents and had a list of questions written in his notebook. He put everything together in a file and tucked it under his arm.

As he left the station, Scott saw Maggie's brother Patrick crossing Rose Hill Avenue, going from his Uncle Curtis's service station, where he worked in the morning, to his Uncle Ian's bar, the Rose and Thorn, where he worked every afternoon and evening.

Patrick Fitzpatrick had the unique ability to be bone-idle even though it appeared as if he worked all the time. All day at the gas station he chewed the fat with the old men who hung out there, gossiped with the customers who came in and joked around with the mechanic who was working on the cars. He flirted with every female within sight, no matter what age, and if business was slow, he would hang out at the Dairy Chef, where he could keep an eye on the station while gossiping, flirting, and keeping their staff from working. All evening he leaned on the bar at the Rose and Thorn, polishing glasses and serving drinks while chatting and flirting with the crowd there.

Scott followed Patrick into the bar, which was full of ski tourists and students from the college as well as a few locals. Booths lined one wall of the long, narrow space, with the bar area opposite, and there were round pub tables in the middle and front. A few musicians or a small band sometimes performed on a small raised stage area at the back, usually Celtic or Bluegrass music, because anything Irish (or influenced by the Irish) was Patrick's passion. If customers wanted food it was pizza delivered from PJ's across the street, but Guinness and Harp were always on tap, and bottles of Bushmills, Jameson, and Locke's Irish whiskey stood proudly on the top shelf behind the bar.

Mandy was waiting tables, and the owner's wife, Delia, a tall, slender brunette of more mature years, was tending bar. The owner, former police chief Ian Fitzpatrick, a stout, balding man in his late sixties, was entertaining some tourists at one end of the bar, using a thick Irish brogue he claimed gave the place "atmosphere." It was so warm and humid in the bar that the front windows were fogged, and it smelled like damp winter coats, cigarettes, and beer.

Scott ordered a soft drink and sat at the opposite end of the bar from where Ian was so he could speak privately to Patrick.

"I know what you're going to ask me," Patrick said before Scott could begin. "Theo was in here Saturday afternoon, and Ian kicked him out. He was outside with Willy around midnight, giving me grief, and then in here without him just before we closed, around 1:15. He was plastered, trying to buy a bottle of whiskey, which I refused to sell to him, and that's the last I saw of him. Mandy was working, you can ask her."

"You didn't see him after you closed?" Scott asked him.

"No," Patrick said, "and I didn't kill him either, no matter how much he deserved to die. The last time I tried to kill Theo was twenty years ago, and you were there. It was after he bent your snout and almost drowned my little brother."

"How do you walk home from here?"

"I walk Mandy home to the trailer park, and then I go down Marigold."

"Did you notice anything odd that night, on your way home?"

Patrick shook his head and said, "The fog was so heavy you couldn't see much of anything."

"Anybody fight with Theo while he was here?"

"No more than usual."

"Anyone leave right after him, follow him out?"

"Not that I noticed."

"If you see Willy Neff will you let me know?"

"If I see little Willy Nilly, I'll put a coffee cup down over top of him and call you to come get him."

Patrick went down to the other end of the bar to wait on some customers. Mandy greeted Scott as she came up to the bar to put in an order.

"How're you? How's Tommy?" Scott asked her.

Mandy's son Tommy was the paper carrier who worked for Ed.

"Oh, we're just fine," Mandy said, in her Chattanooga twang.

"You're keeping busy, looks like."

"It's about to wear me out, but the money's good. These city people know how to tip a waitress. They could teach these here losers a thing or two."

She gestured to the local men sitting at the bar, but they ignored her. She confirmed Patrick's version of events the night Theo was murdered.

"Did you see Ed in here Saturday night?"

"Ed's in here most nights," Mandy said. "He comes in about eight and leaves about ten. It takes him two hours to drink two beers, and he gives me a two-dollar tip. He's a nice guy, though, and never gives me any trouble, unlike some people."

She looked pointedly at the men she had just accused of being stingy tippers.

"Did Theo ever give you any trouble outside of this place?"

"Naw. He knew Patrick would skin his hide if he did."

Scott thanked Mandy, and she went back to work.

Patrick came back to Scott's end of the bar and said, "Ian wants a word."

Scott took his soft drink and file folder down to the other end of the bar to sit next to Ian.

"You've only been chief for three weeks, and you already have a murder on your hands," Ian said. "Looks like I got out just in time."

"Thanks a lot."

"How's the investigation going?"

"It's early days yet," Scott said.

"That county filly taken over?" Ian asked, scowling at Scott.

"Yes," Scott admitted tiredly. "The sheriff's office has taken charge of the case."

"They may 'officially' be in charge," Ian said to him. "But don't you let those county clowns forget this is your turf. You find out who killed the bastard first, and show 'em what they're dealing with."

"I'll do my best," Scott said. "Patrick said Theo was in here Saturday."

"Aye, he graced us with his presence for a few hours, drinking Maker's Mark and scrapping with anyone who'd have him. Delia was glad to take his money all afternoon, and I was happy to throw him out when I got here, around 4:30. Patrick said he threw him out as well, around closing time."

"Anybody seem suspicious to you?"

"Everyone seems suspicious to me. It's one of the lasting side effects of being a police officer; that and a craving for hot coffee and doughnuts."

He patted his large, soft belly and winked at Scott.

"Tell me what you think about these."

Scott handed Ian the copy of the threat card and photo, and the file on Brad's death. Ian put on his half-moon reading glasses, and with a look on his face as if he had suddenly developed indigestion, he grunted at the card with the threatening message and the accompanying photo and then flipped through the contents of Brad's file.

"What do you want to know?" he asked.

"Everything," said Scott.

Ian regarded Scott for a moment from underneath wild, bushy eyebrows.

"I thought Theo killed him," he said, surprising Scott by agreeing so exactly with the opinion of Scott and his friends. "It may well have been horseplay that got out of hand, with a tragic result, but nothing that could be proved. There was not a mark on him, and his lungs were full of water. The county boys had jurisdiction, and they determined he'd swum across the lake and back, got a cramp and drowned."

"In shorts, a t-shirt, and tennis shoes," Scott said, and Ian shrugged.

"Ted Eldridge was a powerful, wealthy man," Ian said. "Theo was the surviving male heir. How smart would it have been to deprive him of the first son on the heels of losing the second, when there was no evidence, and no witnesses?"

"So Theo got away with it."

"That he did."

"And this?" Scott gestured to the photocopy of the card with the threat.

"An awful coincidence, that. If the postmark was Rose Hill on Saturday, Margie would have put this in his box Saturday morning. Don't these cards usually come in an envelope just a little bigger than the card? Where is that?"

"I thought that was weird too," Scott said. "This came in a nine by twelve envelope with a computer printed label on the front, with just Theo's address, no return address."

"You talk to Margie yet?" Ian asked, and Scott shook his head no.

"You're between a rock and a hard place there," Ian said. "You need to know if she saw someone drop it off, but asking her means the whole town will know what you're up to before you get back to your office."


Sarah was already seated in one of the booths at the diner, drinking coffee and looking irritated. Scott sat and signaled to Pauline he wanted coffee. When she brought it, Scott asked her where Phyllis was; Pauline's daughter usually covered this section.

"Her Majesty called in sick," Pauline said. "So I'm doing her work and mine, too."

Grandmother Gladys was running the register, and Pauline's husband Phil was cooking while grandson Billy, a sulky teenage troublemaker, cleaned tables and washed dishes. Scott decided it would be kinder to wait until things calmed down a bit before questioning the diner staff about Theo's altercation with Ed.

"What did you find out?" Sarah asked impatiently, and Scott realized he was supposed to have been asking people about the coin.

"Nothing yet," he said. "Something came up."

"This town has one stoplight and a hundred people in it. What could happen?" Sarah demanded. "Somebody steal an apple pie out of a kitchen window?"

"There are over five hundred year-round residents in this town, and there's a college with over eight hundred students in it at the end of this street. Add to that the thousands of tourists we get coming through here who think the laws don't apply to them because they're on vacation, and the transient people who work in the resorts but can't afford to live up there. The police force is me and two deputies, one who only works part-time. I know it doesn't seem like much to you, but it's sometimes more than we can handle."

Sarah put up her hands, saying, "All right, all right. Don't get your boxers in a bunch."

Scott was embarrassed at how easily she got to him and worse that he'd let her see it. Sarah was equally patronizing to Pauline, which irked him too. Because nothing that happened in his little town could possibly compare to her experience working in Washington, DC, she never let anyone forget it. Scott ate his patty melt in silence while she briefed him on her interview with Doc Machalvie.

"Evidently Theo had several compressed discs in his back," she said. "The doctor says he refused to have surgery. The types of painkillers prescribed were strong narcotics, but the doctor can back everything up with medical records and x-rays. None of the drugs were illegal, and the records are consistent with increasing the dosage as he became more resistant to the effects of the drugs. The doctor said the multiple kinds of painkillers reflected attempts to try different approaches to pain management when one would fail. He said he was just waiting for the pain to become so great Theo would give in and have surgery. The toxicology report isn't back yet from the post-mortem, but it sounds to me like he was drinking on top of some seriously strong drugs. I wonder about this doctor of his. The pharmacy is owned by his brother."

"Who is also the mayor," Scott told her.

Scott had known Doc Machalvie all his life; the man had been his doctor since he was a boy. He didn't doubt what he had told Sarah. When he said as much, she rolled her eyes as she looked away, obviously not caring that he saw.

"Paragon of virtue he may be," Sarah said, "but I still want you to look into it."

"I'll do it," Scott said.

"You need to stop being so naïve," Sarah said. "Just because you've known these people all your life doesn't mean they aren't capable of committing crimes."

"I appreciate the advice," he said, through clenched teeth.

"You can't afford to be sentimental in law enforcement. You can't worry about what anyone thinks of you," Sarah said. "You've got to be willing to arrest your own mother if you have to."

"I'll be sure to keep an eye on her," he said, suppressing a smile at the thought.

"I'd suffocate in a town this small," she said. "I don't know how you stand it."

"Comes with being naïve and sentimental, I guess."

She surprised him then by saying, "I have two tickets to a political fundraiser next Friday. It may be awfully boring, but you could meet some people who might be in a position to help you someday."

"Help me what?" Scott said.

"Move up, of course," she said. "You don't want to stay buried alive in this dump, do you?"

"Not everyone is as ambitious as you are, Sarah," he said. "I'm fine right where I am, thanks anyway."

Sarah smiled at Scott in a flirtatious manner and said, "We'll see. You help me solve this case, and it will look good for both of us."

Scott knew better than to count on Sarah sharing any credit. He'd seen her in action before when higher ups were around; it was all about her. Scott couldn't wait for her to leave, which she soon did, but not before admonishing him to "get on" the coin thing.

Scott called Ian's wife Delia, who collected antiques, and asked her if she knew any coin experts. She told him bank president Knox Rodefeffer dealt in coins, so Scott went to the bank to see him.

Scott asked to see Knox and then was kept waiting for several minutes in his outer office. During this time Knox's secretary, named Courtenay, made a point of adjusting her open-necked blouse to better reveal her lacy, push up bra, hiking up her short skirt by crossing and re-crossing her long legs, and suggestively sucking on the end of a pen. All this she coordinated with frequent tosses of her big blonde hair while pretending to work.

Scott didn't mind the floorshow, and he couldn't deny it had a pleasurable effect, but he was anxious to get moving on this case and was relieved when Knox finally opened his door and beckoned for him to come in.

Knox Rodefeffer was a tall, ungainly man, and so unnaturally tan for this time of the year he had an almost orange glow about him. His dark toupee was expensive but not fooling anyone, and his capped teeth were so white Scott thought they probably glowed in the dark. He clothed his pronounced gut and collection of chins in the good old boy uniform of blue oxford button-down shirt, red tie, navy blazer, and khaki pants, all of which seemed to cut off his circulation and caused him to sweat profusely.

Scott noted he still chose to wear multiple pieces of what Maggie referred to snidely as "man jewelry." He had on a big gold watch with diamonds on the face, diamond cufflinks, a diamond tiepin, a diamond and gold wedding band, and an insignia ring on one pinky.

Knox may have impressed some people, but they had gone to grade school together, and to Scott, he would always be the big crybaby who bullied smaller kids, bragged about himself all the time, and lied at the drop of a hat. There was really no point in asking him anything because whatever he told you was bound to be at least fifty percent bullshit. Still, Delia said he knew coins.

He seemed particularly interested in the photos Scott showed him and examined them through a magnifying glass.

"Thrace," he said. "Lysimachus, 323-281 BC."

"Pardon me?" Scott asked, but Knox continued to study the photos, ignoring him.

"This side features the head of Alexander the Great, wearing the royal diadem and the Horn of Ammon. On the other side is Athena, Goddess of War, holding up Nike, Goddess of Victory. Lysimachus created it after Alexander's death when he ruled Thrace."

"So, I'm guessing you've seen it before."

"Where did you get this coin?" Knox demanded, looking up from his magnifying glass.

"Not telling," Scott said, and enjoyed the angry flush that spread over Knox's face at being talked to that way. No matter how old they got, or how much money Knox accumulated, it was always recess on the playground, and Scott was bigger and stronger.

"It could be worth anywhere from two to four thousand dollars," Knox said. "I used to have one in my collection."

"What happened to yours?" Scott asked, and Knox hesitated before he answered.

"It was stolen."

"So this might be your coin?"

"Hmmm, could be," said Knox. "I made an insurance claim on my coin, you see, which makes it a tad awkward for me to say."

"Right," Scott said. "I get it."

Scott held out his hand for the photos, and Knox reluctantly gave them back.

"What will happen to it now? To the coin, I mean."

"It's evidence in an investigation."

"Theo's murder?" Knox asked.

"I'm not going to say."

"Well, if it ever gets released from custody I'd be willing to buy it."

"I'll let someone know," promised Scott. "Were you involved in any business dealings with Theo?"

"Theo kept a small account here, for his convenience," Knox said, with a curled lip. "But I believe most of his banking business took place in Pittsburgh."

"Was there any personal business between you two?" Scott asked. "Investments, real estate deals, that sort of thing?"

"Certainly not," Knox said. "Theo Eldridge was not someone with whom I would lower myself to do business. I believe my brother may have worked with him in the past, but you would have to ask him about that."

"I'll certainly do that," Scott said. "Sounds like there was some bad blood between you and Theo. Would you care to enlighten me?"

"It's common knowledge that Theo swindled my grandfather out of the family's glassworks property. He took advantage of a senile old man and stole it right out from under us."

"That sounds a lot like a motive for revenge," Scott said. "Tell me, Knox, where were you Saturday night?"

Knox smirked at Scott and replied, "In DC with Senator Bayard. I'm doing some consulting for his office, and he invited me to a dinner with some very senior White House officials."

Scott was not impressed with anyone who kissed political ass and called it work. He thanked Knox for his time and left the office, catching Courtenay applying fresh gloss to her pouty red lips.

"Don't be a stranger," she told him and waggled her gloss applicator at him as he hurried past.


Scott went to the bookstore to see Maggie, but she was out. He figured she was at her parents' house giving her father and grandfather some lunch, so he headed down toward the river, to their modest two-story house on Marigold Avenue. Scott let himself in when no one answered his light knock at the front door. Maggie's maternal grandfather, Tim MacGregor, was sound asleep in his recliner in the living room, and her father Fitz's recliner was empty. Scott assumed Maggie's father was in the bathroom because King Fitz only ever sat on one throne or the other.

Fitz's big shaggy red dog, Laddie, known as "Lazy Ass Laddie," was sprawled out on the floor in front of the heater, snoring. He didn't wake up when Scott came in. Duke, the vet's cat, was curled up in Grandpa Tim's lap. Duke opened one eye and regarded Scott but did not move.

"Hey Duke," Scott said as he shut the front door behind him. "You better not let Bonnie catch you in her house."

Duke just resettled himself and closed his eye, as if he was not a bit worried about something that wouldn't happen for a few hours yet. Grandpa Tim snored loudly, his teeth in a glass on a TV tray next to the recliner.

Maggie was in the kitchen with her Aunt Delia and Hannah, watching a home improvement program on a small television while they ate some delicious smelling vegetable soup. Delia jumped up when Scott came in and offered him soup and tea.

He declined the soup, saying, "Tea would be great, though."

Scott was amused to see Maggie's and Hannah's eyes were riveted to the television, where a muscular man in a tight t-shirt was helping a clueless couple build a deck on the back of their house.

"What are you watching?" he asked them.

"Shhhh," Maggie said.

Delia said, "They're watching a good looking man working on a home improvement project without being nagged into it."

"It's like our porn," Hannah said, and Delia swatted her with a kitchen towel.

Scott sipped tea and conversed in low tones with Delia until the show ended, and Maggie turned off the television.

"That man is too handsome to be real," Hannah declared.

"Your man isn't exactly an eyesore," Delia admonished her.

"You're pretty easy on the eye yourself, Scott," Hannah said. "Don't you think so, Maggie?"

Maggie ignored her.

"How's the case going?" Maggie asked Scott. "I saw Miss Albright in town earlier."

Hannah said something under her breath that made Maggie laugh, but Scott didn't catch it. He had found it was often better not to know.

"You know Scott can't discuss the case with you," Delia said, putting on her coat, preparing to depart. Maggie hugged Delia and thanked her for bringing lunch.

"Now you can tell us," Maggie said as soon as the door shut behind her aunt, but Scott shook his head.

"Nope, I've been too lax already, and you two cannot be trusted."

"C'mon," whined Hannah. "We can help you, Scott. I have direct connections to several key scanner grannies, and they will tell me anything I want to know."

"Don't let Sarah beat you to it," Maggie coaxed. "We can help you find out who killed Theo before she does."

Despite his previous insistence they stay out of the case, Scott planned to ask for their help, but it was nice to be begged. He liked the tiny amount of power it gave him, however briefly. Scott didn't want to show both of them the photocopy of the threat card in case Maggie might be more forthcoming about her brother Sean when alone, so he showed them the coin photo and told them what Knox said about it. What he could remember, that is.

"How did Knox's coin get in Theo's bedroom?" Hannah asked.

"They were lovers?" Maggie suggested.

"I don't think so," Scott said. "Have you seen Knox's secretary?"

"You mean his latest condom application specialist," Hannah said. "The gossip on those lovebirds is smokin' hot. They have a lot of 'strategic planning meetings' behind closed doors, and the cleaning lady has found some mighty interesting things in Knox's trash can afterward."

"Unless Theo was involved somehow, I don't want to know," Scott said.

"She could be the thief," Maggie said. "Maybe she stole the coin from Knox and gave it to Theo."

"Or Knox sold it to Theo," Hannah said, "and reported it stolen to get the insurance money."

"Or traded it for drugs," Maggie said.

They all nodded in agreement, but then Hannah asked, "Wait a minute, what about Knox's wife, Anne Marie? Maybe she gave it to Theo as a little token of her love."

"I don't think so," Maggie said. "The gossip among the students who work for me is that Anne Marie is sleeping with a tennis player at the college; she likes 'em young."

"But who likes 'em Theo-style?" Hannah asked, grimacing. "He was so gross."

"Phyllis Davis," Maggie said.

Hannah nodded, saying, "Oh yeah, I forgot about ole Phyllis."

"What?" Scott asked, clueless.

"Phyllis Davis, the waitress at the diner," Hannah told him. "Theo has been known to frequent her trailer many a night, late at night."

"And early in the morning," Maggie said.

"How do you know that?" Scott asked.

"They have noisy fights and noisy makeup sex, and Mandy lives next door."

"Why didn't I know about that?" Scott asked them.

"Because you don't listen to evil gossip," Hannah said. "Plus, you're the police."

"Yeah," Maggie said. "You're the heat."

"The long arm of the law."

"The fuzz."

"The pigs."

"Okay, okay, I get it," Scott said. "I guess I need to talk to Phyllis."

Scott spent a few minutes visiting with Maggie's father Fitz, who seemed a little vague and was slurring his words. Scott knew Fitz took strong pain medication and also drank a bit to ease the pain of his back injury, and thinking he must be in a lot of pain, he didn't linger.

Phyllis was still off sick from the diner, and her mother Pauline was too busy picking up the slack for questions about Theo's fight with Ed. Scott stopped in at the station to ask Frank to follow up with Phyllis and Pauline and to find out if Skip had found any clue as to Willy Neff's whereabouts. Skip had come up empty so far. The last anyone had seen of Willy was when he left Hannah's place with Theo around 12:30 the night of the murder.

No one they interviewed had heard the break-in at the veterinary clinic, although all the neighbors in the area heard the party in the insurance building going on until well after 2:00 in the morning. A couple of neighbors remembered being awakened by their dogs barking in the night. Scott wished people in real life were more like people on television programs, and could report something happened at "12:07 exactly" instead of "sometime after midnight."

Scott consulted his notes and then asked Frank to follow up with Trick on the sale of the glassworks, and Gail Godwin, who cleaned Theo's house, to see if she knew who had stood Theo up for dinner. He asked Skip to call in at every business in town to see where Theo went during his last day, and whom he harassed. Both officers had been putting in a lot of extra time, so Scott told them they could expect overtime wages, which made them happy. Scott really appreciated his team and knew Frank's family could use the extra money. He would worry about balancing the station budget later.

Scott did an electronic background check on veterinarian Drew Rosen, which came up clean, and then called the emergency vet clinic where he used to work. His former supervisor only had good things to say about him, and the office manager said there had been no malpractice claims made about his work.

"We miss him," the office manager said. "We keep hoping he'll be back."

Scott spent some time updating his notes, crossing things off his many lists, and then looked over the evidence again. The photo of him and his friends as teenagers, along with the threatening note, had him stumped. He knew he shouldn't involve Ed, but he needed to ask him who had access to photos he took as a teenager.

Scott found Ed at work, the knot on his head a little less swollen but still a lurid purple and yellow. Ed was on the phone and did not look glad to see his best friend. It felt awkward in a way that pained Scott, but until this case was solved his visits to Ed, no matter how well-intentioned, would always seem official.

Scott waited to speak until Ed hung up the phone.

"I don't believe you had anything to do with Theo's death," Scott said. "I'm sorry I haven't been able to keep you in the loop with what's going on, but I can't give Sarah any reason to shut me completely out, you understand?"

Ed's jaw worked a bit, but he looked Scott straight in the eye as he responded.

"My job sometimes places me in difficult situations, too. I do understand."

"I need your help with something, off the record. Way, way off the record."

Ed looked surprised.

"I'd be glad to help, Scott. You know you can trust me."

Scott showed him the photocopy of the threat card and the photo.

"Jesus," Ed said, sitting down on a stool at the worktable. "This is one I took. Where did this come from?"

Scott told him about finding it in Theo's unopened mail.

"So he never saw it."

"I don't see how he could have."

"Who do you think sent it?"

"That's what I need help with. Who would have copies of your photos from that summer?"

"I didn't get multiple copies of my prints back then; I couldn't afford it. My Dad sent my rolls of film to the place that developed the photos for the paper. My prints and negatives came back with his, and the cost came out of my delivery money. Look at the date stamp on the front and the company imprint on back of the paper; this is the original."

"So who had originals of your photos?"

"Well, you, Brad, Sean, maybe your mom or Sean's mom. My dad had some. The thing is, I don't remember giving this photo to anyone. Doesn't mean I didn't, I just don't remember."

"I haven't looked for any at my house, but I don't remember having it either."

"That leaves Brad and Sean."

"Would you have given any to Caroline or Gwyneth?"

"Maybe Caroline, but I don't remember doing it. I was beneath contempt as far as Gwyneth was concerned."

"I guess someone could have stolen it from you, without you knowing."

"Gail Goodwin cleans my house, but I can hardly picture her as a photo thief and poison pen writer. Other than Gail and you, Sam and Patrick are the only people who come to my house."

"Well, think about it, and let me know if you remember anything."

"Lots of people thought Theo murdered Brad," Ed said, "but who would go to the trouble of sending him a threatening letter, and why now?"

"It's just too much of a coincidence in the timing," Scott said. "It has to be connected."

"Does Sarah think I sent it?"

"Sarah's not too impressed by it. She thinks it's just a prank."

"Have you talked to Margie at the post office?"

"No," Scott said. "I'm putting that off for as long as I can."

Ed chuckled, saying, "I can see why."

Scott stopped in at the Rose and Thorn again, where Ian had just returned from school bus duty and was enjoying his first beer of the day. Instead of resenting the older man's strong views, Scott found himself glad to have someone with whom to discuss the case. With his best friend a suspect, he needed someone to bounce ideas off of, and Ian, for all his opinionated bluster, had been a pretty good chief of police, could keep a confidence, and knew everyone involved. Scott went over his notes with Ian, and Ian gave him a few suggestions.

"Doc Machalvie is a good doctor and an old friend," Ian said. "But he is enough like his brother Stuart to bear watching."

"Really? I would've thought they couldn't be more different. Doc is such a gentleman, and Stuart's so... "

"Greedy? Manipulative? Conniving?"

"All that. Doc, on the other hand, is always going out of his way to help people, whether or not they can pay."

"Still, I wouldn't be surprised if he was supplying Theo with prescriptions for imaginary ailments."

"For money?" Scott asked.

"Doc likes to gamble a bit and may have found himself in a tight spot. Or maybe Theo found out something about Doc which would hurt him if it got around."

"Blackmail?" Scott said. "Do you know what it could be?"

"I might," Ian said. "Let's just say I once caught Doc in a place he had no business being, with a person I was surprised to see him with, doing something he wouldn't have wanted his wife to know about. I got the feeling it wasn't the first time."

This gave Scott a lot to think about. Theo as a blackmailer, on top of cheat, arsonist, and all 'round bastard, was not that big of a stretch.

"You'll have a hard time finding someone who isn't glad Theo's dead," Ian said. "Most folks will think whoever did it, did the whole town a big favor."


Scott stopped by Doc Machalvie's office, above his brother's pharmacy, and found him filling out paperwork. He greeted Scott warmly and asked him to sit down.

"I thought when I went to medical school I'd spend most of my time healing sick people," he said. "I actually spend most of my time referring people to specialists and filling out forms for health insurance companies."

Scott asked him about Theo.

"Ah, yes," he replied. "Someone from the county sheriff's department was here about him as well. What an awful thing to have happen, even to a fellow as unappetizing as Theo. His father was a good friend to me when I was just starting out, and I always felt it was a pity the younger son drowned and not Theo. Life is such a mystery to me. I shared his records with the deputies who came with a search warrant; do you need to see them as well?"

"No," Scott said. "I want to know if you had any personal dealings with Theo outside of your doctor/patient relationship."

Doctor Machalvie looked surprised, and more than a little offended.

"What are you insinuating, Scott?"

Scott felt the rebuke, and it made him uncomfortable.

"Any business dealings, investments, leases, things like that," he said.

"Heavens, no," Doc said. "Business deals are my brother's forte, not my own. I personally found Theo repellant, and would not have given him two nickels for a dime. I can't think of anyone who will miss him."

"I have to ask everyone this," Scott said. "Where were you the night Theo died?"

Doc took a deep breath and appeared to be thinking about the question carefully before answering.

"I was at home in bed with my wife," he said finally. "I'm pretty sure the lodge meeting was the night before."

"It was," Scott said.

"Well then," Doc smiled broadly and stood. "I guess we're all done here, and I can get back to my forms."

Scott was mollified, as he was intended to be, and left the office knowing he had let himself be handled, but at a loss as to what to do about it. He just couldn't picture Doc Machalvie stalking Theo with a baseball bat.


Later that evening Knox's wife Anne Marie was awakened, still high and very drunk, by her husband, who dragged her out of bed, and then dressed her in the clothes she'd worn earlier in the day.

"Where we goin'?" she asked him, repeatedly, but he just hummed to himself and would not answer.

He slung her up over his shoulder, carried her to the garage, and then heaved her not so gently onto the backseat of his car and shut the door. Cradled in the soft, warm leather, she allowed herself to drift, listening to the classical music Knox always played when he drove.

Maybe he was taking her to rehab again, she thought. It hadn't been too bad; the spa part had been relaxing, and she had lost some weight. She felt dizzy but not sick, which was exactly the feeling she liked best, most often followed by unconsciousness or sex, although sometimes she'd wake to find both seemed to have happened without her remembering.

She lost track of time as he drove, but she was conscious of the curves in the road, and the swaying motion of the car lulled her to sleep in the warm, leather cocoon. She woke up to a sudden blast of cold air upon her lightly clad body, and it was enough of a shock to her system to sober her up a tiny bit. Knox hauled her out of the back seat, leaned her back against the side of the car, and then slapped her face lightly until she protested.

"Pay attention to me," he said. "I'm getting out here, and you have to drive yourself home."

Anne Marie looked around, and they seemed to be parked on the right-hand side of Pine Mountain Road, the nose of the car pointed downhill. It was dark, snow was pouring down, and Knox seemed to be insisting she drive somewhere. He pressed the keys into her hand and walked away to where she could see another car was waiting farther up the road, on the other side, facing in the opposite direction.

"Hey!" she yelled, and the effort caused her to slip and fall into the snow bank created by the snowplows.

"Shit!" she shrieked. "Knox! Come help me up, ya big jerk!"

She heard the other car pull away, going uphill, toward Glencora. She struggled out of the snow bank and stumbled against the car.

"Knox!" she screamed after the disappearing taillights, "I can't drive; I'm drunk!"

This struck her as really funny, and she laughed out loud before saying more quietly, "I am so screwed."

She had dropped the keys when she fell, and now had to scrabble in the darkness on her hands and knees, feeling around with rapidly numbing fingers until she finally found them in the snow. She let herself in the driver's side of the car, shivering uncontrollably, covered in wet snow from where she'd fallen. She started the car and turned up the heater, almost falling asleep as soon as she was warm.

"No, no, no, no," she told herself then, pinching her arms. "Must stay awake."

She glanced in the rearview mirror as a car passed her, but it wasn't Knox. It had been a familiar car, but whose?

"Jerk," she said to the rearview mirror, although Knox was long gone.

What kind of crazy game was he playing? She closed one eye to try to halve the double vision plaguing her and when that didn't work, shook her head, trying to clear it, which only made her dizzier. She was sensible enough to know she couldn't stay there with the heater running. She'd run out of gas eventually and freeze to death.

"All right," she said out loud, and pressed the satellite assistance button, but nothing happened.

"Bastard," she said, thinking Knox must not have paid the bill. She looked for her handbag to retrieve her phone, but it wasn't in the car.

"Son of a bitch," she said, rubbing her eyes in an attempt to get them to focus.

She considered her options, now that she realized the jerk was not coming back for her, and no one knew where she was. Snow alternating with freezing rain was falling, and Anne Marie knew it was only a matter of time before the road became dangerously icy. She put the car in drive.

"I can do this," she said. "Leave me on the side of the road, will you? I'll show you."

She pulled the car off the narrow shoulder and began her descent of Pine Mountain.

After a long day of running around chasing leads but not getting very far, Scott called Maggie to see if he could come over, and she told him to come up the back way to her apartment. She was cleaning, she said, and when he got there, she was scrubbing the bathroom floor. She took off her rubber gloves and put the kettle on in the kitchen, while he brought her up to date, sitting at her kitchen table. Once seated with a pot of tea and two mugs between them, she looked at the photocopy of the threat in the card and shook her head at the image of the young boys, including her brother Sean.

Sean was now an attorney who worked in the trust and estate planning department for a large national banking corporation in Pittsburgh. The way Maggie described it, Sean created hiding places in which wealthy people could store their money so neither they nor their heirs had to pay taxes, but Scott thought there was probably more to it.

Maggie insisted Scott needed to talk to Sean about the card and photo.

"We all thought he was probably out there," she said, frowning. "He and Brad were joined at the hip every day and night that summer. He said he spent the whole day working with Brian at the service station and Brian backed him up. The thing is, he never stepped foot in the place if he could help it, and he and Brian couldn't stand each other. We all thought it was fishy, but neither of them would budge on the story."

"It was the first time something really bad happened to one of us," Scott said.

"After Brad died, Sean was so upset Mom sent him out to Uncle Curtis' farm for the rest of the summer. Hannah said he spent every day in the woods and would come home filthy and starved at sunset. Back then they didn't send kids to counselors. Everyone just left him alone to get over it."

"We didn't know what to say to him," Scott said. "He didn't seem to want to talk about it."

"He got really serious afterward, and worked his tail off in school; got a scholarship, graduated early, left us, and never looked back."

"I hate to make him look back, but I have to."

Maggie pushed her chair back, stood up, and stretched. Scott admired her, even dressed in sweats, but didn't let her catch him doing so. She reached for the landline to call Sean, and even though the smile of pure affection and pleasure on her face when she got her brother on the phone only lasted a second or two, Scott was completely undone by it. He just had no resistance to this woman, no matter how many times she rejected him.

Maggie handed Scott the phone, and he told Sean about the card and photo. Sean said he was available Thursday morning if Scott wanted to talk.

After he hung up, Scott stood as if to leave, but she said, "Stick around, and as soon as I'm through cleaning, we'll order a pizza."

Scott could hardly believe his good luck. Instead of lounging around, Scott pitched in and mopped the kitchen for her while she took a shower. He went to the front room to wait for the kitchen floor to dry. Maggie had multiple photo albums, and he went through them, ostensibly looking for pictures taken around the time Brad died, but also to look at pictures of Maggie.

The first album held photos of her grandparents and parents when they were young, and all her aunts, uncles, cousins, her three brothers, and Maggie up to the age of twelve or so. The photos of her father, Fitz, taken before his accident, show a lively, robust man, much the size Patrick was now. He was pictured wrestling with his boys, working at the bakery, bowling with his league, standing with his arm around wife Bonnie, and holding baby Maggie as if she were a fragile china doll.

There were several photos of Uncle Ian and Aunt Delia's son Liam, who died of leukemia as a child. His sister Claire was close in age to Maggie and Hannah. Maggie's Aunt Alice and Uncle Curtis were pictured with their four boys and scrawny little Hannah, who always seemed to have scraped knees and a dirty face.

The next album held photos taken after Fitz fell off a ladder while painting the trim on the second story of their house. Scott could remember him lying in the hospital bed they put in the front room when he first came home from the hospital. He looked like a pale, skinny ghost of his former self. Scott thought about how quiet the house was afterward.

There was a photo of sunburned pre-teen cousins Claire, Maggie, and Hannah, along with Caroline Eldridge, at a pajama party at Claire's house, with Aunt Delia in the background, talking on the phone. Claire was tall and skinny with dark hair and bright blue eyes; Maggie was also tall and thin, but covered in freckles, with her curly red hair in pigtails. Hannah was tiny and always looked like she was up to something.

There were several before-the-school-dance photos of her eldest brother Brian with his wife-to-be Ava, and Patrick with a varied collection of girls. There were plenty of Brian and Patrick in their football and baseball uniforms, trying to look macho with unfortunate haircuts. All the Fitzpatrick men were athletic, so every family get-together featured touch football in the yard, and there were several of those photos.

There were only three snapshots of Ava and Brian's wedding, but they were blurry and poorly developed. It had been a hasty affair when Ava was just sixteen years old, and Brian was about to leave for college.

There were school and graduation photos, and all Hannah's brothers' weddings. There was one photo of Fitz, Ian, Curtis, and all their sons, standing out in front of Fitz's house in their best suits on the day of Grandma Rose's funeral. Rose had been the formidable Fitzpatrick matriarch, who famously did not get along with any of her daughters-in-law, and doted on her boys. In the photo, Curtis and Ian were obviously holding up their brother Fitz between them.

There was one of Maggie's brother Sean with his beat-up Honda, packed to the roof, leaving for college. There was one of Brian working at the service station with Uncle Curtis, and several of Hannah and Patrick working at the Rose and Thorn with Aunt Delia and Uncle Ian. There were only a couple photos of Maggie working at the bakery. She worked there alongside her mother and aunts for several years after her father had his accident, up until she bought the bookstore.

There were photos of Hannah's husband Sam Campbell, at a party held just before he left for the Gulf, handsome and indestructible looking in his uniform, with his former high school sweetheart Linda by his side. The pictures of him afterward at his welcome home party showed a skeletal, haggard version of the same man. He looked smaller and much older, slumped in his wheelchair, with haunted, shadowed eyes. There was no girlfriend by his side then, just his brittle, bitter mother, who looked as if her expectations in life had been amputated along with her son's lower limbs.

Scott skipped ahead, past photos of Sam working out with the high school wrestling team, sled riding with Patrick, Ed and himself, going off to MIT; slowly building a new life. There were many shots of Hannah and Sam's wedding, a much happier time, and then the farm, as family and friends helped them turn it into a place Sam could negotiate with his wheelchair.

There were several photos of Ava and Brian as young newlyweds in the enormous run-down Victorian house which later became the Rose Hill Bed and Breakfast. All the Fitzpatricks and their friends worked many long hours on the house, restoring it to the grand lady it had once been. There were snaps of Ava's and Brian's daughter Charlotte taken before their son Timmy was born. Ava was so photogenic there was no way to take a bad picture of her, and Brian always hammed it up for the camera. Charlotte was a miniature of her beautiful, dark-eyed mother, and Timmy was just as red-headed as his father and Aunt Maggie.

Then there was Scott's wedding. He looked so happy, as did Sharon. The only unhappy person pictured was his mother, who had red-rimmed eyes and a miserable look on her face. She had fainted during the service and had to be carried out.

There were photos taken during the time he was married, while Maggie and her boyfriend Gabe lived in the house up Possum Holler, and socialized with Scott and his wife, Sharon.

'We all look so young,' he thought, although it had been only six years or so since the photos were taken.

Sharon looked pretty and sweet. Scott was working on the Pendleton police force at that time, and Sharon was doing her best to make a home for them, built on dreams of a family he could not fulfill. He'd heard she was married with children now, and he sincerely wished her well, but they did not stay in touch. He was mostly sorry to have wasted even a few years of her life.

Scott looked at the photos of Gabe with his arms around a beaming Maggie and felt an aching pain in his chest. After Gabe left and her house burned down, a light went out in Maggie, and although Scott occasionally saw it flicker, he knew she believed that with Gabe had gone her only chance for happiness. He studied Gabe's face in the photos and felt conflicting feelings: sadness at losing a friend, anger at what his friend had done to someone he loved, and guilt for his part in it; but mostly regret, for there was plenty of hurt to go around.

Toward the end of the same album, there were a few pictures of a New Year's Eve party Maggie and Gabe had hosted, with everyone crowded in the living room, listening to some friends of Patrick's playing the mandolin, fiddle, and tin whistle while Patrick played the drum badly but sang really well.

Sam was there in his wheelchair, a silly hat on his head, with a drunk and disorderly Hannah sitting on his lap. Scott was cuddling Sharon on the loveseat, looking very cozy and happy. Brian and a very pregnant Ava were laughing and pointing at something just out of frame, probably Ed's dog Goudy, who used to go everywhere with him and farted all the time. A couple of Hannah's brothers and their wives were there. Scott thought he remembered their cousin Claire being there as well, along with her husband Pip, but they weren't in any of the pictures.

Ed was behind the camera, as usual, a part of them but always apart, observing and recording. His wife Eve claimed to be too ill to come, but everyone knew the truth was she couldn't stand to be around his friends, who didn't seem to care enough about political issues or world affairs to argue passionately with her about them. She left Ed six weeks later on Valentine's Day, and as the year progressed, the lives of several other people in the party photos fell apart as well. On this night, however, everyone looked young and happy, and it seemed as if it would never be any different.

Photos of the blackened wreckage of Maggie's house were the last in this album. It was late April, but there was still snow on the ground. Scott, Ed, Brian, and Patrick were shoveling debris into a big dumpster, under the supervision of Uncles Curtis and Ian. The sky was gray, the trees scorched, and everyone looked grim. There were no pictures of Maggie taken at that time, but Scott would never forget the grief-stricken look in her eyes.

Maggie came out of the bathroom wearing jeans and a man's flannel shirt, her hair hanging in dripping ringlets down her back. Scott felt the attraction between them like a thermal layer, surrounding them, connecting them. Her color was high, maybe from the shower, or maybe from the same thing he was feeling. She walked up behind his chair, leaned over it, and looked at the last page of the open photo album on his lap.

"I don't look at them much," she said. "Ava had Timmy a week later, and by summer Brian was gone too."

Scott couldn't think of the right thing to say. He put the album aside, got up and hugged her. What was meant to be a comforting gesture quickly changed into something more. He looked in her eyes, and her pupils were large and dark. He looked at her mouth, and was drawn toward it; hypnotized by her fragrance, her warmth, and the closeness she was allowing him to experience. He could feel them drawing together in the sparking magnetic field they created between them, and he was more than willing to take advantage of this opportunity.

His phone rang and broke the spell. It was Skip, reporting Anne Marie Rodefeffer's car had gone over the side of Pine Mountain road.


The snowplow driver who reported the accident claimed it was a lucky thing he came along shortly after it happened.

"Otherwise, the sleet and snow would have covered up the skid marks within five minutes."

Because of the treacherous road conditions, Maggie's Uncle Curtis was already out on another wrecker call with two others waiting, so a wrecker from Glencora was employed to pull Knox's Lincoln up out of the ravine. Anne Marie was unconscious but alive when they pulled her out.

"She didn't have a coat on," the wrecker operator told Scott. "No pocketbook and no ID. I got the name from the car registration."

Knox, on a business trip to DC, was reportedly flying to Pittsburgh, where Anne Marie was being airlifted by helicopter. She had sustained multiple fractures, the paramedics suspected internal injuries as well, and her condition was considered critical.

ROSE HILL by Pamela Grandstaff

# Chapter Five – Tuesday

Maggie Fitzpatrick unlocked the front door of her bookstore, Little Bear Books, and pulled her chalkboard easel outside onto the recently shoveled and salted sidewalk. The bear design painted on the top of the easel looked like a chalk drawing and matched the colorfully painted wooden sign that stretched across the top of her storefront windows. On the left-hand side was the logo, a bear cub balancing a large open book on his little bear legs as he appeared to read through big glasses perched on his cute little bear nose. "Little Bear Books" was written across the rest of the sign in a fairy tale font. It was all way too cutesy for Maggie's taste, but customers would buy anything she put the logo on, from mugs to t-shirts, so she kept it.

Benjamin, her best barista, had already been at work for half an hour when Maggie came downstairs and opened the bookstore. She liked Benjamin because he was reliable and easy to work with, besides being an excellent barista. But most of all, he didn't talk her ear off first thing in the morning, when she was feeling grumpy. He picked up the bakery order, shoveled the sidewalks, performed all the opening procedures, and the café was ready for customers by 7:00 a.m., all without any irritating chit-chat.

Dreadlocked songbird Mitchell, on the other hand, was prone to chat too much and screw up orders, but was so charming the customers loved him. The other three baristas she employed were also college students, all three were blonde, and their names were Kristen, Kirsten, and Christine. They were all reliable, sweet girls, but Maggie never got their names right.

As she secured the easel to the nearest lamp post, Maggie saw Mamie Rodefeffer rounding the corner in front of the bank, wrapped in multiple layers of dress, cardigans, and scarves topped with a moth-eaten coat, tote bags swinging and cane banging the pavement. She was listing right and then left as she made her way forward toward the bookstore. Mamie was legally blind and wore thick lenses, but her hearing was supernaturally sharp.

"Mary Margaret!" she yelled. "You're late again!"

Maggie shook her head and sighed. The minute hand of the bank clock on the corner had just ticked past 7:03 and dawn was barely peeking over Pine Mountain. It still looked more like a clear, moonless night, and twinkly stars were visible in the dark sky over the hilltops to the west. A sudden drop in temperature overnight had sucked up all the humidity, leaving the air crisp and sharp.

Mamie was the oldest surviving heir of Gustav Rodefeffer, the original owner of the now-closed Rodefeffer Glassworks. She lived in a large, sprawling Gothic Revival style house up on Morning Glory Avenue, with a small staff to care for her.

"I guess you heard about Anne Marie," she said.

"Yes I did, Mamie, I'm so sorry," Maggie said.

"That woman never did have the brains God gave a goose," Mamie said, and glared at Maggie, daring her to disagree.

Maggie just murmured again that she was sorry to hear about the accident, and then fled back into the bookstore.

Mamie settled herself at a central table on the café side so she could better hear everyone's conversations and interrupt with her own commentary. Benjamin waited on her every morning and was ready for her usual interrogation and insults.

"Are you still working here?" she demanded.

"Yes, Miss Rodefeffer," Benjamin said. "You know I work here most weekday mornings."

"Don't you have a degree in something?" she yelled over the sound of the espresso machine.

"Theoretical Physics," Benjamin told her, and grinned at Maggie, who mouthed, "I'm so sorry."

"Where did you say you got your degree?" Mamie demanded.

"Caltech," Benjamin told her.

Mamie addressed the room at large, which held only a few customers waiting for their cappuccinos to go.

"Then why in God's name are you working here? Did you have a nervous breakdown? Was it drugs?"

"No ma'am," Benjamin said, a smile lurking just beneath his straight face. "I work here to pay my expenses. I like it here."

Mamie acted as if it was the most insane thing she had ever heard, every day.

"Why are you so short?" she asked him, as he served her cappuccino and a scone.

"My parents were short, Miss Rodefeffer."

"You can hardly be blamed, then," she said, satisfied. Thus concluding their daily interaction, she tucked a large paper napkin into the collar of her blouse and started nibbling on her scone.

"This scone doesn't have many sultanas in it!" she complained.

"That's because it's cranberry," Maggie said through clenched teeth and escaped even further back on the bookstore side.

Maggie tried to stay out of the old woman's limited sight line and spoke to her customers as quietly as she could. The store had the usual morning clientele, despite the cold weather and icy sidewalks.

When a young woman from the bank came to pick up a large order, Mamie told her, "You tell my lazy nephew Knox to come and get his own damn coffee. I'd like to speak to him."

The girl smiled nervously at Mamie, with fear in her eyes, and hurried out when her order was ready.

Some students from the college came in.

"The least you could do is to get dressed properly before you go out in public!" Mamie told one young girl. "It's ten degrees above zero outside, and I can almost see your personal business!"

The young woman just laughed at her.

Mamie accosted Maggie as she crossed the room to clean off a table.

"You hear about old Theo getting his head bashed in?" she asked loudly.

"You know anything about it?" Maggie asked her.

"I know he stole our family business right out from under us, and then drove it straight into the ground. I know he tried to cheat my nephew out of a large sales commission. If you ask me, he got exactly what he deserved."

"I bet Trick was pretty mad about that business deal," Maggie said.

"His name is Richard," Mamie said crossly.

Trick had been nicknamed in grade school, where "Richard" started as "Rick," became "Tricky Dick," and was eventually shortened to "Trick."

"Richard and Knox came to dinner on Sunday night," Mamie said. "Brought their idiot wives with them, and told me all about it."

"Pretty big sum of money, was it?" Maggie asked.

Mamie, maybe realizing she had just suggested her nephew had a motive to kill Theo, immediately changed the subject.

"You're getting awfully fat, Mary Margaret," she said. "You need to lay off the desserts."

Maggie jumped up, fuming, but bit back the dozens of retorts that sprang to her mind as she walked up to the café counter and hid behind it.

"You know, my name is Mary Margaret too," Mamie yelled at her retreating back, "but my father liked to call me Mamie."

"Short for 'cockamamie,' no doubt," Maggie whispered to Benjamin, who hid behind the espresso machine and giggled.

"I heard that!" Mamie said and wagged a shaming finger at them.

Grocery store owner Matt Delvecchio stopped in for his latte at 8:15, just after he opened his store.

"You sure you're Sal's son and not the milkman's?" Mamie asked him. "You look a lot more like that Pollock Kazminsky than that Dago Delvecchio."

Maggie started to say something, but Matt just winked at her and said, "She's a live one."

He was the nicest man in the town, married to one of the biggest bitches Maggie could name, yet she'd never seen him angry. They never charged him for his latte, so he always left a three-dollar tip in the tip jar.

As Matt left, Mamie said, "I can't decide if he's a retard or just an idiot."

"All right, Mamie, that's enough," Maggie said.

Mamie stood up, gathered her things, and muttered about Maggie not appreciating her patronage. As she left, she said the same thing she always said when she left in a huff, and Benjamin mouthed the words to Maggie as Mamie said them.

"Good-bye and good riddance. I probably won't be back."

"We should be so lucky," Maggie said quietly.

"I heard that!" Mamie retorted and teetered out the door and down the sidewalk.

"What is it with this town and the name Mary Margaret?" Benjamin asked Maggie.

"Funny isn't it," Maggie said. "There's me, Margie at the post office, crazy old Mamie, Meg at the pharmacy, Mary at the bank, Madge at the IGA, Margaret the crossing guard, Midge who's secretary at the church, and let's see, Sister Mary Margrethe."

"You should have a club," Benjamin said.

"We do," Maggie replied. "It's called Sacred Heart Catholic Church."

Dr. Drew Rosen found Maggie in her office later that morning.

"Can I buy you some of your own coffee?" he asked. "We keep saying we're going to get together, but we're both always too busy."

"I know, I'm so sorry," Maggie said. "Let's do it now. I need an excuse to take a break, anyway."

Drew placed an order at the counter and Maggie directed him to join her at a table by the front window, the closest thing she had to a more private section of the café.

"Have you been allowed back into the clinic?" she asked him after he sat down.

"They let me put together a kind of emergency call kit so I can make home visits," he said. "I have to take Skip or Frank with me when I pick up supplies. All the calls are forwarding to my home phone."

"That can't be too good for business."

"Actually I think people prefer home visits to dragging their dogs and cats to my office. Plus they're curious about what happened."

"Asking you a lot of questions, I expect."

"Yeah, it will be a relief when they catch whoever did it and things get back to normal."

"You have any ideas about that?"

"I didn't know Theo all that well, but he seemed like someone who frequently made enemies," Drew said. "Not a nice guy."

"You know I used to live in the house next door to you."

"Scott said something about Theo burning it down."

"He was trying to buy up every piece of property up Possum Holler," Maggie said. "I wouldn't sell it to him, so he set it on fire, with me in it."

"That's terrible. How did you get out?"

"Have you met Lily Crawford, who lives on the farm at the end of the road?" Maggie asked, and Drew nodded. "The Crawford's dog woke me up howling under my window. The whole downstairs was on fire by that time. I had only enough time to wrap my photo albums in my grandmother's quilt and fling them out the window. I climbed out onto the porch roof and into a crabapple tree and stayed there until Lily's husband Simon came running down the road with a ladder; he pitched it up and helped me down. By the time the fire truck got there, it was too late to save any of it."

"You didn't have smoke detectors?"

"I had several. Someone had taken all the batteries out. We found them in the ashes later."

"So he didn't mean to just scare you."

"No, he meant to kill me."

"If you knew it was Theo, why wasn't he arrested?"

"Phyllis Davis gave him an alibi. He laughed about it in the Thorn later, said he'd warned me it was a fire trap. The fire chief investigated and concluded it was the wiring, although we had all that upgraded when we bought the place."

"We?"

"My boyfriend Gabe and I bought it together. Well, I bought it, and he and my brothers did all the renovations. We lived there for three years."

"Was he there when it caught on fire?"

"No, he'd been gone for a few weeks by then. Just went out for a walk one night and never came back."

Maggie looked away and Drew touched her hand briefly.

"I'm so sorry. Both of those events must be painful subjects for you."

"It seems like it all happened to someone else now. That was six, almost seven years ago."

"When did you buy the bookstore?"

"The very day I got the insurance check for the house burning down I ran into the owner of this store. She had opened this for her retirement, not realizing how much work it would entail. I think she saw herself more as a gracious literary hostess, spending her days recommending books and having intellectual discussions with members of the college faculty. In reality, she spent most of her time managing inventory and covering shifts for employees who didn't show up for work."

"I always assumed bookstore employees read all day."

"It cracks me up when people say that. All these books don't unpack themselves and jump onto the shelves, you know. She also wasn't prepared for eight months of winter, and it can feel really isolated up here when you're not used to it."

"I can vouch for that."

"So you can understand why she was desperate to sell and accepted my measly offer."

"Had you always wanted to own a bookstore?"

"Never considered it before in my life. I love to read, but I was a library girl, town and college; I couldn't afford new books. My real motivation was being sick of living and working with my mother. This building came with an apartment upstairs, the business was breaking even most months, and I was pretty sure I could get the college textbook business if I tried. I had my brother Sean look over everything, and he pronounced it a crazy idea but backed me up anyway."

"It was a really brave thing to do."

"I didn't feel brave. In a way, I was as desperate as the previous owner was. I wanted my own business, my own space, my own life."

"Fate brought you together."

"I don't know about that, but it was lucky for me."

"So are you glad you did it?"

"Some days I wonder what in the world I was thinking."

"I have days like those myself," Drew said.

"I've been dying to ask you why you moved here," Maggie said. "Start at the beginning."

"It's not a long story," he said.

Drew's answer was interrupted by a staff member calling Maggie to the phone, and by the time she was finished dealing with the call Drew had to go.

"We'll continue this conversation soon," Maggie said. "Promise me."

"Absolutely," he said, smiling. "Besides, I want to see that great apartment you've got upstairs. Hannah has been raving about it."

Maggie realized Hannah had been doing some matchmaking, which was her third favorite hobby after eating and gossiping. She didn't really mind it, though, come to think of it. Drew Rosen was a nice, attractive man, and when he touched her hand, she felt a little spark.

Scott was on his way back to the station from lunch at the diner when his phone rang. He answered it to Maggie saying, "You need to get over here to the bookstore right away."

Scott stopped in his tracks.

"Why? What's happened?"

"Theo's sister Gwyneth is in my bookstore, Chief Gordon," Maggie hissed, "and if you don't come and remove her within the next five minutes, you'll have another dead Eldridge on your hands."

She hung up with a loud bang. Scott shook his head and started back in the direction of Little Bear Books. Talking to Maggie Fitzpatrick could be like a right to the chin, a left to the stomach, and a knee to the groin, all before you could get your wits about you and your dukes up.

When he arrived at the bookstore, the situation looked civil enough, although Scott could feel the tension crackling in the air like electricity around a transformer before lightning strikes it. The staff members were covertly watching, some with worried expressions and some with delighted anticipation.

Gwyneth Eldridge was obviously the elegant blonde to whom Maggie was serving cappuccino. She had all the stereotypical accoutrements of an affluent city dweller, including a severe blonde haircut and a business suit. Her expensive looking clothing, handbag, and phone were all black. Everything about her was young and fashionable except for her gnarled looking hands and drawn, gaunt face, which seemed to have a peeved expression permanently etched upon it. When she spoke, Scott noted she hadn't lost her affected British accent, much like the one her brother Theo could turn on and off at will.

As he approached the table, Gwyneth was saying to Maggie, "I'm surprised you don't have more requests for soy. This is nonfat milk, though, correct?"

"I get it fresh from anorexic cows every morning," Maggie said through clenched teeth, and Gwyneth, not knowing how dangerous it was, actually tut-tutted in return.

"My private psychology practice in Manhattan is largely devoted to young women with serious eating disorders, Aggie, and even though that is something you obviously don't suffer from, you really shouldn't joke about it."

The pink blotches on Maggie's cheeks deepened to a hazardous level red, and Scott swooped in between the two women before Maggie could pick up Gwyneth's twig-like frame and snap it in two.

"Hello Gwyneth, you probably don't remember me," he said. "I'm Scott Gordon."

He offered his hand for her to shake, which she did, with a couple of cold, limp, bony fingers, as he said, "I'm the chief of police here in Rose Hill."

"I certainly would have remembered you had I met you, Todd," Gwyneth said appreciatively and gestured for him to sit.

"It's Scott," he said as he sat down, "and it was a long time ago. This was a clothing store back then."

"I wouldn't even be in here, Todd," she said, looking around with distaste, "were I not in desperate need of a decent cup of cappuccino. I should have known it would be impossible to find one this far from civilization."

"It's Scott," he said again, "and I think their cappuccino is really good."

"Obviously you have never had a real cappuccino," Gwyneth assured him. "In Manhattan, the baristas perform the theater of espresso. It's really as much performance art as a kind of urban communion."

Scott couldn't think of any appropriate response to such a statement.

"I'm so sorry about your brother," he said instead, thinking it wise to change the subject before ceramics were launched from behind the café counter.

Gwyneth immediately teared up in a dramatic but studied way and touched her eyes with the paper napkin Scott handed her. With her eyes full of tears and her lower lip trembling, Scott finally saw the sulky teenager he remembered from so many years ago, lurking behind the sophisticated façade.

"That is so kind of you to say, Todd. I was shocked at the news, of course, and immediately rescheduled all my patients so I could be here, to manage things."

"Well, it's certainly good to have you back in our little town," Scott said.

"Little town? It's more like a stage set for a farce," she said. "The Irish own the pub; the Italians own the pizza parlor; it's just so stereotypical, so rife with clichés."

Scott saw Maggie's head pop up from behind the counter and held his hand up to stop her.

"So Italians in Manhattan don't own Italian restaurants?" he asked. "And there are no Irish pubs?"

"Touché, Todd, touché," Gwyneth said. "Still, it's such a primitive way to live, n'est ce pas? With murderous hillbillies roaming the streets, attacking innocent, civilized people."

"As opposed to Manhattan, I guess," Scott said, "where it's so safe."

"You're one of a type yourself, aren't you, Todd?" Gwyneth said. "The polite, dimwitted sheriff of a one-horse town. Do you have a town drunk and a town whore as well?"

Scott hadn't even seen Maggie approach the table, but there she was next to Gwyneth, cheeks a melt-down level of code scarlet, pulling the fragile blonde up by the shoulder of her expensive jacket and jerking her towards the door. Scott scooped up Gwyneth's handbag and hung it over the frightened woman's free arm. He didn't want to stop Maggie, he wanted to help.

"Your brother was the town drunk, Gwyneth," Maggie said, "so I guess that position is open; and although I'd vote for you as town whore, our men like a little more meat on the bone. Not that I'm joking about your obvious eating disorder so much as I'm pointing out what a dried up old rack of bones you've turned into. If you step one foot in this store ever again, so help me God, I'll soak you in hillbilly cappuccino and throw you to one of our stereotypical dogs to gnaw on."

Gwyneth protested all the way to the front door, using declarations that began, "Well, I mean really," and "You can't possibly," and "What do you think you're," ending with, "I can't believe you just..." as Maggie shoved her out the door, slammed it shut, and locked it behind her.

There were at least twenty people in the bookstore watching this happen, and they all applauded and cheered as Maggie strode to the Banned Customer Dry Erase Board of Shame, and wrote Gwyneth's name in large block letters at the top.

Scott clapped and whistled. Lord, but he loved that woman.

As Scott walked back towards the station, Ed flagged him down and asked him to come back to the newspaper office for a chat. Once inside, he offered Scott some sludgy black coffee that Scott knew from experience he should decline. They sat at the solid oak worktable next to the gas stove, which kept the newspaper office snug and warm. Ed's new black lab was sound asleep on Goudy's old bed in front of the stove.

"What's his name?" Scott asked.

"I couldn't decide between Helvetica and Harrington, so I'm calling him Hank."

"Looks like he feels right at home."

"He's doing great. Somebody must have worked with him at some point because he already has good manners. I still can't leave him alone with any food or garbage."

"He learned some survival skills in the wild, huh?"

Ed nodded, looking down at the lab with warm affection.

"You know Tommy," Ed said, changing the subject.

"Mandy's boy."

"Delivers my papers," Ed said. "Tommy saw something the night Theo got killed, and it's worrying him. He said I could tell you about it."

"What's that?"

"He heard Theo and Phyllis's son Billy fighting outside their trailer. He said he was sleeping when the yelling woke him up, and when he went to look he saw Billy run off, and then Theo hit Phyllis."

Scott sat back, and said, "Whoa."

"Exactly," Ed said.

"What time of night was it?" Scott asked him.

"He said his mom comes home at 2:00, and she wasn't home yet. He thinks it was around 1:30."

"It must have been right after Theo got kicked out of the Thorn. Did Tommy see anything else?"

"He says not," Ed told him. "But he's really worried about Billy finding out he told, and about being in trouble with his mother for what he called peeping."

"Meaning he often sees what goes on inside Phyllis' trailer?"

"I think he probably does."

"Well, that's mighty interesting," Scott said. "I'm going to need to talk to him about it. Do you think he'll talk to me?"

"I think Tommy's more afraid of getting beaten up by Billy or grounded by his mom than talking to the police. I could arrange for you both to meet here if it's okay with you."

"He should have his mother with him when I talk to him," Scott said.

"I told Tommy he needed to let her know what was going on," Ed said. "He said he would."

Scott slapped his hand down on the table and said, "That's settled then. You let me know when they can be here and I'll stop by."

"Will do."

"Are you okay?" Scott asked him, pointing to the bruise on his head.

"Oh yeah," Ed replied. "Gave me a hell of a headache. But you know all about those."

Scott started to say he was sorry about everything that had happened, but someone came in, so he left.

Later in the afternoon Scott got a call from Ed and was able to interview Tommy in the backroom of the newspaper office. Tommy said he told his mother about it and she said it was okay for him to talk to Scott if Ed was there.

Scott reassured the boy right away that he was not in trouble for seeing what was going on at Phyllis's. Tommy hid his eyes under his floppy brown hair as he haltingly told him what he had seen. Scott looked over the gangly, skinny twelve-year-old and saw he was growing much faster than his mama could keep up with clothing-wise. His jeans were a good three inches too short and his skinny wrists stuck out way beyond his coat sleeves.

"What was the fight about?"

Tommy shrugged.

"Could you hear anything that was said?"

"Naw, just yelling. Theo was really mad, and he went after Billy, but Billy ran."

"Then what happened?"

"He hit Phyllis in the face, and she fell down."

"And then?"

"He yelled at her again and left."

"What did he yell?"

"I don't remember."

"Which way did he go?"

"Down the alley."

"Then what happened?"

"Phyllis got up and went in the house."

"Where was Billy?"

Tommy shrugged.

"Did you hear Billy come home afterward?" he asked.

Tommy shook his head.

"So what did you do?"

"I went back to sleep."

Scott doubted the boy was able to go back to sleep so quickly after seeing such a violent fight, but he didn't want to traumatize him over his reluctance to admit it.

"Was there anybody with Theo you could see, besides Phyllis and Billy?"

Tommy shook his head.

"If you think of anything else, Tommy, you tell Ed, okay?"

Tommy nodded, his whole body leaning toward the door in his strong desire to go through it.

"Okay, you can go," Scott said. "I appreciate your help."

After the boy left, Scott said to Ed, "I think he might have seen more, but I'm afraid if I push harder he'll just clam up."

"Do you want me to pressure him?" Ed asked.

"No," Scott replied. "I think if you let it go completely he will be more apt to tell you, given time."

"Do you remember how I came to hire Tommy?" Ed said.

"Sorry," Scott said. "I don't remember the details."

"Jane Anne Porter was the paper carrier when I came back after Dad died," Ed said. "You remember her?"

"Pitcher for the girls' softball team," Scott said. "Wicked right arm and swore like a sailor."

"That's her. When Jane Anne graduated from high school and left for college, there must have been fifty kids who applied for the job. Fathers offered me bribes, kids brought me letters of recommendation, and their mothers baked me cookies and cakes. I took a couple weeks to decide, and gained five pounds."

"Smart move," Scott said.

"Tommy showed up every morning at 4:30 during those two weeks, and offered to help me out until I made my decision. He wasn't pushy, he didn't whine or beg, and no one called, wrote, or baked on his behalf. I took one look at the shabby clothes, the long hair, and the rickety bike, and I was not impressed."

"He's not exactly Boy Scout material," Scott said.

"That's an understatement. Goudy, on the other hand, who by that time in his life rarely left his bed over there unless it was time to eat or take a piss, jumped up and greeted Tommy like his long lost friend. So I decided to give him a chance. After the two weeks were up, I decided the kid wasn't too irritating and gave him the job."

"Goudy always was a good judge of character," Scott said. "I remember he used to wag whenever he saw Doc Machalvie but would growl at his brother Stuart."

"He hated Theo too. Theo made all the hair stand up on Goudy's spine. Not too many people got that reaction. There was one weird exception, though. Goudy really liked Willy Neff. I never could understand that."

"Dogs do love bad smells, I guess."

"Well, anyway, when Goudy got so he could no longer jump up into the truck cab, Tommy helped me lift him every morning. The morning Goudy did not wake up, we took him to the end of Possum Holler and buried him on the hill behind Lily Crawford's barn. That fat old dog once caught a rabbit up there that was as surprised about it as he was."

"He was a good dog," Scott said, while Ed wiped his eyes and cleared his throat.

"I've been pining over that damn dog for months," Ed said. "Then Hannah found me this one."

"He looks like he's recovered from surgery all right," Scott said, wincing at the thought of what had been removed.

"He won't even miss 'em," Ed said, and then laughed.

Things felt closer to normal between them, and Scott was relieved.

"What are you going to do now?" Ed asked. "I know Tommy's worried Billy will find out he told."

Scott shook his head, saying, "That won't be a problem. Phyllis and Billy live in a trailer park surrounded by nosy neighbors. Any one of them could probably tell me the same thing Tommy did. I'll do a little trailer-to-trailer inquiry as a cover. You might want to let Tommy know."

Scott left Ed's office, turned right, and crossed the alley to look at the new antique store. He could see the people who had purchased the building had been renovating the outside in preparation for a late spring opening. It looked as though they were pouring some serious money into it, installing new wrought-iron handrails and sprucing up the facade. The dumpster in the alley was overflowing with their renovation trash, and Scott picked up a couple pieces of the old pipe handrail and some broken glass that had fallen out of the dumpster and threw them back in.

Scott walked the length of the alley to Peony Street and then turned left and crossed diagonally to reach the trailer park.

Built in the fifties, Foxglove Mobile Home Park consisted of a "U" shaped drive around which a dozen or so trailers were situated, with garden space in the middle. Scott talked to all the trailer park residents who were home. All had heard the fight but were used to hearing Phyllis, Theo, and Billy carry on. This latest fight didn't seem out of the ordinary to them. No one would admit to seeing anything; they didn't want to get involved. Scott got the feeling they were all a little afraid of Billy, a bully who was known to break things when he got angry; the kind of frustrated, restless teenager who liked to torture younger kids, set off loud fireworks, or shoot out the streetlights with a BB gun.

'Kind of like Theo used to be,' Scott thought, uncharitably.

Billy's mother Phyllis was a year older than Scott and had been a wild child in high school. One of those girls who developed a woman's body before she had the brains to manage it, Phyllis cut a wide swath through the male population of Rose Hill before and after the teenage pregnancy that resulted in Billy. She never named the father, maybe couldn't have, and Phyllis's mother Pauline raised her difficult grandchild as best she could. Phyllis and Billy bickered more like siblings than mother and son, and because both worked in the family-owned diner, their frequent fights were like a floor show for the customers.

Scott went to the back door of the diner, where he found Billy was as surly and belligerent as he remembered. Ian and Scott both had warned him on several occasions that he was now an adult and subject to the laws of the adult world, without much good effect. Ian always said it was just a matter of time before he was arrested for something.

Billy came out the back door to the alley with Scott and immediately lit up a cigarette. He had a generous white apron wrapped around his body, but whether it was to protect the underlying black t-shirt and raggedy jeans or to protect everything else from them, Scott wasn't sure. Billy was tall and brawny, one of those kids who's nineteen but looks thirty.

When he asked Billy about the fight, the young man shrugged and said, "Yeah, so?"

"Your neighbors said it got pretty violent."

Billy communicated what he thought of those neighbors using several profane words.

"Did Theo hit your mother?"

"Yeah, he popped her one," Billy said. "Bitch deserved it."

"That's your mother you're talking about," Scott said.

Billy smiled slyly as if he realized he'd touched a nerve in the grownup, and loving the effect, pushed his luck.

"She's a huge pain in my ass," Billy said. "She's always bitchin' about something, raggin' on me all the time. She did the same thing to Theo. When he got tired of it, he'd pop her one. They did it all the time. I think they got off on doing it."

Scott had an urge to knock the smart-ass look off the boy's face, but he didn't give in to it.

"So you weren't angry with Theo when he left the trailer that night? After the fight?"

Billy flipped his cigarette, and intentionally or not, it came pretty close to Scott as it sailed by.

"Theo was all right," Billy said, "for an old guy."

"And you weren't angry that he hit your mom?" Scott said.

Billy laughed and showed the consequences of a chronic lack of dental hygiene when he smiled.

"No, man, she deserved it. I told ya. She was asking for it."

"Did Theo ever take a swing at you?" Scott asked, and Billy immediately puffed out his chest.

"He wouldn't a had the cojones, man! I woulda..." and then he seemed to realize what he was about to say and stopped mid-sentence, his mouth gaping open.

"Woulda bashed his head in with a baseball bat?" Scott completed the sentence for him.

Billy spread his arms wide, saying, "Hey man, don't try to hang that crap on me. My mom'll tell you, I was home with her when that shit went down."

Scott wanted to drop kick the boy into the nearest snow bank, but instead, he said, "Great, I'll ask her." He went in the back door, through the kitchen, and on into the dining room, where Phyllis was waiting tables.

"You do that," Billy said from behind him, and Scott heard Billy's grandfather tell him to shut up and show

120

some respect. Billy was mumbling under his breath as Scott walked back through the kitchen with Phyllis, whose look shot daggers at Billy as she followed Scott out the back door.

"What did you do now?" she hissed at her son in passing.

"Nothin'," Billy grumbled.

Scott closed the door behind them and gave Phyllis his jacket. She thanked him and wrapped herself up in it. Scott could see the black eye which bloomed underneath the new bangs she had artfully arranged to dip over it; it showed through the heavy makeup she had spackled over it. The white of her eye was blood red at the side, which could not be covered up. In her mid-thirties, Phyllis was still an attractive woman, although she looked hard, with her hair dyed a little too dark and her makeup applied heavily.

"I heard there was a little trouble outside your trailer on Saturday night. What can you tell me about that?"

She looked scared, and he could see her hands were shaking as she lit a cigarette.

"Oh, Scott, you know how Theo was," she tried to laugh it off, but the fear in her eyes gave her away. "When he got few drinks in him he got a jealous notion and went off."

"Who was he jealous of?"

"Well, you know me and men, Scott. I probably flirt a little more than I should, but like I told Theo, 'if there's no ring on this finger don't try to lead me around by one through the nose.'"

She tried a girlish laugh, but it turned into a smoker's cough. Scott waited for her to catch her breath.

"Did he hit you?"

Phyllis unconsciously reached toward her eye, caught herself, and put her hand back down.

"No, of course not! I misjudged how far I was from the counter in there, bent over to pick up my pen and bam! I decked myself pretty good."

"I heard Billy and Theo got into it."

"Some friggin' nosy neighbors I've got, huh?"

"Did they often fight?"

"Well, you've talked to Billy," she said. "Every time that kid opens his mouth I wanna smack the snot out of him."

Scott almost laughed because he agreed.

"So Theo, Billy, and you had a noisy fight in and outside your trailer the night Theo died."

"Yeah, I reckon there's no point in denyin' it," she admitted, "when ten outta ten nosy friggin' senior citizens all agree."

"Did Billy follow Theo when he left?"

"No," Phyllis said quickly. "He came right back soon as he saw Theo was gone."

"What time was it?"

Phyllis pretended to think about it.

"I don't rightly know," she said. "I'd had a few myself by that time, and I wasn't exactly watching the clock. It was after midnight, I guess."

Scott didn't doubt Phyllis was too drunk to know what time it had been, which he now knew was between 1:15, when Theo was kicked out of the Thorn, and 2:00, when Tommy's mother came home.

"Did you see anyone waiting for Theo, or hanging around the trailer park?"

"Nope. Just the usual nosy parkers peeking out the curtains at me. Don't have any thrills of their own so they gotta have a good look at mine."

"Tell me about the fight Theo had with Ed in the diner. I heard it got pretty heated."

She rolled her eyes and waved the notion off like a pesky fly.

"That was just business as usual for Theo," she said. "That was his normal way of dealing with people who disagreed with him or got in his way."

"You didn't think it was serious?"

Phyllis laughed.

"Everybody knows Ed Harrison wouldn't hurt a fly. He might get a bug up his ass about a damn dog, or politics, or global friggin' warming, but he wouldn't lower himself to get physical about it. No, good ole Ed would write about it in that cat box liner of his."

She cackled at her own attempt at humor.

"Did you love Theo?" he asked.

"No," she said, but tears appeared in her eyes as she said it. "It doesn't pay to love anybody that ornery and mean."

Scott took his coat, and she went back inside, where he could hear her screaming at Billy, but he couldn't make out what she was saying. He took one whiff of the stench of cigarettes and perfume on his coat and carried it back to the station held out in front of him rather than putting it on. He left it hanging outside the back door the rest of the day to air it out.


Skip and Frank had worked out a timeline for Theo's last day, and they went over it with Scott. Theo had gone around town on Saturday being his usual disagreeable self, picking fights and stirring up trouble, before going home to prepare a dinner for someone who it seemed did not show up. They reported that Gail Godwin, Theo's housekeeper, said she didn't know who he had invited to dinner. Theo came into town, fought with Patrick outside the Rose and Thorn, took a drive with Willy Neff out to Hannah's farm, went back to the Rose and Thorn for another altercation with Patrick, went to Phyllis's, and then went to the vet's office and got killed.

Nobody saw Willy Neff after Theo left Hannah's farm with him.

They compared notes and Scott made assignments for the next day. He wanted Frank to talk to some of Theo's latest dog breeding customers to find which one was angry about the experience. Scott then let them go home for some much-needed rest, although he could have used some himself. He was used to stretching himself thin so his staff could lead normal lives. He made a fresh pot of coffee, spread out his notes, and had just settled in for the duration when the phone rang.

Being called to the mayor's office was a lot like being called to the principal's office, and Scott thought he knew what was coming. Mayor Stuart Machalvie was ostensibly Scott's boss, although he had officially been hired by the town council. There were only five town council members, and all of them were either cronies of Stuart's or somehow related.

Stuart took turns being mayor with his wife Peg, who ran the local funeral home. Each always won by a wide margin and served on the town council during the four years they weren't busy being mayor. The truth was, in a town of around 500 permanent residents, only about 150 people actually voted, and no one wanted the mayor's job but those two.

There was not a lot of power attached to the job, but what there was they abused with a grin and a wink. Nothing illegal, understand, just favors for friends, which was pretty much how the town operated on its own anyway. The real money for a town that size was in having a hydroelectric dam or a wind farm within the city limits, or a huge shopping complex on the outskirts of town, and Peg and Stuart were always pursuing those pipe dreams. It didn't help them that the Little Bear River was not big enough to support a hydroelectric dam, or that the congressional representative for their district was against any project that might damage the local environment.

Surrounded in Rose Hill by large Italian, Irish, German, Hungarian, Lebanese, and Polish families, the Machalvie family was descended from one of the few Scottish families who settled the town, and they were fiercely proud of their heritage. The Kilt and Bagpipe Club of Rose Hill may have had fewer members than a man's got fingers and toes, but they always had a float in the annual Heritage Festival parade and marched in their kilts to the wail of the piper. Every year they tried in vain to launch a highland games competition during the festival, but few people were willing to balance on logs floating on Frog Pond or heave a telephone pole across the meadow while wearing a short skirt with no underwear, so it failed to catch on.

Stuart's office walls were a showcase of historic Scottish regalia and Celtic worship, complete with shields, swords, and framed, autographed photos of Sean Connery and Billy Connelly. There was a first edition of Robert Burns' poetry, some elaborately decorated sporrans, and several collectible bottles of Glenlivet proudly displayed in a specially made case (along with a drinkable case in the coat cupboard). There was a huge "Braveheart" movie poster on the wall behind the desk, and the whole collection lent a bizarre, slightly menacing effect to meetings with the mayor.

Stuart greeted Scott and asked him to have a seat. Scott waited for Stuart to begin, and the silence stretched to a point where other men may have become uncomfortable, but Scott preferred the silence to anything Stuart had to say.

"You know don't you, Scott, that Gwyneth and Caroline Eldridge now own the vast majority of property in this town."

Scott nodded his head in agreement but said nothing.

"Theo's sisters will inherit all the family holdings, including the college president's home, the lodge, the glassworks, the Eldridge Inn, and several other valuable buildings in the town."

"Hmmm," Scott nodded as he pictured the falling down firetraps Theo owned down on Lotus Avenue, up Possum Holler, and the empty buildings on Rose Hill Avenue now collecting dust. He was glad he didn't have such "valuable" property hanging around his neck.

"Were you involved in any business deals with Theo?" Scott asked him.

Stuart shook his head.

"Not a one," he said. "That might be construed as a conflict of interest, me being mayor. I did, however, encourage any venture he put forth that would benefit Rose Hill's tax base."

"Such as?"

"What you may not know, Scott," Stuart explained, "is that Theo's family owns several thousand acres between here and the State Park."

"Hmmm," Scott replied, even though he did know because he'd seen the development plan on Theo's pool table.

"Thousands of acres of property which could be developed in the future," Stuart said. "At one point I know he considered building a ski resort and luxury condo development. It was just a matter of waiting for certain restrictions to be lifted, and I understand it was in the works when he died. Peg and I advised him to lease some of the property to a wind farm concern we had been in touch with, and he was considering it. There were fracking companies lined up. The town could annex that property and reap huge tax benefits. Theo was on board."

"So what was the holdup?"

"Flying squirrels," Stuart said and offered Scott a cigar.

Scott declined it, saying, "Pardon me?"

"Flying squirrels," Stuart reiterated. "Small, gray, flea-covered, flying rats, which are considered an endangered species, and therefore are more precious to the environmentalists than their own children's futures."

"Ah, Congressman Green," Scott said.

"A mental midget," Stuart said, lighting his cigar.

"Hmm," Scott said, which seemed to be interpreted as agreement.

Stuart pointed his cigar at Scott and said, "Exactly."

Scott actually agreed with Congressman Green's platform on environmental causes and always voted for him. He didn't see why every pristine piece of woodland property had to be scalped and paved so people would never be more than ten minutes away from a Mega Mart or a fast food restaurant.

"So I think you understand, my boy, why Gwyneth Eldridge should be handled with kid gloves in this town. Why it is important she be made to feel welcome and appreciated."

"And not, say, tossed out of the bookstore on her ear?" Scott suggested.

"While the chief of police watches and applauds," Stuart said pointedly, and then puffed meaningfully on his cigar.

Scott, sensitive to smoke, blinked against the rank fumes.

"I shouldn't have applauded," Scott admitted. "But the bookstore is a privately owned business, it was well within the owner's rights to escort an unruly customer out of it, and Gwyneth deserved it."

Stuart shook his head and wagged his cigar at Scott.

"Except the longer term result, my son, is that you have created a powerful enemy out of someone I want to do business with."

"Does this mean I'm fired?" Scott asked.

"Not if you apologize and make it right with her."

Stuart blew some smoke rings at the ceiling, and Scott started feeling nauseated.

"Hmmm," Scott said, noncommittally.

"And it wouldn't hurt if you could get Maggie Fitzpatrick to do the same."

Scott snorted unintentionally and then laughed out loud.

"Well, that's not going to happen. You might as well ask Congressman Green to approve plans for a nuclear power plant in Gerrymaine Valley."

Stuart leaned forward with a weird, zealous gleam in his eye.

"It would be a wonderful windfall for this town, Scott, and there'd be jobs for everyone."

"And the flying squirrels would glow in the dark, so they'd be easier to spot," Scott joked.

"You want to know a secret, son?" the mayor asked with a smirk.

"Probably not," Scott said, and stood, preparing to leave.

"Those squirrels," Stuart began, pointing an imaginary gun, using the hand without the cigar in it.

"No, don't tell me," Scott said, backing toward the door.

"They're mighty good eatin'," Stuart said, and laughed uproariously at his own joke, pounding the top of the desk.

"He's quite a character, isn't he?" Scott said to Stuart's secretary, Kay, who sat at a desk in the outer office, where she could hear everything.

Kay smiled and shook her head.

As he left the outer office, Scott could still hear Stuart laughing, which turned into a cough, which sounded as if a lung might come up.

"You make up with Gwyneth!" Stuart choked out between coughs as Scott shut the door behind him.

Sarah was sitting in her car outside the station when he got back. He invited her in and made some coffee. Scott told her about what Knox said about the coin, about Anne Marie's accident, Drew's background check, and about Billy, Phyllis, and what Tommy saw. No one had any leads on Willy Neff or his vehicle. He did not tell her about his plan to go see Maggie's brother, Sean, on Thursday. She made some notes and thanked him for the work.

He walked her back out to her car, where she hesitated before getting in.

"I'm going to talk to Phyllis, Billy, and Tommy," she said. "Afterwards I'd like to compare notes with you. I'll bring pizza."

Scott didn't want to encourage Sarah, but he did want to know what happened.

"Sure," he said.

Maggie stopped by a little later to give Scott his to-do list from the Winter Festival committee meeting he forgot to attend. Scott told her all about Tommy, Phyllis, and Billy.

"Do you think Phyllis or Billy could have killed Theo?" Maggie asked Scott.

"Phyllis may have been mad enough," he responded. "But I think it had to be someone much bigger and stronger."

"Billy's big enough," Maggie said. "But he only bullies people weaker than he is. I think he would be too scared of Theo."

"I thought maybe Billy might do it in retaliation for Theo hitting his mom until I talked to him," Scott said.

"Phyllis and Billy hate each other. I wouldn't be surprised if one day Billy hauls off and smacks her one himself. She constantly puts him down and makes fun of him in front of people."

Sarah came in carrying a pizza box and a six-pack.

'Damn,' Scott thought. He forgot she was coming back.

The two women were barely civil to one another, and Maggie was obviously not pleased to see the pizza and beer come in along with her petite nemesis. She left after giving Scott a dirty look.

Sarah served the pizza to Scott as if it were her kitchen and not the station break room, made teasing comments about his bachelor life, and gave him the distinct feeling she was about to make another blatant pass.

Sure enough, after she reported on interviewing Tommy, Billy, Phyllis, and the neighbors (without finding anything more out than Scott did), she batted her eyes, smiled up sideways at him, and commenced her assault. Scott feigned cluelessness until she made it perfectly clear what she was interested in, and then he said he had a policy not to get involved with anyone he worked with.

"I'm only keeping you involved in the case as a courtesy, Scott," she said. "I wouldn't call that working together."

Scott wouldn't budge, and she finally left in a furious snit. Scott thought he probably could have been talked into sleeping with Sarah if she wasn't so condescending about everything. She was good looking, willing, and Lord knows he was deprived. It would ruin things with Maggie though, for sure, and he hadn't given up on her yet.

When he got back inside, he called Maggie, but her line was busy. Completely exhausted, he flopped down on the couch in his office to rest a moment before trying her number again, and fell sound sleep.

Maggie went home seething about what looked to her an awful lot like a date between Scott and Sarah. She called Hannah to bitch about it and found her cousin less than supportive.

"You don't want him, but you don't want anyone else to have him either," Hannah said. "How fair is that?"

"But not Tiny Crimefighter!" Maggie moaned.

"You wouldn't like anyone he dated," Hannah retorted. "You're just as bad as his mother,"

Maggie gasped and hung up. The phone immediately rang again, and she picked it up, saying, "I am nothing like Scott's mother," and a voice that wasn't Hannah's said, "Okay, you're not."

It was Caroline Eldridge, calling from South America. They had been friends since kindergarten, although they hadn't seen each other for many years. Caroline would occasionally send a postcard or call and catch up for an hour or two, but those instances were sometimes years apart. She traveled extensively, often on behalf of charitable organizations, and did not have a fixed address.

Caroline said she had recently returned from a foray into a rural area outside the city of Concepcion, in Paraguay, where she was assisting a relief organization in distributing much needed medical supplies. Talking to Caroline always made Maggie realize how spoiled and rich she was compared to most of the world, and the way she dealt with the guilt was by making a contribution to whatever charity Caroline was working with at the time. She asked Caroline for the mailing address, and Caroline told her she could make a donation through their website, and she would e-mail Maggie a link.

"I've been out of touch, so I just found out about Theo," Caroline said. "I talked to Gwyneth and told her I can't be at the funeral. It sounds like she has everything well in hand."

When Maggie told her she was sorry about Theo dying, Caroline said, "I'm not upset about it. Theo was a miserable guy most of his life, and he made everyone around him unhappy too. Maybe next time he will do better."

Maggie knew better than to ask about "next time" lest she be treated to another long, loopy lecture on karma and reincarnation. Caroline sounded tired but still as cheerful and optimistic as ever. She told Maggie about the people she'd met and the plans they had to build a Buddhist retreat center nearby. Maggie listened patiently and tried valiantly to keep from rolling her eyes every two minutes. She loved Caroline, but her groovy new age version of Mother Theresa act wore thin quickly. Maggie preferred to send money to support the effort rather than have to hear her friend lecture about it for an hour. Maggie knew it was shallow and selfish, but it was how she felt.

She told Caroline Scott was investigating the crime and asked if Theo had any enemies she knew of.

Caroline laughed, and said, "I don't think he had many friends, do you?"

"Is there anything else you can think of that might help? Anything you know Theo was doing he shouldn't have been?"

"Theo never confided in me, so I haven't a clue what he was doing. There is something Scott should check out, though," Caroline said. "Out at the lodge there's a room above the study. You can get to it through the closet ceiling, but we were not allowed to go up there. Dad said his father used to keep booze up there during prohibition, and who knows what Theo used it for. There should still be a key to the house behind the lantern on the front porch; Theo always left one there for me."

Maggie told Caroline about Theo's dogs, which probably weren't really the purebred dogs Theo said they were.

"They weren't mistreated, were they?" Caroline asked.

"Not at all," Maggie reassured her. "Hannah just needs to know if you want to keep them or should she find homes for them?"

"I really don't know what I'm going to do. They won't read the will until after the funeral so I won't know what property's mine and what's Gwyneth's until then. I travel so much with this organization that I certainly won't be able to take care of them, and you know how much Gwyneth hates animals and children. Tell Hannah to find good, loving homes for them with my blessing."

Before she got off the phone, Caroline said she would let Maggie know when she was coming home. Caroline said, "Namaste," to which Maggie said awkwardly, "Right backatcha," before they both hung up.

Maggie lay awake for a long time thinking about the secret room, trying to decide whether to tell Scott and let him deal with it (probably should) or enlist Hannah to go with her to check it out instead (probably would).

ROSE HILL by Pamela Grandstaff

# Chapter Six - Wednesday

Maggie woke up on Wednesday morning right before the alarm rang at 6:00, and thought about what had happened the night before. She pictured Scott and Sarah lying entwined in tangled sheets and an actual pain shot through her chest, propelling her out of bed. Convinced Scott was seeing Sarah romantically, she decided she would not tell him about the secret room in Theo's lodge home. She would wait until she saw Hannah this morning, tell her about the room, and then they would decide what to do about it.

It turned out she didn't have to wait long. Hannah called her right after the bookstore opened to see if she was free to go out for breakfast.

"A big one," Hannah said. "I want everything fried and covered in gravy."

"We won't have time," Maggie said. "Come pick me up, and I'll bring you something. We're going on a treasure hunt."

Maggie made Hannah an extra-large latte with extra caramel syrup and whipped cream and filled a bag with baked goods before going out back in the alley to wait for her. As soon as she got in the cab of the truck, she gave Hannah the cup and bag of food.

"Yummy," Hannah said.

"Caroline called me last night," Maggie said. "After you insulted me and I hung up on you."

Hannah had already latched onto a cheese danish, so she could only say, "Mmm, hmmm?"

"Our Miss Caroline is on a missionary trip in Paraguay–she told me the name of the city, but I can't remember it now–and just found out about her bastard brother getting himself murdered," Maggie said. "She's flying back in a few weeks, as soon as she wraps up what she's doing down there and can get flights booked."

Hannah asked, "Where's whatsit-guay?" with a mouth full of pastry.

"South America," Maggie told her. "Anyway, she said the lodge has a secret room you can get to through the closet in the study. She said her great granddad used to hide booze in it during prohibition."

Hannah put the truck in reverse and backed into the alley so fast they slid.

"How do we get in?" she asked, and Maggie grinned.

After an interminable crawl up Pine Mountain Road behind a slow-moving eighteen-wheeler, they went on a four-wheel drive adventure up the lodge driveway. The state road crew was plowing it a couple times a day for Hannah, as a favor, so she could get to Theo's dogs, but they hadn't done it yet. Hannah's truck slid to rest almost against the porch of the large house, and they waded through three-foot high drifts to get to the front door. Up here on the ridge top, there was a clear blue sky, while down in Rose Hill it had been overcast and gray; they had climbed above the bad weather.

Maggie fumbled behind one of the big lanterns that flanked the door and found a key on a long, frozen leather shoelace, right where Caroline said it would be. She carefully lifted the yellow police tape that was draped across the doorframe from lantern to lantern and Hannah held it up for her. When the key turned the lock on the massive door, they more or less tumbled into the foyer of the big house, bringing a lot of snow in with them.

Hannah whistled low and said, "Wow, I forgot how big it is."

They shed their coats, hats, gloves, and boots on the rug right inside the door. Maggie handed Hannah some big yellow rubber gloves and one of the flashlights she brought from the bookstore. Hannah laughed, making a queenly wave with one of her gloved hands.

"Some cat burglars we make with our big yellow hands," she said.

"It was all I had," Maggie told her.

They went through the library to the billiard room, where they stopped long enough for Maggie to pull the sheet off the development model on the pool table and take a good look at Eldridge Point. They studied it from several angles, pointing out different features.

"This must be Theo's house," Maggie said, pointing to an elaborate mansion at the end of a cul-de-sac, the largest home featured, with a view of the mountains, lake, and golf course behind it.

"Isn't all of this property protected land?" Hannah asked, noting the miniature wind farm on several of the mountain ridges.

Maggie was glowering at the development, looking like she might destroy it with one swipe of her huge yellow hand. Hannah reminded her cousin what their intentions were, saying, "Let's go see what the bastard has hidden in the ceiling."

In the study, there was a closet, right where Caroline said it would be, back in the corner. The closet was three feet deep and wide, and full of boxes of Eldridge Point logo merchandise. They laughed at the stupid looking logo before moving all the boxes into the study. Maggie used a flashlight to look at the ceiling of the closet. The cedar-paneled enclosure had a cedar plank ceiling, and looking carefully, they could just make out how it was not flush against the molding where it met the walls. They borrowed the rolling ladder from the library and pushed it into the closet as far as it would go.

Maggie went up first and found the ceiling panel was hinged on one side, which allowed it to swing upward into a dark space above the closet. With the upper half of her body through the opening, Maggie shone the flashlight on all four walls of the space, roughly the same size in circumference as the closet.

"If I see one spider this mission is aborted," Maggie told Hannah.

"You're such a big sissy," Hannah said. "Spiders wouldn't stop Miss Marple. Spiders wouldn't stop Harriet Vane. Spiders wouldn't stop Kinsey Milhone. Spiders wouldn't stop Cordelia Gray..."

"All right, shut up," Maggie said.

Maggie was momentarily disappointed to think this was the secret room itself. Then the beam from the flashlight revealed a series of iron rungs attached to one wall. Maggie pointed them out to Hannah, who was steadying the ladder beneath her. After testing the strength of the rungs first, she climbed up into the dark, empty shaft above the closet. It was hard to climb and shine the flashlight up at the same time, so she went slowly, pausing every so often to shine the light above and around her. The walls were cedar lined, just like the closet beneath it, and the rungs were made of thick iron pipes bolted to the wall. It was dusty and cobwebby in the corners, but to Maggie's relief, they seemed to be dust webs and not the spidery kind.

After she climbed what seemed like ten or twelve feet, she discerned a door on the wall behind her. She calculated she must be at the second-floor level looking toward the back of one of the bedrooms, but she felt a little disoriented. Up another eight feet, the shaft ended in a cedar plank ceiling that seemed to be firmly fastened to the walls all the way around.

Maggie turned and shone the light on the door in the wall behind her, a yard away. She reached out and turned the old iron doorknob, which had no locking mechanism, and pushed the door inward. She pointed the light into the room and frightened herself by shining it into a mirror on a far wall and seeing herself looking back. She told Hannah, close behind her, what she was doing, then turned and leaped into the room.

She stumbled over something and had just righted herself as Hannah got high enough on the iron rungs to point her flashlight and look in.

"That was graceful," Hannah said.

Maggie stood up in the middle of the room and flinched as something swung against her cheek. She batted frantically at what she thought was probably a giant spider, much to Hannah's amusement. It turned out to be the pull chain to a light bulb in the ceiling. She pulled it, and the light came on, throwing everything in the room into dim relief by its low wattage light. Hannah leaped into the room, avoiding the ottoman Maggie had stumbled over.

Maggie estimated the room was ten feet square at most. There was an old velvet armchair next to the ottoman with a fringed floor lamp behind it. The mechanism on the lamp showed its age, but when Maggie pulled the short chain, it worked, helping to light the small room even more. On the other side of the chair and ottoman was an old iron safe, about two feet cubed, with an old-fashioned dial and handle, and on top of it was a half-empty bottle of whiskey and a glass with some whiskey residue in it. The bottle was new and not dusty. Theo, or someone, had been up there recently.

Hannah meanwhile, was studying the wall across from the chair and ottoman, most of which was covered in photographs.

She turned a grim face to Maggie and said, "Come look at this."

They were all photographs of Maggie's sister-in-law Ava. There were black and white shots of her as a toddler, yellowed color photos of her in grade school, and blown up color photos of her posing as Prom Queen, Winter Festival Queen, and Miss Firecracker. There was even a blurry wedding photo with Brian cut out of it. There were photos representing all the intervening years from her childhood to the present, even some that seemed recent. The almost surgical precision of the cuts revealed Theo had removed anyone who appeared in a photo with Ava, even her children. The recent photos seemed surreptitiously taken, and Maggie wondered who had taken them.

Altogether, the collection told the story of an obsession which seemed to span most of Theo's adolescent and adult life and formed a shrine to the beauty of Maggie's sister-in-law. Hannah pointed at one photo pinned near where she stood, and Maggie leaned over to look. It had been taken through Ava's second-floor bedroom window, could only have been taken from the vantage point of a tree outside, through the space where the lace curtains were parted. Ava was sleeping, one arm thrown over her head and one leg under a sheet. There was a man in the bed with her, but Maggie couldn't tell who it was. Theo had cut him out of the picture, so only his arm showed.

"I'm taking them down," Maggie said firmly, and Hannah said, "I'll help you."

"You don't think Ava was ever involved with Theo, do you?" Hannah asked tentatively as they worked.

"I don't know," Maggie said. "They dated briefly the summer Brian broke up with her, right after he graduated, but it was probably only a week or two at the most."

"Didn't Brian and Ava get married shortly after that?" Hannah asked.

"Yes," Maggie said. "It was the big scandal of the year. She had just turned sixteen. He had to turn down a baseball scholarship at Wake Forrest to stay here and work for Curtis at the station."

Hannah remembered some other gossip about the quick wedding, but she didn't think now was the time to bring it up.

The air in the room was stuffy, dusty, and stale. Maggie didn't want to think about what all Theo got up to in there, with this shrine to her sister-in-law on the wall. Once all the pictures were in a pile on the floor, Maggie checked the safe.

"It's locked, of course."

"What number was it left on?" Hannah asked. "Maybe he forgot to spin it."

Maggie told her the number.

"That's the year I was born," Hannah said.

That gave Maggie an idea.

"Wasn't Brad your age?"

Hannah nodded.

"Too bad we don't know Brad's birth date; that might be it."

"Or Ava's," Hannah said and gestured at the wall they had just cleared.

Maggie knew her sister-in-law's birth date, and sure enough, those numbers opened it.

"That was too easy," Maggie said to Hannah.

"Oh, I don't know," Hannah said. "If I kept a safe in my secret stalker Ava Fitzpatrick shrine, I might make her birth date the combination."

"Thanks, wise ass," said Maggie, and opened the door.

The safe had several manila envelopes and folders in it, plus a handgun, two boxes of ammunition, three thick, bundled stacks of money, a display type coin or jewelry box, a big plastic bag of pot, some small plastic vials of what looked like rocks of brown sugar, and a rectangular shaped object wrapped in brown paper and twine.

"Geez oh wiz, would you look at that! Colombian drug lord Theo Eldridge," Hannah said.

"I'm not touching those things," Maggie said, pointing at the gun and drugs.

Maggie left everything in the safe except the manila folders and envelopes. Those she piled on the ottoman before she seated herself in the velvet armchair. Hannah sat down on the floor and watched her open each one, awkwardly, with her big-yellow-gloved hands.

As Maggie and Hannah opened and examined the contents of each envelope, they realized the collection represented enough blackmail dynamite to blow the quiet lives of several prominent Rose Hill citizens to kingdom come.

There were compromising photos of men and women who didn't seem to realize, in their enthusiasm, that they were being photographed. The two recurring players in these photographs were Phyllis Davis, in various color wigs, looking triumphant and smug, and a man who always had his face covered, or turned away, but who had a distinctive snake tattoo down the underside of both his forearms.

The names on the envelopes included several Maggie did not know, but some she did, including Doc Machalvie, former fire chief Eric Estep, Ed's father, and Maggie's brother Brian.

Hannah was beside herself at first, but eventually could only say, "Ew," at every photo.

After the first six envelopes, Maggie said, "I'm getting sick of looking at naked people, how about you?"

Hannah nodded emphatically, saying, "That Phyllis is like a gymnast at the sex Olympics, isn't she?"

"We'll only look in the envelopes of the people we know," Maggie said.

Maggie handed the envelope with Brian's name on it to Hannah, saying, "I can't look."

Hannah reported, "It's him and Phyllis, and can I just say, whoa, I know he's your brother, but I can see why he was so popular."

Maggie swatted her friend with a folder, saying, "I could have lived quite happily not knowing that."

There were several photos of Knox's wife Anne Marie, obviously wasted and posing in what she must have thought were provocative ways.

"She looks better with clothes on," Hannah said. "I know I'm skinny, but she's scary skinny. I can count every rib. You think those boobs are fake?"

"She's in a coma right now," Maggie reminded her. "Have some compassion."

"You're right. Sorry, Anne Marie," Hannah said to the ceiling. "I hope you get better soon, so you can get back to whorin' and snortin'."

Maggie said, not for the first time, "We are both going straight to hell."

"Well, if we do I bet it will look a lot like this room," Hannah said, gesturing around her, "This is the creepiest place I've ever been in."

After they had seen all the photos they could stand, Maggie put the envelopes aside. The first folder she looked in held a sheaf of letters to "G" from "S." Written on lined notebook paper with a blue ballpoint pen, Maggie thought it looked like it was written by an adolescent hand. She didn't read the letters, but closed the folder and put them aside, intending to examine them more closely later on.

In the next folder was a stack of completed and notarized AKC registration forms with matching DNA and medical records representing several different litters of purebred dogs which Maggie now knew didn't exist. Drew's signature did not appear on any of the documentation, but his predecessor's did.

"That's a relief," Hannah said. "I really didn't want to start over with a new vet."

The next folder revealed documents for a loan made to Brian Fitzpatrick from Eldridge Financial Corporation, Inc. It listed as collateral his home and life insurance policies on both his children and his wife, Ava. There were also copies of those policies. On the date the loan was made, baby Timmy had been two months old. The amount of the loan and usurious interest rate made Maggie sick at her stomach. A receipt was attached showing the balance had been paid in full, on a date soon after Brian had disappeared. Maggie wondered why Brian needed so much money and how he was able to pay it back so quickly.

There was a file on Knox Rodefeffer that contained a lot of newspaper clippings about some incident that happened when he was in college. Maggie also put that aside to examine later.

One file had transcripts of what looked like phone conversations along with cassette tapes, and one had pages and pages of e-mail correspondence printouts between "hotnwild69" and "jailbt4u." Maggie quickly put those aside as well.

"Why did we think we needed to look at everything?" she asked Hannah. "I feel kind of sick now."

"You made me do it," Hannah said. "That's my story."

"What should we do now?" Maggie asked. "We can't just leave it here, and we can't give it to Scott. It would be inadmissible, I think, because of how we found it."

"If any of this stuff got out, it would hurt a lot of people," Hannah said.

Maggie chewed her lip while she thought a minute, and then made a decision.

"Okay, we take Ava's pictures for sure, and Brian's stuff, the letters, and the file on Knox. I sure don't want Doris Machalvie to see Doc's pictures. Anybody you want to protect?"

Hannah chose Ed's father. "He was really good to Sam when he came home from the war," she said. "I don't want Ed to ever see these."

"What about the fire chief?" Maggie asked.

"Well, now we now know why he blamed your wiring when Theo burned your house down," Hannah said. "He was being blackmailed."

"That explains it," Maggie said. "These photos would devastate his wife. We'll take them, too."

Hannah frowned.

"Doesn't it feel like we're playing God here?" Hannah said. "Maybe we should burn all of it."

"Technically speaking, this is all evidence," Maggie said. "We shouldn't be tampering with any of it. One of these people might have killed Theo."

"So we can take the dead ones for sure, because we know they didn't do it," Hannah reasoned. "That covers Ed's dad and Chief Estep. Unless Ed killed Theo because of what he had on his dad."

"I think it's more likely Ed would expose Theo for being a blackmailer. That seems more his style. I never thought for one moment that Ed killed Theo."

"Oh, me neither," Hannah said. "I'm wondering what the police would think. He's already a suspect, and this would give him one more motive if they could prove he knew about it."

"The cops always think the worst," Maggie said, "of everybody."

"Not Scott," Hannah said.

Maggie shook her head but didn't respond.

They sorted the files and envelopes into piles representing people they did or didn't know, then dead people, and people they wanted to protect.

"I don't care what happens to Brian, but this would kill my mother and father," Maggie said, putting his envelope and file in the pile to take.

Hannah was still not completely convinced they were doing the right thing.

"But what if we're questioned about taking this stuff?" she said, in kind of a whining voice.

"Why do you think I brought the gloves?" Maggie asked her, irritated. "This is no time to chicken out on me."

Hannah just sat there.

"What?" Maggie asked her impatiently.

"I'm worried we're going to get in trouble. This isn't just about us protecting our friends and families from being embarrassed, this is dangerous. Somebody may have killed Theo over this stuff, and now we have access to it. I don't want to get whacked on the head the next time my back is turned."

"Okay, we take the stuff that may hurt the people we love, we leave everything else, and we immediately go to Scott and say, 'Caroline told us about this room, blah blah blah.' He'll tell Tiny Crimefighter, and then the county will come and get everything else."

Hannah looked dubious, but she said, "Okay."

They heard a noise. It was kind of a thump, which could have been snow sliding off the roof, or someone in the house. The hairs stood up on Maggie's neck, and Hannah's face lost all its color.

"What was that?" Hannah whispered.

"I don't know," Maggie said. "Let's get out of here."

They put everything they weren't taking with them back the way they found it, more or less, and gathered up everything they wanted to take. Maggie shut the safe but didn't lock it.

"It will save them time," she told Hannah, who looked ill.

They checked the room for anything they'd missed or left behind, turned out the lights, and descended the way they'd come, as quietly as they could, listening for more sounds but hearing nothing.

They wheeled the ladder out of the closet back to the library and then put all the boxes of Eldridge Point merchandise back in. Hannah found a grocery bag in the kitchen in which to carry the evidence they were taking with them.

There was another thump, and it sounded like it came from upstairs.

"There's someone in the house," Hannah whispered.

"Maybe it's Willy Neff."

"Maybe it's the murderer."

"Don't say that!"

"Hurry."

They quickly put their coats and boots back on and pulled their yellow gloves off, replacing them with woolen ones. Maggie felt paranoid but resisted the urge to go back and check their trail through the house. She used the entryway rug to wipe up the water from the snow that had come in with them, locked the front door behind them, put the key back up behind the lantern, and ducked back under the police tape. Hannah took their bag of blackmail to the truck.

Even though they wanted nothing more than to get as far away from the lodge as possible, Hannah quickly let the dogs out and fed them. Maggie stood in the driveway between the truck and the barn, watching for anyone who might leave the house but saw no one. After putting the dogs back in their kennels, Hannah and Maggie ran to the truck, got in, and quickly locked the doors.

Once they were back on Pine Mountain Road, Maggie remembered to tell Hannah Caroline said she should go ahead and find homes for the dogs if she could. Hannah just shrugged. Maggie could tell her friend was worried, and when Hannah was worried, she got quiet. Neither said more than a few words to the other all the way down the mountain. The weather got worse as they descended. Hannah was an excellent driver and had a lot of experience driving on bad roads, as Maggie had, but it was still a scary descent.

Once in town, Hannah pulled in behind Maggie's car in the alley behind the bookstore and waited for Maggie to get out.

"Are you mad at me?" Maggie asked.

"No, I'm scared," Hannah said. "And you might as well know right now I'm telling Sam everything."

"Okay, okay," Maggie said defensively. "If Sam says we should do it differently we will. I will wait to hear from you before I destroy anything or call Scott."

"Good," Hannah said, and took a deep breath, letting it out with a whoosh. "Sam will know what we should do."

She smiled at Maggie but still looked worried. Maggie took the grocery bag with her and waved to Hannah as she left, saying, "Be careful."

Inside her bookstore, Maggie saw there were no customers, and her staff members weren't doing any work. She checked the weather forecast, saw it was only going to get worse, so she sent everyone home and closed the store.

Alone in the place with the music turned off, Maggie could hear the wind howling outside, and suddenly the building felt too empty. She was still mad at Scott, so she called her brother Patrick and asked him to come over, saying she had something she urgently needed to show him. She was relieved when he arrived, even though he immediately helped himself to half the case of baked goods, piling everything up on a tray along with an extra-large hot chocolate. Maggie made him bring it all upstairs to her kitchen after she carefully locked up the deposit and set the alarm.

"Why are you so freaked out?" he asked her as they went up the stairs.

"Wait, and I'll tell you."

Patrick followed her down the long hallway of her apartment and sat on a kitchen chair with his tray of goodies in front of him on the table. Maggie sat the grocery bag of blackmail evidence on the table and put the kettle on while she told him about Caroline's call, and what she and Hannah had done.

Patrick pulled everything out of the bag and looked through it while Maggie made tea and talked. When she got to the part about the photographs of Ava on the wall, and he looked at the photographs, he got really quiet. Maggie showed him the loan documents and explained how Brian used life insurance on his newborn son, wife, daughter, and home, as collateral on a loan. Patrick stayed silent, but Maggie could see him clench and unclench his jaw.

When he saw the photos of Brian and Phyllis, he shook his head, saying, "Good ole Phyllis."

When he looked at the letters, he said, "That's Sean's handwriting," immediately, and Maggie realized that's why it had looked so familiar.

"So 'G' must stand for Gwyneth," Maggie said, and they both curled their lips and said, "Ew."

"I don't want to read them," Patrick said, putting them aside. "And you shouldn't either."

"I wasn't going to."

"Yeah, right."

"No wonder he spent every summer up there with them," Maggie said. "He was always nice to Gwyneth while we all hated her, but I never thought it was anything more than that."

"Sean always was a weird duck," Patrick said. "I never saw him have a date in high school."

"He must have been pining for Gwyneth the whole time."

Patrick looked thoughtful for a moment and then shrugged, saying, "That's one explanation."

He sat the folder on Knox aside, saying he didn't care about that idiot. He also didn't want to see the photos of Doc, Ed's father, or the fire chief.

"Burn it all," he said. "They're worse than dirty, they're dangerous."

Maggie told him Hannah was going to ask Sam what they should do.

"Why should Sam decide?" Patrick demanded. "This is about our family, not his."

Maggie agreed, but said, "It won't hurt to listen to his opinion, even if we do ignore it afterward."

Patrick agreed Ava should see the loan papers, but their mother and father should not.

"And we burn the pictures of Brian and Phyllis," Maggie said, and Patrick shrugged.

"It would only prove something she already knows."

"What about all of Ava's pictures?" Maggie asked.

Patrick was studying the photograph taken through Ava's bedroom window.

"Patrick," Maggie prompted. "I asked you a question."

"Let's give her back the ones he obviously stole, like her baby pictures," Patrick said, "and burn the cut up ones and the ones he took without her knowing. They'll freak her out."

"He must have been obsessed with her. It's so creepy."

"She was never involved with him," he said vehemently.

Maggie said, "Calm down, I know," but privately, she wondered. She also wondered who it was in bed with Ava in the photo Patrick was studying so closely.

Her sister-in-law Ava was an enigma to Maggie. She was a good mother, a hard worker, a devout churchgoer, and Maggie had never heard her say an unkind word to or about anyone. Maggie did think she often played on other people's sympathies, especially Patrick's, as the long-suffering, abandoned wife and mother, but she had never done anything Maggie could look back on now and say, "Ah ha! That must have been when she was secretly meeting Theo!"

Ava was rarely away from her bed and breakfast business or her children, and she volunteered at both the church and the grade school with any free time she had. Just because she was gorgeous, and wouldn't gossip or make fun of people like Hannah and Maggie did, they tended to roll their eyes and call her "Saint Ava" behind her back. Maybe she was just what she appeared to be. Maggie wished she knew.

"I think if I had our brother Brian in front of me right now I might kill him," Patrick said, as he studied the loan papers.

"You were always saying you wanted to kill Theo and now he's dead," Maggie said. "You might want to watch what you say."

Patrick glowered in response and said nothing more. Maggie didn't for a moment suspect her brother Patrick of killing Theo. She could more easily imagine Brian doing it, especially now she knew what he was capable of doing to his own family.

Brian was the first-born, and the apple of their mother's eye. He had inherited Grandpa Tim's red curly hair and bright blue eyes along with his ability to charm the pants off just about any female he set his sights on. Grandpa Tim was a good man, but no one could say he was a faithful man, especially when he was a young man.

Ava may have won Brian by being the prettiest and the most tenacious of his girlfriends, but she was not able to tame or shame him into being a good husband and father. Although he was her brother, Maggie never liked him, and he'd barely acknowledged her presence as long as she'd known him. He may have chased and bedded the female locals, students, and tourists, and wrapped his mother around his little finger, but Maggie thought he didn't actually like or respect any woman. To Brian, a woman was a plaything to be used and discarded, or a nag to be avoided and placated.

"Where are we going to burn all this stuff?" Maggie asked Patrick.

"You leave that to me," Patrick said, and they began sorting everything into 'burn' and 'not burn' piles.

Hannah called and put Sam on the phone.

"Concerning the flammable materials," Sam said. "I think you should go ahead and burn all of it, and not save any of it. It would be dangerous to leave any of it lying around."

"Gotcha," Maggie said and got tickled in spite of the seriousness of the situation.

Hannah got back on the phone.

"The goose will fly at midnight," Hannah said before she hung up, and Maggie was relieved to hear her friend's sense of humor was back.

She looked at Patrick and said, "Sam says to burn it all."

"Let's hide the stuff we want to keep first," he said.

Maggie put Sean's letters in between the pages of a large book of art photographs on her bookshelf and hid the Knox folder behind some books on the same shelf. Patrick folded up the loan documents and slid them down inside his shirt. Maggie tucked Ava's baby and childhood pictures into the front of one of her photo albums, where they seemed to belong. The rest went back in the grocery bag, and they left by the back stairs, so Maggie didn't have to disarm the bookstore alarm system.

Maggie felt much safer now that she was with her brother Patrick. Not only was he big and strong, but he also exuded the confidence of someone who always comes out on top in any physical contest. They walked down the alley and up Pine Mountain Road to the Rose Hill Bed and Breakfast, where they found Ava folding towels in the kitchen while Charlotte and Timmy watched television in the small family room.

Patrick swept six-year-old Timmy up in his arms and pretended to throw him out the back door into the snow, while Charlotte, a dignified young lady of twelve, tried not to look as if she wanted to say, "Me next! Me next!"

Patrick swung Timmy down and gave Charlotte a big smacking kiss on the cheek, to which she squealed, and Timmy told his Aunt Maggie, "That's a cartoon kiss."

Maggie happened to turn and catch Ava looking at Patrick with such tenderness and love in her expression that it felt like an invasion of privacy to observe it.

Patrick spent a lot of time with Ava and the kids after Brian left, and both Charlotte and little Timmy were especially close to him, but Maggie wondered when Ava's dependence on Patrick had turned into something, well, so romantic? How had she missed that happening?

If it was true her mother would not be a bit happy about it, Maggie was sure. Bonnie Fitzpatrick still expected Brian to turn up one day with a good excuse for leaving, and for everything to go back to normal. Bonnie's favorite theory was Brian had been knocked unconscious and had amnesia. No one else was on board that particular denial train with her, but she held fast to her belief in her son's innocence despite all evidence to the contrary.

Maggie watched television with the two kids while Patrick took Ava to the front room. After ten minutes or so, they came back, and Ava's eyes were red from crying.

Patrick said goodbye to the kids, said, "We have some work to do," to Maggie, and went out the back door.

Ava squeezed Maggie's hand and mouthed, "Thank you," to which Maggie mouthed back, "I'm so sorry," before following Patrick out.

"Wait up!" Maggie yelled and caught up with her brother at the end of the walkway to the alley. "Where are we going?"

"If you need a fire, you go where the fire experts go."

"Not the fire station," Maggie protested, but Patrick ignored her.

Maggie had a lot of questions she would have liked to ask her brother about his relationship with Ava, but she knew from experience he would not discuss anything so personal or private with her. Although they loved each other and were fiercely loyal, she and her brother were not that kind of close.

Instead of going to the front door of the fire station, Patrick led his sister around behind it, where a large metal barrel used to burn trash sat on the edge of the parking lot. Patrick took the grocery bag from Maggie, put it in the barrel, pulled a flask out of his back pocket, and with a flourish, emptied the contents over the bag.

He then took a metal lighter out of his jacket pocket, lit a receipt he found in one of his other pockets, and said, "Stand back!" in a dramatic way before dropping it in the can as well.

There was a whoosh and Maggie could hear the paper catch fire and start to crackle and burn. Patrick performed a silly dance around the barrel to make Maggie laugh.

They waited until everything burned, and then Patrick threw some snow in to make sure the fire was out.

"And throughout all that no one came out to see what we are doing," Maggie said, gesturing at the firehouse, which was staffed by local volunteers.

"They're all sleeping or watching TV," Patrick said.

"Or drunk," Maggie said.

"Said Miss Priss," Patrick said. "Lighten up, why don't ya."

Maggie saw Rose Hill's only squad car roll slowly down Peony Street, turn in the alley behind the police station, and creep toward them. As it pulled up next to them, a darkly tinted window slid down, and Scott eyed them suspiciously.

"What in the world are you two up to?"

"We thought we saw a UFO land in the field over there and we came to check it out," Patrick said with a straight face.

Scott looked at Maggie and said, "You look guilty. You better come with me."

Patrick said, "You're on your own, Sis," and jogged away down the alley.

Maggie walked around the car and got in on the passenger side. Scott's scent rolled over her, and she fought the swoon, but it was stronger than she was. When he asked her if she would like to go for a ride, she said, "Sure."

The roads were bad, but there were crews out plowing. As they drove slowly around town, Maggie did not ask him how his date with Sarah was. She didn't trust herself not to throw a screaming fit and fling herself out of the car no matter what his answer might be.

"Caroline called last night," Maggie said instead, studying Scott's profile in the light of the dashboard and streetlights. He looked so handsome.

"What did she say?" he asked.

Maggie hesitated. It felt so warm and comfortable between them right then, but as soon as she told him, he would be angry. However, she knew from experience if she lied now he'd find out eventually and would be even angrier.

"Caroline said there was a secret room in the lodge where her great grandpa kept his bootleg booze. She told me where it was, and I thought you might want to go out there and take a look."

Scott stopped the car, put it in park, and turned halfway around in his seat to look at her.

"Where were you and Hannah today?" he asked her. "I looked everywhere for the two of you, and neither of you answered your phones."

"We went out to take care of Theo's dogs," Maggie said.

"And?" he asked as he raised an eyebrow.

"And we might have stopped in the lodge to see if we could find the secret room," she said.

"And?"

"And we might have found it."

He didn't look at all amused now.

"What was in it?" he asked.

She stared at him, wide-eyed.

"What were you and Patrick doing just now?" he demanded. "Burning something?"

Maggie tried desperately to open the door but this was a squad car, and he had all the controls on his side.

Scott turned back around facing forward, put the car in gear, and drove a little faster than it was safe to back to the station. Maggie wasn't sure what he was planning to do. He slid into the parking place in front of the station so hard the tires bumped the curb.

"C'mon," he said, as he unlocked all the doors and got out of the car.

Maggie crept out of the car as he unlocked the station door. She hesitated, but then followed him inside. Scott flipped on the lights and summoned her back to his office, where he sat down behind his desk and popped a cassette tape in the tape recorder.

"What are you doing?" Maggie asked, from the doorway.

"I'm preparing to take your statement," he said briskly, and not in a friendly tone. "You trespassed in a secured area, you tampered with evidence in a murder investigation, you may have destroyed evidence, and I'm taking your statement before I decide whether to arrest you or not."

Maggie started backing out of the office.

"Oh, no you don't," Scott said and came around the desk after her.

He caught her by the back of her coat as she ran through the outer room, and swung her around to face him. Maggie's heart was pounding. It had occurred to her that Scott would be mad, but it never occurred to her he might do something so official about it. He was holding her by the arms, and although he was angry, there was also that something else that always occurred between them, and it was just as palpable as his anger.

"Let go of me," she demanded, and to her surprise, he did.

They were both breathing a little heavily, and Maggie backed up to put some space between them.

"I know my rights," Maggie said. "If you want to arrest me, go ahead, but I'm not making a statement without Sean here."

"Sean's a corporate attorney," Scott said. "What's he gonna do, draw up a contract?"

"Not another word," Maggie said, edging toward the door, holding out a hand as if to ward him off. "Arrest me and I call Sean."

"There's no phone in the holding cell," Scott motioned toward it. "And I may lock myself in with you, keep you company all night."

"Sexual harassment!" Maggie accused as she pointed her finger at him and backed around the reception desk toward the door.

Scott began to walk toward her, so she turned and ran out the door, and then slid on the icy pavement all the way to the curb, where she caught herself on a parking meter.

Scott came out the door laughing.

"Stay away from me!" she warned, clinging to the meter.

She looked up the street and saw no one was out, but the door to the Rose and Thorn was open as someone was leaving the bar, and she could hear fiddle music, which meant her brother was working.

"Maggie," Scott said from the doorway, and his tone was softer.

"You go to hell, Scott Gordon!" she yelled at him, and then toward the bar, she screamed, "Patrick!"

The local who was leaving the bar leaned back in and called out to Patrick that someone wanted him.

Scott made a move toward her, and she held a hand out toward him to stop him.

"The lodge is Caroline's and Gwyneth's house now, and if Caroline asks me to go in it and look for something I can."

He took another step toward her, hands out, pleading, "Now don't get all freaked out, Maggie, I was just trying to make a point."

"Not another step!" Maggie said, and then again screamed, "Patrick!"

Up the street, Patrick stepped out of the bar to see what was going on. Scott threw his hands up in the air as Patrick came toward them.

Patrick had a way, like some animals do, of drawing themselves up and out to look even bigger than they already are when preparing to defend their territory. He did that, with menace, as he walked towards Scott.

"Now, Patrick," Scott said, holding one hand out as if to say 'hold it right there' and gesturing toward Maggie with the other. "You know I would never hurt your sister."

Patrick considered them both, hands on his hips, and then held out a hand to Maggie, saying, "C'mon, Sis."

Maggie took his hand, and he led her down the street, like a child, back to the Thorn. Maggie heard Scott curse and go back to the station, but she didn't look back.

She looked up at Patrick and said, "I love you sometimes."

He shook his head and said, "I wish you two would get a room."

Maggie jerked her hand away from his and socked him on the arm.

"Ow!" Patrick complained. "What was that for?"

Maggie stalked off down the street towards home.

"You're welcome!" Patrick called after her, and then went back inside the Rose and Thorn.


When she got home Maggie e-mailed Sean to tell him she had the letters Theo was "keeping for him," and she would send them with Scott. She also wrote she loved him and hoped he would visit soon. Although she was tempted to read the letters, she decided not to.

A noise on her balcony frightened her, but when she turned, she saw it was Duke, and let him in.

"I don't have anything to feed you," she told the big cat.

Duke made himself at home, curled up on the newspapers in the recycling box. She left a bowl of water out for him and went to bed. Scott called later as she lay awake, unable to sleep.

"I can't go to sleep knowing you're mad at me," he said. "Let me come over, and we'll talk about it."

"I've had enough police brutality for one day, thank you."

"Don't be like that."

"I'll be however I want, Scott Gordon. You are not the boss of me."

"You can't break the law and then expect me to turn a blind eye, Maggie. I can't do that."

"I didn't break the law."

"There was yellow caution tape across the front door, wasn't there?"

"I don't remember."

"Of course not. Tell me what really happened."

"I'm not telling you anything. You might be recording this conversation."

"You're making me crazy, you know that?"

"Sounds like a personal problem to me. Perhaps you should seek counseling."

"I'm trying to keep you out of trouble and do my job. You don't make it easy."

"Then stop trying, and leave me alone."

"You know I can't do that."

"Sure you can. I'm easy to leave. It's been done before."

"I'm not Gabe."

"No, and you never will be."

As soon as the words were out, Maggie regretted them, but could not bring herself to apologize. After a long silence, Scott finally spoke.

"I would never leave you like he did."

Another silence grew, although she could hear him breathing. She knew she should say something, but she couldn't. Finally, with a sigh, he did.

"C'mon Mary Margaret, don't be mad. I'm sorry I tried to arrest you."

"I don't want to jeopardize your job, and I don't want to go to jail."

"I promise to calmly hear everything you have to say about the contents of the room in question. I am hereby giving you complete amnesty in the matter."

"Not tonight. It's late, and I'm worn out," Maggie said. "This has been a long day."

"You won't stay mad," Scott said softly. "You don't really hate me so much."

"Stop by the café in the morning, and I'll give you some coffee for your drive," she said. "But don't expect me to tell you anything. I have something I want you to take to Sean."

Maggie hung up the phone and stared at the ceiling in her dark room. She heard Duke scratching on the balcony doors, so she got up, let him outside, and watched him make his way down to the ground. After she closed the door, she rubbed a clear circle on the frosted glass, looked out at the snow flying sideways and thought about Gabe. She wondered if it would ever stop hurting.

# Chapter Seven – Thursday

Scott was glad to see Sean, whom he hadn't seen in almost fifteen years. The youngest son of Fitz Fitzpatrick looked like a more refined, compact version of his brother Patrick. His dark curly hair was cut short. He was polished and sleek, and much thinner than his brother, who although muscular and strong, had gone a little soft as he approached middle age.

Sean greeted Scott warmly with a handshake and invited him into his glass-walled office, which featured a panoramic view of the famous convergence of the three rivers. Once seated, Scott asked him what he knew about Theo's death, and Sean said Maggie had told him the details. Scott gave him the envelope Maggie sent, saying they were retirement fund forms, and detected a defensive wall sliding smoothly into place as soon as he did so. Scott had debated the whole way there whether or not to open the envelope, but in the end, had decided to trust Maggie.

"I'm hoping there is something you know about Theo that might help me," Scott told him.

He took a seat in front of the wide expanse of smoky glass which served as Sean's desk. He took out the photocopy of the threat card and photo and handed it to Sean. Sean looked at it, took a deep breath, and seemed to age about ten years as he exhaled. He handed the photocopy back to Scott and put the envelope from Maggie in his briefcase and locked it. He was silent for a long moment and seemed to be weighing something in his mind. He considered Scott carefully before he spoke.

"My sister Maggie thinks a lot of you. How do you feel about her?"

Scott was taken aback by this question but decided to be brutally honest.

"She drives me so crazy sometimes I want to wring her neck. She has an awful temper, and she says exactly

161

what she thinks no matter how bad it bites her in the ass later. I continually disappoint her with the stupid things I do and say, but I never quit trying, because she is the one person I enjoy being with more than anyone in this world. I would do anything to make her happy, and anything to protect her."

"That's good to hear," Sean said. "I'm counting on you to protect her."

"What does Maggie have to do with it?" Scott asked.

Sean straightened some items on his desk and shut down the laptop which was sitting front and center.

"Maggie knows part of this story, but not all of it," Sean said, giving Scott a pointed look, "and I'm not sure I'm ready for her to know all of it; do you understand?"

Scott was perplexed, and said, "I'm sorry, I don't."

Sean rose from his seat and motioned for Scott to follow him. From inside a cupboard by the door, Sean removed and then put on an expensive looking wool coat, wrapped a scarf around his neck, put on some gloves, and gestured to the door.

"I'll tell you everything, but I don't want you to share what I tell you with Maggie or anyone else."

Scott hesitated at the door, shaking his head, "If it's related to Theo getting killed, I can't make that promise."

Sean turned the knob but held the door closed, considering Scott. Finally, he spoke.

"It might be a relief to tell someone," Sean said. "I think Maggie would tell me to trust you."

"Then let's go," Scott said.

Once the elevator doors were closed and they were alone, Sean said, "Up until now I've been able to keep my private and public lives completely separate. I'm reluctant to tell you about the one while in the other. It might matter here or it might not, but I would rather not have to find out just yet."

Scott was still perplexed but shrugged his assent.

Sean, in his elegant, charcoal gray overcoat, black gloves and scarf, and Scott in his jeans, hooded sweatshirt, and parka made an incongruous pair walking down the city street. Sean greeted and nodded at many people. They stopped at a coffee bar on the corner and purchased hot drinks, then crossed the street to walk along the path by the river. To call the wind off the river "bracing" would be a massive understatement, and Scott wished he'd thought to wear long underwear.

After some small talk and a long silence, Sean spoke.

"Brad and I were close, had been close for a couple of years by the time he died. We spent all our free time together and developed, I don't know any other way to put it but bluntly, a romantic relationship."

He looked at Scott for a reaction, and although Scott was shocked, and by nature a little more homophobic than he cared to admit, he was also a "live and let live" kind of person and Sean was an old friend.

"I had no idea," was all he said, and he looked Sean square in the eye as he said it.

"Brad had learning disabilities and I, being an egghead, volunteered to help him with his school work. We grew closer, and as they say, one thing led to another. We met wherever we could: the room over the garage at grandma's house, the gardener's shed at the college, the wine cellar at his house. There were plenty of places to hide, and the risk itself was exciting, but we got careless. One of those times was in the boathouse, and Theo walked in on us."

As he spoke, Sean's face changed from tender remembrance to grief and regret.

"The summer that picture was taken, Theo being homemade everything we did ten times riskier and a hundred times more exciting. You know how it is when you're fifteen; you have to have exactly what you want the minute you want it, and you don't think anything bad can happen to you. Theo had been to enough boarding schools to suspect our relationship was more than platonic and began to tease us about it. Brad decided he needed to prove him wrong."

Some people passed them, and Sean paused in his narrative until they were out of earshot.

"Brad started running around with some of the girls who were hanging out at the lake so Theo would think he was interested in girls. Brad was, actually, interested in girls. He also happened to be in love with me."

They had come to a little riverside park, and Scott swept the snow off a bench that faced the water so they could sit.

"One of the girls was Phyllis Davis; is she still around? She was a wild thing that summer. He got drunk with her one night, and they had sex. He told me everything. He said he liked it, which seemed to reassure him but devastated me. He tried to make both of us happy for a few weeks, but she finally got tired of it and dumped him. He was conflicted about his feelings and alternated between rejecting me and begging me to come back. When we finally got back together, Theo caught us in the act."

Scott was breathing and listening but was afraid to move or do anything that might interrupt what felt very much like a confession.

"It was a nightmare. I'm ashamed to say I got out of there as soon as I got my clothes on. I'm not proud of that."

"You were just a kid," Scott said.

Scott's ears were numb, and his nose was running, but his attention was riveted on Sean.

"I thought we'd reconnoiter later and figure something out, maybe even run away together. But I didn't get the chance. I didn't even get to talk to him again."

Sean's wept then and removed a folded silk handkerchief from his suit coat pocket to wipe his eyes.

"I ran along the edge of the lake to the bait shack and got a ride back to town with one of Dad's friends.

When I got home, I told everyone I was sick and went to bed. I didn't sleep all night. I kept waiting for the phone to ring, to find out Theo had told and everyone knew."

"The next morning I pretended to still be sick so I could stay in bed. I wanted to be near the phone in case someone called to tell my parents. Just before noon, Brian came home looking for me. He told me Brad had drowned, said someone had stopped by the station and told him. He saw my reaction; I fell completely apart. I don't know what he thought, and he didn't ask me any questions. He said, 'don't let Dad see you like this. Come back with me to the station.' So I pumped gas and washed windshields the rest of the day, and everyone who saw me said what a shame I had to work on a holiday."

Sean's voice was full of emotion, and when he wiped his face with his handkerchief, Scott could see his hands were trembling.

"Theo called me the next day and told me he had the letters I wrote to Brad. He said if I said anything bad about him he would show them to my parents. Jesus, can you imagine?"

He wept some more, and Scott had an urge to put an arm around him but felt a new self-consciousness. He told himself it was because he didn't want to embarrass Sean, but the truth was he felt awkward now that he knew Sean was gay. He waited until Sean composed himself before pressing him with further questions.

"How much of this does Maggie know?"

"I don't think she knows about the relationship unless she read the letters Theo had. She doesn't know about Theo threatening me, or about me being with Brad the night before he drowned."

Scott cursed himself for believing Maggie's lie about the envelope he had delivered to Sean. He had no doubt it actually held the letters in it; evidence of blackmail which could be connected to Theo's death; evidence he had handed over to a suspect. Scott didn't think Sean had killed

Theo, but he also didn't think Ed or Patrick did. He was making these kinds of snap decisions at a pace that was starting to scare him.

"I want to ask you something that may upset you, and I apologize in advance," Scott said.

"Please, what could be more upsetting than talking about your first love drowning?"

"If it was suicide," Scott said

"I've thought of that," Sean said. "He was confused about his sexuality, and I'm sure he was worried about everyone finding out about us. It might have been enough..."

"But?"

Sean turned and looked at Scott with tortured eyes filled with fresh grief.

"Except he loved me so much, I know he did. He would have at least talked to me again, or sent me a message."

They sat quietly for a while until Scott realized he'd lost all feeling in his butt cheeks. He stood up to get the blood flowing, and Sean took this as a signal to start back.

"Do you think I sent Theo the card with the photo and then sneaked into town to kill him?"

"Do you have an alibi?"

"It would have been hard to do from Los Angeles. You can ask my secretary if you have to and talk to the people I met with in California."

"Had you heard from Theo or seen him since that summer?" Scott asked.

"No," Sean said. "I made sure our paths never crossed again. I left the past behind when I left Rose Hill, and Theo represented the worst part of the past. I sacrificed my relationship with my family so they would never find out about me and be hurt, and I ended up hurting them all anyway."

Sean looked miserable, and Scott felt sorry for everyone.

"Why didn't you confide in Maggie about what happened?" Scott asked. "She wouldn't have judged you harshly."

"You know our Maggie," Sean replied. "What would she have done to Theo?"

A chill ran up Scott's spine, and not because of the cold air.

Scott hadn't seen any reason to check on Maggie's whereabouts on the night of Theo's murder. She had been home when he called right after 3:00 a.m., and had spent the next hour with him in the station, waiting for Mitchell to wake up. She was certainly tall and strong enough and hated Theo with a passion. Scott couldn't picture himself interrogating her. It wasn't a conversation he could see their relationship surviving.

Sean seemed to read his mind.

"Good luck with that," he said with a sad smile.

Back in front of the bank building, Scott shook his friend's hand and then impulsively gave him a brief hug. Sean looked embarrassed, but Scott decided he was not going to worry about what anybody thought. He didn't want to be that kind of guy.

"Now that Theo's gone, will you come back to visit?"

"I don't think the welcome mat is still out for me," Sean said, as they stood close to the bank building, out of the steady stream of sidewalk traffic.

"We were in the same Sunday school class, Sean. Don't you remember how the prodigal son got the fatted calf killed for him when he returned?"

"I'm not sure they could handle knowing who I really am," Sean said

"Don't underestimate them. You Fitzpatricks tend to stick together."

Sean smiled but just said, "Maybe."

"And speaking of prodigal Fitzpatricks, have you heard from your brother Brian?"

"No," said Sean. "I don't know where Brian is, and I really don't care. He was pretty much always a selfish bastard to me. After that day, he would whisper the vilest things to me when he knew no one could hear. And then he would laugh."

"Thank you for telling me all that, back there," Scott said. "I really think you should come home soon."

"We'll see," Sean said.

Scott stopped by the medical center to see Knox's wife Anne Marie before he left town. He ran into her sister-in-law Sandy in the parking garage. Her face was red and blotchy from crying. She said her husband Trick was waiting, but Scott talked her into going to the cafeteria with him for a few minutes.

He bought her some coffee, and they sat at the table farthest away from the other visitors and staff members. She was nervous and overwrought. Scott, who knew she didn't get along with Anne Marie, thought the reaction a bit extreme. To Scott, Sandy always seemed to be a kind of a silly woman. She was apt to talk nonstop, say tactless things and ask stupid questions, and as a result, no one took her seriously.

He talked to her about what had happened to Anne Marie, and when he mentioned Knox, she got even more upset.

"If something happens to me anytime soon, I hope you investigate that bastard."

Scott asked her what she meant by that, and she laughed shrilly, drawing attention from patrons at other tables, but seemed unaware of it.

"I probably shouldn't say anything more, because my life is worth more to me than that. You should look more closely at my dear brother-in-law, keep a real close eye on him, and if I have an accident like Anne Marie's, you'll know who to hold responsible."

"Why would Knox try to kill Anne Marie?" Scott asked her quietly.

He noticed her hands were trembling so hard she could barely hold her paper coffee cup. He took it from her and placed it on the table.

"Because she's a liability," Sandy said. "He can't control her."

"What's she done?"

"She almost caused a scandal with some boy at the college, until Knox stepped in and smoothed it over with money. She drinks too much and takes all kinds of pills. I don't know where she gets them. Knox cut her off."

"Does Knox abuse her?"

"He doesn't hit her, at least as far as I know, but verbally he tears her to shreds. Knox is not an easy man to live with, and he demands perfection. He wants to get into politics, and no one better stand in his way."

"And Anne Marie is in the way?"

"If she's not careful enough, and he gets embarrassed one too many times."

Scott thought about the gold coin that ended up in Theo's bedroom. Was Theo involved with Anne Marie? Scott wondered if by asking Knox about the coin he had unwittingly prompted the man to rid himself of his wife through a convenient accident.

Sandy was rapidly falling apart as he watched, and when she abruptly jumped up to leave, he was afraid of what might happen if he let her go while she was so emotional.

"You're upset, Sandy, let me take you home."

She backed away from him, saying, "Trick's waiting for me; he'll drive me. It's dangerous to even be seen talking to you. I'll deny everything."

And with that, she ran out of the cafeteria and was gone. Scott was worried about her but was afraid if he chased her, it would only agitate her more.

Only immediate family was allowed in ICU to see Anne Marie, and since Knox was not around, Scott left the hospital and drove toward home. Snow was swirling in eddies across the interstate, but the sun was bright in a clear blue sky. He thought of going a little out of his way to stop in to see Sarah but decided it was more important to get back in time for Theo's funeral.

Anne Marie was not careful, according to Sandy. Had Anne Marie got pregnant by the college student, or was she merely indiscreet? He wondered if she may have been Theo's no-show dinner guest and if she had given him the coin in return for drugs. He ruminated on all the possibilities as he headed toward home.

The Machalvie Funeral Home, originally a grand Victorian home, was located on the corner of Peony Street and Rose Hill Avenue. Over the years multiple rooms had been added on in every direction so that the original structure was now unrecognizable. There were Grecian columns of varying sizes and styles flanking broad steps on all four sides. The front façade featured a wide, deep, southern style porch with large plastic ferns in hanging brass pots and pairs of white rocking chairs on the dark green indoor-outdoor carpeting.

Inside, deep-pile burgundy-colored carpet covered the floors, and you knew when you stepped off newer construction and entered a room in the original house because the old wood floors under the carpeting were slanted and squeaked under your feet. At the windows, heavy draperies of burgundy velvet were drawn back in complicated folds like heavy skirts revealing petticoats of shroud-like, puffy-tiered, white sheers. The lighting was subdued, pre-recorded religious pipe organ music played, and the scent of lilies and chrysanthemums wafted through the air.

Hannah and Maggie stepped inside the overheated front foyer and waited in line to sign the guestbook.

"This place looks like a very religious whorehouse," Maggie said.

"Jezebels for Jesus?" Hannah suggested. "Hos for Hosanna?"

"Look at Peg," Maggie said. "She's had some more work done."

Peg Machalvie, the funeral home director and owner, was greeting guests as they came through the door. Her big perky boobs were only a few years old and were pushed up so far by her foundation garment that they threatened to pop out of the neckline of her form-fitting black dress suit. She wore pointy-toed spike heels, and her dyed black hair was teased out into sort of a bell-shaped hat for her head.

Her face had recently been surgically lifted and was so pumped full of wrinkle smoothers and nerve paralyzers that the only facial movement she could make was a strained grimace. Her eyebrows arched so high she looked permanently surprised. Her tautly stretched shiny face was ghostly pale and covered in a thick layer of foundation and powder, and her eye, cheek, and lip makeup were dramatically dark in contrast. She was greeting people and directing them to sign the guestbook, gesturing with pale fingers tipped by long blood red nails.

"Did you bring any garlic?" asked Hannah, holding up the small gold cross she wore around her neck.

"No," Maggie said, "and I left all my wooden stakes at home."

"There's Satan's spawn," Hannah said, gesturing to the left.

Peg's two thick-necked sons, Lucas and Hugo, chewing gum and looking bored, were stationed on either side of the entrance to the viewing room, handing out small programs for the afternoon's event. Their hair was stiff with gel, and their heavy cologne battled with their mother's perfume for dominance in the hot, stuffy lobby area. Their father and Peg's husband, Mayor Stuart Machalvie, passed between the boys on his way into the viewing room and squeezed each of his sons on the shoulder as he did so.

"Look," Hannah said. "There's Huey, Louie, and Stuey."

Maggie had heard the joke many times before, but it still made her smile.

As they approached her, Peg pretended not to notice them, and instead aimed her rectangular smile over their shoulders at the next guests. When they got up to the guest book, Hannah wrote "Professor Van Helsing," and Maggie wrote "Anne Rice."

Hannah nudged Maggie as they crossed the threshold into the viewing room and could see the crowd.

"Get a look at that, will ya?" Hannah said under her breath as she indicated the fashionably attired sister of the deceased.

Gwyneth, dressed head to toe in black, was perched on the edge of a chair at the front. She reached up underneath the dark veil of an enormously wide-brimmed hat to dab her eyes with a large white handkerchief edged in lace. The mayor was comforting her by alternately squeezing her knee and patting her other hand from the chair beside her.

"I wonder if Joan Collins knows that outfit is missing," whispered Hannah.

"This is even better than I expected," replied Maggie. "I hope Mom saved us seats near the front."

Hannah and Maggie dutifully filed through to look at Theo in his casket.

"He's needed this makeover for about twenty years," Hannah whispered.

"Look at the expression on his face," Maggie said. "He looks almost happy."

"He's thinking of all the trees they had to cut down to make this giant coffin."

They nodded politely to everyone as they looked for Maggie's mother, who was waving her program in the air at the back.

"This place is packed," Bonnie murmured to them as they took off their heavy coats and sat in the seats she had saved on either side of hers.

"I think they all want to be sure he's really dead," replied Maggie, for which Bonnie gave her daughter a sharp pinch on the underside of her arm and a stern look of reprimand. Maggie winced and rubbed the spot.

"I separated the two of you because I know you can't behave," Bonnie said. "Try to act like grown women, the both of you."

Hannah looked as if she didn't know what her Aunt Bonnie could possibly have meant by that remark, and Maggie just looked straight ahead and did her best not to laugh.

Reverend Macon's voice was a deep, resonant monotone, and he spoke in a slow, sonorous manner that some people found soothing, but others found to be a strong sedative. He seemed to be having a hard time finding good things to say about Theo, so instead, he recounted all the good things the Eldridge family had done for the town of Rose Hill since they settled there in 1889. He went on and on and on, until right when it seemed like the group as a whole had achieved the level of boredom which can cause irrational behavior, nausea, or fainting, he introduced Gwyneth, saying she wanted to say a few words.

The mayor helped Gwyneth take her place at the podium, where she lifted her dark veil and looked out over the crowded room. She didn't realize the veil she thought was draped back over her wide-brimmed black hat was actually standing straight up in the air, giving her a bizarre beekeeper-of-the-night look as she spoke. Hannah and

173

Maggie could only look at each other out of the corners of their eyes and suppress their laughter, lest Bonnie deliver another pinch.

Gwyneth's accent was extra-British for the occasion.

"Thank you so much for coming," she began. "I would like to thank Reverend Bacon for his kind words about my family. One is gratified to know all one's family's many valuable contributions to this community are appreciated, at least by some."

Maggie had to press her lips inward and clamp down on them with her teeth. She could feel Hannah trembling with laughter even though she was on the other side of her mother.

"In addition," Gwyneth continued, "I would like to thank the many townsfolk who have gone out of their way to make me feel welcome, and had such kind words to say about my brother."

Bonnie lightly touched the underside of Maggie's arm with her pinching fingers, and Maggie looked at her as if to say "what?" while Hannah smirked.

"Due to my delicate health and sensitive nature, my parents felt it best that I be educated abroad. After returning to the states, I received my graduate degree behind the ivy-covered walls of one of the finest schools in New England. Living as I have for these many years in Manhattan, I daresay I would never have returned to Roseville, but for the unfortunate and premature ending of my dear brother's life."

Maggie looked for Scott and found him, watching her from where he stood against the wall to her left. He winked at her, and she stuck her tongue out at him. Her mother pinched, and Maggie flinched.

"One hopes one's friends will be comforted knowing I shall remain here, shouldering the heavy mantle which has been passed down through many distinguished generations of Eldridges before me. I, too, shall seek to uphold the high standards set by our ancestors as I pledge to look after our tenants and preserve our land, as my dear brother did."

Maggie reflected that Gwyneth was acting as if it was the eighteenth century and not the twenty-first. Maggie also enjoyed knowing that the original Theodore Eldridge from whom Gwyneth was so proud to have descended was an alcoholic younger son shipped to America because his gambling debts were such an embarrassment to his family. He got the money to start his own business by marrying the daughter of a rich low-born Yankee who owned a string of "opera houses" known more for bawdy women than classical music. The Eldridge family legacy Gwyneth so enjoyed the fruits of came from scalping the first growth hardwoods off the surface of the surrounding mountains and then carving the coal out from beneath them. If the town of Rose Hill had the Eldridges to thank for the college and the city park, they could also thank them for the mine subsidence and permanently poisoned spring water.

"My sister Caroline regrets she cannot be here with us today, but she has pledged her support in my endeavor to continue the good works with which our family name has become synonymous. Thank you again."

Gwyneth paused momentarily, as if for applause. The mayor jumped up and almost collided with Reverend Macon in his attempt to reach her side. Organ music swelled as Gwyneth pulled her veil down over her face and allowed both men to lead her out of the side door to a waiting limo.

"She called him 'Reverend Bacon,'" Maggie said to Hannah, as soon as her mother was out of pinching range.

"I know," Hannah said, "and 'Roseville,' for crissakes. She can't even get the name of the town right."

"Her sensitive nature," Maggie said. "What a load of crap. She was only ever sensitive when it came to her own feelings, as I recall."

"The ivy-covered walls of a New England loony bin would have been more appropriate for her," Hannah said.

They were waiting for the rows ahead of them to empty so they could file out.

"The only person making her welcome and saying nice things about Theo is the mayor," Maggie said, "and that's because he thinks she's won the Eldridge lotto."

Impatient with the slow-moving crowd, they edged their way around the people remaining in the aisles, who were clustered together in small, gossiping knots.

"Are we going to the graveside?" Hannah asked. "I half expect to see the earth spit Theo back out."

"I don't want to," Maggie replied. "It's much too cold to stand on the top of Rose Hill Cemetery and watch the mayor slobber on Gwyneth. Besides, they're dedicating a stone, not burying him. His body's going to be cremated."

"Cremated?" Hannah said, shivering in distaste. "Wasn't a silver bullet enough?"

"It's their family thing," Maggie said. "Lots of people do it."

"Maybe it's a British thing," suggested Hannah, and Maggie shook her head.

She knew anything outside the small town culture in which they grew up tended to make Hannah suspicious.

Maggie and Hannah stood outside to wait for Maggie's mother to join them.

"I guess this means Gwyneth is staying in town," Hannah said. "I was hoping she'd go back to Manhattan today."

"No way," Maggie said. "She likes the idea of being Lady Eldridge. She'll be living in the big house up on Morning Glory Circle, looking down on us all, throwing us bits of stale bread and cheese. Noblesse oblige."

"What's that mean?"

"When rich people condescend to help the poor people who hate them, whether the poor people like it or not."

"You know, I think Gwyneth will be great at that."

"I almost feel sorry for her. She wants so badly for everyone to think she's a proper English lady, but she only learned how to do it from books written two hundred years ago. The blue blood she claims to have running through her veins has been diluted by too many Yankee transfusions. She's no more British than you or me."

A procession of black limos carrying Gwyneth and the more stalwart and curious mourners passed them going up Peony Street.

"I wish Caroline was here," said Maggie. "She's nothing like her sister."

"I always thought Caroline was as big a spoiled brat as Gwyneth," Hannah said. "She doesn't fool me with all that saving the rainforest and building the ashrams, or whatever they are. She's only doing that because it's trendy."

"She's delivering medical supplies to needy people in Paraguay," Maggie said. "That's a worthy cause."

"Does she not know there are needy people right here in her own country?"

"We live in one of the richest countries in the world, Hannah. We should be able to take care of our own poor and everyone else's."

"Are you done preaching to me, oh righteous one? Cause I'm just saying, there are plenty of good works she could be doing right here."

"Like, say, paying for a bigger and better kennel facility for the local animal control officer?"

"Who has been taking care of her dead brother's dogs, and offered to find them all homes, free of charge, I might mention."

"Caroline is not like Gwyneth. She gives back. That's all I'm saying."

"We may have to agree to disagree."

"If Brad hadn't died her parents would've let Caroline stay here with us. I think shipping her off to boarding school was cruel. Look at how Gwyneth turned out."

"If Gwyneth were my daughter I would have shipped her off too. She was always a screamy little turd if I remember correctly, all 'she touched me, she's touching my toys, she's getting me dirty.' "

"Due to her delicate health, no doubt."

"Due to her delicate mental condition. Tell me again how you pitched her out of your store. That is my new most favorite story."

Just then, Bonnie Fitzpatrick came up behind them and pinched them both on the backs of their necks.

"Ouch! What was that for?" Maggie complained.

"Whatever you two were saying; I know you weren't reciting Bible verses."

"How about thou shalt not abuse your only daughter?" Maggie said. "You're going to give me the cancer pinching me all the time."

Bonnie was always claiming things were going to give her "the cancer," so it was an effective complaint to make back at her.

"Don't even think it," her mother warned. "Father Stephen says 'wishing is fishing and saying is praying.'"

"Well then, I wish you would quit pinching me, and I pray you will cease and desist," Maggie replied.

"Can you believe she got both the name of the preacher and the town wrong?" Bonnie asked them.

"That's what we were just saying," Maggie said. "I ought to pinch you."

"I don't think you will," Bonnie replied, hugging both girls with either arm as they walked up the hill. "Not if you value your life."

The men of Rose Hill were well trained. While their wives walked in gossip clusters up the hill from the funeral home to the community center, deconstructing the funeral and picking apart the bereaved along the way, the husbands took the food their wives had prepared up Peony Street to the former Rose Hill High School, now the Rose Hill Community Center.

There they unloaded and carried various plastic containers and plastic-wrap-covered trays into the vast commercial kitchen and placed them on the long work island in the middle of the room. Then the men retired to the game room to shoot pool, to the lounge to watch sports on television, or outside to smoke, and the women put out the feast in what used to be the school cafeteria, now called the "common room."

Good sons and daughters were expected to report to the common room to set up tables and do their mothers' bidding, while their mothers took turns making statements that were a special combination of complaining and bragging about their offspring.

"Tony, see if you can get the furnace to come on, please," said Antonia Delvecchio to her son, and then turned to the assembled women. "I'm beginning to think he'll never get married, but he says he can't find a girl who will spoil him like I do."

Beverly Myers countered with, "My Charlie says girls these days don't know how to cook or clean, and he'd rather eat my cooking than anyone else's."

"My Heather keeps a spotless house, and you could eat off her kitchen floor," claimed Alva Johnston, "but that's how she was raised."

Hannah and Maggie rolled their eyes at each other as they unfolded tablecloths and draped them over the tables.

Maggie was obviously looking for someone, and Hannah said, "Scott and Ed probably went up to the cemetery."

"I was looking for Drew," Maggie replied. "I don't care where Scott is."

"Oh well, my mistake," Hannah said, pretending to take offense.

Mamie Rodefeffer came in, dragging her tote bags and swinging her cane around. A mountain of food was spread out on the long buffet tables, and Mamie was first in line, where she loudly criticized everything yet piled her plate high.

"Mamie wasn't at the funeral," Mrs. Myers told Maggie. "She told me Theo was the devil's own son and deserved whatever he got. But put out some free food, and she makes a beeline."

"Anne Marie went and got herself in a car wreck," they heard Mamie tell someone. "We may be doing this again in a few days if she doesn't come out of her coma. This potato salad has pickle relish in it; someone has ruined a perfectly good potato salad!"

Hannah and Maggie retreated to the kitchen, where they washed plastic containers and made sure the lids were reunited with the bottoms that had the same last name written on them in permanent marker. They heard when the bereaved appeared, and then had steady reports on her movements.

Maggie tensed when she knew the funeral party had arrived and Scott was somewhere nearby. She wondered how his meeting with Sean went, and whether he had found out what was in the envelope he'd taken to her brother. Sometimes she appalled herself with the things she'd do to that man. Still, he kept coming back.

Hannah infiltrated the common room to score some cupcakes, and when she got back, she whispered, "Scott's sitting with Ed and Patrick back by the rolling chalkboard where they stack the chairs. Not that you care."

"I don't."

They also got a steady stream of information on Gwyneth.

"She says she isn't hungry," reported Erma Cook. "How could she be that skinny and not be starving?"

"She says she doesn't eat white flour or sugar," said Alva Johnston. "She says they're like poison to the digestive system."

"She's complaining that they don't sell loose leaf tea at the IGA," Beverly Myers said. "I told her to pop open a tea bag; what does she think they put in there?"

Later the women brought the leftover food back to the kitchen and "made plates," which consisted of piling a sturdy paper plate with dabs of everything, covering it with plastic wrap, and taking it home to snack on all afternoon until supper.

Funeral director Peg Machalvie came in to thank them, acting as if they had done it all for her. With those surprised looking eyebrows, painful looking smile, and her shiny pale skin, she looked like she'd been flash-frozen.

She was offered a plate, but said, "Oh no, thank you. I have to watch my figure so Stuart will still want to."

"Looks to me like the mayor's too busy watching someone else's figure," Erma Cook murmured.

As if on cue, Gwyneth came in with the mayor close behind her and thanked the ladies very graciously, if a little condescendingly. Maggie steeled herself, then walked right up to her in front of everyone and stuck out her hand. Gwyneth moved back in fear, but Maggie forced herself to smile and look the woman in the eye.

"I wanted to apologize for my rude behavior the other day," she said. "I hope you will forgive me and accept my invitation to come back to my store."

Gwyneth had her hand to her throat and at first looked appalled. Then, perhaps realizing she had a full house watching her debut in the role of Lady Eldridge, she gave Maggie a tight smile that didn't reach her eyes and shook her hand, albeit with the tips of two limp fingers and only for a second.

"Of course, Agnes, I'd be delighted. I'd already forgotten about it."

The mayor beamed in approval and said to Maggie, "Nicely done indeed. All friends again, see? That wasn't so hard."

Maggie walked back to the sink and started scrubbing the hell out of the nearest pan. The mayor led Gwyneth out, and Hannah rushed up to the sink.

"All right, pod person, who are you and what have you done with Maggie?"

Bonnie Fitzpatrick came up and kissed her daughter on one flushed cheek.

"I'm very proud of you, Mary Margaret. You're a good girl."

Bonnie then fixed her evil eye on Hannah, who threw up her hands.

"Hey, I'm not the one who threw ole Twiglet out in traffic."

Maggie smiled at Hannah, who put her head next to Maggie's and murmured, "Twiglet, the British Bumstick."

Maggie's mother pinched them both and said, "Stop that whispering, it's bad manners."

With ten women working flat out the kitchen was cleaned up in a short time. Maggie walked out with Hannah and her mother and turned down Peony Street toward town. Gwyneth was standing outside next to the funeral home limo, which was parked at the curb, and as the women neared her, Gwyneth asked if she could have a word with Bonnie. Hannah and Maggie walked on and waited at the corner.

After a brief conversation with Gwyneth, Bonnie turned and came toward them. Her cheeks were stained pink, and she wore the kind of look that still made her children want to hide in the nearest cupboard. Maggie could hear her mother muttering the prayer she always used to keep her temper right before she went ahead and lost it.

"What did she say?" Maggie asked.

"She asked if I would be interested in a job cleaning her house. She said her father always told her there was nothing like rough Irish hands to keep a house clean or a garden green."

Scott, who had come up behind Maggie, was able to grab her around the waist as she lunged toward the limo, now pulling away from the curb. He was not, however, able to stop Hannah from removing and throwing her shoe, which just missed the back of the car as it glided up the hill toward Morning Glory Avenue.

A few members of the Fitzpatrick family and some friends congregated back at Maggie's parents' house. Ed and Patrick sat in the living room watching an old western movie with Grandpa Tim and Fitz. Maggie, Bonnie, and Hannah converged in the kitchen to pick at the plates of leftovers and rehash the day's events. Lazy Ass Laddie was sitting right next to Hannah with his furry redhead on her knee, looking up longingly at what she was eating. When Scott arrived, he came straight through to the kitchen.

"I can't believe you apologized to that woman," Scott said to Maggie. "What on earth compelled you?"

Maggie looked pointedly at her mother, who was still nursing her feelings over Gwyneth's insult.

Bonnie said to Scott, "I told Mary Margaret how you'd been called on the carpet in the mayor's office and she'd better make it right, seeing as how you might lose your job."

"And how do you feel now?" Maggie asked her mother.

"Well, as a Christian I know I should turn the other cheek, but now that I've met that awful woman I wish I'd been there to cheer you on when you booted her out of your store."

Scott hugged Bonnie and kissed her on the cheek.

"And such a lovely, rosy cheek it is," he said.

183

"A Scottish bakery owner's cheek," Hannah said. "Not an Irish housekeeper's cheek."

"Stop that nonsense!" Bonnie said and pushed Scott away, but she was smiling.

Scott turned to Hannah, who raised her cheek for a kiss and got one too.

"Ah, Hannah," Scott said. "If you weren't married to my good friend Sam, and if he wasn't an expert marksman, I'd drag you off and have my way with you."

"I know, I know," Hannah said. "It's the flat chest and big feet that draw all the men to me, like moths to a flame."

Maggie's face flushed as Scott dropped to his knees by her chair and took her hand.

"Get your hands off me," she said, but she didn't withdraw her hand from his grip.

"Mary Margaret," he said. "Thank you for apologizing to Gwyneth and saving my job. How can I ever thank you?"

"You better hope she stays out of my way and out of my bookstore," Maggie replied. "Next time I'll make sure there's heavy traffic before I heave her out into it."


Scott and Maggie left together after enjoying a huge feast of funeral reception leftovers and goodies from the bakery. The mood between them was warm and easy as they walked. Small talk soon descended into silence, and as they passed the veterinary clinic, with its yellow crime scene tape flapping in the wind, Maggie stopped and faced Scott.

"I want to tell you what we found at Theo's," Maggie said, "but I don't want to get in trouble, and I don't want to get you in trouble because you know."

"Let's go back to your place," Scott said. "I promise to listen like your friend and not a big bad police officer."

Scott left her apartment an hour later wondering how in the world he could keep bending the law for Maggie Fitzpatrick before he broke it completely. He also now knew why Knox might have wanted to kill his wife. Those pictures in Theo's safe would not help the bank president win any elections. Knox may have an alibi for the time of Theo's murder, but he could also have hired out the dirty work. Scott couldn't tell Sarah any of this, of course. He would have to wait until her team searched the secret room, found the photographs, and put it together themselves.

Maggie had been anxious to hear what her brother Sean had said, but Scott told her only that he had an alibi for the time of Theo's death, and that he didn't know where Brian was. He didn't feel like it was his place to tell Maggie about Sean and Brad. That was Sean's personal business, and if Maggie had read the letters, she might have already figured it out. Scott was disappointed in her use of him to transport those letters but wasn't eager to have that confrontation. He decided to leave it for now.

Ed flagged him down at the corner of Pine Mountain Road and Rose Hill Avenue and took a moment to catch his breath before he spoke.

"I know you said I shouldn't push Tommy, and I didn't, but he's told me something more."

"Good," Scott said. "I need all the help I can get."

"Tommy said Billy did not come right back after Theo left. It was a while later, maybe even after his mom came home at 2:00."

"That boy knows way more than he's telling,"

"It's coming out, little by little. He's really worried about it."

"Well, tell him he did a good thing, and let me know if he says anything else."

"You think Billy could have killed Theo?"

"Or saw who did."

Ed walked on with Scott, and when they reached the corner of Peony Street and Rose Hill Avenue, Ed said, "I thought a lot about Brad today."

"I did too," Scott said.

"I don't understand how someone as good as Brad could be taken at such a young age, and that wretched brother of his lived as long as he did," Ed said. "It doesn't make any sense."

"I know," Scott said. "It's not fair."

"He was nothing like Theo," Ed said. "It's hard to believe they were raised by the same mother."

"Maybe that's why their parents adopted the third and fourth after they had the first two," Scott said. "So they wouldn't repeat their mistakes."

Ed nodded in agreement before the two friends parted and went their separate ways.


Sarah was on Scott's front porch when he got home. Duke, the cat, was sitting next to her, keeping her company, but she didn't seem to appreciate the gesture. He invited them both in, and although Duke declined, Sarah accepted. Scott made Sarah some coffee and put a shot of whiskey in it to help her warm up. Scott caught her up on what his team had been doing with a quick review of his notes.

"No disgruntled breeding customers so far, no sign of Willy Neff or his truck, Knox's alibis checked out for the night of the murder and the night of Anne Marie's accident, and neither Doc Machalvie nor Mayor Machalvie had any business dealings with him."

Sarah nodded and said, "Uh huh," in all the right places, but it didn't seem like she was really listening. He told her Caroline had called about the secret room but did not mention anything was known to be in it, or that anyone had been in it. Sarah didn't get too excited but said she would have a team search it.

He told her what Tommy said to Ed about the night Theo was killed, but she dismissed the information, saying, "That kid's starving for attention. I wouldn't put too much stock in anything he says. Besides, you said yourself the busboy could care less about Theo abusing his mother. They're trailer trash, all of them."

Sarah shrugged off his theory Anne Marie may have traded Knox's rare coin for drugs, saying, "Knox has an airtight alibi; that's a dead end."

Sarah helped herself to more coffee and whiskey and then took her turn sharing some news.

"Your buddy Ed checked out okay. No blood on his clothes or anything belonging to him, and no motive any more serious than the ones everyone else in this town seems to have. The owner of the diner said Theo argued with everyone, and the fight with Ed was no different from any of the others. I don't see any point in pursuing him or Dr. Rosen, so barring any new developments, it looks like we can cross them both off the list. I think we haven't met our murderer yet. We need to focus more closely on Theo's business deals, and my hunch is we'll find our killer there."

"I'll talk to Trick," Scott said. "Maybe he knows something."

"They read Theo's will today," Sarah said. "Since it will be common knowledge by tomorrow I thought I'd give you a heads up."

"By tomorrow, you say?" Scott laughed. "I'd say most of the town probably knows by now."

"But not you?"

"People know I don't like gossip, and I don't encourage it."

"I know I've said this before, and you don't agree, but I often find out important things related to a case by listening to gossip, even encouraging it," she said. "You might want to rethink that stance."

Scott had received this lecture from Sarah many times and was tired of it.

"If I acted on every piece of gossip going around this town, everyone would be in jail for something," he said, but she ignored him as she got out her notes.

"Gwyneth gets the properties in town, the leases, stocks, and half the trust, which adds up to several million dollars. Here's where it gets interesting. Caroline gets the lodge plus the surrounding land, the other half of the trust, and a load of stocks, but all of hers will be held in trust, so she can't liquidate any of the assets. Why do you think that is?"

"A lot of the Eldridge properties were placed in trust back in their great-grandparents' day," Scott told her. "For instance, Theo also had rights to the lodge and surrounding land, but only for the duration of his life, and under the terms of the trust, he wasn't allowed to develop it. Caroline is kind of a 'give it all to the poor,' un-materialistic person. Looks like he gave her only the untouchable assets so she wouldn't be able to break them up, sell them, or give them away. If something happens to Caroline, it all goes to Gwyneth. Unless some bastard child of Theo's shows up, demanding a share, when there aren't any more Eldridge heirs, it all goes to the college."

"How do you know all this?"

"From Ed. It's his business to know everything."

"So Caroline gets the untouchable stuff, and Gwyneth gets the Rose Hill board game Theo created. She'll get to play with people's lives just like he did."

"Gwyneth is only interested in being important, and Caroline is much more interested in charitable works, so they should both be happy."

"It's easy to be charitable and un-materialistic with a multi-million dollar trust fund as a safety net," Sarah said.

"Yeah, but she's a nice kid," Scott said, munching on some cookies Bonnie sent home with him.

He offered one to Sarah, but she declined with a disgusted curl of her lip.

"So what does she do with her time?"

"Caroline? She drifts from cause to cause, still kind of looking for herself."

"How old is she?"

"She's in her early thirties," Scott calculated.

"Wow. You'd think she'd have found herself by now."

"Is that it?" he said, standing so she'd get the clear hint he wanted her to leave.

"No, actually, there's something I want you to investigate."

Scott sat back down.

"Theo left a considerable amount of money to someone named Ava Fitzpatrick. Is she any relation to your chubby friend Maggie?"

Scott's mouth fell open in surprise.

"I'm guessing the answer is yes," Sarah said.

"She's Maggie's sister-in-law."

Scott was trying to remember all Maggie had said about the photographic shrine Theo had created in the secret room, and the details of the loan Theo had made to Brian.

"And how will Ava's husband feel about this?" Sarah asked, with a raised eyebrow.

"He won't know. He disappeared about seven years ago and no one's heard from him since."

"Was there an investigation?" she asked.

"Yes," Scott nodded. "I don't know all the details. I worked in Pendleton then."

"Look into it for me. Theo's murder could have been a crime of passion."

New questions were racing through Scott's mind. Did Theo buy off Brian to have Ava all to himself? Or did he lure him away and kill him? Did Ava have a relationship with Theo after Brian left? Scott couldn't imagine that beautiful woman with Theo.

"So, what about Ava?" Sarah asked. "Did she divorce him?"

"No," Scott said. "Ava will never divorce Brian. They have two kids together."

"So she's just waiting for him to come back? How pathetic."

"She's Catholic," Scott said. "She is also very much beholden to the Fitzpatricks, and his mother still expects Brian to come back."

"Any idea what Ava's relationship was with Theo?"

"I didn't know there was one," Scott said. "Jesus, I feel like I need to get over there."

"You better remember you're a police officer, not a friend, and anything you hear you share with me."

Scott stood and walked to the door, so she couldn't mistake his meaning.

"Find out everything for me," Sarah said as she put on her coat, "so I won't have to upset Ava with my evil, gossip-loving, county sheriff's investigator ways."

"All right," Scott said. "I'll call you tomorrow if I find out anything."

Sarah stopped on his front steps and looked like she wanted to say something else, but Scott quickly closed his door so she couldn't.

After Sarah left Scott put on his coat, left by his back door and jogged down the snow-covered alley that divided the backyards of Sunflower Street and Pine Mountain Road. When he knocked on the back door of the bed and breakfast, Patrick opened it, but stood like a wall, blocking the entrance.

"She's not in any state to talk to the police, Scott."

"How about a friend, Patrick?"

"But you aren't her friend right now, are ya, pal? You're a cop, and unless she's being arrested for something, she's not available to you."

"Any clue why she was in the will?"

"No comment."

"Patrick."

"Thanks for stopping by, Scott. I'll let Ava know you were concerned for her, as a friend."

"I really do want to help if I can."

"Thanks again, Scott, I'll tell her."

Patrick backed into the kitchen, shut the door, and Scott could hear the deadbolt lock being set. He saw Maggie peeking out the window of the family room, and she shrugged at him, mouthing, 'sorry,' before dropping the curtain.

The Fitzpatricks had closed ranks.

Scott left the porch and walked on down the alley to the junction where it created a "T" with the alley behind the service station and the Dairy Chef. He stood there a moment, trying to decide which way to go. Everyone he wanted to talk the case over with was either a suspect or related to one.

"Pssst," he heard and turned around a couple times before he saw Hannah, crouched in the bushes behind the Dairy Chef.

"What are you doing in there?"

"Meet me inside," she said in a loud whisper and disappeared back into the parking lot.

Scott took the long way around the bushes through the side parking lot.

She was sitting in a booth at the far side of the restaurant, near the bathrooms, and it being January, they weren't selling much ice cream. Hannah couldn't go a day without ice cream, so she was just tucking into a giant banana split, and had purchased a hot fudge sundae for Scott.

"You and I ate a gigantic meal not three hours ago," he said. "I saw you eat two pieces of pie."

Hannah shrugged, saying, "Great metabolism, I guess."

"What's all the secret squirrel business about?"

"I'm going to tell you why I was not surprised about Ava Fitzpatrick being in Theo's will."

"I know all about the photos of Ava on the wall in the secret room. Maggie told me today."

"This is much older stuff," Hannah said, "and it didn't come from me."

"If they turn the screws on me I'll swear someone told me in an anonymous phone call," Scott said and crossed his heart with his finger for emphasis.

"Okay. You remember the summer Brad Eldridge died."

"Yes."

"Ava and Brian broke up for a couple weeks over Brian cheating with Phyllis Davis."

"Go on."

"So during that time, guess who is sniffing around Ava, trying to take Brian's place?"

"Theo."

"Yes indeed. Then Ava and Brian get back together, suddenly there's a bun in the oven, a wedding in the chapel, and old stink eye is left crying in the rain."

"Ava was pregnant? You think the baby was Theo's?"

"We'll never know," Hannah said. "Ava lost that baby soon after they got married, so no one got to see if the kid had horns and cloven hooves, or red hair and freckles."

"I didn't know any of that. Maggie never talked about it."

"Well, she wouldn't, would she? It's part of her family's dirty laundry."

"Does everyone else know?"

"It was juicy gossip back then, and you can bet it's making the rounds again now he left her all that money. Theo was crazy about Ava, and the minute Brian went off with Phyllis he was there, giving her a shoulder to cry on. It was Theo who arranged for Ava to catch Brian and Phyllis in the act, parked out at the lake. After she dropped him to go back to Brian, Theo went nuts, got in lots of fights."

"He broke my nose that summer," Scott said, feeling the bump on the bridge.

"And Patrick beat the hell out of him for it."

"That was also around the time Brad died."

"Yep, and Theo left town right after the funeral."

"So you think Theo left Ava the money because he was still in love with her?"

"Listen, I saw the wall of photos he had in that room, and it didn't look like love to me. It was something much worse than that."

"Will you be talking to Ava anytime soon?"

"I could arrange to."

"Tell her I have to talk to her, but it's only a formality, to dot my i's and cross my t's, so to speak, to keep Sarah off her back. If she wants to drop by my house to do it instead of the station, she can. But it has to be done, and soon."

"I'll tell her."

"Thanks, Hannah."

"For what? You never saw me, and I was never here, and if you say I was, I'll deny it. That Scott, he's delusional! I think he might hear voices."

"Bye Hannah."

"If you don't want this sundae I'm going to eat it."

"Be my guest."


Later in the evening, Scott sat at his kitchen table, trying to organize his thoughts with a series of lists on paper the way Ian had taught him. He had a timeline, a facts list, a questions list, a suspects list, and was working on some scenarios.

Hannah and Sam saw Theo and Willy around 12:30 a.m. Patrick saw Theo with Willy at midnight and then kicked Theo out of the bar at around 1:15. Tommy saw

Theo fight with Phyllis and Billy between 1:30 and 2:00 a.m., but said Willy was not with Theo. Patrick walked Mandy home just after 2:00 a.m. Scott hauled Mitchell in just before 3:00 a.m. Ed found Theo's body just after 4:00 a.m. Theo must have been killed between 1:30 and 4:00, and Willy disappeared after 1:00.

Where was Willy when Theo was killed and where was he now? Scott was convinced Willy had seen Theo's attacker and had gone to ground somewhere. Who could have lured Theo to the vet's office, or followed him there, and then killed him?

Phyllis, Billy, Patrick, Mandy, Maggie, and Mitchell were all out after the Rose and Thorn closed, between 1:30 and 4:00. He was heavily inebriated at the time, but maybe Mitchell saw something while serenading his ex-girlfriend, or on the way to her apartment building.

Even though Sarah had dropped Drew from the list of suspects, Scott wasn't ready to. Maybe Drew had still been in his office, unable to sleep and catching up on some paperwork. He could have caught Theo breaking in and killed him, thinking he was a burglar or killed him simply because he'd fired him. He'd lied to them when questioned in the station afterward; what else might he be hiding?

Scott reluctantly considered Patrick. Theo had repeatedly victimized the Fitzpatrick family. Bullying Sean, fighting with Patrick, burning down Maggie's house, buying Brian' disappearance (or maybe arranging it), and whatever the thing was he had with Ava; it was more than enough grounds for any one of the Fitzpatricks to want the man dead. Brian was still missing, and Sean's alibi had checked out, so that left Patrick

Scott walked the streets of Rose Hill many nights on his rounds, and he often saw Patrick leaving Ava's house via the back door after everyone else in town had long gone to bed. If Theo threatened to reveal Patrick's affair with Ava, would Patrick have killed him to keep it a secret? If

Patrick found out about an affair between Ava and Theo, might he have killed Theo in a jealous rage?

He was certainly tall and strong enough. He was also one of the last people to see him alive, having kicked him out of the bar before Theo went to Phyllis' trailer. According to Scott's notes, Patrick got off work at 2:00 a.m., escorted Mandy to the trailer park, and then walked down Marigold Avenue, arriving home by 2:15. Did he overhear Theo making arrangements to meet someone at the vet's later, someone like Willy Neff, and then showed up there after he dropped off Mandy?

Scott knew he was going to have to follow up with Patrick, and he dreaded Maggie finding out. He also needed to talk to Tommy, and see if he had anything more to say. Maybe the reason Tommy was so scared to talk was because it was Patrick he saw following Theo. Tommy and his mother were adopted members of the Fitzpatrick family, and they wrote his mother's paychecks.

If Brian was still alive, and somehow knew about the bequest to Ava, would he come back and kill Theo, hoping to cash in? That was a stretch, Scott knew.

Who else hated Theo enough to kill him?

Knox certainly had both the height and strength but also had a US Senator giving him an alibi. If Theo was sleeping with his wife, supplying her with drugs in return for items stolen from Knox's collections, the fear of scandal might have been motive enough. Those photos of Ann Marie would be explosive blackmail ammunition. Maybe Knox wanted to remove both liabilities to protect his political aspirations. Theo also had some information which might embarrass Knox, as evidenced in the file Maggie had taken from the safe: something that happened when he was in college. If Knox hired the killer, he didn't have to be in town when the crime took place, just as he was out of town when Anne Marie had her accident.

Knox's brother Trick may have killed Theo for cheating him out of his commission on the sale of the glass factory. Trick's wife Sandy would probably give him an alibi, even though he cheated on her repeatedly, and she suspected his brother of attempted murder.

There was always the anonymous "disgruntled business associate" theory, which Sarah preferred, or one of a hundred other people Theo had blackmailed, cheated, or screwed (literally or figuratively) over the years.

Caroline and Gwyneth stood to gain the most wealth from Theo's death. Scott's gut didn't react to the idea, but it was practical police work to find out if either woman was having financial difficulties. He couldn't imagine Caroline doing anything that might detonate such a karmic time bomb, and Gwyneth didn't seem like she had the constitution for such a cold-blooded act.

Immersed in his notes and working on several plausible scenarios, it surprised him to hear a knock at his back door and find Ava on his back porch. She was dressed in a sweatshirt, jeans, and tennis shoes, and was hugging herself in the cold. Scott let her in and put more coffee on.

"They think I've gone to bed, so I can't stay long," she said as she sat down.

Ava Fitzpatrick was the only daughter of parents who were already past middle age when they adopted her, and they had both passed away before their granddaughter Charlotte was born. An astonishing beauty in high school, Ava was still a stunning woman in her mid-thirties, the kind of woman who made many a man's heart beat faster when she was near.

Scott was no exception. He wondered how a man could ever tire of looking at her. She had one of those luminous complexions that required no makeup, sensual lips which were not too full but perfectly shaped, a bright smile, dark eyes with thick, long lashes, and shining dark hair which fell over her shoulders. She was always voted Miss Everything in high school, but amazingly never seemed pretentious or stuck on herself. She was a nice, friendly woman, a good mother, a gracious innkeeper, and

Scott couldn't understand how Brian could have abandoned her and the children.

Scott hurriedly gathered up his notes and slid them into a drawer while Ava pretended not to notice.

"I was as surprised as anyone when I found out Theo left me money," she said moments later, holding a mug of coffee with both hands to warm them. "We dated briefly the summer after Brian and I broke up, but it was only a few dates and never anything serious."

"It may have seemed more serious to Theo."

"He was hurt when I broke it off, but there was never anyone but Brian for me. Everyone knew that."

"And after?"

"Brad died, and Theo went back to England. I guess it was ten or twelve years later when his father died, that he moved back. He would say hello to me in passing, but we never had a real conversation. I honestly don't know why he left me so much money."

"After Brian left, did Theo come to see you?"

"Well, now that you mention it, he did."

"Go on."

"You know at first we thought Brian must have been in an accident or something, and then a few weeks passed, and all the money in our bank account disappeared."

"I didn't know that."

"Well, it wasn't much, but it was all the savings we had—a few thousand. Brian cashed a check in a Miami bank and cleaned us out. I saw the canceled check; it was his handwriting, his signature. We knew then he meant to leave, and that was the last sign we had of him."

"I guess I was out of the loop back then. I didn't know."

"That's one of the things I like most about you, Scott; you don't gossip, and you don't listen to gossip. Everyone in this town must know about the check but you."

Scott thought about what Sarah continually said about listening to gossip being part of his job, and hated to think she might be right.

"And Theo came to see you?"

"Yes, he came to the house one night, very late, when I was alone with the kids put to bed. He said he'd heard about the account being cleaned out and wanted to know if I needed money."

"And you said?"

"Well, I thanked him, but told him the Fitzpatricks were taking good care of me, and I was going to get a job. This was before I decided to start the bed and breakfast. He said the offer was open-ended. Then he left."

"Anything else?"

"I was surprised to see him, and I thought later, you know, he might have been hitting on me, but I was such a mess at the time, I didn't know if I was coming or going. I wouldn't have recognized a pass if he'd been naked with a rose in his teeth."

"And after that?"

"Nothing."

"No anonymous letters, no cash mysteriously showing up when you needed it?"

"The church and the Fitzpatricks always made sure we had everything we needed. It's still tight sometimes, but the bed and breakfast supports us."

"If you remember anything else, will you let me know?"

"Absolutely. Oh Scott, what people must be thinking. You know how people are in this town."

"Don't worry about it. The people who know and care for you won't doubt you."

"Oh please. They'll stand by me, and defend me to the death, but don't think they aren't all wondering the same thing everyone else is."

"I hope that's not true," Scott said.

"That's only human nature, and I can't control that," she said, with a delicate sigh and a look that made Scott want to slay dragons on her behalf.

"Try not to worry about it," Scott said. "If you need someone to talk to, I'm always here."

"Thanks, Scott, you're a doll."

She kissed his cheek and left, and he felt exactly like the second grader he had been when he first saw her in the lunchroom, and she smiled at him. Like he'd been punched in the gut, and liked it.

As Scott was drifting off to sleep later, a thought popped into his head which jerked him wide-awake, and he got back up and dressed. He knew someone who would still be up and might be able to help him follow up on something, and a quick call confirmed it. He made a detour to the 24-hour convenience store by the highway to gas up and buy the doughnuts he knew would be welcomed.

When Scott pulled into Hannah and Sam's driveway, the kennel dogs were in full voice, and both house dogs ran up to meet his SUV. Scott got out and patted Jax and Wally before walking up the wheelchair ramp to a side door, which led into the kitchen.

"Hannah went to bed already," Sam said as he let Scott in. "She had a stomach ache."

"If you'd seen all she ate today you wouldn't be surprised," Scott replied.

"No amount that woman puts away would surprise me. She said it was the cinnamon rolls Bonnie brought to Ava's this evening that did her in."

Sam was a talented athlete in high school, and still had a thick, muscled neck and a body builder's upper torso, which he maintained by using a home gym. He wore sweatpants that were tight over his muscular thighs and then hung loose where his lower legs had been amputated below each knee. He still had the shaved head and goatee look he adopted in the army, and despite the wheelchair, he still emanated a strong physical presence. He took a beer and soda out of the fridge and offered Scott the soda.

"I guess you didn't kill Theo," Scott began after he sat down at the kitchen table.

"No, not that I didn't want to," Sam laughed. "I guess Hannah told you he came out here with little Willy that night and got the dogs all in an uproar, looking for that black lab."

"Hannah said you fired a shot over his head," Scott said cheerfully.

"My wife is not known for her ability to keep her mouth shut, even if it incriminates her husband," Sam said.

"She's a good detective, though. I'm thinking of deputizing her."

"You can't trust her. She'd be telling all your suspects what you had on them. She can't help herself."

"I have kind of a weird question for you," Scott said.

"Shoot."

"If I wanted to track down Brian Fitzpatrick, is that something you could do through your contacts at the bureau?"

"You don't have to," Sam said. "I know where he is."

"I can't believe Hannah didn't tell me that."

"I dearly love my wife, but I don't tell her everything."

"So how do you know where Brian is?"

"You remember Jay Wallace?"

Scott nodded.

"He joined up the same time as me, but he went to Germany. He's in Seoul now, but we keep in touch. He works for the folks in the funny shaped building in DC. He was on his way to Gitmo a few years back and spent a week's leave in Bimini. First night there he walked into some dive and Brian was there, pouring drinks behind the bar. Jay said Brian had a beard, and his hair was long, but otherwise, he looked the same."

"What was he doing there?"

"Working, trying to make a living; same as you and me."

"Did he say why he left?"

"He said he wanted to be somewhere nobody knew him and nobody had any expectations of him."

"So he left his gorgeous wife and two children because he couldn't handle the responsibility?"

"Well, we both know why he really left, don't we?" Sam said and looked at Scott expectantly.

"I'm not so sure. If Theo did pay him to leave town, why would Brian have to pay him back? Maggie said there were loan papers marked paid in full with bank receipts. Brian guaranteed the loan with insurance policies. That doesn't jibe with a payoff to leave town."

"It may have been some shady business deal between them that only needed to look legitimate. When you move around that much money, you better leave a clean looking paper trail," Sam said. "You could order an audit."

"I don't officially know about any of this," Scott said.

"It's not easy being the lone arbiter of morality and justice around here, is it?" Sam said, smiling at his friend. "Especially with the Fitzpatrick women sticking their noses in everywhere."

"You aren't kidding," Scott said. "But you gotta admit life would be pretty boring without them."

Sam raised the long neck beer he was drinking, and Scott met the neck of the glass bottle with his plastic bottle of soda.

"I'll drink to that," Sam said.

"Did Brian ask Jay about Ava? About the kids?"

"Nope."

"I can't believe that Brian. What a jerk."

"I always thought so," Sam said, nodding. "Even before he left."

"Did he say anything about Theo?"

"Nope."

"Did you tell Ava where he was?"

"I told Patrick."

"Patrick knows about this?"

"I told him as soon as I found out. He talked to Jay about it."

"Christ, I'm starting to think I don't know anybody like I thought I did."

"You don't," Sam said in a matter of fact way. "You can never really know another person completely."

Sam's face was unreadable as if to illustrate his point.

Creaking wood floors announced Hannah was up, and the men dropped their conversation. Scratching her head and squinting in the light of the kitchen, Hannah frowned at the sight of Scott.

"Are you here to arrest me?"

"No, I've come to see if you're hungry. I have a box of doughnuts in the car."

"Really?" asked Hannah, and immediately perked up. "Why didn't ya bring 'em in? I'll see if we have any milk."

Sam shook his head as Scott picked up his car keys and left the house, laughing.

# Chapter Eight - Friday

Sarah called Scott first thing in the morning to say she was sending a couple deputies to search the secret room at Theo's house, and she planned to stop by the station before noon; was he free? Scott said, of course, he would make himself available whenever she could make time for him. It was like talking to his mother; he knew what she wanted to hear, and the tone he used was just as important as the words.

Scott went down to the bakery to talk to Bonnie Fitzpatrick, who was at first glad to see him, but when he asked what time Patrick got home the night Theo was murdered she stared at him like he'd sprung horns.

"I have to ask in order to eliminate him as a suspect," Scott said.

"I know you're just doing your job, Scott, but this is Patrick we're talking about."

"I don't think he killed Theo," Scott told her. "I have to make sure no one else can accuse him."

She softened a bit but still frowned.

"If my second born doesn't go home with some floozy, he's in my kitchen eating leftovers by 2:15 a.m. Men, as my mother often told me, are just like dogs, and occasionally like to roll in shit. My son Patrick is no exception. But on that night, he was home."

"You're sure?" Scott asked her.

"He was home," she said emphatically.

It didn't put Patrick completely in the clear, as he could have left the bar at 2:00, dropped Mandy off at 2:05, run down to the vet's office, taken five minutes to kill Theo and still have been home by 2:15.

Scott walked down to Mandy's trailer and had no trouble making it to the vet's office and then to the Fitzpatrick's house within the time frame, at only a fast walk. If Patrick did it, he wondered, was it premeditated or

203

an impulse? If he agreed to meet Theo there or stalked him there, it was one thing. If he ran into Theo and they argued, it was another. Scott was sure Willy Neff had seen it all; if only he could find him.

Scott went to the bookstore and was relieved for once to see Maggie wasn't in. Mitchell was working behind the café counter, and he didn't look glad to see Scott.

"Have you come to arrest me?" he asked Scott, using his big brown eyes to full puppy dog effect.

"No," Scott said. "I have some questions for you about Saturday night."

"I was so wasted," Mitchell told him. "I don't remember much."

"When you went to your girlfriend's apartment, which way did you go?"

Mitchell shrugged.

"From campus down Rose Hill Avenue, left on Pine Mountain Road and down to the corner of Iris Avenue."

"Did you see anyone or anything unusual?"

"Not that I can remember. It was really late, and there was all this fog. It was kinda creepy."

"If you remember anything else, or anybody else, will you let me know?"

"Sure, man," Mitchell said. "And hey, sorry about the mess I made in your office."

"Not to worry," Scott said. "I'm just glad you weren't trying to drive anywhere."

Scott remembered what Maggie had told him about local gossip implicating Mitchell.

"Anyone giving you any trouble?"

"No more than usual," Mitchell shrugged. "Why?"

"No reason. You would let me know though if anyone gave you any problems?"

Mitchell rolled his eyes.

"Maggie told me 'bout that. I think I can handle whatever the blue hair mafia gang hands out. I'll let you know, though, if they get physical."

Scott smiled ruefully and felt foolish. He waved and turned to go.

"You know," Mitchell said, as Scott started to walk away. "You might want to talk to some of the people in Yvonne's building."

"Yvonne, your ex?"

"Yeah," Mitchell sighed. "I guess I need to accept it at some point."

Scott came back to the counter, leaned in close, and said in a low voice, "Never give up, my friend. I'm not saying you should stalk her or bother her, or show up drunk in the middle of the night to serenade her, but keep in touch. If you don't burn that bridge, there's always a chance you can re-cross it."

Mitchell nodded and seemed to consider this sage advice.

"Thanks, man," he said. "I'll keep that in mind."

"And thanks for the tip. I'll stop by and talk to her."

Mitchell sighed heavily again.

"Tell her I'm sorry."

Scott stopped at Trick Rodefeffer's real estate office on his way to Yvonne's apartment and found Sandy at the secretary's desk. She didn't look any happier to see him than Mitchell had.

"I didn't know you were working here," Scott said.

"Have you seen Knox's secretary?" Sandy asked him.

Scott nodded yes, trying not to smirk.

"Then you can see why I'm here. I'm not making the same mistake with Trick."

"How is Anne Marie?" Scott asked her.

"Still in a coma," she said and stuck her head into Trick's office to tell him Scott was there to see him.

When he entered the office Trick came around the desk, pumped Scott's hand, and offered him a beer.

"It's a little early for me," Scott said, noting Trick had already tossed back a few, judging by the fumes emanating from him.

Trick was a slimmer, paler version of his bloated orange brother, with thinning blonde hair. He wore the same good old boy khaki and navy, but without the jewelry, and he was not so carefully groomed. Known to chase anything in a skirt, Trick, with big bags under his red-veined eyes, was not wearing middle age well.

"I am so sorry about Anne Marie," Scott said, taking a seat across from Trick.

"Oh, yea, terrible thing, just terrible," Trick said. "She was visiting a friend in Glencora and got caught in some awful weather coming back. Fog, snow, rain, ice—such a mess—went right over the guardrail."

With his hand, he demonstrated Anne Marie's car soaring through the air.

'Without coat, purse, or phone,' Scott thought but didn't add. Instead, he shook his head and looked sympathetic.

"What can I do ya for?" Trick asked, and Scott was reminded how much he hated when grown men said that, thinking it was funny.

"I understand you were working on a deal with Theo to sell the glassworks property," Scott said, and Trick stared vacantly into space for a moment before abruptly returning to reality.

"The glassworks, the glassworks, oh yes, yes, yes, yes, that we were. We were indeed. Uh huh, uh huh. What about it?"

"I understand Theo was trying to cut you out of the deal," Scott said.

"Oh no, no, no, no, not at all. That was just a misunderstanding, an error on the part of Theo's lawyer, perhaps, a miscommunication, a mistake. That was never Theo's intention."

"I see," said Scott. "What will happen to the deal now?"

"Well, it's Gwynnie's deal now, isn't it?" he said.

Scott doubted anyone ever called Gwyneth "Gwynnie" to her face and lived to tell about it.

"So it's still going through as planned?"

"Oh yes, the gentleman in question is dead set on it. Can't wait to get his hands on it. He's going to put a bicycle factory in there."

"Bicycles?"

"Mm hmm, mm hmm, big business, apparently. Custom cycles, mountain bikes, Tour de France, road rallies, cross country races, or something like that. A big cash cow, according to him. The guy is loaded, really rolling in it, filthy rich. He was a trust fund kid, and then made a fortune selling an Internet company he started up."

"Do you know anything about Theo's land development deal?" Scott asked. "Eldridge Point?"

"I may have advised him, purely in an unofficial capacity, you understand, on the real estate side of it," Trick said. "I didn't have anything to do with the investment side."

"I guess there were some lawsuits," Scott said.

"Might have been, might have been," Trick said. "Nothing to do with me."

"So neither you nor your brother invested?"

"No way, José," Trick said. "Knox hated Theo's guts, always had, since we were kids. As for me, my better half holds the purse strings in this business, and she never liked Theo. She wouldn't have allowed it."

"I have to ask everyone associated with Theo where they were the night he died," Scott said.

"Oh, home, home, home," Trick said. "Home with the wife; she can verify it."

When Scott stood, Trick also did, swaying a bit, and had to steady himself with a hand on the edge of the desk.

Sandy verified Trick's alibi, as he knew she would, before Scott left the office, shaking his head over someone who could get so drunk so early in a day.

Scott stopped by Yvonne's building, which housed Delvecchio's Insurance on the ground floor and apartments above. It was separated by a narrow walkway from the newly renovated antique store next to it, was two doors down from the alley and the newspaper office, and across the street from the veterinary clinic. Scott wondered if you could see the back entrance to the clinic from the upper floors.

By the downstairs door to the interior stairway, there were four doorbells with names written on masking tape next to them, and Yvonne's was one of them. Scott buzzed her apartment, but when her roommate came down, she said Yvonne wasn't in. The roommate couldn't remember seeing or hearing anything after the party except Mitchell the night Theo died, and no one else who was home in the building had anything more to add. Scott went up and looked out the top floor hallway window, which had a clear view of the back of the veterinary clinic.

Scott left his card with a note on the back for Yvonne and headed back to the station via the alley. As he crossed Peony Street, he looked up the hill and saw Duke sitting on the front porch of Machalvie Funeral Home, surveying his progress. Scott almost waved but thought it might look odd to anyone watching. He did, however, nod his head briefly, out of respect.

Back at the station, Sarah was waiting impatiently and spent some time getting Scott caught up on her progress on the case.

"I don't know if I shared the post-mortem info with you or not," Sarah said, taking out a report. "Theo being so prominent a citizen put him at the head of the line with the coroner's office. We don't usually get these back so fast."

Scott shook his head.

"It was pretty much what we thought. He was struck on the back of the head with enough force to crush the skull into the brain. There was internal as well as external bleeding. A blow like that would render someone instantly unconscious, and if no medical intervention were made, that person would most likely bleed to death within a half hour. He probably didn't know what hit him and was out before he hit the floor. We've narrowed the time of death down to between 1:30-4:00 a.m. through our interviews and the post-mortem supports that."

Scott was not surprised but nodded appreciatively.

"The toxicology tests show he was so full of drugs and alcohol I can't believe he could stand upright let alone walk and talk. These included cocaine, OxyContin, beer, and whiskey."

"That's our Theo," Scott said. "He was a rock star."

Sarah looked at him as if she thought it was an odd thing to say and then continued.

"You'll love this. Those slipped discs the doctor had the x-rays to prove? Either those were someone else's x-rays or Theo had a miraculous recovery, because he didn't appear to have a back problem, just a back pain medication problem."

Scott shook his head over this but did not comment.

"He had advanced heart disease, cirrhosis of the liver, and his lungs had what looked to be precancerous cell activity. He was a walking time bomb, health-wise.

"He had $750 in cash in his wallet, and an assortment of credit cards, so the motive doesn't seem to be robbery. Here's a surprise: the aluminum baseball bat was not the murder weapon. Looks like Theo used it to break into the office, but there was no hair or tissue on the

209

bat that would be consistent with the injury he received. So, we're looking for something shaped like a baseball bat, or another bat, I guess. There were flakes of paint and rusted metal in the wound, so perhaps a metal pipe of some sort."

She concluded her report and looked at him for a comment.

"Thanks for letting me know," was all Scott said.

Sarah continued looking at him speculatively as she returned the report to her briefcase, and then consulted her notes.

"Oh, here's one for you. We found a signature under the label inside the threat card," she said offhandedly. "It was signed by someone named 'Lily Crawford.' "

Scott said, "What?" because it surprised him, and Sarah rolled her eyes at him.

"I know Mrs. Crawford really well," he said. "All right with you if I go out and see her myself?"

"Fine with me," Sarah said dismissively. "It was obviously a prank, and I have plenty to do without following up on practical jokers."

"Anything more on the whereabouts of Willy Neff?" Scott asked her.

"No one seems to know or care," Sarah said. "If we can't find anyone else to hang this on, he may be our default leader in the suspect pool."

Scott must have looked as shocked as he felt because she looked at him incredulously.

"I'm kidding, of course. What's up with you today?"

Scott shook his head and rubbed his eyes, saying, "Lack of sleep, I guess."

"I have a couple guys going out to the lodge to look for the secret room. Unless Mr. Neff's hiding out there with a lead pipe, it's probably a complete waste of our time."

Being it was officially Sara's case and not his, Scott was only supposed to investigate leads if she allowed it. Sarah seemed to have lost interest in the case, and Scott wondered how much effort she was still putting into it. The two pieces of evidence that Scott had contributed, the secret room and the card, didn't seem to have impressed her.

"So, are you making any progress?" he asked, not wanting to seem like he was criticizing, just interested.

"Tig's still working on the files from Theo's house and the mail. Locally, however, there doesn't seem to be anything more to be gained through interviews," she said, in the same dismissive way she seemed to answer all his questions lately. "Everyone despised the man, but no one saw or heard anything."

"You did talk to Tommy again, though, about Billy Davis."

She shook her head, saying, "I don't know how much credence we can give the kid's statement," she said. "Peeping Tom could hardly put a sentence together."

"But you talked to Billy again?"

"No point. Kid's got an alibi, doesn't he? His fat mother says he was home with her all night. Besides, he didn't seem too upset about Theo decking her; seems like it was a common occurrence. Like I told you, they're trailer trash, the lot of them."

Scott tried to be careful how he phrased his next words, saying, "You don't sound confident about solving this case."

Sarah shrugged.

"Not much to work with, unfortunately. Unless Tig and J.T. come up with some dog breeder, investor, or business associate with a murderous grudge, we may have reached a dead end. In addition, I have my hands full with other cases. I am stretched to the absolute limit, resource-wise."

"Then don't let me keep you," Scott said abruptly and stood to indicate she could go.

Sarah eyed him a moment, and then said, "I could fit in some lunch if you're interested."

Scott gave her a tight smile and said, "I can't today, I'm afraid. I'm a bit stretched resource-wise, myself."

Sarah made a face that showed she found that hard to believe, but Scott ignored it. He was fed up with her condescending attitude.

He walked her to the door and swung it open for her, but did not walk out with her. She was clearly disappointed but tried to hide it with brusque cheerfulness.

"Well, good luck with your prankster."

"I'll let you know how it goes," he said. "Thanks for stopping by."

As the door swung shut behind her, he shook his head at Skip, who had heard everything.

"She doesn't give a damn who killed Theo," he told his deputy. "If we don't find out, no one will."


Lily Crawford lived at the end of Possum Holler, a dirt road extension of Morning Glory Avenue that started at the top of the town behind the library and wound around the hillside past Drew's house, Maggie's property, and Rose Hill Cemetery. Her husband Simon, now deceased, had been a farmer who was well regarded for allowing the town to hold events in the large meadow they owned, one of the few pieces of flat ground in a town built on a hillside. The Heritage Festival took place there every September after the hay was baled.

The Crawford farmhouse was over one-hundred-years-old and overlooked the large meadow from the hillside above it. There was a big red barn and several small outbuildings, although the only animals kept at the farm now were the feral cats that lived in the barn, an old basset hound named Betty Lou, and Penny, an elderly pony.

Hannah had pleaded with and begged Lily to adopt the pony after she rescued it from a vagrant traveling through town, selling rides on its broken down back for a dollar. To cinch the deal, she brought Mrs. Crawford out to her farm to meet Penny. Hannah explained her Border Collie Wally was going nuts not being allowed to herd the poor creature every minute, and the pony was agitated by that and all the dogs barking.

Mrs. Crawford took one look at the filthy, shaggy, suspicious pony, and her heart went out to the poor beast, as Hannah knew it would. Penny came to live on Crawford's farm, and Lily eventually won her trust in a time-honored way, using apples and carrots. Now Penny ate grass in the meadow spring and summer, ate pony chow sweetened with molasses during the winter months, and reposed in a warm barn every night.

Betty Lou, the basset hound, was half-blind and had arthritis, but she was still an excellent watchdog and bayed at the top of her lungs when anyone ventured near the house. Scott got out of his SUV and gave her a treat from a bag he kept especially for her, and she snuffled it up greedily before waddling after him up the path, hoping for more. He knocked on the back door, and Mrs. Crawford appeared, drying her hands on a dishtowel.

"Come in, come in," she said cheerfully. "What a nice surprise!"

Scott wiped his feet carefully before entering the big, homey kitchen, which was warm and smelled like apples and cinnamon. Mrs. Crawford was the picture of a sweet old granny, with neat white hair, wire-rim glasses, and a soft cushiony figure, but the image was misleading.

She and her husband had been Harley Davidson enthusiasts, veteran rock festival attendees, and were known to throw some wild parties in their younger years. It was rumored that Mr. Crawford grew a small quantity of potent marijuana in a secret location on his property, and many a high school student still searched for the patch in vain.

"Congratulations on your big promotion," she said. "Simon would be so proud of you."

"I hope that pie isn't spoken for," Scott said. "It smells delicious."

"I'm baking it for Gwyneth," she said. "She's living up at the inn until the college president moves out of the house, and you know Connie doesn't bake anything fresh."

Scott thought Gwyneth probably hadn't successfully digested a baked good in over thirty years but said nothing. Connie was the innkeeper at the Eldridge Inn, known for her obsessive sterilization of anything anyone touched, but not for any culinary expertise.

He sat at the kitchen table, covered in a well-worn vintage cotton tablecloth with a pink and green floral pattern on it. There was a freestanding gas stove in the kitchen, and between it and the heat from the big cooking range, Scott could feel himself starting to sweat. He took off his coat and gratefully accepted the hot coffee and cookies she served him.

"Where is the college president going to live now that Gwyneth has kicked him out of his house?"

"He and his wife are going to move into the inn until they find a place. His wife mentioned an extended stay at her daughter's in Florida, so probably he will stay at the inn until they find something."

"Gwyneth sure didn't waste any time," Scott said sharply.

"It is her house now," she admonished Scott. "Hers to do with as she pleases."

Lily put more homemade cookies on the now empty plate before him. Scott always felt comfortable in this slightly messy kitchen in a way he didn't anywhere else, even in the house in which he grew up. With Lily Crawford, there were no strings attached to her maternal gestures and no strict rules of behavior; she only wanted people to feel welcome in her home.

Scott and his friends had been coming up the holler to visit the farm all their lives. Simon would let them help drive the cows from one pasture to another and take turns riding on the back of his tractor when he plowed or mowed the fields. He enjoyed their company and didn't mind them hanging around as long as they did as he told them, so no one got hurt.

Lily always had something good to eat and time to listen. Every weekend toward the end of summer she would split a watermelon for them, and they would eat big pieces of it seated on the front porch steps, seeing who could spit seeds the farthest out into the front yard. The farm had a good sled-riding hill down into the meadow, and Simon inflated tractor tire inner tubes for them to use as sleds in the winter. Scott still made it a habit every few weeks of coming by to check in, but it was really for selfish reasons. Lily made him feel good.

Mrs. Crawford took the pie out of the oven, and the smell was heavenly.

"You haven't seen Willy Neff anywhere since Theo died, have you?" Scott asked her.

"No, I haven't seen Willy for a long time. I can remember him as a child, coming out here to sled ride with a group of kids. He was always small for his age and never had warm enough clothes on. I knew his mother when we were younger. She ran with a pretty rough crowd. You know he grew up next to the Esteps, and Margie used to be sweet on him before all the trouble."

I didn't know," Scott said, trying to picture the frumpy postmaster as anyone's sweetheart. "It's hard to imagine Margie and Willy."

He grinned, and she shook a finger at him.

"I know you don't think Margie looks like the romantic type, but Willy used to be a nice-looking young man, although he had a horrible upbringing. His mother was a drug addict, and his father or the man everyone assumed was his father, left soon after he was born. Margie's father Eric took a shine to him, and Willy followed Eric around like one of those dogs he always had. I can remember Margie following Willy in much the same way. She had a mighty crush on him."

Scott found it hard to imagine Willy as anything other than the smelly drunk he became.

"What happened to Willy to make him like he is now?"

"Well, Willy's mother passed away, and Eric had his unfortunate accident. Margie and Willy fell out soon after, and then Willy got in trouble," she said.

Scott was impressed at how delicately Lily had just described an overdose, a suicide, and a charge of procuring child pornography.

"I understand Enid is pretty much crippled with arthritis," Scott observed. "Margie still lives at home with her, doesn't she?"

"She does. I know people say bad things about Margie," Mrs. Crawford said. "That she doesn't take such good care of her mother and tampers with the mail. I think she does the best she can for her mother, and I've never noticed my mail being tampered with."

This was the first Scott had heard people said bad things about Margie and how she handled the mail, but Lily couldn't be induced to say more. She brought up the investigation into Theo's murder, asking if Scott had any suspects.

"It's early days yet," Scott said, "not like on TV."

Scott was trying to decide how to bring up the subject of the card, but she made it easy for him.

"You know, I saw Theo twice the week before he died," she said.

Scott made himself all ears as he crunched a cookie and sipped his coffee.

"I went up to the cemetery to tend Simon's grave," she said, "and I was surprised to see Theo there. The only one of his family with a stone there is Brad, as his parents' are back in England, so I assumed he'd been to visit it."

"Theo didn't seem like the sentimental type," Scott said. "He was more likely robbing graves, or dancing on them."

"Now, you never know about people," Lily admonished him lightly. "He talked to me for just a minute, seemed embarrassed to be seen there. He asked me again if I would sell him the farm, and of course, I said no. I went home and found a picture one of you boys gave me the summer Brad died. It was a picture of you all the way I remember you then, full of life and ornery as the dickens, standing on a dock at the lake with some fish you'd caught. I put it in with a card I had and intended to mail it to him."

"Intended to?"

"I saw him again the day he died when I took the card downtown to mail it. He was in the post office, so I handed it to him rather than mail it. He asked me again about selling the farm, but I just laughed. He was tenacious, that one."

"Did he open the card right then?"

"No, he had his hands full, sorting a big stack of mail at the counter next to the trash can. Margie was fussing at him for smoking a cigar in the post office. I didn't want to embarrass him, so I gave him the card, told him I hoped he had a good weekend, and left."

Scott didn't have the heart to tell her what had happened to the card and photo. Someone had obviously taken what was a kind gesture and made malicious mischief out of it. But how had this person got the card and photo from Theo in the first place?

Maybe he accidentally threw it away with some junk mail, or opened it, was irritated by it, and threw it away on purpose. Anyone could then have plucked the card and photo out of the trash, applied the label to the inside of the card, and then put them both in a bigger envelope. The Saturday postmark, however, meant Margie had stamped it and put it in Theo's box after he left. Lily's statement that she gave the card to Theo on Saturday combined with that postmark was pretty good circumstantial evidence that Margie could have done it, or postmarked it for the person who did.

Scott finished the last cookie, groaned about being full, which pleased her, and stood up to leave.

"It was a funny thing, though," she said. "Brad's grave is in the opposite direction from where Theo was walking. I wonder what in the world he was up to."

Scott thanked her warmly and left with a bag of cookies tucked in his jacket pocket. He drove down the narrow lane to Rose Hill Cemetery and turned in under the arched iron entryway. Duke, the cat, was sitting on the stone wall just to the side of the entrance, sunning himself and washing his face. He paused only briefly to consider Scott before resuming his bath.

The same summer the dockside photo was taken, Scott and his friends had a scary experience in the cemetery, and no matter how many years went by Scott still dreaded going there. He reminded himself as he got out of the SUV that he was a grown man, an armed police officer, and it was broad daylight.

'If Mrs. Crawford can come here by herself surely I can,' he admonished himself.

The cemetery was not large, merely two acres of hilltop, and the graves were arranged around a figure-eight-shaped drive. Most of the headstones were modest and plain, but there were the occasional flights of granite fancy, most of which memorialized children or young people who died in the late 1800's and early 1900's. There had been a flu epidemic, tuberculosis, German measles, polio, several mine disasters, a deadly flood, and two world wars since this graveyard had been built.

Scott found Brad's stone with no problem; he had been to visit a few times on the anniversary of his death. There was a small brass plaque on the stone with "George Bradley Eldridge," and the dates of his life engraved on it. The only sentiment was "beloved son and brother."

Scott walked in the opposite direction, where Theo must have been coming from the day Mrs. Crawford saw him, toward the maintenance shack, and felt the hairs rise up on his arms and neck. The feeling of dread which accompanied him into the cemetery became oppressive, making him feel almost panicked to get away. He looked at the surrounding graves but could not find any with what seemed like a direct connection to Theo or his family.

'We will never know what he was up to,' Scott thought.


Now that it was almost noon, and Mandy would be at work in the bakery, Scott stopped back in to have another word with the young woman about the night Theo was murdered. Under the disapproving look of Bonnie Fitzpatrick, Scott took Mandy out in the alleyway behind the bakery to talk to her.

"Theo tried to come in with that pervert Willy around midnight, and Patrick throwed them out of the bar," she said. "He came back later, right after last call, and got throwed out again. He offered Patrick $500 for a bottle of whiskey. I couldn't believe that. I'd a took it."

"What happened then?"

"Theo tried to pick a fight with a couple guys and said somethin' purty rude to me. Then he got right up in Patrick's face and mouthed off, so Patrick told him he could walk out or get carried out, it was up to him."

"What did Theo say to Patrick, exactly?"

"He said 'you'll never have her, I'll make sure a that,' or something like that.'"

Scott wondered if Theo meant Mandy or Ava.

"What did Theo do after Patrick threatened him?"

"Well, what would you do if Patrick was wavin' a baseball bat in your face, tellin' you to get outta there?"

"Patrick had a bat in his hand?"

"Well, yeah, the one we keep behind the bar."

"Is it metal?"

"No, it's wood."

"Did Patrick go out after that?"

"No, we was busy, and he didn't have no help but me."

"So then what happened?"

"We take last orders at 1:00 and then throw everybody out by 1:30 so we can clean up. Patrick puts the chairs up so I can mop while he counts the till and gets the trash together."

"And then?"

"We get outta there by 2:00 most nights. We drop the trash off in the dumpster in the alley, and he walks me home."

"Did you see or hear anything unusual?"

"No. It was really foggy."

"How does he go from your place home?"

"Down Iris or Marigold, I guess."

"But not the alley."

"I don't see why he would," she said. "That's backtracking, ain't it?"

"Does he ever drop you off and then go in a different direction?"

"If he has a date, he might. I never watched him enough to notice."

"And Patrick didn't leave the bar any time before 2:00, even for a short amount of time?"

"Well, he mighta gone to the bathroom, Scott, but I don't remember nothin' in particular."

Mandy looked worried.

"You don't really think Patrick had anything to do with Theo getting his self murdered, do you?"

"No," Scott said. "I want to be sure no one else can say he did."

"Well, I didn't like Theo, and I don't know anyone who did, but you can't just go around killin' people 'cause you don't like 'em. There wouldn't be nobody left in this whole world."

Scott looked in Mandy's big green eyes and saw she was sincere and serious.

"You're right about that, Mandy," he said.

"I know," she said. "It's the truth."

"Was Tommy up when you got home?" he asked her.

"Course not. He delivers the papers of the morning, so he goes to bed early. He's always sound asleep when I get home."

"He told you about the fight at Phyllis' trailer, though, right?"

"Oh Lord, everybody done told me about that fight. They were always fussin' and fightin', those two."

Scott thanked her and left. He thought she was telling the truth about Patrick, but she owed her living to the Fitzpatrick family and would be likely to protect them if she could. Scott was anxious though, to confirm the bat they kept behind the bar was made of wood.

Scott stopped by the service station and asked Patrick to show him the bat. Patrick led him across the street to the Rose and Thorn, unlocked the door, walked around to the back side of the bar, and handed Scott an old wooden bat. Scott examined it before handing it back and then took a seat. Patrick poured him a soda and poured himself a beer.

"We need to have a serious talk," Scott said.

"Shoot," Patrick said. "I'll answer any question you got."

"When Theo said, 'You'll never have her,' or whatever it was he said that night, was he talking about Mandy or Ava?" Scott asked him.

"I don't remember exactly what he said," Patrick said. "It all sounded like typical Theo bullshit to me. He hit on Mandy because he knew it irritated me, and everyone knows he had a thing for Ava a long time ago."

"Did Theo know you and Ava were involved?" Scott asked.

"I was cut out of one of those pictures he had of her; it was taken through her bedroom window. So I would say, yeah, he knew. I burned it up in the trash barrel out back of the fire station the night you tried to arrest Maggie."

"Did he ever threaten to reveal the affair?"

"No, but I wouldn't have cared if he did. The only reason it's a secret is because Ava wants it that way. If it were up to me she would get an annulment, marry me, and what anyone else thinks be damned."

"So he couldn't blackmail you."

"Hell no. Besides, he could hardly use a photo he'd taken that way, could he? He'd be arrested for invading her privacy."

"Maybe he couldn't bring himself to do anything that would hurt her."

"Except leaving her that money is as good as claiming they were involved, at least as far as the whole town is concerned. That's hurting her."

"But it's also providing security to her and the kids."

"It's hard for me to believe the bastard didn't have a nugget of coal where his heart should be, but maybe he really loved her. I don't know, and I don't care."

"He must have really hated you, though. If he knew you and Ava were having this affair, why didn't he try to sabotage it somehow? Seems like it would have eaten him up inside to know you had what he wanted. It wasn't like Theo to let something like that go unpunished."

"He bought the building next door to this one, the one everyone knew I wanted to buy so we could expand this place. Theo outbid me by some ridiculous amount and then put a price tag on it he knew no one would or could pay, so it sits there empty. That might have been his revenge, a way of taking something I wanted away from me."

"But he never got into it with you directly. Physically, I mean."

"He was always telling me he'd like to kick my ass, but when I'd say, 'come on then' he was afraid to throw the first punch. I've never beat the hell out of anybody like I did Theo when we were kids. I really lost it that day. He knew after that I wasn't afraid of him."

"Brad came and got me," Scott said. "When I got there Theo was holding Sean under the water. Brad and I tried to stop him, but Theo was too big. He broke my nose and punched Brad in the stomach, knocked the wind out of him."

"Ava came and got me," Patrick said. "I got there right when he broke your nose. I thought he'd drowned Sean. I don't remember everything that happened after that."

"When Theo saw you coming, he tried to get away, but the water slowed him down. While you whooped his ass, Ava and I pulled Sean out of the lake. Brad ran to the lodge to get help."

"Just think, if I'd killed Theo that day, Brad would be here now, and I would have saved everyone so much aggravation."

"But you'd be in jail."

"I was underage. I might have got away with it."

The two men were silent for a while, remembering that day.

"Did you ever confront Theo about burning down Maggie's house?" Scott asked.

"I told him I believed he did it, that everyone believed he did it, and as soon as I had proof I was coming for him. But I trusted Chief Estep and he said it was electrical, so I couldn't justify going after Theo."

"Maggie said Theo had photos he may have used to blackmail Eric Estep. That's probably why the poor man blew his brains out a year later."

"I burned up those photos too, in case you wondered."

"If it's not directly connected to Theo's death, I'm not officially interested, but Sarah would be. I hope you will remember if she questions you to only answer the questions she asks, and not to volunteer any additional information."

"Don't worry, I'm not that stupid. Besides, she's already been in to see me, and she was more interested in where I'd be when she got off work than where I was when Theo got killed."

"She's pretty aggressive."

"She seems like a scratcher and a biter. I'd watch out if I were you."

"Don't worry, I'm not stupid either."

"Ian's gonna be here in about ten minutes. Unless you want him sticking his nose in, you better wrap this up."

"Just one more thing; I know you know where Brian is. Have you been in contact with him?"

"No. He might as well be dead as far as I'm concerned. He broke our mother's heart and left Ava and the kids. How could someone raised the same as me do something like that? I hope he never comes back, and if he knows what's good for him, he won't."

"No chance he came back and killed Theo, then."

"No way. My brother Brian is a weak man. When the going gets tough, he runs away."

"Why do you think he left?"

"I think Theo had something on him, something he couldn't face. I think Theo paid him to go, and those loan papers were a cover-up."

"You saw Sean's letters."

"Yeah, and I know they weren't written to Gwyneth."

"Maggie still thinks so."

"I'm not going to be the one to tell her any different. I don't care, you know. I'm not that big a jerk. I don't understand it, but Sean's a good guy, and he's the only decent brother I've got left. I think those guys are probably born that way, and there's nothing they can do about it."

"Theo held those letters over Sean's head so he wouldn't tell anyone Theo was the last one with Brad before he died."

"The more I find out about that prick, the more I think we should thank whoever did kill him."

"You were one of the last people to see him alive," Scott said. "Although Sarah doesn't seem too interested in solving the case, you're probably still on her list of suspects. She may not be telling me because she knows how close I am to your family."

"What can I tell ya? I didn't do it, but everyone knows I think he deserved it."

"I wish you had a better alibi."

Patrick shrugged, and Scott got up to leave. When he was halfway to the door, Patrick stopped him.

"I can tell you this," Patrick said. "If it'd been me taking a bat to him, there wouldn't have been enough left of him to ID."

Scott looked around the bar, empty except for him and Patrick.

"Please don't say that to anyone else," he said and left.

When Scott got back to the station, he called Maggie and asked her if she knew about any rumors regarding Margie and the mail.

"Everyone knows Margie snoops in the mail, Scott. Where have you been?"

Scott remembered Mamie claiming Margie stole her *National Geographic* magazines. He spent a couple hours

225

in the files, looking for complaints about the mail, the post office, or Margie, and found plenty in files dated before he came to work there. Put together, there was a damning amount of evidence suggesting Margie had been "tampering" with the mail for many years, and so far, had got away with it.

The complaints included things missing and assumed stolen, like magazine subscriptions and mail ordered items; mail that had obviously been opened and re-sealed; and in one complaint Margie was overhead sharing confidential information she couldn't have known unless she'd read a certified letter before the intended party received it. In one kind of humorous incident, she had been accused of switching envelopes so that a sexy lingerie catalog went to Father Stephen at his office address, and the person meant to receive the catalog got a religious magazine.

More serious, though, was the fact that it was Margie who provided the evidence which sent Willy Neff to prison.

Scott went straight to the Rose and Thorn to confront Ian Fitzpatrick about what he'd found. The old man was offended at being questioned and told him it was all just "women's gossip" and nothing more.

"Her father was a war hero, did you know that?" Ian said. "Eric Estep had a Purple Heart, shrapnel in his leg, and was fire chief of this town before you were a gleam in your mother's eye!"

Scott was familiar with the stone wall which was formed out of Ian's personal prejudices, especially where friends and family were concerned.

"We were in a war together," Ian told Scott, as the younger man stood to leave. "I won't have you dragging his good name through the mud."

Ian and Scott had been the first police officers on the scene after Eric was found, in his office at the fire station, having blown most of his head off with a shotgun.

It was Scott's first year working in Rose Hill, and his first violent death as well, and he still had nightmares about it.

If Eric left a suicide note, Scott wouldn't know. He was out in the hallway puking his guts out while Ian, and Malcolm Behr, Eric's second in command, rearranged the scene to make it look like the accident it was later claimed to have been. Before his retreat to the hallway, Scott had seen what was left of Eric and the position of the gun and knew better, but dutifully supported Ian's official determination.

Scott fumed as he walked down to the post office to confront Margie. He knew he shouldn't undertake any sort of questioning when he was this angry, but he wanted her to know he was onto her, to put her on notice he would not tolerate this kind of thing just because she was the daughter of a local war hero and the former fire chief.

Margie saw Mrs. Crawford give Theo the card, and could easily have plucked the card and photo out of the trash. If a sentimental gesture from a kind woman could be made to look like a death threat, what other horrible things had Margie done no one knew about?

Did Willy really order the pictures that put him in prison, or had Margie just made it look as though he did? Mrs. Crawford told Scott Margie used to be sweet on Willy when they were younger. Had Margie's accusation actually been revenge for his romantic rejection?

Scott was angry with Margie and angry with Ian for protecting her. He had to admit the special treatment he resented Ian for giving out was really no different from what he was doing for the Fitzpatricks in Theo's murder investigation. He was disgusted with himself and disappointed in how easily he had been corrupted. Scott felt dirty and felt like cleaning things up. He decided to start with Margie.

Margie wasn't at work, so Scott went to her home, down near the river on Lotus Avenue. Margie's mother, Enid, was alone at home, and it took her a long time to answer the door. Enid had crippling rheumatoid arthritis, and she could do very little for herself. Scott peeked in the window to show her who it was, and she made her painful way out of a recliner and across the room to the door.

On a small pension and social security payments, Enid was obviously dependent on her daughter to support and care for her. Scott was abruptly reminded of all this as the tiny, bent woman wrestled with the lock and the door handle. By the time she managed to open the door, Scott's face was burning over having caused her so much pain and effort. He should have called first.

Enid smiled up at Scott and asked him in. The house was small, hot, and smelled like camphor and mentholated ointment mixed with talcum powder, but there was also an undercurrent of body odor. He tried breathing through his mouth, and it helped a little.

Enid was dressed in several layers, including a housedress, tan-colored woolen tights, oversize boiled wool slippers, and a heavy wool cardigan topped off by a kind of apron vest like one Scott remembered his own grandmother wearing. Her white hair, what there was of it, was scraped back into a small bun, no bigger than a button mushroom, on the back of her head. She had droopy, red-rimmed, faded blue eyes, and the sagging skin of a woman who had once been much fuller figured, but who had lost a great amount of weight. Her hands were knotted and curled inward, and Scott imagined her feet looked much the same.

"Is your daughter home?" he asked.

"Mary Margaret is at the grocery store," she said.

It took Scott a moment to realize she wasn't talking about Maggie; Margie was a "Mary Margaret" too. Enid offered to fix him a cup of tea or a snack, and he refused politely, apologizing for making her come to the door.

"Well, when you see it's the police you can't ignore it," she said. "I was afraid you'd come to tell me something had happened to my daughter."

Scott cringed inwardly at having also caused this worry on top of the physical strain.

She shuffled her way back to her recliner and gingerly seated herself. She was watching a game show on a tiny black and white TV.

"What'd you want with Mary Margaret?" she asked him.

"I have a question about the mail," he said.

"Well, she's the expert on that, all right," Enid laughed. "She's been working there for over twenty years now."

"How are you doing?"

"I'm fair to middling," she said. "This gettin' old is for the birds."

"Happens to all of us," Scott said because he didn't know what else to say.

"The Home Health girl brought a kitten to visit me a few weeks ago."

She gestured to a calendar pinned to the dark wood paneling near her chair, where January featured a gray and white kitten playing with a pink ribbon.

"It was a pretty little thing, yellow and white striped. I wish I could keep a cat," she told Scott. "But I'm too old for it now. Eric never liked cats. He liked those big old red dogs like Fitz always had; what are they called?"

Fitz always had a big, shaggy, ginger-colored dog, like Lazy Ass Laddie.

"Irish Setters?"

"Them's the ones," she said, clicking her false teeth as she talked. "He always had one of those awful dogs running 'round here, digging up my flowers, and lifting a leg over everything. I wouldn't let a dog in my house any further than the kitchen, so Eric would sit out there with it and smoke his pipe every evening."

Scott nodded appreciatively.

"You wouldn't have believed how that man cried after those animals when they passed. And each time he would swear he'd not get another, and it wouldn't be any time at all but he'd bring home a pup, and we'd start all over again. What was I talking about before?"

She looked puzzled and a little fearful.

"The kitten," Scott said. "Home health brought a kitten to visit you."

"Oh yes," she said, beaming at the memory. "Ruthie brought it. Ruthie is June and Pete Wilkerson's girl; you know them?"

"Yes, ma'am."

"She was a nurse in Pittsburgh for a time, but then came back here to look after her mother. June got the cancer, lost her breast, and had the chemo, but she's okay now. Ruthie joined the Home Health, and she works at that old folk's home in Pendleton, too. She comes over a couple times a week to give me a peanut oil massage. You ever have a peanut oil massage?"

"No ma'am," Scott said.

"Well, they're wonderful. If you ever have a chance, you get one. Ruthie gives an excellent massage, and it helps my rheumatism greatly. I seize up so bad in this cold weather. She married Pudge Postlethwaite. Do you know Pudge?"

"Yes, ma'am. We were at school together."

"Did you go to Rose Hill School or that consolidated nonsense over in the county?"

"I went to Rose Hill."

"That was a lovely school," Enid said, leaning back in her chair. "Mary Margaret got a perfect attendance award at graduation."

Scott nodded appreciatively and said, "Did she?" because he couldn't think of anything else to say.

"Mary Margaret is a good daughter," Enid said, and Scott was seized with an irrational fear she had somehow gleaned his intentions for coming over. "I don't know what I would do without her."

She got emotional then and fumbled for a paper tissue pushed up in the sleeve of her cardigan. Scott mumbled something he hoped sounded comforting and wondered if Margie was coming home soon. He was rapidly losing the steam that brought him to their house and now felt more like escaping than confronting her.

"Oh, I love this part,' Enid said and turned up the volume via a remote control the size of a deck of cards. Enid got caught up in her game show so Scott looked around the front room, as he couldn't see the TV screen.

There was a pile of magazines and catalogs in a basket between his chair and the fireplace. For something to do, he picked up a stack and looked through them, and immediately noticed not one of them was addressed to Margie or Enid. Catalogs, he could imagine Margie digging out of the trash as people flung them while sorting their mail, but subscription magazines seemed less likely to be discarded by the people who paid to receive them.

Scott, seeing Enid was focused solely on her television show, quickly went through most of the basket, until he finally came upon a *Consumer Reports* magazine with his own name and address on it. He also found one of Mamie's *National Geographic* magazines.

Scott returned the stack of catalogs and magazines to the basket. How brazen she was! Anyone could see these–the women who came in and helped Enid or the home health nurses. Could she really feel so entitled to do as she pleased with the mail that she didn't care who saw what she took, or who knew? Scott was suddenly overcome with the desire to search the little house for more evidence and wondered how hard it would be to get a search warrant.

"I knew that one," Enid told Scott, referring to the question that won the game. She used the remote, which actually, physically turned the knob which changed the

231

channels, to go to another show, and he realized they didn't have cable, only the three basic stations, and a set of rabbit ears antennae with foil extensions on each end. Scott looked around. The little house was clean and neat as a pin, but everything was sagging, wearing thin or obviously in need of repair.

He thought about how it must be for Enid, trapped in a body that held her prisoner through pain and limited movement, unable to tie her shoes or button her own cardigan, unable to bathe or dress herself; dependent on the kindness of others and the limited medical help she could afford. He thought of his own mother, with his father's good pension, large life insurance check, and a retirement annuity to see her through old age comfortably.

He also thought about Margie, trapped in this house with her mother, night after night, relieved only during the daylight hours when volunteers and home health workers visited while she worked. She would have to be everything to the helpless old woman every evening and all night, every night, for many years to come. If Margie lost her job and was arrested, it might kill Enid. Now that his anger had abated somewhat, Scott saw the ramifications of what he had been about to do.

"You tell Margie I'll come see her tomorrow at work," Scott said abruptly and insisted Enid not get up to see him out.

He made sure the door locked properly behind him and gratefully breathed in deep lungs full of the frigid evening air as he walked away from the little house, crunching through the layer of snow that had frozen in large patches on the sidewalk.

He backtracked and grabbed the snow shovel off Enid's porch, shoveled the path to the sidewalk, and a large swath near the curb. He sprinkled around a thick layer of rock salt, which they kept in a bucket on the porch, even though he thought it was probably too cold for it to work right now. While he did this, he thought about several things he wanted to do. He wanted to go immediately and buy Enid a new color TV, a gift subscription to cable, and a kitten. What he could do was go see his own mother, make sure she was all right, and hug her.

How, he wondered, could he punish Margie, protect the town from her, and yet not destroy Enid in the process?

Scott set off in the direction of his mother's house. The vet's cat Duke was padding out of the alley when Scott passed it, and the cat had a large dead rat in his mouth. Scott nodded to Duke and kept walking, and Duke ran alongside him until they got to Rose Hill Avenue. Scott watched Duke look both ways before he ran across the street.

"Smart boy," Scott complimented him.

When Hannah arrived to feed Theo's dogs and give them their morning exercise, she met a black SUV with government plates coming down the driveway. The windows were tinted so darkly she couldn't see the driver or passengers. Hannah went ahead and fed the dogs, but felt spooked by the fact that the Feds had been there, and hurried her chores. As she left an hour later, she met a county sheriff's car coming up the drive and thought it seemed odd. Shouldn't they have been there first, before the Feds?

She waved at the county driver, whom she knew, and went back down Pine Mountain Road toward town. She was having Drew and Maggie over for dinner and needed to shop for groceries and get home. She stopped at the station to tell Scott about the Feds, and he said he didn't know anything about the bureau being involved.

Sarah arrived at the station soon after Hannah left. She shut the door behind her after she entered Scott's office and declined his invitation to sit.

"I had a couple guys go out to Theo's, and they found the room, but there was nothing in it."

"Oh my," Scott said.

"The house had been ransacked. You know anything about that?"

"Hannah was just in here, and she said she saw a government SUV out there this morning when she was feeding Theo's dogs. Maybe it was them."

"I need to make some calls," she said and hurried out to her car.

She came back scowling and slammed the door to his office after she entered.

"I don't know what kind of game you're trying to play, Chief Gordon, but if you know anything about that room or its contents," she said, "you better tell me now."

Scott felt sick.

"What did they find?" he asked, stalling.

Sarah looked at him hard for several seconds, and Scott felt as if her eyes were boring into his brain, scouring it for what he was hiding.

"Did you call the FBI?" she asked, in a tone that could best be described as armed and dangerous.

"I didn't," he said, relieved to be able to answer honestly. "I told you about it, and you said you'd look into it."

She stared at him a few seconds longer, as if deliberating, before she spoke.

"I called someone I know at the bureau, and he said they received a tip about the safe and its contents, that it contained evidence pertinent to an ongoing federal investigation."

Scott laughed, "You're kidding me, right?"

"This is not funny, Scott," she said. "They're going to request all the information and evidence in this murder investigation be turned over to them. I could be taken off this case any minute."

"Okay," he said. "Got it."

It was probably not the right time to let her know her "confidential" phone call had most likely been listened to by somebody's great-grandmother, who would, in turn, alert the other members of the scanner granny network, and then Hannah.

Scott thought he had a pretty good idea who called the F.B.I., and although he wished he'd been forewarned, he was mostly relieved to have the responsibility for the contents of the safe transferred into their hands, out of his own.

After Sarah left in a huff, a tall, slim, striking young woman entered the station. Dressed in a ski parka and skintight ski pants, she had dark eyes and long, gleaming black hair. Skip fell all over himself to get to the desk to see if she needed help, but she asked for Scott.

"Yvonne?" he guessed, and her brilliant smile rewarded him for being correct. He could easily see why Mitchell was drowning his sorrows and singing outside her building.

Once seated in the break room, Yvonne flipped her silky dark hair over her shoulders, crossed her long legs and smiled again, revealing straight white teeth.

"Bethany said you were looking for someone who saw anything unusual the night Mitchell got arrested," she said. "I didn't see anything, but my boyfriend Price may have seen something."

"Go on," Scott said, reminding himself he should be taking notes instead of wondering if he was old enough to be her father.

"Price goes to George Mason, so he's back in Georgetown now, but he did mention something he saw on the street a little while before Mitchell showed up."

"Tell me more."

"We had friends over, and Price went out for more beer around midnight. The only thing open that late is the Quickie Mart by the interstate, and it was really foggy. I noticed the time because it was taking so long, and I was worried about him. I called him, and we talked most of his way back. When he got back, it was just after 1:00, and he said there was an old beat up truck parked in his spot, in front of the antique store. He said there was a guy sitting in it. He waited a minute to see if the guy was leaving so he could take the space, but the guy just sat there. He said the windows were steamed up so he couldn't see him real well, but there was definitely someone in there. Price drove around the block, but the guy just stayed there, so he got fed up with waiting, parked down the street, and walked back up."

"He didn't hear or see anything else?"

"No," she said. "He wouldn't have noticed the guy except you know how hard it is to find a parking space on a weekend in this town, especially with the snow plows piling up snow in them. You really should do something about that."

"I'll see what I can do," Scott told her.

He was rewarded once again with a beautiful smile.

Scott took her boyfriend's name and number and thanked her for coming in. Skip had combed his hair and put on some potent aftershave while they were in the break room, and Yvonne made his day by telling him he "sure smelled good" and winking at him as she left.

"That, my friend," Scott told the younger man, "is what a heartbreaker looks like."

Skip just looked dreamily after her, and waved enthusiastically when she waggled her fingers good-bye outside the door. He then ran to the front and smashed the side of his face up against the window, so he could watch her walk away.

"Get back to work," Scott told him. "And wash that stink off. You know I don't allow that in here."

"Sure boss," Skip said, but he wasn't listening.

Scott gave Skip the assignment to call the boyfriend to follow up and hoped that would help break the spell.

As soon as he could get Skip peeled off the front window and back to work, Scott jogged down the street to the bookstore. Mitchell was working. He said he didn't remember seeing a truck parked in front of the antique store when he started his serenade, and Scott knew there hadn't been one when he arrived because it was where he had parked the squad car. So now, Scott thought, he had Willy Neff near the scene of the crime at just after 1:00, but gone by 3:00. Willy had to have seen something. He needed to talk this through with someone.

"Where's Maggie?" Scott asked Mitchell.

"She had some errands to run and then she and the vet are going out to Hannah's for dinner," Mitchell told him.

"Maggie and Drew?" Scott said. "What the hell?"

"Remember the bridge," Mitchell told him. "Don't burn your bridge."

"I'm an idiot," Scott told Mitchell. "Never take advice from an idiot."


Sam Campbell checked his phone one last time before disconnecting from the outside world. If one of his clients had an emergency, or if one of the sophisticated and hacker proof firewall systems he created for them was breached, he would receive an automatic text message on his phone, which he kept clipped to his belt.

His wife had invited some people over for dinner, and even though he dreaded what always felt like an intrusion on his privacy, he usually had a good time when all was said and done. The new vet, whom he hadn't met yet, but had heard good things about, was coming with Maggie, whom he was fond of and comfortable with.

He locked up his office and went out to the kitchen, where Hannah was cooking something that smelled wonderful. She had the phone stuck between her shoulder and ear and was saying, "uh huh, uh huh," at intervals as she tended to several pans on the stove. She acknowledged his presence with a wave of a potholder.

"I'm talking to Claire," she said.

"Tell her to come home," Sam said. "We miss her."

"She's going to Prague," Hannah said. "Where's Prague?"

"Czech Republic," Sam said.

"Where's the Czech Republic?" Hannah asked, but Sam just smiled and shook his head.

Sam got a couple bottles of wine out of the pantry and put them on the table. The dogs were whining at the door, so he put on a jacket and took them out, letting a cold blast of air and some snow in during the process. Even though it was not yet six o'clock, it was dark. The sky was dotted with thousands of bright stars, and the sliver of a new moon was visible in the east. The wind was sharp and shot right down the neck of his coat, so he tightened the collar and flipped up the hood.

He wheeled his chair the length of the walkway to the "dock" by the barn and threw a tennis ball across the meadow. Wally got to it before Jax and trotted back, tail high and wagging. In the barn, the strays barked and whined. The meadow was white with a heavy build-up of snow, the pond was still and shining where it wasn't frozen, and he could see a cat or a fox, he couldn't tell which, darting across the lower end of the fence line near a copse of trees. The mountains surrounding their little valley looked like a dark, undulating wall, encircling their land like a fortress.

Sam threw the ball in the opposite direction, and the dogs shot past him in pursuit. A pain shot through a left foot and ankle he no longer had, but instead of having an emotional reaction, like he once would have, he mentally detached himself and observed it dispassionately, thinking, 'that feels like a cramp in my Achilles tendon.' He didn't judge the feeling, or try to argue with it, or deny it was happening. He stayed with it, and let it be whatever it was.

The feeling faded, and he was able to return his attention to playing with the dogs. It was in this way, this detached, observing, accepting mode that he was able to get through each experience of phantom pain. He used to let them haunt and torment him, and now he let them be. He was still learning to observe and let go, to think 'that's interesting,' as a way to keep moving forward. It worked most of the time.

He did a quick emotional check, like his counselor had taught him, and identified he was worried about how this new person might react to his physical appearance. He reminded himself that whatever happened he could deal with it, and his wife would not invite someone into their home who would offend him. He reminded himself that Hannah needed more people in her life than just him, for her emotional wellbeing, whereas he believed he only needed her.

Sam loved his best friend Patrick, good friends Ed and Scott, and Hannah's family and friends, but unless they reached out to him, he never sought their company. His autonomy and independence meant everything to him, and he meant to keep them for as long as he could. If he let them, his wife, her extended family, and their well-meaning friends would do everything for him, and as much as he appreciated their devotion, Sam saw their willingness to take over as a deadly trap to be avoided at all costs.

He heard the sound of Maggie's VW bug coming over the hill towards the farm and turned around, calling the dogs back. They ran barking past him, up the drive to meet her car, tails wagging in a happy greeting.

Maggie had picked up Drew at his house and tried to avoid looking at the property she owned where her house had burned down. She didn't go out there much, as there was no reason to. Theo had offered to buy it many times, and although she had no plans for it, she always told him she would be damned if she let him get his filthy hands on it.

She beeped the horn instead of going to his door, as it was just too cold to do the reverse chivalry thing, and he ran out almost immediately. She quickly cleaned off the passenger seat and threw everything in the back. He got in, and Maggie could smell his particular personal smell, a mixture of disinfectant from the veterinary clinic, soap, and laundry detergent. It didn't have anything like the effect Scott's smell had on her. Primarily, Drew smelled clean.

Maggie liked the look of him, though. Hannah described him as "crunchy granola," due to the longish brown hair and sideburns, and the mountain hiker/biker outfits he wore. Tonight he had on a heavy wool sweater, a denim shirt, and faded olive colored pants. Maggie thought his face looked open and honest, with grayish green eyes and a goofy smile, and she also noticed he had a crooked eyetooth when he smiled. He seemed a little shy, but earnest somehow. He had, as Hannah liked to refer to the qualities of honesty, integrity, and helpfulness, "that Boy Scout thing."

"How do you like your house?" she asked, as she turned her car around in her old driveway.

"It's pretty crappy," he said.

"Maybe we can find you something better."

There was not much real estate available in Rose Hill, and students snapped up the year 'round rentals, subletting to tourists each summer. There were slumlords like Theo who charged exorbitant rental rates to students and tourists for falling down firetraps, and there were occasionally houses for sale, but someone usually had to die for property to come available for sale.

Due to Rose Hill's proximity to the ski resorts, more and more people from outside were buying up houses in the area to use as vacation homes. This drove the housing prices up, which drove the property taxes up, which would eventually make Rose Hill too expensive for local people. They had watched this happen in Glencora, and then the towns surrounding it, and now the "rich tourist effect" was rolling down the mountain toward smaller towns, like a slow-motion economic avalanche.

Maggie thought about the empty space on the second floor of her own building, across the hall from her apartment, which held overstock and junk. She had considered renovating and renting it out, but she wasn't sure she wanted anyone in her building with her. What if they had loud sex every night or partied every weekend, or worst of all, wanted to hang out with her all the time? She shuddered at the thought.

"I'm hoping whoever inherits it will be willing to do some work on it," Drew said.

Maggie turned right at the end of Possum Holler and went down Peony Street to Rose Hill Avenue, where she turned right again.

"That would be Gwyneth or Caroline, his sisters," Maggie informed him. "Gwyneth is a bit of a pill, but Caroline's all right."

Drew shifted in his seat, so he was facing her.

"I've been looking forward to this all week," Drew said. "It seems like every time you and I get a chance to talk we get interrupted."

"That's my fault," Maggie said. "There never seems to be enough hours in the day for all I have to do. Plus, I can never tell anyone in my family 'no' when they ask for something. In case you haven't noticed, the Fitzpatrick family owns every other business in this town. At least it seems like it."

"Tell me about your family. Hannah says you have three brothers, but I only know Patrick."

"Nope," Maggie said. "Last time we got together I told you my bookstore story. Tonight it's your turn. Why in the world did you buy Owen's practice?"

"Fair enough," Drew said. "The first thing you have to know is the 24-hour veterinary emergency center I worked in was in a tough part of Philly, and it was intense. When I first started, I loved the fast pace and the constant adrenaline rushes. After eight years of it, though, I was feeling pretty burned out.

"I had some money saved, so I decided to take a year off and basically live in a tent. I thought by the end of the year I would know what I wanted to do next. I started in Glencora, during the big bike race last summer. It was July, and you know how great the weather is then."

"During the six weeks of summer we get," Maggie said.

"Exactly," Drew said. "I was living in a tent in the state park, hiking and biking every day, and feeling happier than I had in a long time. I didn't know how miserable I was in my job until I was away from it in such a peaceful, beautiful place."

"Where were you supposed to go next?"

"I was going to meet some friends in Virginia and hike a big piece of the Appalachian Trail, do some white water rafting on the New River, spend a couple months in the Smoky Mountains, and go farther south as it got colder. I planned to spend January, now, that is, in Key West."

Maggie nodded outside at the snow and the night sky and said, "No dockside sunsets here."

"But you have to admit my house is not much better than a tent."

"True. So then?"

"I came down to Rose Hill for provisions and saw a notice on the bulletin board in the grocery store, advertising the vet practice for sale. I decided there was no harm in having a look. It felt like fate, you know?"

Caroline Eldridge was another one who talked about fate and karma, and even if she was dubious, Maggie understood what he meant and nodded.

"I met Owen's wife, Pat, and looked at the practice. She let me examine the books, and it was a small business, but it was turning a profit. I pictured myself living and working in this beautiful place, riding my bike to work, hiking, and canoeing on weekends, and I was hooked. I took what was left of my savings, cashed in some stocks, bought the place, modernized the surgery, and moved here."

"Did your family and friends think you'd lost your mind?" Maggie asked.

Drew laughed and nodded.

"Yeah, pretty much. My parents are MD's, and so are both my sisters, so when I went to vet school instead of med school that was their first clue I wasn't going to toe the family line. When I decided to take a year off, they all thought I would come back afterward and go to med school. Then after two weeks, I did this instead." He waved to indicate the snowy landscape outside. "I'm sure they thought I'd had a breakdown of some sort."

Maggie eyed him curiously.

"And had you?"

Drew looked away from Maggie, out the window, and answered with a shrug.

"I wanted to make a big change in my life, to simplify it, and to have some peace and quiet in order to think."

"So what do you think now?"

"I like the practice and the people, and even if I'm not a 'local,' everyone has been kind to me if a little reserved."

"They're waiting to see if you stay or not," Maggie said. "If you last through a couple winters then they'll start thinking about warming up to you."

"We'll see, I guess," he said. "I have to tell you when the leaves fell and the snow started flying in October, I thought it was beautiful."

Maggie laughed.

"You didn't know you wouldn't see green grass again until May."

"It sometimes feels like winter will never end," he said, and he sounded so forlorn Maggie's heart went out to him.

"Well, most people here don't have it snowing inside their houses," she said. "That's probably why it's harder on you."

As they drove down the long driveway toward Sam and Hannah's house, the dogs ran out to greet them, and Maggie could see Sam not far behind.

"Did you know Sam's in a wheelchair?" Maggie asked Drew.

"No," Drew said. "What happened?"

"War," was all Maggie said and Drew surmised the rest.


Sam prided himself on making accurate, instant assessments of people, and his initial impression of Drew was of an intelligent, soft-spoken man who was definitely attracted to Maggie. Drew kidded around with Hannah in a way that connoted only friendship and nothing more. Sam had been a little concerned at how much "Drew says," he had heard from his wife since the new vet arrived in town, but now that he could see them interact, he decided he could rest easy.

Drew was mostly focused on Maggie, and Sam watched him draw her out with questions and defer to her opinion about whatever they were discussing during dinner. Hannah was a merciless matchmaker, and he could see she was overly pleased with herself on this night.

Earlier, she told Sam her goal for the evening was to convince Drew to stay in Rose Hill, and if a romance with Maggie was what it took, then so be it. Sam felt sorry for Scott, but he was familiar with the ruthlessly fickle ways of women.

Sam thought Maggie could do much worse. Drew was intelligent and funny, with a dry, quick wit he could appreciate. His attention was making Maggie feel warm and flattered, Sam could tell, but not bombarded or manipulated. Having battled with depression over the years, Sam thought he could recognize the signs in other people. Maggie had been sad for a long time, and it was good to see her relax and enjoy herself.

Hannah carried on, like she usually did, and made it easy for everyone to laugh and have a good time. Sam was quiet and observant, but when he asked Drew some questions about his office technology, Hannah threw a roll at him.

"Don't start that!" Hannah protested. "If you let him, Drew, he will lure you into his gingerbread house of technology, fatten you up on gigabytes and megabytes, and we will never see you again."

Sam smiled ruefully and let Hannah change the subject.

The subject of Drew's appalling living conditions came up, and they brainstormed about possible alternatives.

"It will be months before the estate is settled," Sam advised. "I wouldn't count on Gwyneth or Caroline to save you."

"I think Mamie has a garage apartment some staff used to live in," Hannah said. "It's full of junk now, but we could clean it up. I'll get on that first thing tomorrow."

"If I could work out a decent place to live," he said, "I'd love to stay." Sam noticed he started his statement looking at Hannah but ended it looking at Maggie.

When Hannah brought up Theo's murder, Drew told them all about the dog breeding scam, and although they already knew about it, they were careful to act surprised.

"Who do you think killed him?" Hannah asked Drew, who shrugged.

"I haven't a clue. It's some real serious karma for whoever did. I wouldn't want murder on my conscience."

"You and his sister have a lot in common," Maggie said, and then proceeded to tell Drew about Caroline's philosophies and her charitable work.

Sam watched amused as Hannah tried to steer the conversation back to Theo's murder and away from Caroline, Drew's stint in the Peace Corps, global warming, and third world hunger, with no success.


Maggie and Hannah cleared the table and washed dishes while Sam took Drew out to see the kennel and feed the 'prisoners.' Hannah asked Maggie if she had heard anything new about Theo's murder, and Maggie got her caught up on what she knew from talking to Scott.

Mentioning Scott made Maggie feel a little disloyal for enjoying Drew's attention so much, but then she reminded herself she and Scott were not a couple, and he had been spending plenty of time with Sarah lately.

Hannah told Maggie about seeing the Feds up at Theo's lodge, before the county sheriff's car arrived.

"I got a call from one of my scanner grannies this evening," Hannah said.

"What's going on?"

"Tiny Trollop, our crime-fighting kitten, was sitting out in front of the police station today, making phone calls."

"Silly kitten."

"She was calling someone at the Federal Bureau of Investigations."

"Well-connected kitten!"

"Quite. Seems little Sarah was not too happy about the FBI cleaning out the safe before her boys got there."

"They took everything?"

"Evidently."

Maggie felt a little sick at her stomach. She hoped they covered their tracks well enough.

"Anything else?"

"Whoever it was she called said the Feds are going to take over the case because they think it may be connected to a larger investigation they have going on."

"Damn."

"I know."

"So somebody we don't know may have killed Theo over what we found in the safe."

"Somebody important, maybe."

"What does Sam say?"

"That I shouldn't worry."

"Are you worried?"

"No, not really. Think about it. The county people didn't know what was up there, so they can't know anything was taken before the feds got there. We had on gloves, so we didn't leave any prints, and we had a perfectly legitimate reason to be up there, taking care of those dogs. Which reminds me, I have got to find homes for those dogs."

Maggie handed Hannah the next dish to dry. She wasn't so convinced they were in the clear, but she wanted Hannah to be right.

"I can think of a dozen hunters in this town who would jump at the chance to work with one of those dogs."

Hannah wiped the plate and shook her head.

"The problem with that is they were all bred to hunt, but none of them actually has. They might all be gun-shy and impossible to housebreak."

Maggie washed and rinsed the pans, and then handed them one by one to Hannah.

"Mom and Dad would take one, as long as it got along with Lazy Ass Laddie, and you know Ed loves dogs."

"Ed's a one-dog man, and he recently got that black lab. Let's see what happens this week. Maybe Willy will sober up and come back, and then he can take care of them out there."

Maggie stopped what she was doing and put her head close to Hannah's.

"Can I say something completely horrible?"

"Always," said Hannah. "In fact, I demand that you do."

"I hope Willy never comes back, and if it's because he's dead, I won't be sorry."

Hannah bumped her friend's shoulder and nodded.

"Lots of people feel the same way, not just you. Don't feel bad."


On the way back to town, Maggie felt shy and backward being alone with Drew. He, on the other hand, was in a great mood, telling Maggie all about the camping, hiking, biking, and whitewater rafting he planned to do with friends over the summer. One of the vets he used to work with was going to come down to cover his practice for a few weeks so he could take a vacation.

"You should come, too," he said to Maggie.

"Oh no," Maggie said. "My idea of roughing it is staying in a motel that doesn't have a restaurant attached."

"No, you'd love it, I know you would."

Maggie, who was not kidding, knew what it was like and knew she would hate every minute of it. Gabe had finally quit begging her to go fishing with him after she accidentally on purpose knocked a coffee can full of live bait into the water as they loaded the canoe.

"I really don't think you want me along," she said. "I burn to a crisp after five minutes in the sun, I hate bugs, and I'm not a big fan of either blisters or sweating."

He hardly seemed to hear her, and instead regaled her with tales of hikes he'd gone on in the past. Maggie was reminded of how men only seem to hear what they want to hear. She listened to him go on and on and tried to seem interested.

When she stopped the car in front of his house, he said, "Thanks for the great evening," leaned over, and kissed her. Maggie was surprised, but it was a pleasant experience.

"I had fun too," she said when he stopped.

"Come over tomorrow night," he said, "and I'll cook dinner."

"Sure," Maggie said, a little buzzed from the kissing.

"Okay then, see you tomorrow," he said and got out of the car.

Maggie was glad it was dark enough so that the instant hot flash she knew was making her cheeks burn was not easily detected. She drove home feeling fizzy and girly, smiling and giggling to herself like an idiot.

She parked in the alley behind her building and when she got out of the car, saw Duke running by with some small, unfortunate rodent clamped in his jaws.

"Your landlord's home now, Duke, you better get a move on."

Duke kept on at a trotting pace and didn't waver from his path.

Maggie let herself in the back stairwell and locked the door behind her. From this small alcove, she could walk up the back stairs to the hall outside her apartment or go on through to the bookstore. Someone had shoved a note under the back door, and she stepped on it with snowy, wet boots before she saw it, stuck to the bottom of her right foot. She shook off her gloves and picked it up, holding it under the stairwell light to read.

"Call me when you get home," was written on it, and it was signed "S" for Scott.

Maggie instantly felt deflated, guilty, and irritated. She sat on the small folding chair she kept by the door and pulled her boots off, then took her coat and scarf off and hung them on a hook.

She put on the slippers she had left by the back door earlier, disarmed the security system, and slipped through a connecting door to the bookstore, which was closed and dark, with only a few lights left on for security. She went to the front counter and reached over it to retrieve the daily sales log, to see how they'd done during the day, and the number was good. Ski season was always good for business, there was plenty of snow, and now that the students were back, they used the café to meet friends, study, and keep fueled with espresso and coffee drinks.

Maggie was too wound up to go to bed. She wanted a few minutes to try to regain the sweet feeling she'd had with Drew before she saw Scott's note. She knew Scott was probably out walking around, keeping an eye on her apartment for a light to go on. She wasn't ready to let go of the happy, romantic feeling Drew's company had provided in order to re-enter the complicated world of whatever it was she felt about Scott.

They were friends, and if they both could undergo some sort of personality transplant, maybe they could be more. Right now, though, it seemed too difficult. There was a physical attraction that was too strong to deny, but there was also what seemed like too much history, and what Maggie believed were unrealistic expectations on his part. They talked around it sometimes, but they didn't talk about it, and it left things between them feeling, Maggie thought, 'unfinished,' for lack of a better word.

Maggie leaned back against the counter and closed her eyes, going back over the events of the evening, ending with Drew's kiss, and felt her face flush again at the memory. She wanted this feeling. She wanted a new romance untainted by the past or tangled up in family relationships. Drew seemed like a genuinely nice man, and he was interested in her. Why couldn't it be that simple?

Maggie knew why, and suddenly felt she was doomed to sabotage any new romantic possibility. She heard a noise, turned, and saw Scott framed in the window of the front door, watching her. She felt her blood run hot throughout her entire body, not in the tame way Drew's kiss made her feel, but in a runaway train way that frightened her and made her heart pound. They looked at each other for a few moments, and then she walked forward to unlock the door.

"Hey," he said, as she opened the door.

Maggie backed up to let him in, and with the first whiff of his particular personal smell, she forgot Drew completely. Somewhere inside her, when her defenses were down and Scott was near, a fire blazed into life, and the heat was almost unbearable.

She locked the door behind him. She was not quite able to meet his gaze, which she could feel boring into her.

"Do you want some coffee or tea?" she asked him, gesturing toward the café side.

"No," he said quietly.

It seemed like he was trying to read her mind and succeeding. She felt an immediate need to put a physical barrier between them. She quickly crossed to the other side of the store, went behind the café counter, and filled the hot water pot. When she turned around, he was sitting at the counter, still looking at her intently, with a questioning expression on his face.

"What's up?" she said in what she hoped was a light tone.

"Did you have a good time at Hannah's?"

Although she willed it not to with all her heart, her face flushed in what she thought probably looked, even in

251

the dim light, very much like shame. She turned away and made herself busy getting a mug and teabag ready.

"I did have fun. Hannah is campaigning to keep Dr. Drew in town, and we were all brainstorming about finding a decent place for him to live."

"Was that all she's campaigning for?" he asked, and Maggie could hear how miserable he was, as if he could hardly bring himself to ask the question or hear her answer.

It stung her, and she felt horrible for making him feel the same way she felt when she knew he was with Sarah. How could she think she was free to start anything with Drew when she was still so wrapped up in whatever this was with Scott?

"You know Hannah," she said. "It's hard to tell what she's cooking up in that dingy head of hers."

He came around the counter and turned her toward him so fast she was startled. He looked into her eyes for just a moment before he backed her against the counter, took her in his arms, and kissed her. This wasn't a friendly, sweet kiss like Drew's. This was demanding and all-consuming. Her senses reeled as she at first gave in to what her body wanted so badly to do, but then she pushed him away, saying, "I can't do this!"

"You can, Maggie, but you won't," he said. "Gabe's gone and he's not coming back. You need to accept that and get on with your life."

Maggie's face crumpled as she dissolved into tears. Scott's anger seemed to evaporate instantly, and he took her in his arms again, this time gently. Maggie, who rarely cried, and certainly not in front of anyone, willed herself to stop, but the tears kept flowing.

"Why can't we just be friends?" she asked him, as she struggled not to relax into the warmth of his embrace. "Why does everything have to be so complicated?"

He kissed her forehead, her eyebrow, her cheekbone, her neck, and then one corner of her mouth as he rubbed her back.

"It might not be easy," he said. "But it doesn't mean we shouldn't try."

His breath on her face was warm, and his scent was all around her. His hands and lips were so insistent. Maggie felt all her resistance melting away, replaced by a feeling of inevitability, as if she was letting go of the side of a boat she'd been clinging to, slipping under the dark water, sure to drown, but not much caring anymore. It felt so good to give in.

She had just opened her mouth under his to say, "Okay," when someone pounded on the front door of the bookstore, breaking the spell.

Scott cursed and went to the door. He flung it open and Skip almost fell into the store.

"Cal Fischer found Willy Neff—he drowned in the river!" Skip said.

Scott turned back to Maggie, who was standing in the shadows.

"Go," Maggie said. "You have to go."

"I'll come back if I can," he said. "If it's not too late."

Scott left with Skip, and Maggie locked the door behind him.

"It's already too late," she said.


Out at the farm, Sam was wide-awake, fighting the urge to go down the hall to his office and do some work. He knew he should wait until Hannah fell asleep, lest he incur her wrath.

"I really think they make a cute couple," she said as she got into bed. "And God knows it's about time Maggie got back up on that particular horse."

"Speaking of which..." he said, as he wrapped his arms around her and nuzzled her neck hopefully, but Hannah pushed him back.

"Oh no, Romeo," she said. "You kept me from finishing my chores earlier today, don't you remember?"

Sam grinned and said, "I certainly do remember, but you can't blame a man for trying to get more of a good thing."

Hannah considered him a moment and then laughed.

"You sexy, rotten bastard," she said. "How can I resist that face?"

Sam lunged after her on the bed, making her squeal and laugh.

Afterward, they lay entwined and breathless. Hannah brushed the hair back from her face and said, "I'm hungry."

Sam laughed and rolled over, and as if on cue both dogs jumped up on the bed and settled at the end.

"You think Drew and Maggie did anything?" Sam asked her.

Hannah scoffed at the notion.

"Maggie's like a crock-pot, not a microwave," she said. "He'll have to heat her up in stages."

Hannah yawned, curled up in the crook of Sam's arm, and fell asleep within minutes. Once her breathing slowed, he eased his shoulder out from under her head and moved gingerly to the edge of the bed, where his wheelchair sat waiting.

"Bastard," she said with a yawn, but turned over, hugged her pillow, and fell right back asleep.

"I love you too, honey," Sam said, as he maneuvered himself into his wheelchair, and headed for the office.

Sam had an encrypted e-mail response from his friend who worked for the bureau, thanking him for the tip about Theo's safe. Sam had hesitated before getting the Feds involved, but when Hannah described what was in the safe, he thought everyone would be safer if they had the contents instead of the local sheriff's office. Blackmail was a nasty business, but blackmail involving powerful politicians was especially dangerous.

Volunteer firefighter and certified water rescue diver Calvert Fischer had been rowing his boat, with a dog, a spotlight, and a shotgun, across the Little Bear River at around 11:00 p.m. when he saw something beneath the surface of the water. His plan, when he took the barriers down at the end of Pine Mountain Road and backed his boat into the river, was to hunt down and shoot a ten-point buck he'd seen earlier, feeding on the opposite bank. When he realized he was looking at the reflection of his spotlight on the submerged windshield of a small pickup truck, those plans changed instantly.

The truck was facing upriver, held in place underwater by the current pushing it against a dam built to control water flow just below town.

Cal quickly rowed back, hauled the boat out, stowed the gun and the dog, woke up his wife, and made the call. By the time Scott and the volunteer fire department's recovery crew arrived, Cal was in his wetsuit, smearing petroleum jelly all over his face in preparation for entering the frigid water. They took the rescue boat out and lowered Cal in. Within minutes he was back up, having attached a towing chain to the front axle of the truck. Curtis Fitzpatrick was waiting on the shore with the wrecker to pull it out.

By the time someone from the county morgue picked up Willy's body, it was past two in the morning. Everyone was frozen and exhausted, but Cal asked Scott if he would come inside his house so he could have a word. Cal changed into warm, dry clothing, his wife Sue made coffee, and the two men sat in the kitchen at the table, where Cal told his tale.

"Let me get this straight," Scott said quietly afterward, but not without a certain amount of anger in his voice. "On the night Theo was murdered, you took the barriers down so you could back your boat into the river, row to the other side, and illegally hunt for out-of-season deer. Then your dog ran off, so you didn't get back home until after two in the morning."

"Yes," Cal said nervously.

"It was closer to 2:30," his wife Sue said. "The fog was so thick I was afraid he was lost in the woods."

Scott continued addressing Cal, his voice level.

"While you had the barriers down, Willy either accidentally or intentionally drove his truck into the river."

"Yes," Cal said. "The barriers are padlocked, and I'm the only one besides the chief who has a key."

"You know how drunk Willy gets," Sue said.

That's no excuse," Cal told his wife. "He'd still be alive if I hadn't taken those barriers down."

"Maybe," Scott said.

"I am so, so sorry, Scott," Cal said, near tears.

"It was an accident," Sue said.

"And you've told me everything?" Scott demanded.

"Everything, honest to God, Scott. I couldn't live with myself telling a lie about a thing like this. I was hunting, and I did leave the barriers down, and I knew it was wrong. If they'd been up, he would've hit them and not gone in the water. He would still be alive."

Cal broke down then and cried into his hands, and it was pitiful to see. Sue rushed to his chair and put her arms around him, comforting him, and turned a pleading look to Scott.

"It was an accident," she cried. "You've got to believe us."

"I do believe you," said Scott. "I'm just trying to figure out what to do about it. For crissakes, Cal, stop crying."

"Are you going to arrest me?" Cal asked him, hiccupping slightly, and Scott felt his anger evaporate, replaced by irritation at the difficult place in which Cal had put him.

Cal's English setter looked back and forth from his master to Scott with sad, pleading eyes. Cal's wife went back to hovering in the doorway to the kitchen, wringing her hands.

"Does anyone else know about this?" Scott asked him.

"No, I haven't told anybody but you and Sue."

He started to cry again, but in more of a nose-running than a tears-running way.

"Okay. Here's what happened," Scott said, as he handed Cal his handkerchief. "Last Saturday you took your dog for a run on the other side of the river, he took off, and you got lost in the fog, period. Don't mention deer, don't mention guns, none of that stuff. You did leave the barriers down, which you will confess to your boss, and for which he will punish you accordingly. Malcolm Behr is a fair man, and he probably will not fire you for that. Tonight you took your dog across for a run again, God only knows why when he ran off the last time, but that was all you were doing when you saw the truck. Got it?"

"Thank you, Scott. I'd lose my job if I got arrested," the big man said and started weeping again. Cal's day job was as a security guard at the power plant in the next county.

"All right," Scott said, standing up. "No one's arresting you, but for God's sake don't let the game warden catch you hunting anything out of season. He hates me and your boss, and would love nothing better."

Cal's wife ran over, hugged Scott, and kissed his cheek, saying "thank you" repeatedly.

"He won't do it again," she said. "I'll make sure of it."

Scott's head started to hurt as he left Cal's house. What in the hell had happened to put Willy in the river and Theo dead in the vet's office? Had Willy been dead before he hit the river, or did he drown? Was it suicide, an accident, or murder? He would have to wait until the county did a post-mortem to find out.

Whatever happened to Willy, at least he knew it happened between just after 1:00 a.m., when Yvonne's boyfriend Price saw the truck, and 2:30 a.m., when Cal put the barriers back up. Scott still could not imagine someone as small and weak as Willy killing Theo, from a standing position, with a single blow to the back of the head. However, he may have seen who did do it and paid for it with his life.

When he got to the corner of Pine Mountain Road and Lotus Avenue, he saw Duke sitting on top of his SUV, which was parked by the side of the road.

"Are you following me?" Scott asked him, but the big tabby cat hopped down and ran up the railroad tracks behind the glassworks.

"If you're one of those crime-solving cats, please feel welcome to jump in at any time," Scott called after him, but Duke disappeared into the darkness.

# Chapter Nine - Saturday

Maggie struggled up from a deep sleep to find sunlight streaming through her front room windows and down the hallway outside her bedroom. She jumped up with a start, wondering how she could have overslept. The clock showed 8:47 as the time, and she could hear plenty of activity on the street from her front room windows.

After Scott left the night before, she went upstairs to her apartment feeling so unnerved, both half-hoping and half-fearing he would return. She couldn't decide if she would let him in or not, and the anxiety over her indecision made her feel sick at her stomach. She lay awake for a long time, and when she did sleep, she had disturbing dreams.

She felt her forehead now, and it felt hot.

'I must be ill,' she thought. 'I might be coming down with something.'

It felt to Maggie as if Scott was all around her, that her personal space was no longer her own. It was a feeling she had not experienced in a while, and in this instance, it felt like an invasion. She half-liked it, but it also made her feel a little nauseated; that couldn't be good. She dreaded the day ahead.

She dialed the store number, and Jeanette answered, "Little Bear Books," in a friendly voice.

"Oh Jeanette, thank goodness, is everything okay?"

"We figured you had a late night. Don't worry; everything's fine down here, no reason to rush. Jonah's here with me, Mitchell and Kirsten are in the café, and everything is under control. Mamie's already been in, complained about the romance selection, and gone again. Take a day off, for Pete's sake! I'll take the deposit when I go to lunch."

Maggie was relieved but embarrassed and hung up the phone thinking maybe she would take the day off. She didn't feel at all well. Maybe she was getting the flu.

She called her mother to apologize for not bringing her a cappuccino, and her mother brushed her off.

"You don't have to do that every day. I am perfectly capable of brewing myself a cup of coffee."

Maggie said she would go over to the house and feed her father and grandfather lunch at noon, but her mother cut her off.

"I'll have Patrick do it; he'll be there anyway. Honestly, Mary Margaret, you don't have to wait on us hand and foot. We're not helpless. We can survive one day without your services."

Maggie hung up, feeling reprimanded and in the wrong for no good reason.

The phone rang, and it was Hannah.

"Good morning, sleeping beauty," she chirped, and then in a lower tone, "are you alone?"

"Yes," barked Maggie, a little louder than she meant to.

"Don't bite my head off," Hannah said. "I'm downstairs, can I come up?"

"Of course, sorry," Maggie replied and opened the door to the central hallway before she retreated to the bathroom to try to regroup.

Hannah had a key to the downstairs door, so she let herself in and ran up, calling, "Morning, Sunshine!"

Hannah closed the apartment door behind her and went down the long hallway back to the kitchen to make Maggie a cup of tea. She had purchased a large cup of strong coffee with extra sugar and cream in it for herself, so she sat her cup on the chrome and Formica dinette table, then filled the kettle and put it on the gas ring, turning it to high.

By the time Maggie appeared, standing in the doorway, still in her robe and slippers, with wild looking hair and a cranky look on her face, Hannah was steeping some English Breakfast tea for her.

"You know if I had a kitchen like this I would stay home and cook all day every day," Hannah said.

"You'd go stark raving mad after three days," Maggie said. "Like a bee in a jar."

"And you don't use a tenth of it," Hannah continued, ignoring her friend's response. "It's a shame really."

Maggie gestured to it all, saying, "Take it, then. I could survive with a toaster and an electric kettle."

"I can't imagine what it took to get it all up here," Hannah said as if she was seriously considering the offer, "let alone getting it back down."

Maggie shuffled to the French doors that led to her small iron balcony and noted the bright blue sky and the few puffy white clouds. Several blackbirds were sitting on the telephone wire between a utility pole and her building, swaying in the wind. The whole town woke up and got going without her; why was that such a shock?

"The forecast is for one hell of a storm tonight," Hannah said. "You'd never know it to look at it now."

Maggie just grunted and wandered around the kitchen, poking around in drawers, looking for a hair clip.

"Well, don't you look like someone who was kept up late doing goodness knows what," Hannah said. "Confess! You've had your way with that nice young man, haven't you?"

Maggie pulled her hair back into a wild, messy twist and clipped it with a big barrette she found in a drawer by the sink.

"Certainly not," she said, cocking a stern eyebrow at her cousin as she sat down at the table across from her. "I left him in the same chaste condition in which I found him."

"That's a pity," Hannah said. "You could use a good roll in the hay."

Maggie thought of how nearly she had rolled on the café floor with Scott the night before, and her face felt hot.

"You did do something," Hannah accused with a wagging finger. "You're blushing."

"Drew gave me a perfectly nice kiss, thanked me for a lovely evening, and that was that."

"He didn't stick his tongue down your throat or slobber all over your face, did he?" Hannah asked. "Cause you don't look too impressed."

"No," Maggie said. "It was short and sweet. It was very nice."

"That's the end of that, I guess," Hannah said.

"Why do you say that? I like him. He's cooking me dinner tonight."

"Look, I want you to be happy, and Drew's a great guy, but if the first kiss doesn't steam up your windows, nothing else he does will, either."

"You don't know that," Maggie said in a cross tone. "I hate when you do that. I don't want to talk about it anymore. Let's change the subject."

They talked about Willy Neff being found in his truck in the river, and as awful as it was, neither could drum up much sympathy.

"I've got to go to Pendleton to pick up some new prisoners," Hannah said. "And since I know what you love most in the world besides chocolate cake and root beer is a pepperoni roll from the IGA in Pendleton, I thought you might want to ride along."

She looked hopefully at Maggie, who she could tell was about to say no. Hannah jumped in again before she could.

"I talked to Jeanette, the bookstore is covered, and we can take care of Bonnie, Grandpa Tim, and Fitz before we go."

Maggie pointed a finger at Hannah.

"Hah! My mother informed me this morning that she doesn't need me waiting on her hand and foot," Maggie said. "And what's more, the sainted Patrick can take care of Grandpa Tim and Fitz."

"Then there's no reason not to go," Hannah said. "C'mon! Can't you just taste the pepperoni grease soaked up by the warm, squishy roll?"

Maggie gestured to her hair, saying, "I need a shower, and you know this bird's nest takes at least an hour to be put right."

Hanna looked at the tangled, semi-matted mess on Maggie's head, and nodded her head in agreement.

"Okay, how about this? You take a quick shower. I will get the special comb and carefully, ever so tenderly detangle this wild wig of yours while your highness sips your tea, and if I can make it look presentable, we can go."

Maggie sighed deeply and went to take a shower.

"You know, most people would love to have this hair," Hannah said fifteen minutes later, as she started the detangling process from the bottom, using a wide-tooth comb. "It's a gorgeous color, and people pay a lot of money for this kind of curl."

Maggie winced and groaned as Hannah worked the tangles out.

"It's not hair, it's an affliction," Maggie said, "and 'most people' can have it."

"Everything you have going for you, which most people would feel blessed with, you consider a curse," Hannah said. "You are the most contrary person I know."

"Don't lecture me," Maggie said. "I have a mother for that."

A half-hour later they left the bookstore just as Scott was walking down the street toward them. Maggie felt panicked, and her heart raced.

Hannah yelled, "Jinkies! It's the cops! Make a break for it!"

Scott briefly acknowledged Hannah's greeting, but his intense focus was on Maggie, who could see Hannah watching with piqued interest.

"Where are you two off to?" he asked.

Maggie replied, "To Pendleton to pick up some inmates," looking everywhere but at Scott.

He stood directly between Maggie and the passenger side door of Hannah's truck, and Hannah might as well have not been there for all the attention he paid her.

"While you're there," Scott said, "would you mind stopping by the retirement home and talking to Ruthie Postlethwaite about Margie and Enid?"

"Sure," Maggie said, shrugging, but still not making eye contact. "Why?"

"Just to see how they're doing. Remember the thing Lily Crawford mentioned that I asked you about?" he said.

"Oh, yeah," Maggie said. "Will do."

"When will you be back?"

"I don't know. We might go to the city and do some shopping."

It was obvious from her double-take that it was the first Hannah had heard of this plan. Maggie could see her taking note of the body language and palpable tension between Scott and her.

"Call me when you get back," he said. "I'd like to finish the conversation we started last night."

He smiled at Maggie then, in a knowing, intimate way that could not be mistaken for anything other than serious lust, and Maggie felt the flush start in her chest and zoom up through her face.

"All right," Maggie said, as she pushed him aside to open the truck door. "I'll call you."

Scott grinned at Hannah and said, "You girls be careful now."

He stood on the sidewalk, grinning from ear to ear, watching them until they were out of sight.

"What in the hell was that about?" Hannah demanded before they were a block away from him.

Maggie hid her burning face in her gloved hands and would not look at Hannah. She mumbled something Hannah could not make out.

"Mary Margaret Fitzpatrick," Hannah said, smacking her on the arm, "you look at me and tell me what happened between you and Scott Gordon."

Maggie shook her head and kept her face hidden in her hands.

"This happened last night?" Hannah asked. "After you dropped off Drew?"

"Yes," Maggie said, the word smothered by her gloves.

"You brazen hussy," Hannah said. "Seducing men right and left, one after another."

Maggie's head popped up.

"I did not!" she said, trying to give Hannah a mean look, but smiling sheepishly instead. "Scott was waiting for me when I got back last night. It was awful."

Hannah could hardly keep her eyes on the road.

"Awful? You had sex with Scott Gordon and it was awful?"

"No, no, no," Maggie laughed. "I'm saying it was awful because it made me feel awful, afterward."

"After the sex," Hannah insisted.

Maggie smacked Hannah on the arm, yelling, "No! There was no sex!"

"Okay, okay, don't get physical on me. There was no sex. You don't have to tell me anything."

Hannah appeared pissed off and made a pretense of concentrating solely on the road ahead. Maggie knew it was an act, but went along with it. She needed time to think.

Maggie had hoped Scott would pretend nothing happened, at least in front of other people. She could see now it had been a foolish hope. Scott wasn't going to keep it a secret and didn't care who knew it. She had kept him at a safe distance for the last couple of years, across a minefield of bickering and continual rejection. That battleground had been crossed the previous night, and he wasn't planning on retreating. As soon as she weakened and let her defenses down, he was acting as if he had already captured the castle.

Maggie dreaded the days ahead. She felt she had only two choices: she could reject him completely and finally, and hurt him terribly, almost certainly laying waste to the close friendship they had developed over the years; or she could give in and subject herself to what felt like the complete surrender of her safe, orderly world.

She wanted him, oh my, yes. She secretly wished he would come back to her last night and finish what he started. But she knew him so well. There could be no long-term hot affair with Scott Gordon, no way. As soon as he was in her bed, he would be pressuring her to marry him, and once she was married to him, it would be Mother Marcia and her in the center ring, with Scott as the prize, 'til death did they part.

She was so fond of the man, she did love him, and there was no doubt the physical attraction was intense, but she had these nagging doubts. It hadn't felt like that with Gabe. Maggie would have married Gabe in a heartbeat. Maggie would have followed him to the ends of the earth if he'd asked her to. She had assumed she and Gabe would eventually get married, have children, and then grow old together. Unfortunately, during the three years they were together Gabe never proposed, and then one night Gabe was gone.

Maggie knew Hannah wanted everyone she knew to be paired up and making babies. She would not, could not understand why Maggie didn't want that, too. Nevertheless, she was Maggie's best friend in the world and knew her better than anyone. She might not understand, but she loved Maggie, despite her pricklish nature, and would accept whatever Maggie decided to do, regardless of whether she approved or not. She owed Hannah the truth.

"He was waiting for me when I got back last night," Maggie began and then told Hannah all of it.

Hannah said, "Mm-hmm," in all the proper places, and didn't interrupt, keeping her eyes on the road.

When Maggie finished recounting the events of the evening, ending with Skip's timely interruption, she concluded by saying, "And that's what he wants to talk about when I get back."

"I don't think it's talking he wants to do, little missy, and neither do you," Hannah cackled.

"I can't do it. I won't."

"You want him," Hannah said. "But you don't want to marry him."

"No, I don't," Maggie said. "And there's no halfway with that man. If I sleep with him, he'll have Father Stephen over to breakfast the next morning, giving us premarital counseling over coffee and doughnuts."

"I know this seems simple, and you've probably thought of it already," Hannah said slowly as if she were talking to a child. "But do you think maybe you could just tell him all this? And talk about it? You know, like adult people?"

Maggie shook her head.

"I will, but he won't listen. He still thinks being in love solves everything."

"He should know better from marrying Sharon."

"He'll say that wasn't meant to be and this is."

"Well, you can't lead him on," Hannah said.

"I won't lead him on," Maggie protested. "You know I'm not like that."

Hannah shook her head, saying, "What a mess."

Maggie nodded in agreement.

"Poor Drew, too," Hannah said.

Maggie, who hadn't thought it possible, felt even worse.

Several minutes later Hannah, who was singing "Brown Eyed Girl" (loudly and off key), along with a Van Morrison on the radio, suddenly stopped and interrupted Maggie's reverie.

"Hey, why are we going to talk to Ruthie about Enid and Margie?"

Maggie told Hannah what Scott suspected about Margie.

"Jesus, Mary, and Joseph!" Hannah yelled. "Our little town is a haven for blackmailers, murderers, and mail-tamperers! This is a job for Tiny Trollop, the crime-fighting kitten! Turn on the slut signal, Mary Margaret!"


Pendleton was about twelve miles west of Rose Hill, and Hannah took the scenic route to get there rather than the faster highway. The curvy, two-lane blacktop road wound through a narrow gap between the hills, covered with hardwoods and evergreens, all frosted with snow. She waved at almost every vehicle they passed, and Maggie kidded her about it.

"These are my constituents," Hannah said. "My job is a politically appointed position, you know."

Maggie didn't remind Hannah she was continually re-appointed because no one else wanted the low-paying, thankless, nigh impossible job.

Pendleton was much bigger than Rose Hill was, with a Mega Mart and several fast food restaurants right outside the city limits. The Mountain View Retirement Home was on Main Street, situated between a medical office building and a funeral home.

Hannah pointed to the businesses on either side of the retirement home, and said, "It's like an assembly line."

Hannah pulled the truck into the semi-circular drive as if to drop Maggie off, and Maggie said, "Aren't you coming with me?"

"No thanks," Hannah said. "These places are like no-kill shelters for old people. I like to see my grannies in their natural habitats."

"Wait 'til your old man dies and Alice can't remember how to pull up her own panties; you might feel differently."

"Thanks so much for the visual. Now get out!"

Maggie entered the lobby through two sets of automatic doors which formed a windbreak. Just inside was a large, airy room with a semi-circular reception desk, decorated much like a hotel lobby, and a large sitting room area just beyond. There were several people seated in soft chairs and wheelchairs in the sitting room, watching a morning talk show on a big screen television. A cheerful woman dressed as a hotel reservationist asked Maggie if she could help her. Within minutes of her request Maggie's old friend, Ruthie was hugging her and offering to show her around.

"Scott called me," Ruthie said. "He said you were coming by to talk about Enid."

Ruthie took her down to the end of a long hallway that led through the "north wing," where there was a physical therapy room, a craft project room, a full-service hair and nail salon, and a gift shop. The "south wing" held a huge dining room, a meeting room, and a snack bar with game room. Both wings enclosed an atrium garden area with benches and tables. Beyond the atrium, Ruthie told her, in the west wing, was the more hospital-like extended care facility.

Maggie's first impression was it looked like a luxury hotel for people in wheelchairs. She had secretly been anticipating abandoned-looking old people drooling and yelling in the hallways, and was ashamed of herself now she saw how nice it was, and how friendly everyone seemed.

Ruthie bought her a soda in the snack bar and took her back to the office, which she shared with several other people. Nurses were dressed in colorfully printed scrubs, and office workers wore identical khaki's, white shirts, and navy blue blazers. Ruthie had on the office worker uniform, and her badge said, "Intake Registrar" below her name.

"I'd like to move in as soon as possible," Maggie said, as she sat down across from her old friend at her desk.

Ruthie laughed.

"We're lucky," she said. "Our owners are sincerely dedicated to good care. Our ratio of caregivers to residents is one of the highest in the industry. We hope they never sell us."

"It must cost a fortune," Maggie said.

"It is expensive," Ruthie admitted, "but we have a waiting list of people wanting in."

"How could someone like Enid Estep ever afford it?" Maggie asked.

"Some people deed their homes over to the company to pay for it," Ruthie said. "If Enid owns the house she and Margie are living in, that's definitely a possibility. Otherwise, we have a program funded by grants and bequests for people who have limited means, and she might qualify for that."

"Have you talked to her about it?" Maggie asked.

Ruthie frowned and leaned forward, saying in a quieter voice, "Many times. I work part-time here as an intake nurse and part-time as a Home Health nurse, and I see Enid at least twice a week, depending on our rotation schedule. I don't want to imply she is in any way neglected..."

Ruthie paused here, and Maggie filled in, "But?"

"I don't know exactly what Enid's late husband's pension payments are, or what his social security benefit is, but my mother has the same pension plan from my dad having been a fireman in Rose Hill, plus his social security, and she lives a whole lot better than Enid."

"So what do you think is going on?"

"Her daughter has drummed it into her head that they are poor and can't afford anything, but I think Margie must be squirreling away money, or spending it somehow. I told Margie about a new drug treatment program that may help her mother's arthritis, but she shut me down, saying it was just another way for the drug companies and doctors to get rich, and they couldn't afford it."

"Won't her insurance pay for it?" Maggie asked.

"They will pay the larger part," said Ruthie. "Enid would have to pay the rest, but if it would improve her quality of life? I can only tell you if it were my mom I wouldn't hesitate."

"I haven't been in their house," Maggie said. "What's it like?"

Ruthie looked around to see who was nearby before speaking in even more hushed tones.

"It's not exactly squalor, not bad enough to say she's being abused," she said. "But it's depressing as hell, and she's so isolated."

"Would she leave it, though?"

"When I told her about this place she said it sounded wonderful, and she wished she could afford it. She didn't say, 'oh I could never leave Margie,' or 'I could never leave my home.' She said she would love to come but can't afford it. She also said she wished Margie wasn't stuck there at home with her."

Maggie and Ruthie stared at each other thoughtfully for a moment, and then Maggie said quietly, "Scott is investigating Margie for something bad she may be doing, and it could be Enid will need somewhere to live as a result."

Ruthie's eyebrows popped up.

"Is there anything I can do to help?"

"I'll let you know," Maggie responded and made the lock motion with her fingers in front of her lips, the same way they had as children when promising to keep a secret.

"Don't worry," Ruthie said. "I won't tell a soul."

As she walked Maggie back out to the lobby, Ruthie asked, "Who do you think killed Theo Eldridge?"

"Hard to tell," Maggie said. "Lots of people hated the guy."

"I had the biggest crush on his brother Brad," Ruthie said. "Gorgeous George, we used to call him, do you remember? He hated that."

"I had forgotten that," Maggie said. "His full name was George Bradley Eldridge."

After Ruthie hugged her and walked away the full import of her offhand comment sank in for Maggie. It was then she realized Gwyneth was not the only "G" Eldridge her brother Sean could have been writing to.


When Maggie got back to the lobby, she could hear Hannah's voice. She followed the sound to find her friend, who was in the sitting room handing out small kittens to anyone willing to hold one. The delighted looks on the faces of the residents as they held and stroked the little gray-and-black-striped balls of fur were touching to see. The kittens mewed, purred, and rubbed their little faces on the hands and arms of those who held them.

Maggie bumped her friend with her hip and Hannah said, "What?"

One of the caregivers asked Hannah if she would come back sometime and Hannah said, "Sure, I'm through here all the time, and there's no shortage of kittens in Rose Hill."

Maggie was visibly aghast at this response and bumped her again, but Hannah just looked at her and repeated, "What?"

Eventually, Hannah gathered up the kittens and put them all in a vented carrier lined with shredded newspaper. Everyone thanked her repeatedly and made her promise to come back soon. Before they left, Hannah suggested in a low voice to the caregiver that everyone should maybe wash their hands pretty soon, and the caregiver showed her the bottle of hand sanitizer she was carrying in her pocket. She began squirting a dollop of it in everyone's hands, one by one.

Maggie held her tongue until they were in the cab of the truck, with the crate of mewling kittens seat-belted between them.

"What changed your mind?" Maggie asked.

"The visual of my mother you gave me, thank you very much," Hannah said disgustedly. "Cause you know none of my lazy, good-for-nothing sisters-in-law are gonna take that crazy woman in. I thought I'd better check out my options."

"What did you think?"

"I think it's the nicest raisin ranch I've ever seen," Hannah said. "I put down a deposit on a cheap room for Alice."

"You did not."

"No, I didn't, but mark my words, the first time she can't remember my name I'm packing her bags and leaving her on their doorstep with a check pinned to her sweater."

"What's the story on the kittens?" Maggie asked.

"Mama got hit by a car, so they need hand-fed for a few more weeks, and then I'll try to find homes for them."

"Good luck with that, right?"

"I thought I heard you say you'd take two."

"No way," Maggie said. "My eyes are itching just being this close to them."

"You let Duke sleep in your kitchen all the time."

"Duke only crashes at my place occasionally. We're just friends; it's not a serious commitment."

Hannah rolled her eyes and said, "Heaven forbid."

Maggie ignored the dig.

When they stopped at the grocery store, Hannah left the truck running to keep the kittens warm and hurried into the IGA to get Maggie's pepperoni rolls. Maggie used a nearby pay phone to call Scott and tell him what Ruthie said.

"Thanks," he said after she was through. "I'll go to the bank now and get somebody to show me Margie's account, try to see where Enid's money is going."

"Don't you need a warrant?" Maggie asked.

"I'll just mention to Knox that I know what Theo had on him," Scott said.

"Are you sure that's wise?" Maggie asked. "I'm just thinking of what happened to Anne Marie."

"I'm not afraid of Knox."

"Just don't drink anything he offers you."

"No worries. I'll tell you all about it later tonight when I see you."

"If you see me."

Scott laughed wickedly and hung up.

When Hannah returned to the truck, she was waving a plastic bag of pepperoni rolls over her head.

"I got 'em," she said breathlessly, as she got in the truck on a wave of cold air. "I had to knock several old people out of the way and wrestle the last bag away from a crippled orphan, but I got 'em."

Maggie opened the bag and inhaled the aroma of greasy sticks of pepperoni encased in soft yeast rolls.

"My mother would kill me if she knew we were doing this," she said.

On the way home she thought more about what Ruthie had told her, and about the possibility that Sean was writing love letters to Brad Eldridge. If her brother was gay, it would explain why he was so secretive, and why he stayed away from Rose Hill for so long.

A small town can be a wonderful place to live, but Maggie knew to some people it could be a prison or a public court of small-minded opinion. It's probably easier to protect your privacy in a big city, she thought. Scott hadn't told her much about his visit with Sean, except to say he had an airtight alibi. He hadn't mentioned the letters, either, so he must not have looked in the envelope. Maggie thought again about how much she abused his trust, and how ashamed she always was after the fact.

'Why does he put up with me?' she wondered.

When Maggie got back to the bookstore, she picked up an urgent message from Ava, and ran out the back door, down the alley, and up Pine Mountain Road to the bed and breakfast. She was breathless when she got inside, where it felt warm and cozy, and greeted Gail Godwin, who cleaned for Ava on the weekends. Ava was in the kitchen and put a finger to her lips to caution Maggie not to speak. Ava put the kettle on, and Maggie sat on a stool facing her across the broad kitchen island.

As soon as Gail went upstairs, Maggie said, "What's up?"

"I think Brian has been calling me."

Maggie felt her mouth fall open.

"You think?"

"Well," Ava said, putting a tea bag in each mug, "for a couple days now I have been getting these calls, and you know how overseas long distance sounds? Lots of clicking and static? This sounds like that."

"What does he say?"

Ava poured hot water into both mugs and Maggie took hers, adding a heaping spoonful of sugar from the sugar bowl while Ava drank hers plain.

"He doesn't say anything, just listens to me say, 'hello' over and over, until I hang up."

"I know this is an obvious question, but how do you know it's him?"

Ava leaned back against the stove, holding her mug with both hands. One of the things Maggie did appreciate about Ava was how normal she seemed even though she really was an amazingly beautiful woman. Maggie forgot that from time to time but was reminded now. Clad in an old faded sweatshirt and jeans, with the barest makeup and her hair pulled back in a ponytail, she still looked stunning, like a movie star playing a bed and breakfast-owning single mother of two.

"I know it sounds crazy," Ava said, "but since Theo died I've been expecting to hear from Brian, waiting for the phone to ring, or for him to walk through the door. If Theo was blackmailing him, I can understand why he couldn't come back as long as Theo was alive, but now..."

"What will you do if he does come back?"

Unexpectedly, Ava got big tears in her eyes, and apologized, as if embarrassed to be crying.

"Don't be embarrassed," Maggie said. "This situation would overwhelm anyone."

"I'm not crying because I still love him, or because my feelings are still hurt he left us," Ava said. "I'm crying because I don't want him to come back, and I'm afraid if he does Father Stephen and your mother will make me take him back. I know to anyone else it would sound crazy, but you know what I mean."

She was really crying now, and Maggie, who was not a hugger, knew she should do something like that, but really didn't want to.

"Who could blame you?" she said instead. "Let's see. He wasn't a good husband when he was here. He cheated on you repeatedly, left you with a little girl and a newborn baby to raise on your own, and cleaned out your bank account. Turns out he also borrowed money on your home and the lives of you and your children, for God knows what reason. You haven't heard from him in what, six or seven years?"

Ava nodded, sniffing and blotting her eyes while Maggie continued, "I'm his sister, but if he does come back I think we should staple antlers to his head and declare open season on his ass."

Ava smiled, and Maggie wondered how it was that when Ava cried, she looked dewy and lovely, but when Maggie cried, she looked like she had a face full of bee stings.

Life was not fair.

Maggie left Ava feeling better, went back to the bookstore, and called Hannah.

"Where are you?' she asked her.

"I took the kittens to Drew's, picked up my dog from Dad's, and now I'm driving up Rose Hill Avenue looking for a place to park. Who are all these people?"

"They're tourists," Maggie told her, "and they all buy cappuccino and books, so don't complain or do anything that might drive them away. Park behind my car in the alley, and I'll meet you at the back door."

Maggie went behind the café counter and made Hannah a hot chocolate to go, and put two croissants in a bag. She made a cappuccino for her mother and got outside right as Hannah pulled in.

"What's up?" Hannah said as soon as she opened the passenger side door. Maggie got in next to Hannah's husky mix Jax, who greeted her with an attack of licking kisses.

"Yuck, stop!" Maggie told him, but Jax seemed to think she was just kidding.

She handed Hannah the hot chocolate and bag of baked goods around Jax's interested nose, and when Hannah looked inside she said, "Sweet! Thanks!"

"I've just come from Ava's, and she is getting these calls that sound like long distance, but nobody speaks," she told her. "She thinks it's Brian."

"I think it's Theo calling from Hell," Hannah said, "to complain about the heat."

"A call from the great beyond," Maggie intoned, "from the underworld he is forced to roam."

"I hope he's shoveling hot buckets of flaming poop all day every day," Hannah said.

"I just hope he's well and truly ashamed of himself," Maggie said. "That would satisfy me."

"So does Princess Ava want your brother back?" Hannah asked, backing out into the alley.

"She most certainly does not," Maggie said.

Maggie hadn't discussed her discovery of Patrick and Ava's tender feelings towards one another with Hannah and didn't plan to.

"Well, why would she?" Hannah snorted. "She's the queen of this town's pity party, and everybody fights over who gets to wipe her nose whenever she sniffles."

Hannah was not a big fan of Maggie's sister-in-law. Sam had once confessed to having a big crush on Ava in high school, and Hannah had never forgiven her.

"She's teetering on the pedestal now, though," Maggie said. "Theo leaving her all that money has the town gossiping, and it doesn't matter if she's innocent or not; as far as they're concerned she's guilty by association."

"Why do you think he left it to her?" Hannah asked, as they reached the college end of the alley, turned right, and slowly drove down Daisy Lane, a narrow road between the college and the town, to reach Rose Hill Avenue.

"You saw the shrine on the wall," Maggie said. "It must have been one of those unrequited obsessions which festered over the years. Everyone knows Theo was selfish and stingy, so he must have really been nuts about her, and wanted to be sure she was taken care of if something happened to him."

Hannah was driving slowly, so she could steer, eat, and drink her hot chocolate. They turned left at the light onto Pine Mountain Road.

"You know Sam's cousin Edie, who works for the county clerk?" Hannah asked.

Maggie nodded.

"She saw the will, and she said Theo left Ava all the money in a trust, in such a way that Brian would not be able to touch it."

"Really?" Maggie said. "I didn't have the guts to ask her about it."

"Edie said that Caroline got the lodge and all the acreage, and don't you just bet that Gwyneth is fit to be tied about that."

"Good," Maggie said.

Hannah double parked to let Maggie out, saying, "Here you go, Madam, door to door service, one block away, the long way."

"I wish Caroline would come back," Maggie said and patted Jax goodbye as she opened the door.

"What religion is she now?" Hannah asked as Maggie got out.

"Buddhist, I think."

"Is that the one where they don't eat cows?"

"No, that's Hindu."

"Wasn't she in a vegetarian one once? One time she fixed us rice and peanuts you had to scoop up with flatbread."

"That was when we visited her at the Krishna palace; that's what you're thinking of."

"I liked the rice and peanuts, but that bread had no taste at all."

"Trust you to remember the food, but not the philosophy."

"I'm sure she'll tell us all about it when she gets here," Hannah said with a sigh.

"Just try stopping her," Maggie said

"Hey, speaking of food, where are we eating lunch?" Hannah asked as she finished the last of her second croissant.

Maggie shook her head and shut the door.

Scott spent the rest of his morning making phone calls and talking to a few key people before he felt armed well enough to tackle Margie. He wanted to complete as much of his own investigation as possible before the Feds came in and took over. They would be even less likely to involve him in their inquiries than Sarah was, and he would be powerless to protect the people he cared about most.

Knox wasn't in, but Courtenay gave him no trouble at all with his request, merely looked up the account, verified what Scott suspected, and printed out the past two years' worth of activity while giving Scott a peek down her blouse as she did so.

Armed with both hard evidence and a hell of a bluff, Scott stopped Margie at the back door as she was leaving work at noon.

She let him back in, wary, and not meeting his eyes, saying, "I can't stay long. I have to get home to Mother."

He outlined all the mail-related complaints he'd found in the station files, what he had discovered about Lily Crawford's card, and the stack of magazines addressed to other people he'd found in her house.

She stood with her arms crossed, refusing to meet his eyes, and said, "No one will ever believe you. You can't prove any of it."

Scott felt confident he had enough evidence to get her fired. He didn't plan to arrest her, but he wanted her to think he might. It all depended on what she would or would not admit.

His voice was steady and quiet as he delivered his bluff.

"I also have evidence that you took child pornography photos mailed to someone else, put them in an envelope addressed to Willy Neff, and then turned those photos over to the police, claiming they were Willy's."

She gasped, and all the color drained out of her face. It was the first time she looked him in the eyes during the confrontation, and what Scott saw there was pure animal fear.

He had her, so he drove his bluff home, saying, "I went back over the evidence, and it was all stuff you put together. As soon as I get you fired, we can reopen Willy's case. Do you know what the punishment is for someone, let alone a U.S. postal service employee, who tampers with the mail? You made a false accusation that sent a man to prison. What do you think a jury will do, Margie? You'll probably be in federal prison for the rest of your life."

Margie's eyes were wide and fixed, gazing into the distance as if she was picturing what was about to happen to her.

"I didn't mean for it to go that far," she said quietly.

Scott held his breath as she did exactly what he hoped she'd do. She confessed.

"I only wanted to embarrass him," she said.

"Because he was kind to you, and you thought it meant more than it did."

She turned on him then, and her nasty streak showed itself before she could stop herself.

"He said he didn't mean anything by it, that he just wanted to be my friend. He felt sorry for me. He was the biggest loser in this town, and he felt sorry for me! I'm glad he went to prison, and I'm glad he's dead."

The look on her face was one Scott hoped never to see again. All that rage, contempt, and hatred, all because Willy had been kind to her, but not in love with her.

Too late, she realized what she'd just done. Scott could see the wheels turn in her head as she tried to think of a way out.

"My mother," she said, with new, big tears glistening in her eyes, and lower lip trembling. "This will kill her, Scott. Don't arrest me. I promise I will never mess with the mail again. I need this job, and I am all she has in the world. Please, Scott, I'm begging you; for my mother's sake."

She was crying pitifully now, but Scott had prepared himself for that.

"Is this the same mother whose pension and social security payments have been depositing directly into an account with your name and hers on it? An account with over $150,000.00 in it?"

Margie's head popped back, and her mouth dropped open.

"What a devoted daughter you are," Scott said. "Stealing your mother's money while making her live in poverty."

"I'm saving that money in case something happens to me," Margie protested. "It's to pay for her long-term care if she has to go into a nursing home."

"I understand your mother wanted to go to the new facility in Pendleton, but you told her she couldn't afford it."

"She didn't; that's a lie!"

Margie started sobbing hysterically, so Scott gave her some wet paper towels from the bathroom to clean her face, watching all the while to make sure she didn't make a break for it when he left the room.

Hiccupping and occasionally letting out a ragged gasp, she eventually calmed down, eyed Scott shrewdly, and asked, "Why don't you just arrest me, then?"

Scott shrugged, as if it mattered not in the least to him, and said, "I still might."

"Why might you not arrest me?" she asked.

"I'm willing to offer you a deal," Scott said and watched her eyes light up at that.

Looking at her tearstained, swollen face, Scott was repelled by the predatory energy that jumped right back into her demeanor. She was willing to do anything, he was sure, to escape public shame and jail. Scott doubted she would ever repeat her confession, and didn't think he could re-open the case and get Willy exonerated without it. He just wanted her to think it was possible.

"If you agree to sign a power of attorney document appointing a trustee to be in charge of your mother's finances and medical care," he concluded, "I will put all the evidence I have somewhere secure, and no one ever has to know."

She was nodding to everything he said.

"I will," she said. "I will."

"But," Scott warned her, "you give me even the smallest reason to doubt your sincerity where your mother is concerned or get in the least bit of trouble somewhere else, and I will reopen the case and have you prosecuted."

He barely listened to her as she promised to do all that, and thanked him, virtually prostrating herself before him.

"I have people watching your bank account, so don't try anything funny there," he warned her. "And when you get home you'll find I've ordered private around-the-clock Home Health workers to be with your mother until I can get her moved to Pendleton, so you will never again be left alone with her. You will call in sick tomorrow, and take as much sick and vacation time as you have left until you can quit, and then you are never to step foot in this or any other post office again, do you understand?"

Scott could tell she was seething over what he had managed to do to the life she thought she had full control over, but she just kept agreeing to everything he said.

"I'll be watching you and so will several other people, so don't think you can do anything but what we have agreed upon today."

Scott had the feeling that it was not safe to turn his back on her, and even if that was just paranoia, he honored it. He kept her in sight as she set the alarm, locked the back door, and handed him the keys. As she trudged around the corner towards home, Scott suddenly felt so weary his knees wobbled, and he felt the tiniest twinge of a headache.

Maggie was in her office and didn't look glad to see him when he arrived, but Scott was feeling so crappy he didn't care. He ignored the look on her face that said "go away," shut her office door and plopped in the chair next to her desk.

"Do you have any aspirin or ibuprofen?" he asked her. "My head hurts."

"I'm sorry, I don't," Maggie said. "Where are your migraine pills?"

"At home," he said. "I'll run up and get one in a minute, but first I want to tell you what's going on."

Scott told her about Sarah's visit and that the Feds were taking over the murder investigation.

"Probably because of all those drugs in the safe," Maggie said. "Theo was probably a big drug dealer."

"I think it's more likely to be about the blackmail. I think it may involve some powerful people."

"Do you think they will figure out what Hannah and I did?"

"Not if you don't go around talking about it, and for crissakes, quit telling each other stuff on the phone."

"I tell you what I am going to do," she said. "I'm going to get on my phone and tell Hannah the Feds are investigating people who eavesdrop on private citizens using scanners, and they've narrowed it down to twenty people in Rose Hill. That should shake up the scanner grannies."

"It may also cause a few heart attacks," Scott said. "I wouldn't do it if I were you. Just be careful."

Scott told Maggie how the confrontation with Margie had gone, about the threat card and photo, what she had done to her mother, and what she had done to Willy.

"I knew Margie was a vicious gossip, but I never thought she'd do such awful things. Poor old Willy; I treated him like dirt. I guess there's nothing I can do for him now."

Scott told her he was going to take up a collection for Willy's burial, and then he returned to the subject of Margie and Enid.

"I'm going to make sure Enid has a big color television in her room at Mountain View," Scott said. "High definition with every channel known to man."

Maggie laid her hand on his arm, which was resting on her desk, and said, "You are a good egg, Scott Gordon."

Scott felt as if she'd kissed him, and said softly, "Thanks. I think you're a good egg, too."

They sat there a few seconds, enjoying the warmth of the moment.

"Thank you for helping me try to figure this out," Scott said. "It seems like no one cares who killed Theo but me."

"I just want it to be over so we can get back to what passes for normal life around here."

Scott was feeling pretty warm and comfortable with Maggie, and ventured, "Can I cook dinner for you tonight?"

Maggie smiled at him sweetly at first, and then abruptly removed her hand from his arm.

"I can't, I'm sorry. I promised Drew I'd come to his place for dinner."

"You have another date with Drew?"

"No, no, not a date," Maggie said hurriedly, but she didn't look him in the eyes when she said it. "It's just a friendly dinner."

Scott stared at her for a moment and then stood, shaking his head.

"Have a nice night," Scott said as he left.

As soon as Scott left the bookstore, Gwyneth Eldridge accosted him outside, her rich perfume falling over him like a toxic cloud, causing his throat to close.

"I need your help, Todd," she said, standing way too close for his comfort.

Scott disengaged her hand from his arm and stepped back from her, repelled by her touch as much as her strong perfume.

"Scott," he said. "It's Scott."

"I thought Aggie and I had resolved our differences, but evidently I am once again banned from the bookstore. You owe me a favor for doing nothing to stop that Amazon from assaulting me in the first place," Gwyneth said. "I desperately need a soy cappuccino with a double shot."

She started digging through her enormous handbag for money.

"I thought you hated her coffee," Scott said, with some satisfaction.

"Well beggars can't be choosers, now can they?" she said. "My espresso machine has not arrived, and for some reason once again I cannot go in there and buy anything."

"For some reason?" Scott said. "You're the one who sat in her café and insulted her business and everyone in this town. Then you asked her mother, a successful business owner, mind you, to be your cleaning woman, just because she has an Irish last name."

Just then Gwyneth spotted the mayor down the street, and with a brief, acid-soaked, "Thanks for all your help, Todd," she ran toward Stuart, teetering on spike heels while trying to dodge icy patches on the sidewalk.

Scott hoped she landed on her ass. His headache was starting in earnest now, thanks to her perfume. He needed to go home and take some medication before it turned into something much worse.

He crossed the street and walked towards the corner, right as Billy and Phyllis spilled out of the diner onto the sidewalk, screaming at each other.

"I hate you!" Billy yelled at her. "I wish you were dead!"

"You better watch your mouth, little man," she yelled, "or I'll drop you in some deep shit! Don't think I won't!"

Billy saw Scott, looked scared, and screamed, "Go to hell!" at his mother before running down the hill and making a right into the alley, without looking back.

Phyllis was trembling with rage. She turned to look at some tourists watching the performance and hissed, "What're you looking at?" with enough venom that they turned and went in the opposite direction.

When Scott ran across the street and approached her, she held out a hand to ward him off.

"Not now, Scott, I'm just a little upset with my psychotic son."

She seemed more than a little psychotic herself, he thought. Scott was trying to decide whom to pursue, Phyllis or Billy, and decided Phyllis was a bird in the hand.

"Let me take you somewhere to cool down," he offered, smiling in a way he hoped would disarm her. "Cause you're being a little naughty out here on the sidewalk."

"That would be great, honey," she said, smoothing down her skirt. "Let's get out of here and find someplace cozy."

Scott was amazed at how quickly she transformed from she-devil to sex kitten, and wondered if she had turned just as quickly on Theo, and killed him.

Scott cursed his luck at not having his personal vehicle close by, so he steered her toward the police cruiser, parked right up the street. Phyllis linked her arm through Scott's and allowed herself be led to the passenger side, and then crossed her legs seductively as she got settled in the seat. She peeked up at him from underneath her bangs in a practiced way, to see if he was noticing. Scott was glad she wasn't wearing a lot of perfume. The cigarette and booze smell was bad enough.

"Where to?" he asked her.

"Let's go to the Roadhouse," she said. "They're used to me being naughty out there."

There was no headache medicine left in the bottle in the cruiser, and he didn't dare stop anywhere and give Phyllis the chance to sober up, have second thoughts, and escape. All the way to the biker bar, located out near the four-lane highway, Scott flirted with her. It was easy to do, as everything seemed to remind Phyllis of something sexual.

When they arrived at the Roadhouse, there were several cars and motorcycles parked in the lot. When the police cruiser pulled in, a few people quickly left while trying to look casual and invisible.

"What're you doing bringing the law out here, Phyllis?" someone asked her as they walked in, and Scott saw her instantly sober up a bit and lose some of her nerve.

Once seated, Phyllis kept touching her face, unconsciously drawing attention to the black eye she meant to hide. She still wore heavy makeup over it, but despite her new hairdo, he could still detect the swelling and the odd color.

"You want to tell me the truth about that shiner, Phyllis? Theo give you that?"

"You gonna seduce me or interrogate me?" she asked, but Scott just smiled at her and ordered them some drinks.

"You help me, and I'll help you," Scott said.

After a couple rounds she loosened up considerably.

"So how long had you and Theo...?"

"Been having sleepovers?"

"Yep, you tell me everything," Scott said. "Don't lie to me, and I will do what I can to make sure you and Billy are treated fairly."

"I didn't kill him," she said.

"But you know who did."

"No," she said. "Not for sure."

"All right then. Tell me about you and Theo."

Scott sipped his beer and Phyllis knocked back another shot, chased it with beer, and lit a cigarette. Scott wanted to ask her to put it out but thought it might piss her off and cause her to clam up, so he didn't.

"Theo started sniffing around me when I was a teenager. The summer between sophomore and junior year, you remember, the year his brother died?"

"I remember."

"I ran around with Brad for a couple weeks that summer. Hell, I ran around with a lot of people. That was the best summer of my life. It's been downhill ever since."

"Was Brad Billy's father?"

"Maybe," Phyllis said, with a cagey smile.

"Billy doesn't look like him, or you, for that matter."

"You never knew my granddad, Scotty-boy. Billy looks the spittin' image of him at that age."

Phyllis took a long drink of beer and wiped her mouth with the back of her hand, wiping off most of her lipstick.

"So did Theo know Brad might be Billy's father?"

"No, he didn't," she said and blew smoke in Scott's face. "Not 'til Saturday night."

Scott felt the headache escalate; it was going to be a bad one. On top of the smoke, there was a kerosene heater somewhere in the place, and those fumes were noxious.

"And you're sure about Brad."

"I don't know for sure. It could have been one of several other lucky losers I palled around with that summer."

"Does this have anything to do with Theo being murdered?"

"Buy me another drink, and I'll tell you," she said.

"Sure thing," Scott said and signaled the waitress. "None for me, thanks."

"You are such a mama's boy, Scott Gordon; always have been, always will be. You think Maggie Fitzpatrick wants a mama's boy in her bed? She doesn't. Now me, I wouldn't mind it. I wouldn't mind it at all."

Phyllis ran her foot up the side of Scott's calf, and he gritted his teeth.

"C'mon Phyllis, you do your part, and then I'll do mine. What happened that night?"

She rolled her eyes and put out her cigarette, but immediately lit another. Scott didn't know if he was going to be able to stand it much longer.

"Theo came over in a crappy mood. He was still mad about the damn dog Ed stole from him. He was drunk, as usual. He wanted to stay, but I wasn't in the mood. We fought. Then he started on Billy. When was he going to get a real job or go to school? Why did he wash dishes all day and play video games all night? Why didn't he have a girlfriend? Well, I agree with most of that, but Billy's my kid, and only I get to yell at him. Billy and Theo got into it then. I tried to break it up, but they were going at it pretty fierce."

She signaled for another drink, and Scott willed himself not to be sick at the table. The nausea part of the migraine had arrived.

"Go on," he said. "And make it the short version. I haven't got all night."

"All right, keep your shorts on. You brought me here, remember? You're asking me the questions. I'm helping you out. You remember that."

"I'm just impatient to get you out of here and alone somewhere, Phyllis. You know how it is. Tell me what happened."

"You know Billy's got a mouth on him, and it seemed like he couldn't back down. Finally, Theo dared him to take the first swing and Billy ran off. Then Theo turned on me. Theo said something about how Billy was a worthless excuse for a person, no better than the white trash he came from, and I said, 'then you're calling your little brother white trash, cause Brad's his Daddy.' Well, that set him back on his freakin' heels, I'm telling ya. He just stood there with his mouth hanging open and this crazy look on his face. Then he up and popped me one."

"Did he say anything else?" Scott asked, and closed one eye to stop the double vision he was now experiencing.

"Said he'd see me in hell before he'd let me or Billy have one dollar of his family's money."

"What then?"

"Well, I told him to leave, so he left, and I went to bed."

"When did Billy come home?"

"Oh, right away, right after Theo left," she said.

"What time was it?"

"I don't know. Theo usually shows up after last call at the bar, so it must have been around 1:15, 1:30."

"Anything else happen?"

"I went to bed with a bag of frozen tater tots on my eye. I don't remember anything after that."

"Why didn't you claim Billy was Brad's son earlier, after he died, or when their old man died? You could have got some money then."

"Well, the truth is, Scotty-boy, I did get me some money from that old man. A little while after Brad died I went to ole Teddy Bear and asked for help, and he paid me a little something every month up until he died, and no one was ever the wiser.

"After the old man died and Theo came back, he and I started seeing each other. I wasn't sure Brad really was the father, and I thought maybe I could get Theo to marry me; he was always saying he would. By then they had those tests, you know, those DNA tests. If I claimed Brad was the father, and a test showed he wasn't, I'd have blown it with Theo. I thought marrying Theo was a safer bet. Some stupid idiot, I was. I know it's a crapshoot, but if Billy really is Brad's kid, we are owed some serious money. We're gonna get us a lawyer."

"Let me ask you something," Scott said. "How do you think you're going to prove Billy is Brad's son now? Brad's been dead almost twenty years."

"I watch those crime shows," she said. "They can check DNA even after you're dead. They can dig him up."

"Brad was cremated," Scott said. "Just like Theo was this week. Brad's ashes were scattered over Bear Lake after the funeral. If you'd bothered to be there, you'd know. There are only grave markers at the cemetery, not bodies."

Phyllis looked shocked but quickly recovered.

"Gwyneth and Caroline have the same DNA as Brad; we could check Billy's against theirs."

"I've got news for you, Phyllis," Scott said. "Brad and Caroline were adopted."

Phyllis had gone pale, and now the yellow, puffy bruise around her eye was easy to see in contrast.

"So there is nobody to get Brad's DNA from," Scott said. "And Brad was not related to the family by blood, so his sisters would not have the same DNA."

"That's not true," Phyllis said. "Theo would've told me."

"No, he wouldn't have, Phyllis," Scott said. "You didn't mean anything to Theo. He didn't trust you. He didn't care about you. He used you. You were disposable to him."

Scott was seeing bright auras now around all the lights in the bar.

"How did you know about that adoption thing?" Phyllis hissed.

"Because Brad told us; we were his friends. It was one of the things Theo picked on him about," Scott said.

He pressed on his temples to try to relieve the pressure, which felt like a steel band squeezing the top of his head. It hurt so badly he thought he might pass out.

"Oh my God," Phyllis said quietly, as of to herself. "It was all for nothing."

"Did Billy kill Theo?"

"I don't know," Phyllis said. "He disappeared after Theo left. When he came back, he had blood on his clothes. I was afraid to ask him. He's my son ... but I'm afraid of him."

With that admission, Phyllis jumped up and ran out of the bar. Scott's headache had reached the point of no return now. He was starting to get the tunnel vision which presaged a major migraine. He took out his phone but couldn't focus well enough to punch in the numbers to call for help. He stumbled on his way to the bar, and several people laughed at him. He got the bartender's attention, showed his badge, and told the man what number to dial.

Maggie answered her phone on the first ring.


Scott had been getting migraines for as long as Maggie had known him. He was able to ward them off with medication if he took it as soon as he detected the telltale signs one was coming on. Once it took hold, there was nothing he could do but rest in a dark, quiet room until it passed.

Maggie knew these headaches were the main reason Scott never sought to move up into county or state law enforcement. The county and state required a more thorough pre-employment screening process that would include a review of his medical records, which would disclose the condition. Some people still considered migraines a psychological disorder rather than a medical condition. If he were branded as having psychological problems he would be unemployable in law enforcement.

Maggie thought Scott was through the worst of it tonight. She had been horrified to find him slumped over in the front seat of the squad car in the parking lot of the Roadhouse. On the drive home, Maggie called Patrick, who had been with Scott before during these attacks. He was waiting for her when she got to Scott's house. He helped her get him inside, clean him up as best they could, and managed to get some water down him. It was just as important to keep him hydrated as medicated; she knew this from previous experiences with him.

He had been lucid enough at one point to tell her about Phyllis and Billy, and to plead with her to call Sarah and tell her. As soon as they got him put to bed, she went through his wallet, found Sarah's card, and gave her a call.

Sarah was surprised to hear from her, and although she didn't understand why she couldn't talk to Scott, who Maggie claimed had a bad case of food poisoning, she took Maggie seriously, listened to everything she had to say, and said she'd take it from there.


Tommy was eating a bowl of cereal and watching TV when he heard Phyllis come home. He peered through the curtains and saw her get out of a car he'd never seen before, and she was stumbling drunk. Phyllis went inside her trailer and Tommy could hear Billy and her screaming at each other. He heard Billy yell he was going to kill her.

He felt paralyzed and didn't know what to do, but when he heard the sound of glass breaking, he thought, 'I will go tell Ed. Ed will know what to do.'

He left the trailer as quietly as he could. Several neighbors had come out to see what was going on, but none of them paid any attention to him. Tommy rode his bike as fast as he could over the icy bricks of the alley to the newspaper office, but Ed was not there. He didn't know what else to do, so he turned back toward home.

As Tommy turned down the alley, Ed rounded the opposite corner in time to see him go, and then was horrified to hear a car come crashing down the alley. Ed heard a loud bang, and what sounded like trash cans being bounced around, before Billy slid his mother's big Buick out of the alley and fishtailed up Pine Mountain Road. He ran a red light, narrowly missing another car, and left behind a cacophony of horn honking and a few near fender benders.

Ed ran down the sidewalk into the alley with his heart in his throat, fearing the worst. He passed the mangled bike and reached the jumble of trashcans just as Tommy got to his feet. He picked the boy up in his arms and carried him all the way back to the newspaper office, where he gently placed him on top of the worktable before calling his mother.

Mandy ran into the office, breathless and panicked, still wearing her hairnet and a flour-covered apron from the bakery next door. Ed suggested, over the boy's protests he was fine, that they take Tommy to the 24-hour medical center out on the highway, to be looked over, just in case. Mandy and Ed helped Tommy into the cab of Ed's truck, and Ed drove slowly over the icy streets, out toward the interstate, and the nearest emergency medical help.

Mandy held Tommy tightly to her and wiped his face as he cried, telling her what happened.

"I thought he was trying to kill me," Tommy said, in between ragged sobs.

"Why in the world would anybody want to kill you?" Mandy asked him, and Ed said, "I can tell you."

He told Mandy about Tommy seeing Billy follow Theo the night he was murdered and being worried about Billy finding out he told.

"You told me you told your mama," Ed said to Tommy sternly, and then to Mandy, "I'm so sorry, Mandy. I should have told you myself."

Mandy told Tommy not to worry about it now, they would sort it all out later, and then she gave Ed the evil eye.

"You and I will talk about this later," she told him.

Snow was coming down steadily, and the temperature was dropping fast. Snowplows were out, and they made traveling the roads slow going. When they finally reached the little strip mall which held the medical center, they helped Tommy in, told the receptionist why they were there, filled out paperwork, and took their seats in the waiting room.

Ed was so mad at himself for believing Tommy when he said he'd tell his mother himself. He was also mad at himself for not protecting the boy better.

'He could have been killed,' Ed thought.

A nurse came out and took Mandy and Tommy back, and Ed went to the payphone to call Scott. He got his voice mail, so he called the station and told Skip what was going on.

Mandy came back out alone and crooked her finger at Ed to follow her outside, her face reflecting strong emotions. Ed prepared himself for the tongue-lashing of his life and was amazed when Mandy threw her arms around him and burst into tears. Unaccustomed to such emotional outbursts, let alone young women throwing themselves into his arms, Ed just stood there for a minute or two and let her cry before coming to his senses, fishing out a semi-clean handkerchief, and helping her dry her eyes.

"Thank you for saving his life," she cried, and Ed noticed, though not for the first time, that despite her red eyes, flushed face, hair stuffed up in a hairnet, and body wrapped in a flour-covered apron, what a pretty woman Tommy's mother was.

Back inside, Mandy untied her apron and pulled off the hair net, shaking out her long blonde hair. Ed watched, fascinated. She had green eyes and a dimple in her cheek. She smelled like freshly baked bread and a pretty perfume.

Tommy had two cracked ribs and several bumps and bruises, and although they didn't think he had suffered a concussion, the doctor on duty wanted to keep him under observation overnight, just in case.

Tommy had pulled his old buddy Ed's bacon out of the fire by claiming he'd saved his life in the alley, and none of Ed's protestations to the contrary could convince the grateful mother otherwise. Evening turned into night. Ed and Mandy waited in Tommy's examining room, where first Tommy told Ed and his mother everything that happened the night Theo died, and Ed was appalled at the magnitude of the secret the young boy had been keeping. Mandy and Ed then spent the night talking in the curtained off area, with the young boy sleeping between them.

After Maggie called her, Sarah jumped into her county vehicle, and by using the lights and siren, and despite the treacherous roads, was in Rose Hill within forty-five minutes. Frank met her and a deputy at Phyllis's trailer, but Billy was gone by then, along with Phyllis's car and some money she had hidden in the freezer.

Phyllis, drunk to the point of losing consciousness, was not helpful with inquiries. As Sarah left the trailer, she saw a neighbor lurking nearby and went up to her.

"Did you see Billy leave?" she asked her, and the woman shook her head no, and quickly went back inside.

Sarah drove to Scott's house and was infuriated to find Maggie there. Sarah was used to intimidating people and didn't know how to handle Maggie's firm refusal to let her in.

"Unless you have a warrant to arrest him or to search this house," Maggie said, "you are not getting past me."

Sarah glared at Maggie for a moment before stalking back to her police cruiser.

"I will make you regret this," Sarah said before she got in the car.

"Bite me, Tiny Crimefighter," Maggie said, and then shut the door.


Maggie sat with Scott for several hours, putting fresh ice packs on his head and the back of his neck, thirty minutes on and thirty minutes off, which seemed to help.

Fierce, protective feelings rose up inside her, manifesting as anger toward anyone who might hurt him, and a willingness to do anything to make sure he was all right. If someone was going to look after him, she thought, it was going to be her, and not Sarah Albright. Whether that was love or something less honorable, she stayed until she was sure the other woman wasn't coming back.

When he finally seemed to fall deeply to sleep, she put his next dose of medication and a glass of ice water on the night table, cleaned up the bathroom, and left.


When Scott awoke, he had a migraine hangover he'd gladly have traded for the more manageable alcoholic version. He was in his own bed, a glass of water on the bedside table along with one tablet of his migraine medicine, and a note from Maggie that read: "I called Sarah–take one pill–get some rest. M." He reached for his pill and swallowed it with some water. His throat was sore, and the cold water felt good.

Scott heard the combination "bubububub" and "wheeeeee" purr which was Maggie's vintage VW bug starting up in the driveway and realized she must have awakened him by closing the door as she left. What did "I called Sarah" mean? He was too weak and sick to think about it, and he no longer cared about anything except, where was Maggie going? When was she coming back? Those questions were his last lucid thoughts as he drifted back down into a peaceful, unaware state of less pain, less pain, and finally, no pain.

# ROSE HILL by Pamela Grandstaff

# Chapter Ten - Sunday

When Scott raised his sore head to look at the clock on his bedside table, he saw it was 7:15 a.m. Outside, the snow was pouring down, darkening the sky so that it seemed more like night than day. There were ten to twelve inches of snow on his front porch, and the weather forecaster on the radio said they were likely to get six to eight more before it was over. Scott took a shower and got dressed, moving slowly, still feeling clammy and shaky.

He discovered Maggie had turned off the ringer on his phone, and he had fifteen messages. Instead of listening to them he called the station and Frank brought him up to date. Someone had just reported finding Billy, who had crashed his mother's car in a sharp curve on Pine Mountain Road the night before. Tommy had been in an accident as well but was okay, and Sarah was going to interview him as soon as he got home from the emergency room. Scott reluctantly called Sarah, got her voice mail, and left a message, relieved not to have to talk to her.

Scott was looking for a coffee filter when someone knocked on his back door. It was Curtis Fitzpatrick, his tow truck idling behind him in the alley.

"That sheriff lady's back in town looking for you. We're headed up the mountain to get Phyllis's car; thought you might want to ride along."

Scott put on his warmest coat, boots, gloves, and hat, and joined Patrick and Curtis in the wrecker cab. Patrick handed him a bag full of doughnuts and a cup of hot coffee.

"Compliments of my mother," he told Scott.

"God bless her," Scott said before sipping the scalding hot coffee.

Curtis drove them up the alley to Morning Glory Avenue, took a right and drove to the junction of Pine

Mountain Road, where they met a waiting snowplow. The snowplow driver led them up the mountain at what felt like ten miles per hour. Over the scanner radio, they listened to the ambulance driver report Billy's condition as critical at the scene of the wreck.

"Driving that old Buick with bald tires in this weather..." Curtis said grimly.

Patrick asked him how his head was and Scott said, "Okay, now. Were you there?"

"Yep," Patrick nodded. "But it was Maggie who stayed."

Slowly, they climbed the mountain, and at one point, an ambulance crept past them going in the opposite direction, lights flashing but with no siren. They could see the paramedics inside, working on Billy as they passed.

"How'd they find him?" Scott asked.

"Snowplow driver coming down the mountain saw the guardrail down, and the trees broken over in the ravine and knew they hadn't been that way when he went up earlier," Curtis said. "Glencora paramedics pulled him out. He's lucky he didn't freeze to death."


On the drive home from the emergency clinic, Mandy was quiet and kept her eyes fastened on the road ahead, looking as if she believed she could keep the truck from sliding if she were vigilant enough. The falling snow covered the roads again as fast as they were plowed. Ed took them home and helped Mandy get Tommy to the bathroom and then to bed.

"Thank you for everything," she said, with tears in her eyes.

He smiled at her, said, "I will check on you both later," and left.

Ed stopped at the press office long enough to wake up Hank, take him for a short walk in the alley to pee, and then he delivered the town's papers, several hours late. He didn't even bother to roll them, just carried a paper to each subscriber's front door and apologized for the delay. It felt good to do something repetitive, and not have to think too hard about it. After his task was finished, and the vending machines were loaded, he shut down the computers and lights in the office and locked the front door.

He saw an ambulance, with lights blazing but no siren, rolling slowly down Pine Mountain road before it turned right at the light. The lights were on inside the ambulance and Ed could see the EMT's working on someone. He wondered if it was Billy.

Ed turned around and unlocked the door to the news office, and Hank looked at him, head cocked to the side as if to say, 'what are we doing now?'

"I also write the news," he told the dog.

There were few vehicles out on Pine Mountain Road save road crews and emergency workers. The road to Glencora stayed plowed no matter how bad the weather, in order for tourists to be able to get to the ski resorts, and the state road workers driving the big plows waved to the men in the wrecker as they passed, plowing in the opposite direction.

"They'll be out all day," Curtis said. "This is a nor'easter."

Scott was glad for the coffee to counteract the sedative effects of his migraine medication. He was also glad to be with Curtis and Patrick, who seemed invincible and impervious even to the forces of nature. Patrick, usually the chattiest member of the family, was unusually quiet, and Curtis, a quiet man, was his usual self. They listened to the scanner and followed the snowplow, keeping their thoughts to themselves.

Scott was trying to piece the case together in his mind, with the view that Billy killed Theo, and trying to account for the threads that didn't fit the scenario. He thought about Phyllis thinking Billy could be Brad's son and thus heir to part of the Eldridge fortune. If Billy had

303

heard any part of the exchange between Theo and Phyllis and thought by killing Theo he could inherit the Eldridge family's money, there was a powerful motive.

But how had Willy ended up in the river? Was it just an accident? He wondered if Billy would live long enough to answer any of those questions. He figured Sarah would meet the ambulance at the hospital and question Billy if he were in any shape to be questioned.

He wondered if he should have listened to those fifteen messages on his voice mail. He thought, and not for the first time, that he was not a very good policeman. Maybe he could become a firefighter instead. Except the smoke would give him a migraine and incapacitate him. Maybe he could tend bar at the Rose and Thorn, deep fry doughnuts at the bakery, or pump gas at the service station. Maybe Maggie would hire him as a barista in her café. He could get fat on pastries and sweet coffee drinks and just be nice to people all day. That sounded good. There was no need to carry a gun or investigate your closest friends in that job.

As much as he loved his job, Scott thought maybe he wasn't cut out to be the chief of police. Rose Hill deserved someone brave and unflinching in the face of any challenge; someone who stuck to the strict letter of the law no matter who got hurt; someone who didn't care what anyone else thought of him; someone who couldn't be so easily corrupted by redheads with long legs, big boobs, and bad tempers. He was about as good of a protector as Hank, snoozing by the fire in the newspaper office, or Lazy Ass Laddie at Bonnie and Fitz's house.

'It's no wonder Maggie doesn't want me,' he thought. 'I'm a lazy, incompetent coward, stopped dead in my tracks by perfume and cigarette smoke.'

His gloomy, depressed thoughts matched the scene outside: snow flying sideways against a gray sky and barren black trees frosted with white.

"Cheer up," Patrick said and elbowed him in the ribs. "It could be worse."

"How's that?" Scott asked.

"You could be dead."

"You're right," Scott said. "At least we're not dead."

"It's still early, boys," Curtis said, as they pulled off the road at the site of the wreck, marked by flares. "Let's not celebrate right yet."

Going back down the mountain a few hours later, with Phyllis's Buick winched up behind the truck, the tire chains jingled like bells on a sleigh. Frank radioed from the police station to say Billy was dead on arrival at the county hospital. Scott thought but didn't say that with him went all hope of a confession, and any of Scott's questions answered.

In Rose Hill, snow was pouring down in big downy clusters, and both sky and landscape were clad in its ghostly gray and white cloak. The city looked deserted, and most of the businesses were closed.

Curtis parked the wrecker beside the service station and went inside to relieve his brother Ian, who was covering his shift. Patrick and Scott went to PJ's and ordered some pizza to be delivered across the street to the bar. When they entered the Rose and Thorn, kicking the snow off their boots and removing their heavy outer garments, Ian was already there, sipping his first beer of the day.

"I'm glad it's Sunday and we don't have to open," the older man said. "We probably wouldn't have any customers even if we did."

Scott realized he had once again missed church and a meal at his mother's, and called her, prepared to grovel and make excuses. She surprised him, however, by telling him Maggie had stopped her before church to tell her about Scott's migraine.

She further surprised her son by adding, "I've always liked Maggie. You ought to bring her for dinner sometime."

Scott hung up thinking he should probably write this date down somewhere so he could remember when his mother's first dementia symptoms began.

After they ate, Scott decided to go see Tommy and take his statement, hoping to save the boy from being interrogated by Sarah. He was asleep when Scott got to their trailer, and Mandy wasn't about to let anyone wake him up. She went on and on about how Ed had saved his life and had driven them to the emergency clinic in a blinding snowstorm. Scott listened patiently, foreseeing many free drinks and doughnuts in Ed's future.

Scott went down to the newspaper office and found Ed working on his account of Theo's murder for Pendleton's daily newspaper.

"They can have it in tomorrow's edition, but I won't have another Sentinel published until next Sunday," he said. "I thought about putting together a special edition, but the God's honest truth is I'm just too damned tired. You don't look so good yourself."

Scott sat down at the work table, and Ed sat across from him.

"How do you know what happened?" Scott asked. "Did Billy confess to someone?"

"Tommy told us," Ed said. "After the fight at Phyllis's, Tommy saw Billy follow Theo down the alley. Tommy was afraid to be in the alley with them, so he ran down Iris Avenue and hid in the walkway between the antique store and the insurance office, to see where they went. He saw Theo banging on the windows of Willy Neff's truck, which was parked in front of the antique store, and then cursing when he couldn't get in. He saw Theo take the bat out of the bed of the truck, cross the street, and go behind the vet's office. Billy, who was hiding in the alley, followed Theo, carrying a piece of the iron pipe railing which used to be in front of the antique store."

"The murder weapon," Scott interrupted, and Ed nodded.

"A few minutes later Billy came back with the piece of pipe still in his hand. Tommy said Billy looked in the windows of Willy's truck, then pushed in the vent window, reached inside the truck to unlock the door, got in, started it, and drove the truck down the street into the fog. Tommy heard the truck door slam, and then heard the truck roll down the hill into the water, but he couldn't see anything through the fog. He also couldn't see where Billy went afterward."

"Wait a minute," Scott said. "If the fog was so thick Tommy couldn't see the river, then he couldn't have seen the barriers were down. That means Billy couldn't have known they were down, either. How far down the street did Billy take the truck before he let it roll?"

"Tommy couldn't see," Ed said. "My guess is he let it roll from the intersection of Pine Mountain Road and Lotus Avenue, so it only had to roll a couple hundred feet. He had Willy passed out in the truck, so if he just wanted to plant the murder weapon on him, he could have left him parked on the street. I think he knew the barriers were down, thought Willy would be found drowned with the murder weapon, and everyone would assume Willy killed Theo."

"Tommy didn't know Willy was in the truck?"

"Willy must have been passed out across the front seats. Tommy didn't know Willy was in the truck until they pulled it out of the river. He thought Billy was just getting rid of the pipe in an empty truck."

Scott thought the pipe was probably still in the cab of Willy's truck, which was sitting in the parking lot behind the station.

"That poor kid, he must have been terrified."

"He said he waited a few minutes to make sure Billy wasn't coming back, and then he went home. Said he got home right ahead of his mom, and got in bed, pretended to be asleep. Of course, he couldn't sleep. He heard Billy come home later and crept out to the front room so he could see what he was doing. Tommy saw him come out again, carrying a bag. He disappeared into the fog, and Tommy doesn't know where he went."

"Getting rid of the clothes he wore when he killed Theo."

"That's my guess," Ed said. "Tommy said he went back to bed but didn't fall asleep until morning. He really did oversleep, and that's why he didn't show up for work. He felt bad about it. He had no idea I would be the one to find Theo."

"And he's been keeping this secret all this time."

"He hoped that by telling us he saw Billy follow Theo it would be enough to put us onto him. He was too afraid to tell the rest of it for fear Billy would hurt him or his mom. When he heard about Willy being drowned in the truck, he panicked. Then last night he heard Billy threaten to kill Phyllis if she didn't keep her mouth shut, and came to get me. I wasn't in the office, so he turned around and went back down the alley, just as I turned the corner and saw him. Then I heard a car come crashing down the alley..."

Ed's voice became hoarse, and he had to pause as he recalled what he thought had happened to Tommy. Scott went back to the fridge and took out two beers. Ed opened his and took a long drink before continuing.

"I thought from the sound of it Billy had run over Tommy, but he jumped in time."

"I wonder if Billy tried to hit him or just didn't see him."

"It's pretty dark back there, and he was flying."

"How is Tommy?" Scott asked.

"He has a couple of cracked ribs and some bruises," Ed said. "He's lucky to be alive, but he's okay. His bike is history."

"We can get him another bike," Scott said.

"I'm taking care of it," Ed said.

"Do you know where Phyllis is?" Scott asked, thinking someone had probably given her the news of Billy's death by now, and not wanting her to be alone.

"She's at her mother's," Ed said. "Doc Machalvie sedated her. Bonnie, Delia, and Lily Crawford were there with Pauline and Gladys when I called. There's probably a house full of church women over there by now."

They sat in silence for a few moments, drinking beer. The phone rang, and Ed got up to answer.

Scott let his mind wander, looking out at the snow flying. If Billy had lived, Tommy would have had to testify against him in court. Scott wasn't sure Tommy could handle so much pressure or attention. Even now, the strain of being questioned by Sarah would be traumatic. What was the point, really? Theo was dead. Billy was dead. Poor old Willy was dead. Whom would it help?

"That was Frank looking for you," Ed said. "Someone at the hospital called to say Anne Marie Rodefeffer woke up this morning."

Both men sat in silence for a moment, processing this new information, and thinking about all they would need to do as a result. Ed would have to write it up for the paper, and Scott would have to interview Anne Marie, to find out if her husband tried to kill her.

"I'm thinking of resigning," Scott said.

Ed shook his head, smiling.

"I used to think about quitting," Ed said. "But think about it. You're a cop like I'm a newsman. What else are we gonna do? I could quit, but I'd still poke my nose in everything and write about it. I can't help myself. You could quit, but you'd still be running around this town looking out for everybody. A bloodhound needs to track, and a collie needs to protect the herd. We have to accept our roles in life and quit thinking we can do anything different."

"But I'm not sure I'm making anything better," Scott said. "Maybe someone else would do a better job."

"Don't be so hard on yourself. People are always going to do bad things to each other. This town isn't perfect, the people in it aren't perfect, and you and I aren't perfect. We can be bitter and miserable about it or find a way to be happy in a world that isn't ideal. A man's got to do what he thinks is right, learn from his mistakes, and know when to let sleeping dogs lie."

Scott looked over at the black lab snoring by the stove and then smiled at his friend.

## ACKNOWLEDGMENTS

My love and gratitude go to John and Betsy Grandstaff for all their support and encouragement. I give many thanks to early readers Terry Hutchison, Joan Turner, and Ella Curry, who gave me great feedback. I am grateful for the professional assistance and friendship of Kim Cohen and Kara Gray. Love to my good friends Joan, Nancy, Cassie, Mary, and Opal, and thanks for all the good laughs we've shared. Love also to Beth Ann, and to Shay and Dale, who introduced me to the joy of reading mysteries.

Thank you to Tamarack: The Best of West Virginia, for selling my paper books in your beautiful building.

And last, but not least, I want to thank the people who buy and read my books. Thank you so much.

If you liked this book, please leave a review on Amazon.com (Thank you!)

For more information go to RoseHillMysteries.com

# Morning Glory Circle

Rose Hill Mystery Series Book 2

## Chapter One – Monday

Margie Estep sealed the entrance to the hiding place where she kept all her secrets, or rather, the stolen evidence of other people's secrets. A frisson of fear and excitement ran up her spine at the prospect of setting into motion one of the most clever schemes she had ever concocted. One day, after she disappeared and was living her new life somewhere far away, she hoped someone would figure out what she'd done and how she'd done it. Her only regret about leaving the town she had lived in all her life was not being able to witness the havoc she would leave in her wake.

The home health nurse was with her mother in the front room. The young blonde woman glanced at Margie with barely concealed dislike as she entered the room. This one was called Cindy and had a chirpy voice that grated on Margie's nerves.

"We need to eat our dinner now, Mrs. Estep," Cindy said. "We can't let good food go to waste, now can we?"

Cindy had draped a dish towel across the cardigan and housedress that encased the older woman's sagging bosom and was trying to coax her into eating a spoonful of tapioca pudding. Enid Estep's hands, crippled with arthritis, lay curled into gnarled fists on each arm of the recliner in which she sat all day.

"Where are you going, Mary Margaret?" Enid asked her daughter in a sharp tone, as Margie took her coat off the peg by the door.

There was tapioca on her mother's chin, glistening in amongst the few long whiskers growing there. It seemed to Margie that everything about her mother was worn out and failing, from the sagging, spotted lids of her pale blue eyes to her swollen ankles and misshapen feet. She was helpless, and something about this great vulnerability enraged Margie, made her snap out answers instead of being patient and kind.

"Out for a walk," Margie said, averting her eyes. "I won't be gone long."

"She does this every night," Enid said to Cindy. "I keep telling her she shouldn't go out alone after dark, but she won't listen."

"I'll be fine," Margie said through clenched teeth.

"I'm going to Mountain View tomorrow," Enid said to Cindy. "She can't wait to get rid of me."

"I'm sure that's not true," Cindy said.

Margie waited until the door was shut behind her before saying quietly, "It is true."

Margie and her mother lived in a small house on Lotus Avenue, in the shadow of the defunct Rodefeffer Glassworks building, which sat next to the railroad tracks by the Little Bear River. Most everyone on Lotus Avenue heated with coal, so the smell of coal smoke permeated the air. It had also permanently stained the peeling white paint on the houses built by the coal companies to house workers in the early part of the 20th century. It was, as Margie knew all too well, considered the wrong side of town, and only the poorest people lived there.

Down at the end of the block Margie spied Sue Fischer unloading groceries from her car and carrying them into the house she shared with her husband, Calvert. Cal and Sue had purchased one of the neighborhood's small houses and fixed it up. Margie resented their optimism. As she approached Sue, the woman nodded at her in as bare an acknowledgment a civilized person could make without being rude, and Margie took that as an invitation to speak. Sue stopped, with six heavy bags of groceries dangling from her arms and hands, lips pursed and countenance straining to conclude as quickly as possible whatever conversation it was Margie wished to have.

When Cal Fischer came out the front door a few minutes later to see what was keeping Sue, he found his wife threatening to dip Margie in tar and roll her in feathers before forcibly running her out of town. As he hurried down the steps to the front walk, Sue dropped her groceries in the snow and advanced on the small dumpy woman with what looked like every intention of following through on her threat.

"What's going on?" Cal asked as he rushed forward to restrain his wife.

"Margie's up to her old tricks," Sue said bitterly. "She's just picked the wrong person to try it on this time."

Margie just smirked and said, "You think about what I said and get back to me."

"I'll see you in hell first," Sue said, and Cal took his wife more firmly by the arm.

"Sue!" he said, and she seemed to come to her senses.

As Margie walked away, Cal helped Sue gather up the grocery bags and retrieve the items that had rolled out when she dropped them.

"What in the world did she say to you?" he asked her.

"We'll talk about it inside," Sue said, looking around to see if anyone could have overheard her argument with Margie.

"I really thought you were going to hurt her," Cal said. "That's not like you."

"Somebody needs to do something about that woman," Sue said. "And if she doesn't watch herself someday I will."

Margie walked up Pine Mountain Road past the newspaper office and bakery, which were closed for the evening. Davis's Diner was open, and she could see some college students and a few regular customers seated inside, but no one with whom she had business dealings. She turned right, crossed the street, and walked down toward the college. She stopped in front of the post office, which up until a few weeks previously she had been postmistress of for over twenty years. It was closed as well, of course, so she could only stare into the dark interior and feel her resentment build. With a vengeful smirk on her face, she drew out a thick handful of stamped, addressed envelopes from her coat pocket and dropped them into the mailbox outside the building. To anyone watching it would have looked like a perfectly ordinary, innocent activity when actually it was as wicked of an act as a madman poisoning a well.

Maggie Fitzpatrick came out of Delvecchio's IGA grocery store just as Margie was dropping her letters and although Maggie greeted her, it was no friendlier than Sue's greeting had been. Margie felt stung by the snub; she had never done anything to actually harm Maggie, even though she easily could have. Margie didn't think there was a person in town she didn't have something on, some little nugget of unpleasantness she could take out and polish when her feelings were hurt. Maggie Fitzpatrick's family provided a treasure trove of such gems.

'That stupid policeman must have told her lies about me,' Margie surmised. Her resentment at losing her job was still fresh in her breast, and her frustration at not being able to get back at the person she blamed was driving her mad with desire for revenge. Taking it out on

Maggie was the next best thing to getting back at Police Chief Scott Gordon, so Margie lashed out with the only weapon she had left: over twenty years' worth of vicious Rose Hill gossip.

"Heard from Gabe?" she asked Maggie in a syrupy sweet voice.

Maggie was so visibly taken aback that Margie knew her poison dart had found its mark.

"Why would you even ask me that?' Maggie said, and her face could be seen under the streetlight to become suffused by a deep red flush.

"I bet you'd give a lot to know what really happened to Gabe," Margie said.

"You know, Margie," Maggie said. "Scott told me about all the awful things you've done, and I would think you'd need to be on your best behavior right about now."

"I bet Scott would give a lot for you not to find out what really happened to Gabe," Margie said with a cackle.

"You don't know what you're talking about," Maggie said. "Stay away from me and mind your own business."

Margie felt all her anger and bitterness rise up and burst out, and it felt good to let it fly on someone instead of bottling it up and storing it somewhere deep, dark, and dank.

"Everyone knows your father's a drunk and Theo Eldridge was screwing your sister-in-law," Margie said. "You've got no right to look down your nose at me."

Maggie advanced on Margie much the same way Sue Fischer had a few minutes earlier.

"Don't you hit me," Margie yelled. "I'll have you arrested."

"You listen to me, Margie Estep," Maggie said. "I wouldn't pollute myself by touching you. Besides, there's not a thing I could do to you that's worse than what you've done to yourself. You're hated in this town, truly hated, and there's not a person here who'd miss you if you went to jail, which is where you belong."

"Maggie, what's going on?" Matt Delvecchio said as he came out of his grocery store to see what the yelling was about. "Margie, are you making trouble again?"

"You'll be sorry you said that," Margie said to Maggie, and then looked at Matt. "You'll all be sorry."

But Maggie Fitzpatrick had already turned her back and walked away, crossing the street to her bookstore.

"You better keep your nose clean, Margie," Matt said. "You've just about worn out your welcome in this town."

"You better keep a closer eye on that wife of yours," Margie snarled. "I hear she's been spending a lot of time in the hardware store, but she never buys anything."

"You'll never learn, will you?" Matt said, shaking his head. "You better go on home now, and try to stay out of trouble."

Matt went back inside the grocery store, and Margie stomped back the way she came. She wished she had time to exact revenge on everyone who dared to underestimate her. She retraced her steps to the center of town where Pine Mountain Road and Rose Hill Avenue met. The heavy snow that was forecast began to fall, and the last vestiges of daylight disappeared behind the mountains to the west, on the other side of the Little Bear River.

She crossed Rose Hill Avenue and trudged uphill, toward the higher streets in town where the homes were bigger and sat on wide, manicured lawns. From Lilac Avenue Margie crossed through Rose Hill City Park and lingered in amongst the trees at the far edge, where she could stand unobserved but with a very good view into some of the finer houses on Morning Glory Avenue. She was particularly interested in Morning Glory Circle, the cul de sac at the end of the street where the wealthiest Rose Hill residents currently resided.

There, in a Gothic monstrosity of a mansion, lived Mamie Rodefeffer, the great-granddaughter of the glassworks founder. The cranky old woman spent her days bullying her staff and walking around town acting like she owned it. She personally blamed Margie for any rise in the cost of stamps, and flung her mail on the counter in an imperious manner rather than put it through the slot like everyone else. Margie took her revenge on Mamie by making sure some of her mail never reached the intended recipients, and by occasionally stealing the old woman's National Geographic magazines. She also knew something about Mamie she was pretty sure the old lady would not want to have revealed.

In a Federal style home next to Mamie's lived Knox Rodefeffer. He was Mamie's nephew, president of the local bank, and his wife had recently been seriously injured in a car accident that Margie suspected Knox had engineered. She didn't have any actual proof, but sometimes, Margie had found, an accusation was worth as much as real evidence. Knox never lowered himself to come to the post office, preferring to send that whore of a secretary instead. Anyone who looked at her could tell she had the morals of an alley cat. Margie had heard from the cleaning woman at the bank the kinds of things found in Knox's garbage can after he had closed-door meetings with his secretary. Her imagination could easily fill in the blanks. Everyone knew Knox was poised to run for political office and couldn't afford a scandal.

At the very top of Morning Glory Circle sat a large Edwardian home in which lived Gwyneth Eldridge, one of the two Eldridge heiresses who inherited a fortune when their brother Theo was murdered back in January. Margie didn't have anything on Gwyneth, but she knew plenty about Theo and thought his sister might be willing to pay plenty to keep those secrets hidden. Gwyneth was positioning herself as a powerful influence in town and would be anxious to keep any unsavory information out of her spotlight.

The Eldridge Inn was next door to Gwyneth's house, and the walled grounds of Eldridge College could be seen behind. Margie could see movement where she hoped to. She took a small pair of binoculars out of her pocket and focused them on the object of her interest. It all looked very promising.

A few hours later Margie pulled her dead father's coat close around her as she turned down the alley behind the fire station. The snow, flying sideways, stung her cheeks and ears. She made her way down the narrow lane by walking in the deep ruts that the city snowplow's tires had made the night before. The tire tracks, already filled in with a couple inches of fine, white powder, ended behind a building that used to house a tire store, closed now for several years. Stacks of used tires still lined one side of the narrow lane, with many weeks' worth of snow plowed and drifted up against them, creating a white wall of whitewalls.

She had stayed away the night before, when the drop off was supposed to have taken place, not wanting to take the chance that anyone would be waiting for her. Better to come like this, before sunrise the next day, when most folks were still in bed or just waking up. Margie was certain her victim was just as anxious as she was to maintain confidentiality, and hardly likely to send the police to arrest her. With way more to lose than most people in this town, in terms of reputation, wealth, and power, she was certain this target would pay just about any price to eliminate the merest breath of scandal. The wealthy, socially prominent citizens of Rose Hill may have enjoyed a certain amount of power, but their status carried with it a vulnerability to scandal that Margie found irresistible.

Margie's focus was on a rusted metal barrel that stood next to a set of stairs leading up to Rose Hill Avenue. Down in the bottom of the barrel, she found the grocery bag, placed just as she had instructed it be done. The weight of it seemed to indicate the money was in there, but she used a small flashlight to make sure. It was during this brief lack of attention to her surroundings that someone moved out of the shadows behind the wall of discarded tires, grabbed Margie around her waist, and clamped a gloved hand over her mouth and nose. That hand held a cloth soaked in a strong smelling chemical that choked her as it filled her lungs. Although Margie struggled she also gasped in the fumes, and passed out within seconds.

Over the years, many people in Rose Hill had discovered that Margie Estep had a tendency to stick her nose in where she ought not, to seek out and spread vicious gossip, and to create malicious mischief wherever and whenever she could. These people often complained to each other that something should be done about Margie Estep. A few people in town also knew that Margie was dangerously malicious and vindictive, and incapable of feeling either empathy or remorse.

One person, in particular, knew very well what awful acts Margie was capable of committing. This someone had finally had enough, was not going to put up with it anymore, and was willing to wait for a long time in the cold and dark for the opportunity to finally do something about Margie Estep. Once the deed was done and Margie's body was disposed of, all that was left to do was retrieve the money, eliminate the evidence, and let Mother Nature do the rest. Snow had a way of making everything in Rose Hill look clean and innocent, even the scene of a murder.

Morning Glory Circle is available on Amazon.com